Kensington Heights

'Her eyes closed. Her eyelids were almost transparent. She breathed regularly. He eased her skimpy body down on to the bed. With the cup he went to the door, looking back at her once before going out. He took the cup into the kitchen and washed it under the tap. Whatever was he going to do with her?'

Leslie Thomas was born in Newport, Monmouthshire in 1931, the son of a sailor who was lost at sea. His boyhood in a Barnardo's orphanage is described in his hugely successful autobiography *This Time Next Week*, and he is the author of numerous other bestsellers including *The Virgin Soldiers*, *Tropic of Ruislip* and *Revolving Jones*. He lives in Salisbury with his wife Diana.

LESLIE THOMAS

Kensington Heights

Mandarin

A Mandarin Paperback
KENSINGTON HEIGHTS

First published in Great Britain 1996
by Methuen London
This edition published 1996
by Mandarin Paperbacks
an imprint of Reed International Books Ltd
Michelin House, 81 Fulham Road, London sw3 6rb
and Auckland, Melbourne, Singapore and Toronto

Copyright © 1996 by Leslie Thomas
The author has asserted his moral rights

The extract from Stephen Spender's poem
'The Room Above the Square' on p. vii
is reproduced by kind permission
of Faber and Faber Ltd

A CIP catalogue record for this title
is available from the British Library
ISBN 0 7493 2295 0

Typeset by Deltatype Ltd, Birkenhead, Merseyside
Printed and bound in Great Britain
by Cox & Wyman Ltd, Reading, Berkshire

To the Clarke family,
Keith, Ros, Jody, Eric and May,
with my thanks for their generosity

The light in the window seemed perpetual
When you stayed in the high room for me;
It glowed above the trees through the leaves
Like my certainty.

STEPHEN SPENDER

One

January the second seemed as good a day as any for trying to find somewhere to hide. The first rain of the year, a sparse drizzle, thickened to spiteful sleet. Noon in London was dim, clouds low, with airliners, incoming and unseen, sounding heavily. Traffic was thin on the ground.

People looked as furtive as Savage felt; collars up, hats and hoods pulled low, noses raw and damp. Women who had been at the New Year sales clutched bags of bargains as though fearful they might be snatched back. It was like watching a shifting shadowgraph.

At Waterloo he had not been able to give the taxi driver an address because he had none to give. 'Suggest somewhere,' he said.

The driver, only a little surprised, treated Savage to a quick but professionally prudent examination in his mirror. He saw a lean man, forties, five-ten, he thought, although his passenger was now seated, hunched as if attempting to make himself less conspicuous, his raincoat collar like a rampart around his head and neck, a damp hat over his forehead, his only luggage a supermarket shopping bag that bulged.

'Hounslow, Chiswick,' the man suggested hopefully. Then less so: 'Hammersmith, Fulham, Kensington.' They were all on his way home.

'Kensington,' decided his passenger. 'That will do.' He was staring out at the streets, the wet pavements reflecting the dumb lights from the shops. 'I'll drop you at Kensington High Street then,' the driver said.

'All right, drop me there,' said Savage. The tone was blunt, non-commissioned military.

Now he sat, upright and motionless, not even turning to look from the window. Outside Kensington High Street tube station the driver called: 'This do you?' His passenger seemed to wake and said it would, paid, and got out. As he was about to move off the driver threw a practised glance into the back of his cab and his eye caught the edge of the plastic bag. Hurriedly he pulled into the side. You never knew these days.

Getting out and opening the rear door he saw the bag on the floor in the far corner and was eyeing it apprehensively when Savage reappeared, hurried but decisive. 'My shopping,' he said.

Relieved, the driver leaned into the cab, brought out the plastic bag and handed it to Savage. 'Thought it was a bomb,' he laughed.

'No, it's just shopping,' said Savage seriously and now more easily. The driver looked uncomfortable and said: 'Right, I'll be on my way then.'

'Yes. Thanks . . .' The man was climbing back into the driving seat. Savage followed him to the door and, plunging his hand into the shopping bag, brought out a ten-pound note. He gave it to the driver. 'Thanks for stopping,' he said.

'Cheers,' said the taxi man. 'That's very nice.' He pocketed the note and drove off shaking his head. It took all sorts.

Savage bought an *Evening Standard*. Next to the newspaper seller was a young beggar playing a penny whistle badly, squatting cross-legged on the damp pavement. Savage put the change of a pound in his hat. 'Happy New Year,' said the young man.

'I never want to see another like the last,' muttered the news vendor. Rain dripped from the peak of his cap like the overflow from a gutter. He nodded at the front page of the *Standard*. 'But it's not going to get any better.'

'It'll get worse,' forecast the piper like a financial analyst. He resumed his playing.

'It will,' agreed the newspaper seller. 'For the likes of us.'

Savage began to cross the High Street. A descending plane sounded heavily, its belly just above the low grey clouds. The traffic lights altered, the only bright colours in the scene. He waited on the island in the middle of the road. A woman with a Barkers bag thought how ill he looked and smiled at him sympathetically. 'Happy New Year,' he said unsurely. She had not expected him to speak and she mumbled: 'And you,' and hurried over as soon as the lights changed.

As he crossed the street Kensington slowly rose in front of him, a gradually ascending hill with winter-bare beech trees clasped above it, sturdy Victorian bay windows on either side, some with left-over Christmas lights blinking behind the glass, and pricey cars parked front to back against the pavement. A white child walked by holding the hand of an Asian woman. A man buried below a dozen ragged coats slept on a bench. No one else was about.

There was a lonely light in the window of Wolfton's Estate Agents and inside someone was moving about. Transferring his plastic bag to the other hand he pushed down the door handle and went in. A pasty, hollow-eyed young man wearing an untidy striped tie looked up from the drawer of a desk. The glance was furtive, as though he had been caught red-handed. 'We're closed today,' he said.

'The door was open,' pointed out Savage.

The youth took in the spectral figure. Savage said: 'I need a flat to rent.'

'Well, as I say, we're not really open,' mumbled the young man. 'Would you come back tomorrow?'

'I need a flat today.' The words were clear and the delivery short, like an order.

'Today? I don't think we can do anything for today. Not as fast as that.'

'Why not?'

There was an aspect about the man that made the estate agent hesitate to answer firmly. He stood, medium height and square built; his hands were powerful but pale. But he was a little unkempt, his hair lank, his shoulders a touch rounded, as though he had spent a long time sitting in a chair.

'Well,' said the young man after a pause. 'If you found somewhere . . . we found somewhere for you . . . even if that were the case, there are references and banks and contracts and all that sort of stuff. The usual.'

'I have the money. Here,' said Savage. He opened the carrier bag and displayed its contents to the agent who looked startled. Then Savage put his hand in and took out a dense wad of notes secured with an elastic band. He riffled along the edges like an expert card dealer. 'Fifty-pound notes,' he said. Reaching in the bag again he produced another thicker bundle of fifties with one hand and a wide bunch of twenties with the other. He could only just fix them between thumbs and fingers. He had thousands. 'I can't provide references,' he said. 'I don't know anyone who would give me one.' He put the bag on the floor.

The estate agent swallowed. 'It just can't be done in a couple of minutes.'

'I've got all day. I'd like to see somewhere. I would like to be high up. But quiet.'

'The one above sees all,' laughed the youth uncertainly.

'And remains unassailable,' said Savage.

'Like a cat on a roof.'

'Like an eagle in a tree.'

As if making up his mind the young man held out his hand: 'I'm Freddie Spencer-Hughes, by the way.' Savage shook it. 'Frank Inigo Savage,' he said.

'There *is* someone I *could* ring,' decided Spencer-Hughes. 'Mr Kostelanetz. He moved out before Christmas and he's looking for someone to rent his flat.'

'And it's . . . high up . . . and quiet?'

'High and quiet,' confirmed the young man. He renewed his study of Savage. His hand went to the telephone. 'It's twelve hundred pounds a month,' he confided with a blink.

Savage, with a decisive movement at odds with his clumsy appearance, picked his carrier bag from the floor and Spencer-Hughes swallowed thinking he was going to walk out. Instead he placed it on the desk and counted out two bundles of fifty-pound notes. To this he added another four. The estate agent watched with scarcely restrained astonishment. He pushed the money back to Savage and glanced towards the glass door. 'Better put it away,' he suggested.

He picked up the telephone and fingered out a number which was answered immediately. 'Mr Kostelanetz,' he said brightly. 'Sorry to bother you over the New Year . . .

Oh, no, I see. It's not your New Year. How interesting. We must remember that.'

Savage heard Mr Kostelanetz ask what he wanted. Yes, he knew who it was. 'I know the voice of Wolfton's,' he said. The young man coloured. 'Yes, it's Freddie Spencer-Hughes. I have a gentleman who is interested in renting your apartment at Kensington Heights . . . Yes, yes, he knows the rent. Yes . . . I've seen it . . . It's cash. Six months. You will? Splendid, Mr Kostelanetz. Jolly good. We'll meet you there in, say, fifteen minutes.'

Smiling boyishly, he replaced the phone. 'First business this year,' he said to Savage. 'Sorry I wasn't very welcoming when you first came in.'

'You thought I was a tramp.'

'Hah, hardly. But all sorts of people wander in here and I wanted to get away. I've left my girlfriend in my flat and I'm not at all sure that she'll be there when I return. It hasn't been a happy Christmas.'

'Why don't you telephone?' suggested Savage.

'No, no, perhaps this is the distraction I needed. If she's there when I get back then she is, if she isn't then she's not.' He hardly paused. 'Normally we ask for references.'

'From girlfriends?'

'From prospective tenants.' He laughed tentatively and glanced at the shopping bag. 'But I suppose that will do. Mr Kostelanetz understands cash.'

'Many people do,' said Savage.

'Right you are,' said Spencer-Hughes. He smiled at Savage. 'Let's get started.' He attempted the hearty tone of an amateur comedy actor. 'Wait, wait,' he added at once, although Savage had not moved. 'We *do* have some details.'

After a moment's fumbling through a pile of photo-copied sheets he said: 'Ah,' handed them over and then read aloud from a duplicate. 'Kensington Heights,' he recited. 'Built in the eighteen-nineties – a hundred years ago.' He glanced up as though this might be a surprise. 'Yes, part of one of the old Kensington estates. This area was almost countryside until then, you know. Fields, milkmaids, all that stuff.'

There was a poor photograph at the top of the sheet and another on the reverse. 'It looks solid enough,' mentioned Savage. He studied the baronial building, its wide, old windows, and turrets and finials on the roof. He counted the six floors. 'And this apartment is at the top?'

'Couldn't be higher,' confirmed the young man. 'Up there with the pigeons.' He pointed to a pair of windows below one of the turrets. 'That's the actual one, I think.' He frowned at the murky picture. 'And, as you say, solid. They knew how to build in those days. With real bricks. Thousands of bricks. Imagine how many bricks went into that pile. It was meant to last for a hundred years.'

'Which is now up,' pointed out Savage.

Spencer-Hughes soon recovered. 'Longer, I should say. Much, much longer. These places, these mansion flats, will be there when half this modern stuff is falling down.'

He let Savage out of the door and locked it behind him, turning to take a precautionary peer back through the glass. 'Right you are,' he repeated. 'Kensington Heights it is.'

Together they walked up the steady slope, the day dead around them. Savage's steps were level, ordered, spaced; although he seemed to be moving quite slowly Spencer-Hughes had to hurry to keep up. 'Personally I'd dearly like to be in Africa, the Indies, the East, anywhere at this time of the year,' grumbled the estate agent pulling his collar high. A thought struck him. 'Did you have a nice Christmas?' he enquired.

Savage, who had spent the Christmas alone, said: 'Quiet.'

'I wish mine had been,' sighed the young man. 'Got pissed on Christmas Eve. Breathalysed. Positive. I'll have to get myself a bike. It's going to be difficult taking clients around on a bike.'

'Hard work,' agreed Savage.

Spencer-Hughes stopped on the pavement and surveyed the grey general scene, the substantial Victorian houses with their moribund Christmas door wreaths and morose illuminations. 'Strange how Christmas lights look all dead now,' he observed. Drippings from a bare branch plopped on his forehead. He glanced up as though someone might be perched there. Giving the tree a patronising pat he said: 'When these were planted, put in, or whatever they do with trees, this was a pretty refined area. Butlers, nannies, boot boys, all sorts of lackeys. It's changed but it's still reckoned to be the best area in London, well, one of the best, to live. There's a lot of dosh around Kensington.' He looked pointedly at Savage's carrier bag. 'Although I can't say I've seen a Tesco's bag loaded like that before.'

Savage said: 'It was all I had to carry it in.'

They continued walking. 'Good shopping, good restaurants,' the young man said. 'Museums, if you like fossils.' He paused as if wondering whether to mention something. 'There's a few fossils at Kensington Heights, by the way. Been there years some of them. A bit dotty maybe, but harmless.'

'Fossils are quiet,' said Savage.

'Yes, of course. That should suit you. Very genteel

some of them too, a little faded, old-fashioned posh, you might say. I always think going in there is like entering a bit of a time warp. Like pushing through cobwebs.' He appeared embarrassed. 'Not that there are any cobwebs,' he assured. 'The place is kept shiny bright. There's porters for different blocks and television security and all that. Keeps the baddies away.'

'They can't all be fossils,' suggested Savage. They had passed the modern monolithic town hall and library.

'By no means,' said Spencer-Hughes hurriedly. 'There's business people as well, youngish a lot of them. You can see the lights going on when they get back in the evening. I went to a party in one of the flats last Hallowe'en and it was a rave.' He glanced sideways as though again worried he had said the wrong thing. 'But there's not many parties, I wouldn't think. It's all very sedate, private, you know. Not many children because there's nowhere for them to play, except the park. And the walls are thick as a prison.'

They crossed an intersecting street and Kensington Heights loomed before them, solid and silent, its upper ramparts, its corner towers, giving it an air of the Scottish baronial. There was a main entrance with glass doors and a uniformed porter lurking within. 'You won't have to use that door,' said Spencer-Hughes. 'Mr Kostelanetz liked to use the side entrance, around the courtyard. He came and went at odd hours I believe.' He walked past the lobby entrance and around the side of the building. They went into a yard with a barren central flower bed and walls on three sides. The estate agent pointed skywards. 'It's the top flat, the window with the little balcony, although it's not a fabulous view because you've got the other wing of the block in your way. The main window faces south and that looks for miles. There's the entrance in the corner, you'll have a key to that. And there's a separate lift.'

He ushered Savage around the front of the building again. 'That's your main outlook,' he pointed. 'Right at the top. Sixth floor, right across London, well Kensington anyway, and you get a view of Holland Park on that side, just, and Kensington Gardens on the other. And Kensington Palace, of course, where the various royals hang out.'

Savage was looking at the highest window. Spencer-Hughes had the uncomfortable feeling that it was the look of a marksman. 'And it's quiet,' Savage said again.

'Deadly quiet,' the young man assured him. 'You could shut yourself away in that apartment and keep the world outside. Nobody need know you're there.' He examined Savage speculatively. 'If that's what you want.'

'That's what I want,' said Savage.

Mr Kostelanetz eyed the money respectfully but muttered that he would still like a reference. Spencer-Hughes appeared downcast and checked his watch. Savage said: 'The only reference I can give you is my army discharge papers.'

'Ah, a soldier,' said Mr Kostelanetz who looked as though he might have been one, perhaps a guerrilla, himself. He was a squat man, wearing a heavy camel overcoat. Underneath was a luminous blue suit with wide stripes. He had short grey hair and a long grey moustache. His eyes were scoured by rings. 'How long since?'

'Since I was in the army?' Savage seemed to have difficulty remembering. 'More than a year. And I have been in hospital a lot of that time.' He felt inside his coat pocket. The apartment was windowed on two sides; the ragged winter sky travelled past towards a bruised horizon. There were a wide living room, two bedrooms, a bathroom and a kitchen. Most importantly the kitchen had a freezer. He thought it was the right place for him. Ideal.

'You have been sick?' enquired Mr Kostelanetz doubtfully.

'Wounded,' corrected Savage. 'I was in Northern Ireland.'

'Somewhere there is always fighting,' muttered Mr Kostelanetz shaking his big silver head. 'Always some war.'

Spencer-Hughes sat down on one of the armchairs as though retiring from the conversation. 'Where did you get the wound? I mean where on your body?' asked Mr Kostelanetz.

Savage ran his finger across his head. Mr Kostelanetz became deeply interested and asked to have a closer look at the scar. Savage bent his head obligingly. His dark, almost black hair had turned grey along the length of the healed wound. Mr Kostelanetz formed his lips into a huge but silent whistle. 'A nice parting. Another centimetre and it was goodbye,' he calculated. 'Maybe less. Maybe only a millimetre.'

Any reassurance he needed was apparently provided by the wound. He waved away the discharge papers but then, out of added interest, decided to see them. 'Staff Sergeant,' he said. 'Staff Sergeant Frank Inigo Savage.' He nodded deeply as though approving both the rank and the name. 'Very good,' he said. 'Excellent indeed,' and held out a big, brown and cracked hand. 'I was a soldier also.' He glanced towards Spencer-Hughes. 'These days young men do not become soldiers.'

'I was in the Officer Training Corps at school,'

claimed Spencer-Hughes defensively. 'But I can't see straight. It doesn't matter when you are an estate agent.' Holding the photocopied details before him like an actor attempting some lines, he began to pace out the apartment. 'Main room twenty-four by twenty,' he said. 'Outlook, outlooks I should say, south and east.' He indicated the windows. 'East window has a single door.' He went across and tried the handle. 'Locked.'

'There is a key,' said Mr Kostelanetz flatly. He rolled his ringed eyes towards Savage and shrugged.

'There *is* a key,' Spencer-Hughes repeated to Savage as though he could not have heard. 'Small, very small, balcony outside. Looks as though the pigeons use it mostly. Good views of adjacent apartments.'

'Miss Bombazine,' said Mr Kostelanetz.

Spencer-Hughes paused as though waiting for enlightenment but then moved smartly over to the opposite door. 'Main bedroom,' he announced opening it. 'Eighteen by fifteen. Window facing south again. You can see lots of roofs including those of the buses in Kensington High Street. Radiator. All heating and hot water comes with the service charges. Which are . . .' He peered at the details. 'Thirteen hundred pounds a year.' Mr Kostelanetz was becoming impatient. Relieving the young man of the sheet of details he strode to the second bedroom. 'Bedroom, little,' he said. 'Window.' He pointed outside. 'Miss Bombazine.'

'Who is this Miss Bombazine?' asked Spencer-Hughes.

'A chanteuse,' said the big man adding nothing more than a lifted eyebrow. He strode to another door. 'Kitchen. Good size, eh? Big freezer. All other machinery. Like dishwasher.'

'Washing machine?' suggested Spencer-Hughes timidly but not wanting to be left out.

'No. They jump, jump, bang, bang. It's like the war. Go to launderette.'

'Oh yes.' The youth glanced at Savage. 'Just up Church Street in Notting Hill.'

Mr Kostelanetz ignored him and went to the final door. 'Bathroom,' he said. 'Toilet. Bidet, if you have a lady friend. Also shower.'

'It's fine,' said Savage. 'It's what I'm looking for.'

'My apartment is yours,' said Mr Kostelanetz seriously. He motioned with his eyes towards the estate agent who picked up the advance money from the table, then turned them on Savage. 'You are a wounded staff sergeant.'

Spencer-Hughes said that he would bring around some papers to be signed unless Savage would like to call into the office. 'Bring them around please,' said Savage. 'I don't plan to go out very much.'

'There is no need,' agreed Mr Kostelanetz. 'You can see everything from here.' He went heavily to the window and spread his camel-coated arms to take in the roofs of London. 'And nobody knows you are here.'

'That's the reason,' nodded Savage. 'I want to be quiet.'

'Like a man you call a hermit.'

'Exactly. A hermit.'

At last he was alone. He had heard them talking outside, the booming voice of Mr Kostelanetz and the subdued responses of the estate agent, and then came the lift's whirring arrival, the clanking of its elderly doors and the echo of its descent. The sounds were to be part of his life, the whirr and the clank and the echo; someone coming, someone going.

Walking to the window he positioned himself where Mr Kostelanetz had stood and viewed the tilted roofs, tiled turrets and small towers that occupied the slope towards Kensington High Street. There was winter mist in the bowl of the valley mixed among television aerials and satellite dishes, and grubby afternoon clouds above. But as he watched there came a brief, dishevelled break in the doleful sky and a beam of tenuous sunlight picked out the royal parapets of Kensington Palace.

He knew little of London. His childhood had been spent in the West Country and he had joined the army straight from school. He had served in the Falklands, in Germany and two tours in Northern Ireland. His experience of London had been during brief periods of leave and he and Irene had spent their week's honeymoon in a hotel on the northern side of Hyde Park.

Standing at the wide view now he thought he had probably come to the right place. He was going to be alone, isolated, a Robinson Crusoe above the London roofs. His view down the conglomerated incline was hedged by the high trees of Holland Park on one side and those of Kensington Gardens on the other, their winter heads lean and hard against the skyline. The second, smaller, window to the left of the sitting room looked due east with a partial interruption from another arm of the six-storey block of apartments, below which was a paved yard and the secondary entrance to the block. A helicopter, clattering under the skirts of the clouds, dropped towards Kensington Palace. At this time, on a January early afternoon, there were lights in the rooms opposite. Curtains were drawn across some of the windows but he had a partial view of other rooms, part of a chair, a lamp, a glowing television set, half a woman pouring tea. Scraggy pigeons flew about the brickwork; on summer nights, he was to discover, the roof was the haunt of urban owls.

Savage was pleased that he had come across such an eyrie so readily. Up there he could be what he wanted to be, private, safe, solitary. He needed it. He surveyed the room. The furnishings were over-elaborate for someone accustomed to military surroundings. The settee and chairs were brocaded in pale blue. There was a thirty-inch television in a lacquered cabinet and a sideboard with some Middle Eastern vases and ornaments; a bookcase untidily lined with paperbacks, mostly French and Greek and Arabic, but also with biographies of Mustafa Kemal and Margaret Thatcher. There were prints of what he judged were Eastern Mediterranean scenes and a last year's calendar showing December and a modestly naked girl.

He was about to look into the main bedroom again when he heard the lift ascending followed by the old-fashioned clash of its gates. The buzzer on the door sounded. He waited, tempted to ignore it, then walked three swift strides and called loudly: 'Who is it?'

'Spencer-Hughes. Freddie.' The voice sounded surprised, a touch hurt, to be asked. Savage fractionally opened the door. The vertical mid-portion of the young man's face was revealed. 'I didn't realise you'd be back so soon,' Savage said.

Spencer-Hughes, catching a little of Savage's caution, stepped into the apartment and looked about as though he expected it to be already radically altered. 'It *is* nice,' he re-emphasised. 'Very nice.' Professionally he sniffed around. 'Victorian builders,' he assured Savage. 'Solid as the pyramids. And quite genteel considering some blocks in West London. Gone downhill some of them, the inmates a bit iffy, you know, but Kensington Heights has a bit of old-fashioned class about it.' He squeezed his eyes at the main window and said: 'The one above sees all.'

He remembered why he had come. 'I thought I'd just trundle around with this agreement for you to sign.' He took the document from his pocket. 'Might as well get it done and then I can leave you in peace.'

'What happened to your girlfriend?' asked Savage casually.

'Oh, I told you, didn't I.' He seemed amazed that the information should have been taken in. 'Well, I rang my place and there was no answer. She may have been in the bath or she may have flitted, I don't know. It's a shame if she's gone. I was getting used to her. Are you married?'

'Just about,' responded Savage. 'But not for long I suspect.'

'Oh, it's like that.' He studied Savage with lack of hope. 'It gets like that, doesn't it?'

'It can do.'

Spencer-Hughes seemed uneasy at the answer. He appeared to want to continue with the subject but instead said: 'You'll want to read the agreement.' Opening out the document he placed it on the table. 'You can sign it now or take your time to read it,' he said. 'It's not very complicated. Mr Kostelanetz liked you and in some ways he's a simple man.'

'In some ways he's *not* simple then?' suggested Savage.

'No,' conceded the young man carefully. 'He's a bit mysterious.' He glanced around the room as if he suspected Mr Kostelanetz might still be there. 'I asked him once what he did for business and he said that he comes and he goes. I thought that was a bit odd.'

Savage read the document. 'He doesn't want a separate deposit then?' he asked.

'No. Normally he would be entitled to ask for one but a month's rent in advance suited him. And it's quite enough anyway.' He hesitated. 'There aren't many people who turn up with thousands of quid in a plastic carrier.' Savage smiled and said he would have to get a new bank. Spencer-Hughes said: 'I think the cash from the shopping bag impressed him.' He regarded Savage quizzically. 'I've never seen anyone do that before.'

Two

Savage paced out the apartment as though staking out his territory; the ample main room, the large first bedroom and smaller second bedroom. The bathroom and kitchen had identical measurements. The place was comfortable but bare in the way that rooms are bare when personal touches have been removed. It was somewhere to begin again. This was to be his domain, his fortress, his own place. Here he would patiently wait to recover, wait privately for his life to come back. He had time to decide what to do next.

By now the afternoon had dropped and faded into early damp dusk. Street lights were misty. This is what London must have looked like in the old times. At four o'clock there was a streak of red to the west, thin and apologetic, a sorry shrug from the sky after a dreary day. He switched on the three table lamps and the corner standard lamp and drew the curtains. It gave him no sensation of claustrophobia as he had faintly feared it might; it gave a feeling of enclosed well-being.

He sat in each of the armchairs in turn and then in both positions on the sofa. Then he shifted one chair a fraction so that he would have a half-view out of the window, mostly of the sky. It would be necessary to get a clock; Mr Kostelanetz had apparently taken his with him. He needed his typewriter and he would have to return to their house to get it with his other things. Irene would not be there but going back would not be easy. And there was the gun.

First he would have to get some food. He went into the kitchen and opened the empty freezer, feeling the iced air jumping up to his face.

After what he had done that day – all that in a *single* day – his confidence was high, so high that he felt tempted to ring Dr Fenwick and tell him. In any event he was certain that he could go out of the building and find a corner table in a small restaurant close by. Almost every street had a restaurant. It would be easy although he would have preferred to stay in.

The doorbell rang. There had been no sound of the lift. He stood in the centre of his room and then abruptly went towards the door, slowed, and cautiously opened it. Outside stood a rotund man, his uniform cap already raised. ' 'Evening, sir. It's Mr Tomelty, the head porter. I look after the block and Mrs Tomelty. She helps too.'

Savage invited him in. 'I'm going to need you, Mr Tomelty,' he said shaking hands. The man had a face of broken reds and strands of blue, his eyes bright and busy, his nose like a knot.

'Most people do, sir. Some more than others.'

'It's just that I want to keep people away as far as possible. I want to be alone here.'

'Doing a Greta Garbo,' nodded the porter knowledgeably. 'Ah, we've had a few of those. Mrs Barley was here for years, twenty years at least, in this block and she wouldn't have anybody a single inch over her doorstep. Nobody. She said they would disturb the dust. The first people to go in there were the undertaker's men.'

'I don't think I will be quite so isolated,' said Savage. 'But I've been in hospital and I just want some quiet.'

19

'The army, sir, wasn't it?'

'Well . . . yes. But I need some solitude. There's some writing I want to do.'

'Reminiscences of soldiering, sir?'

'No.'

'Don't blame you. I didn't take to it. National Service. Royal Irish Fusiliers.' Savage did not answer. They were both standing in the middle of the room, Mr Tomelty looking around with his bright, interested eyes. 'Haven't been in here for a long time,' he said. 'Mr Kostelanetz kept his business quiet.'

'What is his business?'

'Spying, so I understand, sir. But he's retired now.' He switched his thoughts. 'Will you be wanting any shopping? Mrs Tomelty will be going down to the Indian. He charges a lot but he stays open late.'

'I think I might eat as far as possible from the freezer,' Savage said. 'But if Mrs Tomelty wouldn't mind getting me something to eat tonight . . .'

'Rations,' suggested the porter.

Savage smiled slightly. 'Yes – rations.'

'I'll ask her to come up, sir.' Tomelty raised a finger. 'Don't go telling her anything about yourself or it will be as far as Fulham by morning. She talks more than me.'

Mrs Tomelty arrived eagerly. She was a lanky woman, her piled-up hair making her lankier, wearing black trousers that stuck to her narrow legs. Her faded blue sweater lay flat against her chest and carried the slogan: 'Save All Souls'.

'Tomelty told me not to keep you,' she said confidingly. 'I'll bet you didn't hear me coming.'

'You didn't use the lift,' Savage said. He had made a list of groceries. It was lying on the arm of the chair. Mrs

Tomelty picked it up and ran her nose down it. 'No problem,' she summed up. She smiled with false teeth. 'Tomelty tells me off for saying that – "no problem" – but it's on account of the foreign residents. No, I don't use the lifts. You never know in a place like this. And we only live downstairs. Bottom flat. There's "Porter" written on the door. So it's only six floors. Keeps me like a stick.'

As she faced him her nose went up and down much as it had done with the list. 'Are you getting better?' she inquired bluntly.

'Improving,' he said with caution.

'Tomelty said you'd been wounded.'

'And I was ill after that.'

She tutted sympathetically. 'People getting shot,' she muttered. 'Disgusting.' Her expression cleared. 'Anyway you should be nice and lonely up here. Mr Kostelanetz was, although he was inclined to go out in the dead of night.' She lowered her voice. 'On account of him being a spy.'

'So I understand.'

She folded the shopping list as though ready to leave. 'You forgot trifles like washing-up liquid,' she observed. 'I'll get anything I think you'll need. Who is going to keep the place tidy? Do the housework?'

'I thought I might do it.'

'Being a soldier I suppose you would,' she reasoned. 'And it will be quiet for whatever you have in mind. There are quite a few residents here in these flats who don't go out much. They keep to themselves. Getting on most of them. Mrs Blenkinsop will tell you that she buried her husband in the basement.'

'Did she?'

'No. It was her dog. She just says it to sound interesting.'

The porter's wife went out and returned in half an hour with two bags of shopping which she took into the kitchen and began to unload. 'Tomelty said you wanted your freezer stocked up,' she observed. 'Well, that's another job. I could do it bit by bit if you like. Now I've got you some chicken portions and some bacon and eggs, and bread and milk, and sugar and things like that. I've got some tins of baked beans.' She put them on the kitchen worktop. 'I don't know how you feel about baked beans.'

When she had finished she made towards the door. 'I like to see the *Nine O'Clock News*,' she said. 'The outside world.'

'How much was the shopping?' he asked.

'Tomelty will give you a bill,' she told him. 'It's the best way if we're going to be doing a few things for you. And I expect we will. I might help you clean up in here. The Indian is expensive and not much good but he's open up to midnight.'

They wished each other goodnight and she closed the door firmly. He had not eaten since he had a cold pie and a cup of coffee on the train to Waterloo. Now he fried some bacon and eggs and had it with baked beans. He sat on the sofa and smiled around the apartment. Then he went to the window and drew back the drapes. The vision was remarkable. Drifting rain thinly curtained London but there were spaces between the clouds and he could see the coloured lights of an airliner dropping towards Heathrow, the cutting searchlight of its landing beam thrust before it.

Immediately below his vantage point was a diagram of lights, liquefied by the rain. On that second night of

January they spread in formations and colours, some flashing intermittently, some gaudy, some dutifully lining the wet streets of the Royal Borough of Kensington and Chelsea. But all was dumb, no sounds came up to him at his window. There was a segment between the roofs where he could see part of what he would come to know was Kensington Church Street, rising towards Notting Hill. Cars and buses drifted up and down but sparsely. It was a quiet night.

As he was about to draw the curtains, withdrawing into his new enclosed world, he heard again the low clatter of a helicopter. He peered up from the window, saw it clearly come over the roof and drop towards the glow of Kensington Palace.

Nothing else seemed to be happening out there; the lights illuminated little but the misty rain, although another distant and hushed airliner had appeared below the clouds, its belly blushing with silvery reflection.

Eventually he pulled the curtains together again, turned on the television and sat in the armchair facing it. It was five minutes to nine. He watched a politician, cornered as a rabbit, in a documentary programme and then sat through the news, observing it blank-eyed as though it came from a remote planet. There were reports from various wars and famines, men, three inches high, festooned with ammunition, playing at soldiers, children with their ribs showing. In Ireland the ceasefire was just about holding. They screened a film sequence with a reporter at the once notorious Crooked Cross. He leaned forward abruptly. That was where it was, that was where it *happened*. The reporter was in a car moving through the district. Savage caught his breath. *There* was the pub on the bit of green, *that* was the half-tree, all that had been left of it, and *there* was the telephone box, now replaced, where they had planted the explosive. He reached to turn it off but remained rooted. The images crossed the screen. The report finished. He put his hands across his eyes. The doorbell rang.

He half-stood, his gaze on the door. He felt shaken; he was sweating across his forehead. His sub-machine gun was back at his house. 'Who's there?' he called, not moving. He leaned forward and touched the button to turn the television off. 'Who is it?'

'Police,' returned a strong voice. 'Mr Savage, we'd like to have a word.'

Savage, astonished at first, then swore quietly, wiped his face with his sleeve, and after a faltering moment, moved towards the door. Before he could unlock it, there was a tentative knock and a woman's sharp voice called: 'It's just routine. We won't keep you long.'

He stood inches from them on the other side. 'What is it you want?' he asked through the wood. 'It's Detective Sergeant Gander and Constable Deepe,' itemised the male voice.

Savage turned the key in the lock, opened the door narrowly and regarded them through the crack. He now noticed that there had been a security chain on the door at one time but that it had been forcibly broken and the damage to the woodwork shoddily repaired. A man's nose appeared the other side of the aperture. 'Mr Savage,' the voice repeated with a sort of patience. 'It's us, the police.'

'Have you got identification?' he asked, ready to throw his weight behind the door.

A warrant card was passed through the gap. It said: 'Humphrey Gander, Detective Sergeant, Metropolitan Police.' He handed it back then opened the door.

Gander was huge enough to have forced his way in

anywhere. He wore a check sports jacket with imitation leather patches on the sleeves, his tie was sportingly striped but his shirt looked as if it was coming to the end of a protracted day. He had a low-slung moustache and the front of his head shone baldly. His eyes, blue and flat, surveyed the room.

The policewoman was in uniform. She was slight, almost skinny, with short dark hair and tired eyes. She studied him carefully as if filing him away for future use.

'What is it?' sighed Savage.

'Do you mind if we sit down?' asked Gander.

'It's been a long day,' said the woman.

Savage motioned them towards the settee. 'You haven't by any chance got the kettle on, have you?' asked Gander. 'Jean will make it.'

Savage blinked. 'No ... I haven't...'

'Yes, I'll make it,' confirmed the policewoman. She stood and went towards the kitchen. 'Leave her,' suggested Gander. 'She's good at making tea.'

Savage sat down heavily. 'What is it you wanted?'

'Well, first off, sorry we're so late.'

'I wasn't aware you were coming at all.'

Gander shifted uncomfortably, laughed and coughed. 'No, well you wouldn't I suppose, stands to reason. The computer took its time. Some of those things can tell your fortune, but they can't give you the stuff you want.'

'What stuff did you want exactly?'

'Only routine, really, but we thought we'd better get it done tonight, out of the way. Then we can leave you alone.' He nodded towards the kitchen. 'We'd better wait until Jean comes back. She'll get upset if I start without her.' He breathed deeply. 'Women.'

As though to forestall any additional questions he rose weightily and rolled towards the main window. Savage watched him with growing astonishment as he opened the curtains and straightened his big back with a profound sigh. 'Does you good to see London like this, don't you reckon. All spread out right under your nose, no crime you can see, no villains, no kids on drugs, no lost dogs, all decent and quiet. There's hardly a sound gets up here, is there.' His head moved as he saw an aeroplane, fiercely lit, on its path towards Heathrow. 'You can't even hear him,' he said. He lifted his arms and pretended he was aiming a rocket. 'Bang! Whoosh!' he said quietly. He turned with a wicked smile. 'Got the bugger.'

From the kitchen they heard the kettle begin to whistle. It served as a signal because Gander turned back and reseated himself. He looked at his watch, thick-banded about a massive wrist. 'Nine thirty,' he said. 'We're into overtime.' In three distinct movements he looked around the walls. 'You'll be needing a clock here.'

'I plan to get one,' agreed Savage steadily. 'I only moved in today.'

'Right,' said Gander. He took out a notebook and wrote it down.

Savage watched him and said: 'What is all this?'

'Here she comes. Tea,' smiled Gander hugely. Jean Deepe appeared through the kitchen door, pushing it with her police shoe. She had a tray with a teapot, jug, sugar bowl and three cups. 'No biscuits, I'm afraid,' she said. 'Can't find them.'

'I haven't got any,' Savage told her keeping his voice level. 'I didn't even know I had a teapot. You should have come tomorrow.'

'Couldn't,' answered Gander decidedly. 'No way. My day off. Golf tomorrow.' He swung his arms in unison.

'And I'm on a course,' said the woman. Brushing

down her uniform jacket she smiled thinly at Savage and then transferred it to Gander. 'Not a golf course either.'

'So we had to get it done tonight or it would have been the weekend,' said Gander. Jean began to pour the tea. Her colleague mentioned he would like two sugars. Savage said he would do without. 'What, may I ask, is it you have come about?' he insisted eventually. 'I'd like to know. I've had a busy day.'

'You certainly have,' agreed Gander as if he had monitored every move. He sucked heavily at his tea. Jean Deepe drank hers almost primly, her black-stockinged knees tightly together. The detective sergeant produced a computer print-out from his jacket pocket. He flicked his eyes at Savage. 'It was all done at once, wasn't it? In a bit of a rush.'

'What? You mean getting this place? Well, yes it was. I needed somewhere. But I still don't understand what that's got to do with the police.'

'Mr Savage,' said Gander with half a sigh. 'You're a military man . . .'

'I was.'

'Right. Then you've got to realise that this flat, apartment, call it what you will, is in a strategic position. You only have to look out of that window.'

'Strategic?' said Savage astonished. 'For what, for God's sake?'

'Embassies. Royal residences,' sniffed Jean Deepe, her lips half an inch from the rim of her cup, her words ruffling the surface of the tea. 'Helicopters going overhead.'

Savage stared at them. 'Christ,' he breathed. 'That's all I need. I came here because it's high up, because it's quiet, or I thought it would be. I want to be by myself.

Instead of that, half of bloody London has been though here today.'

They laughed together as though in sympathy. The detective sergeant wagged his big head. 'But we hope you'll understand that anyone occupying this spot has to be cleared security-wise.'

'I'm beginning to. What about Mr Kostelanetz?'

'Mr Kostelanetz is confidential,' said Gander a touch huffily. 'But we know all about Mr Kostelanetz.'

'You have to clear somebody with a name like that,' said Jean Deepe.

'He was clear,' conceded Gander. 'In fact he's been quite handy to us one way and another. But this sudden moving-in of yours set the alarm bells ringing even in our nick, and they're not the quickest off the mark.'

'So we had to check you out,' said the woman.

'What do you want to know?' asked Savage wearily.

'We know most of it,' grunted Gander. 'We just wanted to confirm it, that's all. And to give you the once-over, as it were.'

'As a recent member of Her Majesty's armed forces I'm hardly likely to go shooting down any royal helicopters,' responded Savage moodily. 'And I haven't got anything to shoot with.' He had not touched his tea.

'Oh, I don't know,' put in Gander with a sort of whine he might use arguing some point about golf. 'You never can tell. We've had lots of nutters come out of the army and still having a yen for a rocket launcher.'

'Well, this nutter doesn't have a yen for one,' said Savage sharply.

'Sorry, I didn't mean to offend you', returned Gander his expression apparently concerned. 'Nothing personal.' The woman tutted towards her colleague. Gander peered at his print-out as if he had trouble understanding it. His

28

pale, almost blank, eyes came up and he half-rose. 'Wounded in Ulster,' he muttered. He appeared to be distantly confirming the grey streak in Savage's hair. 'In the head.'

'Right lung and left testicle as well,' Savage finished for him. He regarded the man acerbically. 'Would you like to see?'

'Won't be necessary,' said Gander unruffled. Jean Deepe shook her head. Her colleague returned to the print-out. 'Oh, right. Yes, it says here. Lung, right and testicle, left.'

'It must have been nasty,' said Jean.

'Painful too,' added the detective. 'Pity about that.'

'Four of my squad were killed,' Savage told them quietly. 'It was, as you put it, nasty.'

'Cor,' said Gander. 'I wouldn't have been there for a bonus.' He breathed deeply as if thinking about his narrow escape, then continued: 'You ended up in hospital, military hospital?'

'Aldershot,' said Savage deliberately. 'And then to Marshfield Manor. That's the psychiatric hospital, to save you asking. I have losses of memory among other things.'

'How long can't you remember?' asked Gander with genuine interest.

'At first it was weeks,' Savage said. 'I could hardly remember anything that happened in Northern Ireland. Then it got down to days. And now it's much better. It just gets me sometimes. I'm not likely to forget today in a hurry.' He waited and then decided to tell them. 'I also have a fear of crowds and enclosed places – I'm scared of being trapped, I suppose – and I'm subject to occasional bouts of depression. I'm well aware of all my ailments. It's all down on that sheet, I imagine.'

'Not in those words,' conceded Gander. 'Thanks

anyway. So that's why you're up here then. You're above everything, crowds, the lot.'

'Isn't this a bit enclosed?' asked Jean Deepe looking around her. 'Wouldn't you have been better off in the country somewhere?'

'I also have a fear of *exposed* places,' Savage informed her seriously. 'It's not simple. Up here, in the clouds, as it were, seemed like a good idea. Until I got here anyway.'

'We won't bother you after this,' Gander assured him as if making a sporting offer. 'It's only routine surveillance.' He glanced at his colleague. 'Unless somebody higher up wants to know more about you.' He looked back towards the curtains and once again stood and went towards the window. Opening the drapes he bunched then expanded his shoulders as he looked out on the lights below. 'They couldn't build these flats any higher,' he confided. 'Even when they put them up, donkey's years ago, they weren't allowed to build any higher. And in those days there weren't any planes. No helicopters.'

'Do you have any family?' Jean Deepe asked Savage carefully.

Gander strolled to the side window and said: 'You've got a little balcony. Well, you've got the best of all worlds. Not too closed in, not too out in the open. You were lucky to get this place.'

'Yes, I *thought* I was,' replied Savage. He returned to Jean Deepe. 'Well, I do have a wife. We've been married ten years in fact. But traipsing around army bases is not the best foundation for any marriage. In the end we bought a house in Hampshire, near Basingstoke, when I was stationed nearby. I went to Ulster, Irene stayed at home. After I was discharged from hospital we tried to settle down but it wasn't easy. I was in a difficult state, shall we say. And anyway our hearts weren't in it. We decided to call it a day.'

'It happens,' nodded the woman.

'It certainly does,' confirmed Gander as if it happened to him all the time. He was anxious to get away from sentiment. 'What are you going to do here?' he asked.

'Live, I hope,' said Savage. 'That was the intention.'

'Will you get employment?'

'Not for a while,' said Savage. 'I've been in the service all my working life. I have a pension and some savings. And we'll be selling the house.'

'You paid your rent in cash,' said Gander. 'From a carrier bag.'

'Yes. Do you want to see it?'

'I wouldn't mind.'

Savage got up and went into the bathroom. Gander glanced at his colleague and said quietly: 'Funny bloke.' Savage returned and put the plastic shopping bag on the table. 'There it is,' he said. 'Do you want to count it?'

Gander peered into the carrier and whistled. 'I'd put that in the bank if I was you,' he advised. He leaned forward and fingered the notes as if to ensure they were real. 'You never can tell in London.' He appeared to be searching for one last question. 'What will you do?' he asked indicating personal interest. He leaned forward bulkily. 'Just sit up here?' He glanced at the television. 'Watching the box?'

Savage said: 'I'm going to compile an encyclopaedia. When it's finished I'll send you a copy if you like.'

Gander regarded him sideways. 'An encyclopaedia?'

'All by yourself?' asked Deepe.

'Initially. The publisher will want to get other people involved eventually. Editors and suchlike. But for the time being it's just me.'

'You've got a publisher then?' said Deepe.

'No. Not yet. But I'm in no hurry. It might take several years.'

Gander asked carefully: 'What sort is it?'

'The subject? It's about islands.'

'Oh,' said Gander.

'Really,' said his colleague.

'Yes, it will be called *An Encyclopaedia of World Islands*.' Gander looked puzzled, Jean Deepe attentive. Savage said: 'It's been an interest for me, a hobby, you could call it, reading about islands, research, recording material. It helped me when I was in hospital. Now I've got the opportunity I thought I would gather it all together.' As though he thought they still needed convincing he added: 'No one's ever done it before.'

'No,' mumbled Gander. 'I suppose they wouldn't have.' He surveyed the room. 'How are you going to write it, in longhand?'

'I have a typewriter,' returned Savage seriously. 'I have to bring it from my house.'

'And you're going to sit here by yourself and work at it,' summed up the woman constable. She glanced at Gander. 'That sounds peaceful enough. I wouldn't mind a job like that.'

'I'll need to go out,' added Savage. 'To libraries and so forth.'

'And to islands,' she put in.

'Yes, of course.' He wavered. 'Once I've got myself together.'

'Well,' yawned Gander standing up as if there was nothing more to say. 'We'll be on our merry way.' Jean Deepe stood up also. She picked up the tea tray, loaded it with cups and took it towards the kitchen. 'Thanks for the tea,' she said.

'Yes, thanks,' contributed Gander. 'We'd help with the washing up . . .' He laughed. 'But we're on overtime.'

They went towards the door. As he got there Gander paused and squinted around the room again as if he wanted to be quite sure. 'Yes,' he said vaguely. 'Thanks.'

They left. Savage waited inside the door while they got into the lift, closed the metallic grille and descended. Then he walked backwards and sat in one of the armchairs, still facing the door. 'Bloody hell,' he muttered.

Three

He had no nightmares, although he woke once and lay with instinctive caution, inert and unsure. Where was he? What was he doing there? A subdued glow filtered around and through the curtains and he realised his whereabouts. Relieved, he looked at his watch on the bedside cabinet. It was four o'clock.

He next awoke with full daytime outside and with muffled noise rising from the streets below. The half-lights of the windows were open and he could hear the sounds and shouts of dustmen collecting bins, and the movement of cars. It was the bleat of a fire engine which had wakened him. He lay back, glad that he was there.

What was he going to do now? Be there. That was the answer, an answer he had known for a long time; all during the weeks recovering from his wounds, his 'indents' as they had playfully called them in the ward; then the long shaded months in the psychiatric hospital, safe but riven inside, wanting only to be away, isolated from everything. Now he was there, here, within the rented walls, high up, knowing that he was at a new start. Where would it lead? What, he wondered again, was going to happen to him? If anything.

He got up and made tea, drank it and went to the bathroom. He still had his army washbag, the razor upright and keen. He dressed methodically. Dr Fenwick had always been keen on routine as a basis for recovery; milestones through the day he had called them; getting through that day, and the next, and the next.

Now that the depression, the blank of memory, and some of the fears had retreated, he felt certain he could face life, preferably on his own terms. He was pleased that he had made the move from the cold armchair in his vacant house, deep in the damp countryside, to this enclosed and comfortable haven above London. He had carried through his resolve. All he needed to do now was to settle down, slowly to be himself again, although it would never be the same self. That self was gone forever.

He had gone into the service at sixteen, to the Army Apprentices School, overlooking the Severn, where the bridge now crossed from England to Wales. When he drove across the bridge in later life he always nodded recognition at it. Drill, school lessons, more drill, range firing, military history, sports, swimming. It had been a safe, institutionalised life. When he had gone into the real army it had been the same pattern; if you conformed to its rules and its routines the army would look after you. Until you left the service. Or died.

In that distant, vivid moment at Crooked Cross, County Antrim, three men, three men like him, good regulars serving their time, had died. Sergeant Barnard, Henry Barnard, had died later. Another fraction of an inch and he would have been the fifth. Not a bad morning for the Provos. He tried not to think of it but he remembered it every day.

He knew that he would sometimes have to venture out of the apartment; he could not just bolt himself in there. He needed things. He would go, but when he chose. At some time he would have to return briefly to his house. He thought of the gun there. It was bloody foolish that gun, but he had it, he had stolen it, and he still, in a guilty, ashamed way, felt he needed its reassurance. Stupid soldier.

That first day he spent moving things around the flat. There was not a great deal to rearrange but he spent time doing it. He had to buy a clock. At intervals he went to the window. It was always the same scene but different in its details and its light. As the day moved so did the tones of the Kensington roofs. When the windows were closed the noise of the traffic was diminished to near silence but you could hear the rain. It rained, then it stopped, then it rained again. The one constant was the tracking of the spaced planes towards the airport, as though someone at Heathrow were tugging them in on a string.

He was glad to find an ironing board. It had never been used and still had the retaining plastic band around it. It was difficult to imagine Mr Kostelanetz ironing his own shirts. Savage would need to get some temporary clothes himself, enough to last until he went back to his house. Irene had bought his shirts and sweaters. Some were still unwrapped, trousers still in the Marks & Spencer bags. He broke the plastic band on the ironing board and opened it out. Now he would need an iron.

He fried bacon and eggs for his breakfast and had chicken and beans for lunch. He watched the television news and, surprising and pleasing himself, slept for an hour. At four o'clock, when it was almost dark, he put on his overcoat and went determinedly out into the street, the neighbouring world.

The early January hush remained over everything and he was grateful for it. Collar up, he walked down Kensington Church Street, crossing the reflections of the shop windows. The damp and cold of the afternoon were on his face; he looked directly ahead. He went into

Barkers and bought all the clothes he needed and the iron, paying cash. Tomorrow he would have to open a bank account.

He returned to Kensington Heights feeling a small triumph, taking a different route, another rising street under the bulwarks of the massive, brick town hall. A signpost pointed to the public library. There were lights in every window. Sitting on the paving in the space between the different wings of the building was a group of young people, close together, still as huddled pigeons. Two newcomers, a youth and a girl, although it was hard to tell with their layers of clothes and their pulled-down hats, joined them without saying anything. Just as silently the others moved even closer to make room. As they did so the sound of muffled music emerged. Somewhere, at the centre of the pile, a battery radio was playing. A skinny girl in a pink fun-fur coat, hanging damp on her, arrived and squatted next to the human pile. Somebody said: 'Korky's here.' Savage caught a glimpse of her narrow, ashen face in the aperture of a scarf pulled around her head. He thought she looked at him for a moment. Then he moved on.

Again it began to rain and he hurried the few yards along the adjoining side street and into the courtyard formed by the wings of Kensington Heights. He entered by the side door. Emerging from the lift was a worn-looking man, not quite elderly, wearing a dusty, old-fashioned suit and a limp, spotted bow-tie, and with spots of dandruff on his shoulders.

'Ah, ha,' he said with ponderous cheeriness. 'You must be our new resident. In old Kostelanetz's place.'

Hesitantly Savage took the proffered white hand. They introduced themselves. 'Bertie Maddison, flat two-two-

two,' said the man. 'Do you like music? Serious stuff I mean.'

'I don't know much about it,' admitted Savage.

'We love it. All sorts. Opera to a piece for the piccolo. Anything. I'm trying to get some sort of musical interest here in Kensington Heights. I mean, the Albert Hall is only down the street.'

'Well, I . . .'

'It's my wife is the trouble. People won't go with her. She boos. She was blowing raspberries at the Festival Hall last night. Didn't think the conductor was any cop.' He patted Savage on the shoulder. 'Anyway think about it. Hope you settle in. I'll introduce you to some of the gang.'

He went briskly out into the evening. Savage began to climb the stairs. At the top, on the landing in front of his door, he discovered Mrs Tomelty. She began briskly polishing his letter-box. 'Did you sleep all right, Mr Savage?' she enquired blandly.

'Yes, fine thank you.'

'I'll come and see what you want for your freezer. Miss Bombazine didn't disturb you then, coming in?'

'No, she didn't.'

Mrs Tomelty's eyes dropped to her polisher and to the letter-box again. 'She's always late. She's an entertainer, you know.'

Late the following afternoon, twenty minutes before they closed, he took his carrier bag full of money to the bank. The black girl behind the grille glanced at the clock. 'I'd like to join the bank, please,' said Savage.

'You want to open an account?'

'Yes, I want to do that.' He put the plastic carrier on

the counter. She regarded it suspiciously. 'What's that?' she inquired.

'Money. It's the money I want to put in the bank.'

'In that bag? How much is it?'

'Twenty-six thousand, eight hundred and eighty pounds.' He had counted it that afternoon.

'In cash?'

'Yes, it's cash.'

'Don't tell me. You've robbed a bank.'

'No. It's my money.'

She said: 'Shit,' under her breath and rang a bell. A pink-cheeked man in a waistcoat appeared. 'This gentleman wants to open an account,' said the girl.

The man also glanced at the clock but attempted to look pleased. He turned to the girl. 'Well?' he said.

'It's in cash,' she told him stonily. 'In that shopping bag. It's twenty-six thousand . . .'

'. . . Eight hundred and eighty pounds,' finished Savage.

'Shit,' said the man also under his breath. He smiled fulsomely at Savage. 'Will you step into the office, please.'

The woman at the desk in the library was squat and friendly. She gave him the forms to fill and sign. She glanced at the address. 'Kensington Heights,' she said.

Savage took in the lined shelves behind her. It was late and they would be closing soon. 'Can I take some books now?' he asked.

'Yes. Up to four. More on special request. Tell me what you want and I'll know in which direction to point you.'

'Islands,' he said. 'Anything dealing with islands.'

'Ah,' she said a little taken aback. 'There's no section devoted to islands, particularly.' She moved from behind her desk and led him down the central aisle. She stopped and pointed down a long row. 'Travel, Topography and Geography is around the corner,' she said. 'You should find something there.'

When he walked back with four books ten minutes later she was clearing her desk. 'Just in time,' she said. 'We're closing.' She indicated a mildly disgruntled young man standing behind a counter. 'Harold will stamp them for you.' She called across to Harold: 'Won't you, Harold.'

'Oh, yes,' said Harold flatly. He had just started the job and he did not like it. As he stamped the books he thought they could be the last he ever did. He probably would not come in the next day. Savage walked out with the woman. They were going in the same direction. 'What did you get?' she asked as they paced up the easy hill.

'All Pacific,' he answered. 'There were more about the Pacific islands, so I got those. I'll come back regularly for the others.'

'I'll keep anything back I think might be interesting,' she offered. 'Is it any sort of islands?'

'Yes, any islands, anywhere,' he said. 'I'm . . . well, I'm thinking of putting together an encyclopaedia.'

'Of islands? Well, that should be new. I've never seen one that I can recall. You're a writer then.'

'Yes. Sort of.'

'This area is a kind of island,' she reflected as they walked. 'It's separated from London still, even though it's built up on every side. Not all that many years ago it was countryside, big estates.' She paused and he waited too. 'Here,' she indicated, 'Observatory Gardens. An astronomer lived there, Sir James South. He had a telescope there.' She laughed. 'That was in the days when you could see the sky properly, not through a haze of smog.'

She was taking a turn right there. He thanked her and said goodnight. A group of unkempt young people slouched silently along the pavement, keeping close, eyes ahead. The girl with the pink fun fur was with them. It clung damp and dirty about her body. 'Going to bed,' said the library lady. 'If they can find one.'

'I saw them lying in the space in the town hall the other day,' Savage said. 'You'd think kids of that age would have a home, wouldn't you.'

'You would. Perhaps they don't want to go to it,' she said.

Four

After two weeks, having twice put it off, he decided it was time to make the journey back to his house near Basingstoke. It took all his resolve but at eleven in the morning he left Kensington Heights and walked out into the street. There was a man on a ladder cleaning a bay window and a fat woman with a fat dog, both waddling away from him, but no other people. He could see the traffic in Kensington Church Street at the distant junction but, as though the driver had been seeking him out, a taxi rounded the corner and came towards him, its orange light aglow in the dingy morning.

He asked for Waterloo Station and sat back, watching the grey-faced streets, the traffic and the hurrying people.

'Going far?' asked the driver in a bored voice. 'From Waterloo?'

'Hampshire, that's all,' answered Savage.

'Wish I was,' returned the driver as though he had said Tahiti. Savage got out at the side entrance to the station and went in, under the huge, high and sounding cavern of the main concourse. It was a massive space, echoing with announcements, acres of it, wide and pale, above it, like a private sky, a zigzag enclosing roof. He kept walking steadily.

There were few people there at that time of the morning. He was relieved. A scattered group was watching the clicking departure board, every head at an upward angle as though awaiting some great, revealing truth. He bought his ticket from a window which framed an Indian booking clerk in a blue turban, and then got a newspaper and stood, half-reading, observing the departures indicator over the paper's top edge. The Southampton train clicked up. Basingstoke was the second stop.

Circumstances appeared to be working for him. The carriages were almost vacant. He found a corner seat by the window and concentrated on pretending to read the newspaper.

At eleven forty-five the train gave a jolt and moved out of the station. He felt confident sitting in the corner, watching from the window. The train switched and clattered out of the station and began its trail through the older yellow brick South London streets, now diminished and pushed into blind alleys by tower blocks and glass-faced offices.

He began to think about Irene. He ought to have stayed at the hospital for longer, as they had wanted; he should have returned to life less hurriedly. But he had feared that the place might claim him for good. Irene had been the one who stuck with him. She did not deserve it. He thought of her now, her good smile and dark hair, her patience, at last cracked, and her concern for him, what would happen to him when he was alone.

At Woking, the train's first stop, there were six soldiers on the platform, crop-haired recruits, wooden-faced, awkward in their stiff uniforms, slinging their packs and kitbags inexpertly as they boarded the train. They shouted to each other in raw voices. The train pulled away and the landscape opened out, grey-green, wet and sullen on the mid-winter day, the sky sulky, the horizon close but indistinct. A brown river curled like rusty wire through flat farmland, there were lights showing in houses and from the few cars on the rural roads. He wondered if he would ever need to drive again.

It was fifty minutes to Basingstoke. There the young soldiers awkwardly piled out of their carriage. He stood on the platform watching, wondering if they had any idea of what could happen. A sergeant was sorting them out like children. Savage walked past and out of the station.

There was a line of taxis in the forecourt and a military fifteen hundredweight into which the soldiers and their equipment were climbing. The sergeant banged the tailboard with his hand and trotted around to the front of the vehicle where he heaved himself in beside the driver.

As they drove away Savage saw that the sergeant and the driver were laughing. The sergeant was shaking his head. A taxi driver leaned back and opened his rear door. Savage got in. 'High Grenville, please,' he said. 'I'll show you where.'

'Those kids,' mentioned the driver as they drove. 'Those squaddies you was watching. They have a lovely life these days. Proper grub, lots of sport, decent pay, plenty of leave. Not like when I was in.'

He studied Savage in his mirror. 'You been in the cake?' he asked.

'Until last year.'

'I wouldn't do it again.'

'Nor would I,' said Savage.

It was a fifteen-minute drive. Savage pretended to read the newspaper. They pulled up in front of the thatched house, its roof scarcely projecting over a high yew hedge. 'Cosy,' approved the driver. 'Is this where you live now?'

'I did,' said Savage paying him. 'I won't be long. An hour at the most. Will you come back for me?'

'All right,' said the driver. 'I'll book it and either I'll be back or another cab if I've got a job in the meantime.'

That would be plenty of time. He would not need to stay longer nor did he want to. He turned and went through the wooden gate. Its groan gave him a jolt. She had always said that she would listen for it and know he was home again. It was a sign between them, something, at least, shared. The garden looked ragged, wet, making him wonder, but only briefly, if he should come down and try to clear it, tidy it, dig a bit here and there, before they put the place on the market.

He walked the remainder of the short paved path. Under the trees at the side he caught sight of the bicycle. He had forgotten that too. The fact annoyed him, offended his sense of care for equipment. Turning away from the front door he went slowly to it, shaking some of the wet from its frame and brushing the saddle with the newspaper. They had thought that it was going to be useful. Now the chain was rusty. He should have put it under cover.

Regretfully he laid it back back against the tree and turned again to the front door. From his back pocket he took the key, studied it as though he thought it might no longer fit, then tried it in the Yale lock. It turned obediently and he pushed at the door. He had expected there to be a drift of letters and junk mail behind it but there was none. Instead, as he opened it, he came face to face with his wife. When she saw him she began to cry.

They stood a pace apart. 'Hello,' Irene said wiping her face with her hand. 'We've come back at the same time. Funny isn't it. I've only been here a few minutes.'

'Do you mind if I come in?'

'Come in? Of course. Sorry.' She stood back and he stepped into the hall lowering his head to get below the lintel. 'It's your house as well,' she said. She paused. 'I almost didn't recognise you with your hair longer.'

'I should have got it cut,' he said a little guiltily.

They were standing as close as they had been for a long time. It was Irene who offered her arms and put them around him. He responded, hesitant and anxious. She kissed him on the cheek and he kissed her head. 'What a business,' he mumbled inadequately. 'I'm sorry I decided to come here today.'

'I shouldn't have just walked out like that,' she said dropping her head to his chest. 'It wasn't right. Not just before Christmas.'

'I didn't blame you,' he said releasing her. Her face came up. They moved into the silent sitting room with its icy fireplace and lattice windows. 'I would have walked out on myself.'

'What did you do?' she asked.

Savage shrugged. 'I just stayed here. I sat in that chair. Sometimes I watched the television and sometimes I didn't. The fire went out and I didn't light it again. The radiator was on.'

'What about food? I was worried. I tried to ring you.'

'I was all right. There was enough to eat in the kitchen. I unplugged the phone.'

'I went to my mother's. What a Christmas.'

'I guessed you would.' They were standing close in the room. 'It's no good, is it,' she remarked sadly. 'It never has been, has it? Not since you came back. I'm not strong enough for it, Frank.' Her face was desolate.

'Nobody could expect you to be,' he said. 'Really I should have stayed in the hospital until everything was right. Until they'd sorted me out.'

'Then you might have never come out,' she said.

'That's what I was scared of.'

They were standing, almost loitering. 'Do you want a cup of coffee?' she suggested. 'I could do with one.' She turned and went towards the kitchen. They were playing at house in their own house. After a while her call came more firmly through the open door. 'Frank, what did you do after Christmas? Where did you go?'

'To London,' he called back. 'I'm living in London now.'

Irene came back into the room looking astonished. 'London?' But surely . . . surely that's the last place you ought to be. Frank, you need somewhere quiet and . . .'

'Isolated,' he completed with a semblance of a smile. 'Well, I've managed to find that all right. I've got a flat at the top of a block in Kensington. I can look out over everything.'

'And it's quiet?' she asked. She could hear the kettle boiling. She went back into the kitchen.

'It's meant to be,' he answered raising his voice. 'At the start it was less than that. People in and out. But now it's quieter. I'm going to begin work on my encyclopaedia. Remember my encyclopaedia? That's why I came today, to get my typewriter.'

'Your islands,' she said reappearing with the cups. Her eyes rose to him. 'You've always wanted to get on with that.' She put the cups on the coffee table, wiping some dust away. 'Only powdered milk,' she said. She sat and they drank the coffee, already short of conversation. Irene surveyed the unwarmed room. 'This was going to be where we lived.'

He reached forward and patted her softly but awkwardly. 'All I can say is I'm sorry,' he said.

'The man who put a bullet through your head isn't, I bet,' she said with quick bitterness.

'Maybe by now he's had a bullet through his.'

47

She glanced at him. 'Are you due to have any more treatment?' she asked.

'Nothing definite. No set appointment or anything. Dr Fenwick said to contact him, if anything went wrong. I'm taking the right course I think, waiting to see if it will all eventually go away. I've been pretty good recently.'

'You came down by train?' she said realising. 'You didn't drive.'

'No, I haven't got back to driving.'

'Well, I've known the time you couldn't have done that, get on a train.'

'And I managed to make all the arrangements with the flat in Kensington,' he said with a touch of pride. 'All in one day too. January the second.' He glanced at her. 'I took my half from the bank, from the deposit account,' he said.

'Exactly that,' she said quietly. 'I know. Down to splitting the odd seventy-four pence. I had to go in there this morning.' Her eyes went around the room. 'We'll be selling this now. Do you want me to make a start on it?'

'I'd be grateful.'

'It's all right. I can do it. I'll get another job when things get settled down. And you'll be up there in your flat putting your islands together.' They became wordless again but, before the silence could settle, she rose. 'I must be going,' she said with a sort of primness. She suddenly realised that the mantleshelf clock had long stopped. 'It's one thirty,' she said looking at her watch.

She went to the clock, put the hands right, and gave the key a single token turn. It began to tick boldly. 'Not such a deathly hush,' she said. Then she made towards the door and he stood up. The void between them was sagging. 'I'll manage,' she told him. 'I just packed a couple of cases.'

'You'll want a taxi,' he said.

'No need. I've got someone picking me up. A friend.' She turned quickly and sadly held him. 'Don't come to the door,' she said. 'It's just a friend.' They kissed. 'I miss you,' she mumbled putting her cheek against his.

'I miss me as well,' he said. 'One day perhaps I'll turn up from somewhere.'

There was a car noise outside and then in a moment she had gone, opening the front door and hurrying out with her cases. They had, at the final, difficult moment, exchanged telephone numbers. He returned to the room, its cheerlessness now only emphasised by the dogged ticking of the clock, and stood listening while the car moved off. He sat in the chair, in front of the black, yawning fireplace, and finished the lukewarm coffee.

He remembered how far it had been necessary for her to travel to the psychiatric hospital but she had driven it three times a week, sharing, or trying to share, his isolation, trying to fathom his deep inner void. She had sat and held his hand when they had watched a comedy film, sitting in the dimness with other docile patients; then she drove two hours back through the night to this, their forlorn cottage, leaving him in his fortress bed besieged by shadows. Once, while he was waiting for her, he saw her in the garden below talking to Dr Fenwick. They had talked a long time half-hidden at first by the huge spread of a cedar, but then had walked into the open and towards the hospital. With a shock Savage had seen the tears she was shedding and saw that Dr Fenwick was trying to console her. Ten minutes later she had greeted him with her firm smile and lied cheerfully that she had been delayed by the traffic.

When the hospital authorities had finally decided, with

49

patent reluctance, that he could leave, she had held his hand and told him not to look back. From then, from that moment, it was going to be all right, different, the only way was forward. And she would be with him all along the journey. But it was not. Living together again they had become strangers.

Now he sat with the dregs of the coffee, surveying the purposeless room, the dull chairs, the blank television, the closed bureau they had bought at a sale. Moodily he took the cup to the kitchen and washed it under the tap. The water felt hard and cold. A spider had spun a web across the corner of one of the cabinets. Someone was at home anyway. He put the cup on the draining board and then looked around for a cloth. He pulled one of the kitchen drawers open and there was his sub-machine gun.

He stared at it. He tried to remember putting it there. He must have done so just before going to London. Had Irene seen it?

It was in three pieces, a Russian weapon; he picked it up, familiarly, like an old acquaintance. He clipped the pieces together hesitantly at first but then with a sudden resolve, professional facility, and finally, satisfaction. It was something he could do. He balanced the gun in one hand, then the other, and then both. It felt good to him, even now. He regarded it as a man would a secret, shameful vice. He was ashamed that he had stolen it and was not sure why he had done so. But he was glad he had it. After what had happened to him he could not help the feeling that it might come in useful, even if the trigger mechanism was missing and there was no ammunition.

He took the weapon and without noise laid it out on the kitchen table. He put one eye to the barrel, like a telescope, and then putting it to his mouth blew through it so that it made a muted bugle sound. It could go under his bed.

He left it on the table and walked upstairs. There were two hunched bedrooms in the roof of the cottage, warm and cambered below the thatch. He felt their closeness overhang him as he pushed open the black wooden door; their former bed was there, lying neatly abandoned. There was another door leading from the low room into the next. That was a single room where he had stumbled on the nights when he could not sleep. In the three months they had occupied the house together he had spent many open-eyed hours lying in its darkness. Fixed at the highest part of the wall in the main room was a long, scarred mirror and he caught sight of himself in the stained reflection. He had to stoop to look. His face was set as a skull, his eyes hollow, his mouth oblong.

Against the low wall under the thatch was an area where Irene had intended to collect oddments, the sort of lumber that people gathered after occupying a house for years. But there had been no years. It contained only his army suitcase. He tugged it out patterned with dust. His name was stencilled on it in large letters: 'Staff Sergeant F. I. Savage' and his army number. As he pulled it towards the low door between the two rooms, a panicky bird cried out in the thatch and startled him.

The suitcase felt as though it were not entirely empty. He banged it with the side of his hand and blew away some of the dust. The concealed bird was still clamouring. He replaced the small door, restoring its privacy, and it became stilled. Then he lifted the suitcase on to the bed, blowing away more dust. It was locked but the key was in the right-hand hole; he turned it and the hasp flew up at the first press of his thumb. Then he waited, backed away from it, as though with the abrupt thought that he might be uncovering, tampering with, a secret he would rather not know. His own perhaps. Frowning he bent again, transferred the key, turned it and clicked the second hasp. He lifted the lid of the suitcase. In it, crumpled and rolled, was his army uniform.

He tightened his lips and picked it out, lifting the tunic gently with both hands and by the shoulders, stretching them out to their fullest extent, as though the wearer were standing to attention. His crown and stripes were dulled, the khaki fabric creased and giving off a damp odour. Once it had been the stuff of his life; his daily work clothes, his best suit. He relaxed his hold on the tunic. Now it was bent and dishevelled. Disused, like him.

With a grunt almost of disgust he dropped it back into the case. At once he lifted it out again, with the trousers and the belt, and threw them with a faint snarl into a corner. Let them stay there. Briefly he allowed himself to think about the camouflage fatigues he was wearing when the ambush occurred. He remembered them being cut away from him. There had been a lot of blood. Then, resolutely, he went to the wardrobe where his civilian new suit and his sports jacket and grey flannels were hanging, took them and, folding them but not carefully, put them into the case. From the chest of drawers he took out his unworn shirts and underwear, and the things Irene had bought. He threw his regimental tie into the corner after the uniform. Quickly he packed underwear and socks and everything else, even an old scarf, and pushed the lid of the case down with a movement that produced a puff of air and more dust. For the last time his eyes went around the room and then he clambered out of the door and bent almost double down the twisted stairs.

At the foot Savage paused briefly like a soldier

screening a suspected sniper's lair, considering the next cautious advance. But when he moved it was quickly. In the kitchen he took the sub-machine gun apart and placed the components separately in the case, among his shirts. Then, returning to the bleak sitting room, he opened the oak bureau in the far corner and lifted out his old, portable typewriter in its wooden case. He put some books in the suitcase and some tapes and a pocket tape recorder. On a sudden thought he took the ticking clock from the mantleshelf and pushed it in also. One of them might as well have the clock. That was everything he needed. He closed the lid and pushed home the hasps. As he did so there was a sharp knock on the kitchen window and he quickly looked up. All he could see was the dark day held within the window frame like some blank abstract painting. But there *had* been a sound. He stepped swiftly to the window and stood to one side looking out at an angle and then jumped as the bare end of a rose bramble, agitated by the wet breeze, appeared briefly and tapped against the glass. He grimaced.

Now he was ready to leave. Before going from the room he stopped and, as though it deserved some courtesy, let his glance roam for the final time around the sullen walls. When they had first come there Irene had forced herself into hope and enthusiasm. Everything in their lives would be changed, new, all right. This was to be their home once he had finished with the army or, as it occurred, the army had finished with him. But even then, in the days before he was wounded, even as he went for the first time into the confined hallway, paced the rooms and sniffed out into the damp garden, even then he knew he held a doubt, a hollowness, a self-pretence, a suspicion that he was never to live there, that none of it would ever work.

Now he went determinedly from the room and strode with one step through the hallway. There was a small hallstand with a vase containing a few early daffodils. They were fresh, still wet from wherever Irene had bought them that morning. It was a simple gesture, typical of her. He tapped one of the petals with the tip of his finger and a drop of water fell on to the polished wood. He opened the front door sharply and lifted the suitcase and typewriter. At once he was confronted with the startled expressions of two young, clean, bespectacled, meek-looking men in suits. Their mouths opened like birds but they said nothing. They appeared chilled but earnest. One had short fair hair, the other was going bald. 'Yes?' asked Savage.

'We just happened to be passing,' blurted the balding one bravely. 'And we thought you would like to discuss the state of the world.'

'It's in a poor state,' confirmed his companion supportively. He blinked with a touch of hope. 'Don't you think?'

'Terrible,' agreed Savage feelingly. 'Somebody must do something about it. But here's my taxi. I have to catch a train.' The taxi had drawn up outside the gate, its door filling the gap between the wet yews. As though highly familiar with the emergency drill both arrivals now scrabbled into briefcases and thrust pamphlets into his hand.

'We'll drop by again,' said the fair youth with something like triumph. 'We'd like to talk.'

'We would,' confirmed the other. His voice dropped. 'Together we could change things.' Lamely they watched him go out of the gate.

He climbed into the back of the taxi. 'What did they

want?' asked the driver, the same man who had brought him to the cottage. 'Jehovah's Witnesses?'

'Something like that,' answered Savage. 'They were passing and thought I might like to change the world.'

'He's got a lot to answer for, that Jehovah,' muttered the driver. 'A lot.'

They reached the station in such fast time that Savage got on the wrong train, the local stopping service to London, not the through train. It had halted at two insignificant stations before he realised his mistake. At the second station three noisy youths climbed on. They had been drinking and one kept toppling and laughing against the others. They moved to seats at the far end of the carriage, sitting down and rolling and joking. He moved out of their view.

At the next stop a puffy, pale girl with a baby in her arms attempted to get into the train. While she was still struggling on the platform one of the noisy youths got up and called: 'Come on, hand the kid up, love. It's just going.'

'You're holding the bloody train up,' the most drunken of the group called. He stood and stumbled towards the open door. The girl regarded them stupidly and, unsurely, passed the baby into the arms of the youth who had offered to take it. He began rocking it extravagantly. The baby began to cry. Its mother attempted a panicky clamber up on to the train but she was bulky and hung with bags. She shouted unintelligibly. Her plastic rain hood fell over her eyes.

'Give it 'ere to me, Ernie,' demanded the second youth holding out his arms.

'You'll drop the bloody thing,' warned the third who had remained rocking in his seat.

But Ernie handed the swaddled child back to his

companion. The young woman screamed: 'Don't! You'll drop my Deirdre!' Desperately she heaved herself into the carriage. Ernie pulled the door and the train began to jolt from the station. 'Give 'er the kid, Rodney,' demanded the seated youth.

'I'm only minding it,' retorted Rodney turning and letting the infant slide. He caught her with a frantic grab. The baby howled. 'You mind your fucking business, mate.'

'Give me my Dierdre!' demanded the mother trying to reach for the bawling child in Rodney's uncertain arms. 'Come on, you council-house bastard!'

'Bastard!' exploded Rodney. 'I'm not a bastard. Am I, Bill? Here, let Bill have the kid, he's had plenty of bastards, 'aven't you Bill!' He passed, almost tossed, the child to Bill who caught it and began to rock it with drunken ferocity. Now the child was screaming, the mother was screaming. Bill threw the baby to Ernie who heaved it back. 'Me, I'm next!' shouted Rodney staggering forward. He caught the baby, again almost let it slip, but held perilously on to it. The mother was hysterical. 'Stop! She's only nine and a half weeks old.'

'Whoops!' called Rodney trying to balance with the infant as the train rocked around a curve. 'Here you are, Bill. Your turn, mate!' He lobbed the bundle to Bill. The mother sobbed and beat them hopelessly with her fists.

Savage stood up and walked along the central aisle of the carriage. He felt his body stiffen as he walked. 'Give the baby back,' he ordered.

Four of the five participants in the pantomine stared at him as if he had materialised by magic. The baby, eyes squeezed, continued to bellow. 'Give the baby back,' repeated Savage.

'You give it back, mate,' suggested Rodney holding the

bawling child. Its arms thrashed. ' 'Ere, you 'ave it.' He thrust the baby into Savage's arms. Then, while Savage stood transfixed, feet apart to keep his balance, Rodney thrust his knee into his groin and, as he was doubling up, Ernie punched him in the face. Somehow he held on to the baby. The train slowed. 'We're getting off 'ere,' announced Bill affably. The trio crowded to the door and before the train had stopped, opened it and jumped whooping on to the platform, flinging the door shut behind them. White-faced, Savage sat down, sick, still with the baby in his arms. Blood was gushing from his nose. His head was swinging inside. He heard, as though from a distance, the mother's cry: 'You're bleeding all over my Deirdre!'

Through a mist Savage looked down and saw with horror and guilt that the baby's clothes were splodged with his blood. Blood again. His bloody blood. 'Give me! Give me my child!' the woman demanded. Blindly he handed the bundle back. 'Look! Blood all over 'er frock!' howled the plump mother. 'That's her very *first* frock. Now there's bleedin' blood on it.' She clutched the baby and rocked it fiercely. It had never stopped screaming. 'I'm getting off this train,' moaned the woman. She glared almost madly into his splattered face. 'Next stop. 'Orrible, bastard men!'

He forced himself to stand and then staggered back to where he had been seated in his concealed place. His nose was still running red. He had no handkerchief. The train was slowing for the station. 'Have you got something I can use for this blood?' he asked the trembling mother haplessly. 'Anything.'

'Bugger off!' she retorted getting up and, with a struggle, opening the door. 'You bastard men. Look at my baby. Look at 'er frock. 'Er first frock that is.'

The train halted and she almost tripped out on to the platform slamming the door viciously behind her. She began to run along the platform like a rugby player clutching a ball. Savage sat transfixed. They had got him again. He was bleeding.

Five

As he staggered across Westminster Bridge in the late hours of that night he vaguely recognised the shining face of Big Ben, remembering it from *News at Ten* on the television. A wet wind whining up the river buffeted him, he leaned into it. He had no true idea where he was, where he had been, what he had done, nor why he was crossing this bridge.

In the shelter of the Houses of Parliament he attempted to get himself together, standing upright but still, swaying on the pavement, pulling his coat around him, trying to push down his soaking hair. A policeman on the corner of Parliament Square eyed him speculatively but then concluded he was just another windblown drunk or vagrant and aimed his measured stride in the opposite distance. He did not need the paperwork.

Savage was wary of the policeman. He kept trying to think where he was. Was he drunk or was he wounded? There was blood on his coat. Was he mad? Even Big Ben only fitted into the frame of a television picture, but he recognised possible trouble from the policeman and he crossed the rainy street and stumbled back towards the bridge. He considered the front of the tube station, recognised what it was, but dared not risk it. Despairingly he stared at the wall map of the Underground. Some late and voluble people began to come up the stairs and he instantly went on, his head sunk into the hole of his overcoat collar. If only he could sit down he might sort things out. He knew his name and rank but he had mislaid everything else including his suitcase, his type-writer and his sub-machine gun.

At first he went along the Embankment, peering at the lights reflected greasily in the Thames. He did not like the look of the river and the wind remained sharp and spliced with rain, so he waited until the shining wet road was clear and loped oddly across it. There were seats occupied by piled and sleeping figures. He nudged one who was snoring comfortably and asked him to sit up so he could sit down.

'Find your own fucking berth,' suggested the man. He was an irritable, rough and ragged tramp but from below sticking lids he regarded Savage with disgust. 'Look at the state of you,' he blinked. 'Pissed out you are. Where you been?'

'Where?' Where?' Savage repeated.

Sitting up, the vagrant studied him further. 'You don't look all there to me,' he said cocking his head. 'You look a bit bonkers, mate. 'Aven't come out of the barmy house, 'ave you?'

'I did,' agreed Savage.

The tramp remained seated but moved on the bench and assumed a more diplomatic stance. Savage had a good overcoat although there was blood on it. 'Mind,' he said. 'There's more mad than not around 'ere, at this time o' night. Some of 'em don't even know they're nutters.'

Exhaustedly Savage sat on the bench at the distant end from the tramp. 'Where is this?' he asked. 'Where are we?'

'Embankment,' answered the tramp like a correct

contestant in a geography quiz. He added helpfully: 'The Savoy is just along there.'

'But . . . where? I know the clock . . .' He nodded down river.

'The clock? Oh, I get you. Big Ben.' He leaned forward kindly. 'You're in London, mate, England.'

'Yes. Thank you,' Savage nodded gravely.

The tramp folded his arms which were lagged with the sleeves of several tattered coats. 'If I had any loose change I'd give you five pence and you could buy a cup of coffee,' he offered suggestively. 'Just along the road. It's only five pence for the likes of you and me. Or a bowl of soup. It might be just what you need, mate.'

'I've got money,' said Savage with some eagerness.

'You 'ave?' asked the tramp speculatively. ' 'Ow much?'

'Thousands,' said Savage.

'Oh, I see. But you don't happen to have it on you?' His interest drained.

'Enough for coffee,' Savage told him stoutly. He reached for his pocket and took out a fifty-pound note. The tramp's eyes protruded. He examined the note which Savage refused to let go. 'That's plenty,' he managed to say. 'Plenty for two cups.' Then craftily: 'But you'll want *change*. They only take five pences. They don't give no change.' His eyes were still riveted to the note. 'I'll go and get change for you.'

'No, don't bother,' said Savage with childish petulance as he rolled the fifty-pound note tightly in his fist.

'It's not one of them forged fifties, is it?' asked the tramp suspiciously. ' 'Old it up. You can keep 'old of it.' They were like two ragged boys playing a game. Savage held up the note. 'It's all right,' adjudged the tramp. 'Want some coffee?' asked Savage.

The tramp, reluctant to distance himself from such wealth, said: 'Yes, right.' He stood and scratched himself. 'I'll look after you, just see. I'll come wiv you, show you what to do.' He took a couple of apple-sized stones from one of his many pockets and almost daintily placed them on the bench. 'They keeps our places,' he said suggesting that their association might continue. 'It's like, booked.' On the thought he pushed out a filthy hand. 'I'm 'Orace,' he said.

Savage shook his hand and said: 'Staff Sergeant Savage.' His attention was taken by the stones. 'Where did you get those?' he asked as though they might be rarities. Puzzled but pleased at his interest, Horace answered: 'Them? Well, I just pick them up. Anywhere.' He examined the stones as if he thought he might have missed their importance.

'Have you got any more?' Now the tramp began to look apprehensive but took two more stones from his sagging pockets. 'I always 'ave some,' he said vaguely. 'What d'you want 'em for?'

'Just in case,' said Savage.

He accepted the proffered stones and kept them in his hands. The two odd figures went together along the pavement. Ahead of them was the slanting light of the all-night canteen, a caravan parked against the kerb with its flap propped up. 'The soup's all right,' said Horace. 'If you 'ang around and stare at the lady she'll give you extra for nothing.'

Gauntly Savage surveyed the scene ahead. Then he pulled up sharply and held the tramp by the arm. 'Look,' he croaked. 'See them?'

'Who? What?' asked his startled companion, his eyes going wildly about him.

'Out of their minds,' whispered Savage nodding ahead fiercely. 'Look at them. They're exposed, for God's sake.'

Anxiously Horace looked. 'Oh, them,' he said with still-puzzled relief. 'That's the line for the canteen. That's what you 'ave to do. Line up proper. Sometimes there's fifty blokes there.'

To his consternation Savage adopted a crouch and began to lope forward. 'Bloody fools,' he snarled. 'They'll get them again. Out in the open.'

'. . . 'Ere, 'ang about,' suggested Horace. He made to detain Savage but his hand was flung aside and he dropped back and remained still and struck as Savage began to advance at a crouching run towards the lit canteen and the queue of down-and-outs waiting inno-cently. As he went forward he swung his hands holding the stones. Then he halted, straightened from the crouch, and straight-armed lobbed one across the road where it hit the Emankment wall and clattered in the night quiet out on to the empty road. He shouted: 'Down! Get down! Take cover!' Some of the men in the line peered whitely towards him and a woman's pink startled face projected around the open front of the canteen. Savage flung his second stone. 'Down!' Savage bellowed again. 'Get down!' At his strange crouch he ran towards the queue of bewildered men. From behind him Horace bawled: 'Watch out! He's bonkers!'

The warning was late. Savage, his eyes fiery, his coat flying madly, his arms flailing, was among them. He charged into the tramps at the head of the queue just as one was taking delivery of a bowl of soup. The soup and the tramp went flying. The pink woman screamed. Savage battered into the queue shouting: 'Take cover!' The men fell against each other, the line toppling like dominoes, falling, bawling, protesting. They sprawled on their backs on the pavement. Only those at the rear of the queue escaped. 'Get out o' here,' bellowed an Irish voice. 'It's the Provos!'

There was utter panic. Men ran, men struggled to run, men tripped, men tried to rise from the pavement. Almost fainting, the woman pulled down the shutter at the front of the canteen with a bang that some of the vagrants took for the detonation of the bomb. Some began praying volubly. Savage, still shouting, his arms swimming, was sprawled flat on top of those who had been at the front of the line. Those who could regain their feet did so and ran. A police car pulled up at the side of the pavement and three astonished officers got cautiously out.

'It's a bomb!' howled one of the prostrate men, for once glad to see the law.

'That bloke threw it!' a vagrant pointed from behind a metal sandbin. ' 'Im there!'

'Where's the bomb?' demanded the leading policeman. They searched for signs of an explosion. The flap of the caravan was forced up and the woman's now red and distraught face appeared. 'That one,' she indicated with a sob. 'That one there with the nice overcoat.'

Two policemen got Savage to his feet. He stared as if he could not quite place them. They, in turn, quickly took in his appearance, the decent clothes below the overcoat, the wild face, eyes and hair. 'Was it you?' asked the leading constable.

'He's bonkers,' offered Horace smugly from the fringe of the scene.

'I saved them,' protested Savage but now with a touch of doubt. 'I saved their lives.' He paused and looked pleadingly around at the stricken faces. 'I did,' he asked them. 'Didn't I?'

The door opened heavily but carefully. A buoyant-faced police sergeant looked in and then walked in. It was as if he had not wanted to disturb him. 'Nothing like a night in the cells for making the world seem a nicer place,' he philosophised. Savage groaned and sat up stiffly. His face was sore, his clothes clammy, the upper front of his shirt was stiff with blood. He pulled his coat across it. There was blood on his coat as well. He took in the policeman and studied the close walls. 'A spell in custody works wonders,' persisted the officer. 'It's all right to come out now and have a wash and they'll give you some breakfast.'

'What am I doing here?' asked Savage.

'Well,' said the policeman with a modest beam. 'For starters you demolished a queue of tramps, poor old homeless blokes waiting at the Embankment canteen.'

'I did?'

'You did. And we couldn't find any identification on you. Only the return half of a rail ticket from Basingstoke, three keys, a fifty-quid note and some loose change.'

'My name's Savage.'

The man's beam grew. 'Nice one. After last night.'

'Francis Inigo Savage.'

The policeman produced a pad and wrote it down. 'Inigo?' he queried.

'I was named after the architect Inigo Jones,' provided Savage wearily.

'Oh, him,' said the officer hesitantly but beginning to write. 'How does he spell his name?'

Savage spelt it. 'That's what I did?' he queried rubbing his head. 'I don't remember anything.'

'It happened,' confirmed the policeman. 'And your address?'

Savage dictated the address. The officer said: 'Do you

know anyone who can vouch for you? Give you a reference?'

'I don't. I'm ... not in touch with many people.'

'No family?'

'No family.'

The policeman was trying to help. 'Anybody?'

Savage said carefully: 'I know a policewoman. Slightly. But she knows all about me. She's got it on a computer print-out.'

The sergeant frowned as if the situation had abruptly entered a new and more serious area. 'Why did she have that?'

'It was when I moved into my new place, the flat I've just given you the address of. It's in a security sensitive area. They thought I might shoot down Prince Charles's helicopter.'

'Did they?' The man's forehead rose. 'And that's why they had this print-out?'

'More or less. I've been in the army and I was wounded in Northern Ireland, then I was in hospital a long time, complications and so forth. They wanted to check me out.'

'I expect they would. And you know the name of the policewoman?'

'Yes. Her name is Jean Deepe.'

'And her nick? Her police station?'

'She's at West London.'

'Right,' said the sergeant closing the notebook noisily. 'Right. We'll see if we can get hold of her.' He regarded Savage with sympathy. 'You being wounded,' he said shaking his head. 'We don't want to charge you if we can get away with it.'

He had a fried breakfast in the corner of the small

canteen. There was no one else there except for the two white-overalled women who were serving. 'Are you in court, dear?' called one looking at the large wall clock. He said he was not. 'Just visiting,' he told her.

He drank his tea from a half-pint mug and saw the sergeant approaching along the outside corridor. 'Got her,' the man said in his friendly way, sitting down in the chair opposite.

'Want a tea, Mr Trelawney?' inquired the counter woman loudly. 'You will I expect.'

'Not now, love,' returned the sergeant. 'I've got a train robber downstairs. I'll be up later.' He turned his attention to Savage. 'No, she's given you a reference, PC Deepe,' he said. 'And she faxed us this . . . it's all about your head trouble.'

'Inside or out?'

Sergeant Trelawney peered at the fax. 'Both really,' he said. Without embarrassment he examined the line of the wound in Savage's hair and said: 'That was close.'

'I was in a psychiatric hospital,' said Savage quietly so that the canteen woman would not hear.

'Right. Marshfield Manor Hospital,' confirmed the sergeant in his loudish voice. The woman looked up and, turning to her colleague in the kitchen area behind, relayed: 'Psychiatric case.'

The sergeant grimaced briefly in that direction and returning to Savage said: 'Finished?' He surveyed the table. 'We'll go on down.'

Savage followed him from the canteen. The door closed only tardily behind him and he heard the woman say: 'Poor thing.'

'Sorry about that,' said Trelawney as they went into a small room and sat each side of a table. 'All you can say is that they do a good fry-up.' He studied the fax paper.

'She's put in a bit from the hospital report,' he said. 'You've had a rough time, haven't you, mate?'

Savage did not respond. Trelawney said: 'I've shown this to the guv'nor and there's not going to be any charges. The best they could have done was drunk and disorderly anyway.'

'I wasn't drunk,' said Savage.

'Four times over the top,' the sergeant told him flatly. 'Just as well you weren't driving.'

'I don't drive now.'

'Well, anyway, you'll hear no more from us.' With a flick of his hand he produced a plastic envelope in which was an oblong of cardboard. 'Your ticket from Basingstoke,' he said. 'Three keys and fifty-odd quid. What were you doing down in Basingstoke?'

'I remember that much,' said Savage. 'I went down to go to my house. My marriage has packed up. My wife was there, by coincidence. It was a bit upsetting.'

'You had a barney.'

'No, nothing like that. But something happened on the train on the way back. Some yobs started throwing a woman's baby about.'

Both the policeman's eyebrows went up, one after the other. 'Throwing a baby about?' he repeated dubiously. 'In what way?'

'Like a rugby ball,' said Savage not realising Trelawney's disbelief. 'They were drunk and they grabbed this baby and I had to get involved and they did for me while I was holding it. I bled all over the kid and the mother went mad.' He saw the sergeant's expression. 'And I don't remember anything after that.'

'Christ,' said the policeman inadequately. He took a heavy breath. 'Right, well, like I say you're free to go.' He rose but remained looking thoughtfully at the computer print-out.

'But you ought to make an appointment to see this . . .' He checked the fax again. '. . . Dr Fenwick at the hospital.'

'I will. This is going to worry me a lot.'

'I expect it will.'

'I thought I was going to be all right.'

Trelawney nodded. 'I'd put one of the probation officers on to you. But they're all busy trying to sort out the requirements of thieving kids.'

'No. Well, thanks.' They shook hands solemnly. 'And thanks to your guv'nor.'

'I'll tell him.'

Outside he stood on the pavement holding the return rail ticket in his palm. The three keys were for his flat, his house and his suitcase. He had to find the suitcase, his typewriter and, he suddenly remembered with a shock, his *gun*. Oh, shit, who had his gun? He waved a taxi down and went to Waterloo.

He located the Lost Property and, after a moment outside, went diffidently in. They had a typewriter. The man put it heavily on the counter and he identified it and signed the release form. 'That's a museum piece, that is,' said the attendant surveying the wooden case almost reverently. 'All we get these days in here is lost laptops.'

No, they did not have a suitcase with 'Staff Sergeant F. I. Savage' stencilled on it. The man made a double-check but returned as though he were truly sorry. 'Only the typewriter, mate,' he said.

Savage returned to the station concourse. It was hard to believe that it was only yesterday that he had been there, staring as he did now at the Arrivals and

Departures indicator. There were not many people waiting at that time of the day. He looked around him. He was isolated. He began reciting the names of the stations to himself; perhaps that would make him remember: 'Clapham Junction, Woking, Fleet, Farnborough', all the way to Basingstoke.

He felt sure it was the same man framed in the ticket window. He remembered the blue turban and was pleased at his recognition. He bought another return to Basingstoke and caught a stopping train that left fifteen minute later. His relief was repeated from the previous day; it was almost empty. He sat in a corner seat where he could survey the route, where he might get a glimpse, a clue, of some place where he had been; some place where had lost his suitcase and his gun. Then he thought of the clock. If that was still ticking they would think it was a bomb. Oh, God.

The train was about to leave when a young woman with a baby appeared on the platform. It was not the same one but Savage panicked. He made for the door and as she got in he got out. The platform guard took his whistle from his mouth and urged him to hurry. He got into the next carriage. 'Make up your mind,' grumbled the man slamming the door bad-temperedly as he blew his whistle. The train moved away.

He was alone apart from a crouched woman in a mackintosh of pink plastic, so stiff it crackled, who was at the distant end of the long compartment. As each station was reached he examined it from the window, everything he could take in. Nothing touched his memory until they reached Shuffley where a porter was wheeling a laden barrow along the empty platform with a small yappy dog jumping up at him. Something stirred but he had no time to grasp it before the train was moving. He remained staring from the window, desperately trying to place the memory. It refused to be released. At the next station he prepared to get out. The woman in the plastic mac stood up and crackled towards him. 'Do you go up and down all the time?' she enquired. 'I saw you yesterday. You had all this blood on you.'

He stared at her dismal face wrapped in pink plastic. Her eyes lit a little when she realised he was intent on what she had said. 'I go up and down all the time,' she said hurriedly as though she feared he might lose interest. 'Every day. I get from one train to another. Just up and down. I've got nothing else to do.' The train was slowing towards the station.

'You saw me yesterday?' he said.

'Like I said. You was all bloody. Like a bad nose bleed.'

Carefully Savage pulled his overcoat across his front and asked: 'Where did I get off the train?'

She seemed unsurprised at the question. 'I thought at the time you didn't look as if you knew where you was,' she said with satisfaction. 'You didn't seem like you was with us. You just stared straight ahead. I saw you all bloody on the platform when you got off.'

'Where?' he repeated. 'Where did I get off? Which station?'

'The last one,' said the woman. 'Shuffley. Where the cemetery is.'

He returned on the next train. When he got out at Shuffley he saw that the man who had been wheeling the barrow was at the exit waiting to collect tickets, the small brown and white dog sitting attentively by his trouser legs. Apart from Savage only one other passenger alighted from the train, a sedate lady with a stout walking

71

stick. She got to the exit in her own time. Savage loitered, pretending to read a timetable on the station wall, before going towards the door after she had gone through.

He at once saw that the ticket collector recognised him. 'Oh, it's you again,' he said. His hand went forward for the ticket. 'This takes you to Basingstoke then back to Waterloo,' he said screwing his eyes and lifting the ticket to just below his nose. The dog began to whine and scrape his trouser leg with its paw.

'I know,' answered Savage. 'But I want to get off here.' He looked directly at the station man. 'You saw me? When I was here before?'

'Yesterday,' the man said. Surprise and curiosity pinched his face. 'Don't you know?'

'Yes, yes, of course.'

Without questioning the inadequate explanation the man continued. 'Your nose was bleeding like a tap and you had blood all down your shirt.' Savage pulled his coat together. 'You looked like you'd been in a punch-up.'

'I was attacked on the train.'

'The sods. You should have reported it. Mind, you didn't seem to know where you was. You had a big suitcase.'

'I did?' Savage altered his tone. 'I *did*?'

'You just gave me your ticket. That was for Waterloo as well, now I come to think about it. I gave it back to you. Did you go up later? I was off duty at five.'

'Yes . . . yes, I went to London.' He could not think of anything more to ask. The dog was pawing the man's leg more insistently. 'He wants to chase the barrow,' said the man. 'That's all he wants to do. Chase the barrow. It's his enjoyment.'

Savage walked from the doorway. It was a deserted

place. Dead leaves blew across the yard. The elderly woman with a stick had been assisted slowly into a taxi and it was driving away. He walked in the chilly day in the only direction possible, an overhung road which he presumed led towards whatever sort of place Shuffley was. Desperately he tried to remember being there. The taxi stopped and he caught up with it. 'I'll be back in a couple of minutes,' the driver said out of his window. 'When I've dropped Mrs Leadbetter. If you need a cab, that is.'

'How far is the village?' asked Savage.

'Village? There's no village. Just the pub and the graveyard. That's all there is here.' He jerked his chin briefly towards his passenger. 'Mrs Leadbetter lives the other way,' he said. 'Weren't you here yesterday?'

'Yes,' said Savage with a touch of embarrassment. 'I was.'

'Thought so. Saw you come out of the Crossways Arms about half past ten at night. You must have got the last train. If you went to London.'

'I went to London,' confirmed Savage. The old lady at the rear appeared to have belatedly become aware that they had halted. She banged on the driver's glass partition with the rubber end of her walking stick. The driver obeyed and with a quick wave drove on. The woman glared at Savage and wagged her stick.

Unsurely he walked away from the station studying the road. Then he began to remember it, faintly, like a road he had last walked down years before. A dull white wall became visible through the stencilled winter trees. The pub, a solid Victorian block with blank upper windows, was set back from the road. The door was shut but there was a light in the bar. He went in. A recently lit fire was pale in the grate. He saw that the man behind the bar knew him. 'Back again,' the man said. 'I hope you were all right.'

Savage sat on a stool and ordered a whisky. 'Had to open a new bottle,' grinned the barman, fat and wearing huge braces over his belly. 'You drank your way through one.'

'A whole bottle?'

'There wasn't much left. You seemed to be all right, though. A bit dazed, befuddled. But you seemed dazed when you came in.' He regarded Savage wryly. 'Don't you remember?'

'I don't much.'

The barman pulled on his braces as though ensuring their support. 'Well, you sat in that corner, talking to nobody, although there weren't many in, and you put back the Scotch. You were okay or I wouldn't have gone on serving you, and it was over a couple of hours. You walked straight but I wondered where you'd got to. Afterwards I was a bit worried, to tell the truth.'

'I was fine,' lied Savage. He leaned forward. 'There was some blood on me?'

'A lot of it. All on your shirt. I asked if you wanted any help but you said you didn't. What happened?'

'I was beaten up on the train,' said Savage. 'Three yobs. I've been ill and I must have just blacked out because I don't remember any of it.'

'It's a bloody crime these days,' grunted the barman. He poured a whisky and said that one was on him. Savage thanked him. 'So I just came in here and a couple of hours later I went out?'

'Right. Someone said they'd seen you earlier walking up the road from the cemetery. Do you remember that?'

'No . . . no, I don't.'

'That's what they said. But it was gone eight o'clock

when you came in here because I didn't finish my meal until then and I saw you come in, like I say. They shut the cemetery at five in the winter.'

Savage said: 'How is it there's a cemetery here but no village? Nothing but this pub.'

The man appeared surprised. 'It's no ordinary cemetery,' he said. 'It's a military cemetery. It's full of soldiers.'

Savage said: 'When I came in here did I have a suitcase?'

'No. I'm almost sure you didn't.'

'Thanks very much for the drink and the information,' said Savage getting down from the stool. 'Can I buy you one?' 'Another time,' said the barman. 'I hope you find whatever you're looking for.'

'Myself,' shrugged Savage. He went towards the door.

The man looked embarrassed. 'Well, I hope so.' He raised his hand. 'Cheers.'

Savage crossed the empty road. The place was as bleak as any place with trees could be. They rattled and sighed above him as he took the road opposite. A sign said: 'Shuffley Military Cemetery.' An edgy wind came directly up the road and, as if seeking him out, into his face. The way bent around another gaunt bunch of trees trembling together. Beyond them a gatehouse appeared, beside a wide ornamental gate which was closed and a smaller gate at its side which was open. He went through the side entrance and into the gatehouse. A man was just taking off his blue uniform cap to sit behind a long counter.

'Did I leave a suitcase here yesterday?' asked Savage blatantly.

'You did,' returned the man without hesitation. 'Or somebody did. It was standing on a grave.'

Savage swallowed. 'It has my name on the side,' he said. 'Staff Sergeant F. I. Savage.'

'That's it,' said the man rising cheerfully as though Savage had qualified for a prize. 'We've got it here. I was going to take it to the police station.' He had half-turned towards the counter under which Savage could now see his case. He tried to hear if the clock was ticking but there was nothing. The man glanced back over his shoulder and said: 'You didn't by any chance get locked in the cemetery last night did you? You didn't have to climb over the wall?'

'No,' said Savage decisively. 'I just forgot my luggage, that's all.'

The man picked up the case and put it on the counter. 'If you've got some identification,' he suggested. Then conversationally: 'Yes, it seems like somebody got shut in. We're always careful, naturally, we always ring the bell, three times, but it looks like this person got locked in and had to get over the wall. We found one of our ladders up against it this morning.'

'I don't have any identification,' said Savage. 'But I have the key.'

'That's all right,' said the man as though relieved. 'You've told me the name.' Savage produced the key although he hoped he would not have to open the case. No sound of ticking came from it. The man said: 'That's all right,' again and pushed the case across the counter towards him. 'How come you forgot it?' he enquired.

'Lapse of memory,' said Savage with an air of taking the man into his confidence. 'I'm discharged from the service now. I have these lapses.'

'Oh, I get it,' said the cemetery keeper sympathetically. 'Because of ill-health, was it? That's what happened to me. Swamp fever.'

'I was injured in Ulster,' said Savage.

'Oh, I see.'

Savage said: 'It was on a grave, you say?'

The man rose. 'I'll run you down there,' he said kindly. 'I'll show you.'

They went outside. A van was parked around the rear of the building. The man got behind the wheel and Savage climbed in beside him. He kept the suitcase with him, putting it in the rear. 'It's not a bad job, this,' said the man as he started the engine. 'Most people wouldn't want it but in the summer it's lovely. The birds start singing at four. And it's always so peaceful.' He glanced sideways. 'Like it should be.'

They began to drive at what seemed an habitually slow pace, down a long path between lines of white graves. 'I wish some of the kids today would come in here now and again,' said the cemetery keeper. 'They reckon they don't believe in war but some of us *had* to believe in it, didn't we. We didn't have the choice. Like it or lump it.'

At the foot of the drive, where a wall heavy with ivy confronted them, he turned right and after twenty yards stopped the vehicle. 'It was there,' he pointed. 'On number 445 R.'

Savage got out of the van and walked towards a line of simple white stones. 'To the left,' said the man from the vehicle. 'That's the one.'

Savage bent. It was all returning now. The terror, the horror, the panic, all frozen in this deeply silent place with its dumb stones. The inscription on the gave said: 'Sergeant Henry Barnard', and gave a date of birth and one of death. He turned and walked back to the van. 'All right?' asked the driver solicitously.

'Yes,' said Savage quietly. 'I knew him. I was with him when it happened.'

While he was waiting for Dr Fenwick a squat woman wearing a red headscarf wheeled a tea trolley into the room. Savage did not recognise her but he was not entirely surprised when she offered him a cup of tea and, after pretending to pour it, handed him an empty cup before leaning forward solicitiously and asking: 'Would you like sugar, dear?'

He knew the rules there. He thanked her and said he would, sitting solemnly while she spooned in imaginary sugar. 'Two, is it?' He accepted two. 'Nothing like a nice cup of tea this time of the day,' she said. 'If you'd like a refill just call me. I'll be down the passage.'

When Paul Fenwick came in he saw the empty cup. 'I have three of those a day,' he sighed as they shook hands. 'The trouble is we can't decide whether she's fooling us, that she really knows she's pouring phantom tea, and she's seeing how long she can keep it up. On the other hand, she may not know.'

'It's a place for problems,' observed Savage.

'My God, is it just. You should have been at the football match yesterday. Mayhem. Yet everybody's going around today saying what a good game it was.' He reached to the desk and picked up a long envelope. Savage recognised it. 'I'm glad you wrote everything down,' said the doctor.

'As soon as I got back home I got the typewriter out,' said Savage.

'And home is now in Kensington, Kensington Heights,' said Fenwick looking at the letter. 'Where is your wife?'

'She's with her mother.'

'It's not reparable?'

'I'm afraid not. She was very patient but there was a

limit to it. I was relieved when she went. I didn't want to see what I was doing to her.'

Fenwick nodded. 'You got this place in Kensington by yourself?'

'Absolutely.' Savage allowed himself a smile. 'I made all the arrangements and I think it's worked out very well.'

'Until this incident,' said the doctor. Carefully he read through the document again. 'When did you realise *why* you went to the cemetery?' he murmured. 'The reason?'

'At the end. When I went back and saw Henry Barnard's grave. Then I remembered it.'

'When we allowed you to go to Sergeant Barnard's funeral it was a calculated risk,' recalled Fenwick. 'We were amazed you remembered him, considering your general loss of memory, your blotting-out of everything, because he died of his wounds some time after the incident.'

'I remembered him,' said Savage. 'Irene took me to the funeral and she brought me back here. But after that it had gone from my mind.'

'The impression must have remained somewhere deep down,' shrugged the doctor. 'That's what I would expect. So when these men beat you up in the train it's not altogether surprising that you found your way back to the cemetery. Your house is in the Aldershot military area, and the railway goes through Shuffley, the military cemetery, so it's all in the same area, on the same line. In your state after the attack on you in the train you subconsciously recognised Shuffley. When you went to Sergeant Barnard's funeral you were hardly in a state to know anywhere.'

'Anyway, the whole business the other day scared me,' admitted Savage. 'That's why I got it all down on paper.'

'The police had already informed us,' said Fenwick.

Savage sat back in surprise. Fenwick said: 'They were in contact with us the next day.'

'Just to make sure I wasn't dangerous.'

'Exactly. So you blacked out and ended up charging into a lot of tramps waiting for cups of tea.' He did not smile. 'It brought back the canteen and the business in Northern Ireland.'

Savage nodded: 'I thought they were going to be ambushed. It was madness.'

He realised what he had said. Fenwick grinned sympathetically. 'It was something that happened,' he assured. 'Nobody was hurt. It was a temporary aberration, brought on by trauma. Going to your house and seeing Irene there probably upset you more than you realise. Then the fracas in the train. It triggered the whole thing. Then you drank a lot of whisky. It probably won't happen again.'

'God, I hope not. You don't think I should worry about it?'

'I don't think you should dwell on it. Tell me about the place in Kensington. What do you plan to do there?'

'It couldn't be better,' said Savage, a change in his tone. 'Just what I wanted. And I found it first time. If I had needed to traipse around London looking I think I might have found it impossible in the end. I'd have given up.'

'It might have been difficult. But you seem fine now. You look different. I can't believe you're the same man who was here only a few months ago. All you did was read – as though the cover of the book was a shield. You would hardly speak. The only time I ever saw you come out of it was when you were working for those few days while they were refurbishing the army museum at Dorchester.'

Savage wondered why he had said that. Did he know about the gun? Should he tell him now? Fenwick prevented him from doing so. 'Have you made any friends?' he asked.

'Friends?' Savage blinked. 'Well, not really. I didn't intend to be sociable. The more I'm by myself the better I like it. I want to be quiet. I've got a whole lot of books and now I've got my typewriter I'm going to start to put together this encyclopaedia.' He appeared a touch embarrassed. 'You know, the one I wanted to do when I was here. It's about islands.'

'I know,' smiled Fenwick. 'It was encouraged as a therapy.'

'I've become very engrossed. I want to go ahead with it.'

'That's a good idea, I think.' He looked up. 'And what do you intend to do with it?'

'Have it published.' Savage leaned forward eagerly. 'Doctor, no one has ever put together a book like this before. It might take years, but I don't mind. Time is not a problem.'

Fenwick thoughtfully said: 'If I could coin a phrase, no man is an island, not even when he is writing a book about them. You ought to have some friends. Who have you got to know?'

Savage thought. 'Well, there are a few people who live in Kensington Heights, neighbours, but a lot of them are a bit elderly and reclusive anyway. There's Mr and Mrs Tomelty, the caretaker and his wife, and Mr Kostelanetz, the man I'm renting the flat from, and Freddie Spencer-Hughes, the estate agent, and . . .'

'I mean *friends*,' insisted Fenwick. He glanced at the sheaf of papers is his hand. 'Who is Jean Deepe?'

'You heard from her?'

'Yes. She told us of your escapade with the tramps and so on. Wanted our advice. She's a police officer, I believe.'

Savage nodded. 'She is. I didn't realise she had come through to you personally.'

'She wanted to know the score with you. Is she a friend?'

Savage looked doubtful. 'I've hardly met her but I suppose she is. She got me out of trouble after the tramps business.'

'Anyone else?'

'Not really. There's the lady in the library. I don't know her name. She's been friendly and helpful. But I don't know ... I've just not been looking for friends.'

Fenwick folded the papers and pursed his lips. 'You can't live in isolation, not total isolation. You need a friend, Frank, an everyday friend.'

Savage said seriously: 'I'll try and get one.'

Six

At ten in the morning by the clock which he had brought from his house, three weeks after he had first entered the apartment, Savage began writing his encyclopaedia. He had bought and borrowed more books and now had a huge *Times Atlas of the World* spread on the floor. He was cocooned there, mist falling away outside the window like a long cape. He felt better now, enclosed and more confident. A hesitation at sitting down at the typewriter had been pushed aside with the awkwardness of his first attempts at writing an outline of his intentions. Now, with an indrawing of breath, he placed his fingers on the keys and began, at last, to tap: '*Admiralty Islands. Bismarck Archipelago, New Guinea. Tribal islands of . . .*' The clock ticked on the sideboard.

The doorbell sounded. His head drooped and he remained staring over the horizon of the keys into the fog of upper London. He let his hands slide away from typewriter. Perhaps if he remained still whoever it was would go away. Again the bell rang. They knew he was in there. He almost spat. Then he got up from the desk, strode to the door and pulled it open. A group of mostly small people were outside. They were smiling and blinking.

'Remember me?' asked the man in front genially. He wore a dusty formal jacket. The heads of the others nodded unsynchronised in support of the enquiry. 'I'm Bertie Maddison. We met the other morning when you were just coming in. I'm the musical one with the er . . . unusual wife. This is she.'

A plump woman with sparse, rust-coloured hair held by combs, curtseyed.

Bertie said: 'Can we come in? We thought we'd welcome you although it's been a while before we could organise everyone together.' He displayed a half-empty bottle which he carried by the neck like a hunter holding a hare. 'We brought our own amontillado.'

Savage backed from the door. 'I was . . . I was just . . . starting . . . working,' he said.

'He's working!' chortled Bertie marching in with his wife. The others, two old men and three women, trooped in behind him and quickly distributed themselves, the men remaining standing, the women claiming the chairs and the sofa. Savage saw a trail of talcum powder across the carpet. 'Never waste time on work, I say,' Bertie continued. A woman's fragile hand reached out and tugged at his shirt. 'He's working,' she said feebly. 'He's young.' Her veined eyes lifted and she smiled a pale, understanding smile towards Savage.

'We won't keep you,' promised Bertie. 'Not for long. Perhaps we can just borrow some glasses.'

Reluctantly Savage went towards the kitchen. He put some glasses on a tray and returned to the room.

'Is there another bottle of amontillado?' enquired someone. 'There won't be enough.'

'It's before noon,' pointed out one old lady as if quoting rules. 'Halves before noon.'

'Quite right,' acknowledged Bertie. 'Half a glass each.'

Savage had still scarcely spoken. He was given the final glass with a spoonful of clear sherry in the bottom and responded slowly to their toast. 'We hope you'll be very happy here,' said Bertie sincerely. 'Most happy,' put in his wife.

'Happy ... happy ... happy ... happy ...' they murmured between them.

'Thank you,' responded Savage weakly. 'All.'

'These are the older inhabitants, the day shift,' said Bertie with heavy reassurance. 'The younger people, of course, have to go out to work.'

One of the other two men encouraged him: 'Tell him what you told us, Mr Maddison.' He had a metallic grin.

'What was that, Mr Prentice? About what?'

'Oh, Wigmore Hall,' snorted Maddison. He slapped Savage weakly on his shirt. 'You wouldn't want to hear all that,' he said continuing nevertheless. 'It was last night. Chopin recital. Pablo O'Sullivan. I tell you, I've shit better Chopin.'

'He's shit better Chopin,' nodded one of the old ladies.

'Anyway, cheers,' said Bertie raising his glass once more. There was only a trace of sherry in the bottom, like a specimen in a test-tube. He swallowed it and licked his lips. 'I'll introduce you now,' he said decisively but blinked at the assembly as though he had suddenly forgotten their names. 'Well, everybody introduce yourselves to this gentleman, Mr . . .'

'Savage,' provided Frank. 'Frank Savage.'

'I'm Wilhelmina,' said the tallest lady. 'Blenkinsop.' She shook hands coquettishly with two fingers of the hand in which she held her glass. 'I am not married,' she said. 'I was once, for thirty years.'

'I'm Miss Weiz,' said a second woman, pushing herself towards him, her eyes fat and full. 'From Prague I came. Have you ever been to Prague?'

Savage admitted that he had not. 'I will escort you

85

there,' offered Miss Weiz. 'We will go in the summer time. I have many memories.' Her soft hands, only hardened by her rings, enclosed his.

'I'm Miss Cotton,' said the third woman. 'Do come and see me.'

The group began to move towards the door. It was Wilhelmina who was leaving a trail of talcum.

'I'm Percy Belfont,' put in one of the old men. 'You won't see me again. I'm going to Antwerp to die.' He smiled and waited. 'I like Antwerp.' The others ignored him. He went out shaking his head.

'It's nice to know your neighbours,' said Bertie, the last to leave. 'You never know when they might need you.'

The group were waiting obediently on the landing for the everyday drama of the lift. 'It's mended now,' said Miss Weiz sombrely. 'It's always breaking.'

Mr Prentice glanced at them craftily and then swiftly sidled back into the room. 'Have a dekko,' he invited baring his metallic teeth. 'I'll show you. Come over here.'

Unhappily Savage followed him. With a sharp twist of his head to get his bearings Mr Prentice plunged into the smaller bedroom. Its windows looked out over the well courtyard. 'She's right opposite,' he beckoned. He turned, his eyes jolly. 'She's *some* girl. She advertises, they say. Miss Bombazine. Wears black.' He peered from the window. 'She's got her curtains drawn,' he sniffed disappointedly. 'She would.'

They left the bedroom. 'From my place I can only see a bit of her legs,' said Mr Prentice. His teeth clamped shut. 'And then not always.'

Thankfully Savage heard the lift clanking up. They went back to the landing. Some of the residents had descended. The remainder waited, fallen to patient silence, as though out of respect. It arrived and with agile courtesy Mr Prentice stepped forward and opened the door. The remaining residents shuffled in and between them managed to close the cage door. Their eyes, like the eyes of prisoners, looked out through the grille. The lift descended. Wilhelmina waved. 'I'll walk down,' said Mr Prentice. 'I still can.' He shook hands gravely. 'Royal Engineers, by the way. Explosives.'

'Hello, is that Frank Savage?'

'Yes, that's me.'

'This is Jean Deepe.'

'Oh, Jean. Sorry I didn't ... Yes, fine. I wanted to telephone you to thank you for the trouble you took but I didn't want to call the police station. Anyway, thanks.'

'No problem. They didn't press charges, did they?'

'No. As I say, thanks.'

'You must tell me about it some time. Are you settling down there?'

'Yes, at last. I think I am. I'd no sooner begun work than a whole platoon of the residents arrived, the people from the other flats.'

'I bet that was fun.'

'They meant well. They're all pretty old, they call themselves the day shift. Some have been here since the war. That was last Thursday and nobody's bothered me since then.'

'What gave you the idea to write about islands?'

'In hospital.'

'Oh, yes. The psychiatric hospital.'

'Yes, Marshfield Manor. It was something I read there. I was trying to focus my life, my thoughts, and although I've never written anything before, I decided to give it a go. It's more compiling than writing. I've got a lot of notes and it's really a matter of putting them into shape.'

'It sounds as if it's going to take a long time.'

'I hope so. I've done the first draft of the entry on the Admiralty Islands and I've just begun going through the notes on the Aleutians. It's slow work.'

'I'd like to read it some time.'

'I'll show it to you.'

All his grown life he had looked and acted like a soldier and now he knew that he had become careless. He had not shaved that day and he was wearing an old denim shirt underneath an army pullover, creased grey flannels and canvas shoes. He poured himself a Scotch, which he did not even want, and consciously made himself carry the glass into the main room. It was nine o'clock in the evening. Picking up the television channel control he flicked it on, watched flatly for a few minutes and then switched it off.

He went to his desk facing the folds of the closed curtains and picked up the file containing the work he had done so far. He read the latest sheet. *'Aleutian Islands. Bering Sea. A string of about seventy volcanic islands, extending more than a thousand miles from the mainland of Alaska, south-west of Anchorage, almost to the Kamchatka Peninsula in Russia...'*

He read to the end and sighed. Who would be interested? He went to the books, piled haphazardly on the table in the corner and spilling on to the floor and carpet. The solid atlas was at the base of the pile. He pulled it out like a flat slab and hoisted it to the desk. At random he picked Easter Island from the index. Easter Island ... Easter Island ... He turned the large pages and finally opened the atlas fully so that the patterned blues of Capricorn almost covered the desk. There the island lay, alone and famous in the sea, discovered on Easter Day, also called Isla de Pascua and Rapa Nui, lying just under the Tropic. His eye ran over the expanse of ocean across the desk. To the south-east was Juan Fernandez Island, where the real Robinson Crusoe, Alexander Selkirk, had been marooned, and there was Fanning and there was Palmyra, in the Line Islands known to the whalers of New England before the Panama Canal was dug; here the Phoenix Isles and there the Tuamolu Archipelago, Pitcairn and, standing aloof, waiting like a butler, Henderson. Clipperton, the speck where a whole colony of human beings was once forgotten for years, and running out far into, deeply under, the Pacific, the Clipperton Fracture. Then Midway . . . Guam . . .

Savage's finger traced the line of the fracture out into the paper ocean, then he followed the outline of the Marquesas and Tahiti in the flamboyant Society Islands, called by Cook after the sober Royal Society in London. He had never been to any of them. In the hospital he had found a worn and torn atlas dating from Victorian times and had borne it to his bed. Its contours, its bays and seas, its islands, its mysteries had helped to begin to stabilise his mind and his life. Sometimes he would close his eyes on his confined hospital room and wonder what the people in the Celebes or the Ionian Archipelago were doing at that moment. He could almost see the roofs of their houses.

His eye lingered on the spread map, his whisky untouched, the room safe and silent, the walls guarding him. From beyond the curtains came the dulled sounds of traffic. From the pile of books he picked out *Forrester's Navigation Charts: South Pacific*. Sitting in the armchair he opened it and for an hour read about the sea passages, shoals, dangerous reefs and reliable anchorages of Micronesia.

It was midnight when he went to bed. He lay in the dimness, a fringe of city light filtering around the curtains, waiting for sleep. It came only briefly. Music woke him and after a few moments he got out of bed and followed the sound. It stoppped almost at once as if someone had realised it was too loud. He walked into the second bedroom and in the opposite window he saw a naked woman. Miss Bombazine.

Her body was starkly white, her hair black and heavy, her breasts hung forward as she adjusted the window catch. She gazed out for a moment as if idly wondering if anyone had seen her. Then she retreated into the lit room and the curtains were drawn.

Savage sat on the empty, single bed. Sex was one of the things that seemed to have walked away, gone, escaped from his life. Like love. Perhaps one day, in some way, it would come back; something had to. Some time.

He returned to his own bed. Under it was the sub-machine gun; he felt its stock with his bare toe. With the same toe he eased it out from below with the guilt of someone harbouring an obsessive vice or secret. He pushed it away again.

As he was returning to sleep he heard a sound. Someone was trying his door. Alarmed he sat up and his hand dropped towards the gun below the bed. He fumbled and found it. They were coming in. They had a key. He watched through the aperture of the bedroom door as the outer door opened. Three men entered. Savage moved like a soldier. He slid from the bed and lifted the sub-machine gun in the same movement. He reached his bedroom door in two strides and switched on the sitting room light. Revealed in the glare were three short, wide men, one carrying a cricket bat. They blinked and backed away in the sudden light. 'Stay where you are,' said Savage with real menace. He pretended to cock the empty gun. 'Or I'll kill you.'

'Fuck me,' muttered the man with the cricket bat. 'Look at that shooter.'

The middle man nudged him as though to restrain his language. 'We . . . was just wanting to see Mr Kostelanetz,' he said haltingly.

'Is Mr Kostelanetz in?' asked the third. 'By any chance?' He moved his head sideways and grinned ingratiatingly. They were all in their forties, seedy and unfit. The one with the cricket bat had a big paunch, the middle man was hairless and the third appeared shortsighted. He tried to focus on Savage. None could believe the gun. The bald man wiped the top of his head with his hand and said: 'Anybody can make a mistake.'

'Net practice,' mumbled the man with the cricket bat.

'Mr Kostelanetz doesn't live here any longer,' Savage told them. 'I do.'

'Very sorry, guv'nor,' said the bald man. He turned towards the door. Savage snapped at him to stop and pointed the sub-machine gun at his chest. The man trembled visibly. 'Throw the keys you got in with on that armchair,' ordered Savage. All three were sweating, eyes shifting, hands fumbling. The middle man tossed the keys on to the cushion of the chair.

'Right,' said Savage. 'Take your trousers off.'

Together they stared at him. 'Get them off,' he repeated.

'What for?' asked the bald man timidly.

'We only wanted to give Mr Kostelanetz something,' said the man with the bat, pushing it behind his legs. 'We owe him.'

Ominously Savage shifted the gun again.

As though taking part in some sort of novelty race they

rushed to lower their trousers and stood terrified, holding their hands across their underpants. 'Right,' said Savage. 'Now piss off before I decide to shoot you. And don't come back. Mr Kostelanetz is gone. I'm here now.'

Mumbling relief and thanks they backed, trouserless, towards the door while he kept the muzzle of the gun on them. They reached it and with a rush tumbled out on to the landing. He moved forward, kicked the door shut after them, and bolted it. He heard them falling down the stairs. He sat sweating on the armchair. He rummaged behind him for the keys and picked them up. Then he gathered the three pairs of trousers and carried them to the window, opened it and threw them out into the darkness. Legs flying, they floated down to the courtyard below. Restrained calls of appreciation floated up.

Closing the window he returned to the bedroom. He sat with the light on, feeling an excitement, almost an elation, a confidence that he had not known for a long time. He patted the warm, useless, sub-machine gun and slid it back below the bed.

He had reached the Azores. '*Location. North Atlantic, 900 miles west of Lisbon, Portuguese colony. The islands are spread over more than 300 square miles, the most remote group of islands in the Atlantic, the tops of submarine mountains, their bases are two and a half miles deep in the sea and they rise to a height of four miles . . .*'

Some nights, after midnight, he would let himself silently, almost secretly, out of the flat and out of the darkened, sleeping building. Snores trembled behind doors. Milk bottles were marshalled against the corridor walls. He always used the stairs; the lift seemed to clang louder at night.

Once as he left late he met Mr and Mrs Maddison

entering through the street door. 'Albert Hall,' reported Bertie sourly. 'Tchaikovsky. She's been bawling again.'

'Protesting,' corrected Mrs Maddison firmly. She examined Savage as if wanting to ask where he was going at that hour.

'In the middle of *Sugar Plum Fairy*,' retorted Bertie. He directed a grumble towards Savage. 'We've been in the bloody police station for an hour.'

Savage went out into the hushed cold carrying two bundles of washing. Street lamps made the surrounding dark more intense. He walked up Kensington Church Street, up the smeary, rising pavement, below the leaning trees, past the antique shops where old pictures, vases, chairs and oriental figures faced the street. His routine took him to the all-night shop for groceries and the morning papers and then to the launderette. The clothes he washed and dried he would iron the following day; one skill the army had taught him was the use of the iron.

The all-night launderette was a steamy yellow yolk in Notting Hill. There were late cars and taxis cruising by. The police visited it regularly and one policeman always did his washing there. Savage went there once a week and used the washing machine and spin drier, sitting on a damp plastic chair and reading his newspaper while he waited.

Sitting, hunched, there as he went into the launderette was the girl in the dirty pink fake fur; the girl he had seen before with the wandering youths. Her head was wound into a blue and white striped football scarf through which a slice of her dozing face projected. She roused as he opened the door. 'Shut it, will you,' she said drowsily. 'The wind.'

He closed the door behind him. The windows were steamed, the machines damp, the floor smeared. He took his laundry, shirts and underwear, out of the plastic bags and opening the door of the machine put them inside. He inserted the coins and started the cycle. He studied her briefly sitting behind him, slightly over his right shoulder, and then wiped one of the dark seats and sat down. 'I'll keep an eye on it if you like,' she murmured like someone talking in their sleep. 'Cost you a quid.' Her sharp, damp, nose emerged from the scarf, her watery eyes perched above it. 'I'll see it's not nicked.'

Savage said: 'It's all right. There's nowhere I've got to go.'

'Me neither,' she said.

Some shadows formed abruptly outside the opaque window. The muffled girl's head came up sharply, her nose appearing and her eyes suddenly sharp as a bird's. The door of the launderette was pushed open and a youth, embalmed against the cold, appeared. 'We got some, Korky.' His voice was hoarse. 'You coming?'

'Right,' answered the girl firmly. She got up, the wet weight of her coverings making her movements like those of an old woman. As she reached the door she said to Savage: 'Time you was crashed out, home in bed.'

The youth in the doorway thrust a plastic bag towards her. Squeaking she plunged her hands eagerly into it, bringing them out, clutching a mass of steaming chips.

She stumbled out to join the others on the pavement. She had left the door open and Savage got up and went to shut it. As he did so he came face to face with her. 'I was coming back to shut it,' she said, her mouth steaming with chips. The football scarf was hung loosely now and he saw her face was thin and ashen, her eyes like black spikes, her lips raw. 'Where are you going now?' he asked.

'Me? With them,' she answered pointing to the group

moving off along the pavement, clinging together. One turned and shouted: 'Come on, Korky. Stop chatting him up.'

The girl laughed drily and half-turned. 'Cheeky sod,' she said to Savage. 'Did you hear that?'

'I was wondering where you were going, that's all,' he said.

'Up west, I expect.'

She turned and with the dirty pink coat flopping, the scarf dangling, went after her companions on legs like sticks. She wore heavy boots but no socks. Savage watched her go and then returned into the warm, damp, launderette and closed the door. He sat following the revolutions of his washing, wondering about her at large in London on that night.

When he left the launderette Notting Hill was vacant except for a delivery truck and two taxis idling at the traffic lights, their drivers conversing in shouts. He walked down Kensington Church Street, making a detour to put his newspaper on the roof of boxes that sheltered a tramp he had got to know who liked to study the financial pages.

Even now, after weeks, Savage remained cautious and in the desolate and empty street he paused at each corner and peered into each shadow. It had begun to rain thinly, but with growing pace, and he hurried towards Kensington Heights. He could see the all-night security lights and he swung his two laundry bags decisively and made towards them. Soon he would be home.

As he rounded the final corner towards the courtyard of the apartment block, a figure emerged coming the other way. He stopped. 'Sorry,' she said. 'Didn't mean to give you the . . .' Her voice was harsh as if she had a sore throat.

Savage stayed still, looking at her. 'Oh, it's *you*!' she exclaimed. 'Done your washing?'

Her face glimmered, a white patch wrapped in the football scarf, but he could see the steady glint of her eyes. 'Yes,' he said nervously. 'It's done.'

'Fancy us meeting up again like this,' she said as though they were at a social gathering.

'I thought you were going with your friends.'

'Changed my mind,' she answered. 'I always am. I change it all the time. I'm like that.'

'Have you been following me?' he asked her.

'Right, I have.' She sounded genuinely disappointed. 'And I thought I moved like one of them phantoms.'

'I've got to go,' he said. 'We're both getting wet.'

'Sopping,' she agreed. Her voice grated. 'Can I come with you?'

Savage blinked. 'Where?'

'Wherever it is you live.'

He tried to swallow his astonishment. '. . . But . . . look, I can't let you . . .'

'Aw, come on,' she encouraged. 'You can't have a wife or a woman because you wouldn't be doing your own laundry.' They stood five feet apart. Her voice became a plea. 'Just for tonight.' She surveyed the night. 'It's pissing.' Her eyes returned to him and her expression changed. '. . . Raining,' she corrected.

'No, no, you can't,' he argued. 'I've got problems of my own, believe me.'

'All right,' she responded as though she did not care. 'Sod off with your problems.'

Grimacing, he moved towards the door and unlocked it deliberately, trying not to look back at her. She had not moved from her place. She was like a wraith on the pavement. He opened the outside door and let himself in, then deliberately closed it. She knocked blatantly. Savage ground his teeth, waited, reopened it six inches. 'You're not coming in,' he insisted leaning to the aperture. 'I've got enough troubles.'

'I'm no trouble,' she said to the crack. He could see one eye. 'I'm a bit of bother now, this minute, but I'm not generally. I'll be good and I'll go off in the morning and you won't be lumbered with me ever again.' It was a long speech delivered in a croak. Warily he opened the door a few extra inches. Her pinched face was close. 'I've got a cold coming on,' she pleaded. 'I don't feel very well at all.'

She began to cough, heaving and spluttering and clutching her chest. Savage regarded her helplessly. She looked up into his confused face. 'All right,' she said like a threat. She half-rolled away, hugging the brick wall. 'I'll go. You won't hear from me again. Never, ever.' With a final spasm she moved further away until the stark beam of the security light fixed on her. 'Good ...' cough, cough, cough '... fucking night,' she gasped.

Savage forced himself to shut the door. He leaned against it briefly and then began resolutely mounting the stairs. After the first flight he halted, cursed quietly and then went back and opened the street door. She was standing on the step, facing him, her sharp, damp nose only an inch distant, her eyes full. 'I won't bother you,' she promised.

Slowly he let her in. 'You don't realise,' he said lamely. 'I've come here for some privacy. I don't want anybody in the place.'

She had already slid past him and was going sideways up the stairs. 'I won't be staying,' she promised again on the first landing. 'Which number?'

'Keep going,' he sighed. 'It's right at the top.'

'What's the matter with the lift?'

'The lift,' he replied doggedly, 'is too noisy. It wakes people.'

'Stop shouting then,' she whispered, her washed-out face turning quickly on him. 'Talk quiet.'

He got her to the top of the stairs. As he rummaged for his key she summoned up another coughing spasm. 'No,' he pleaded holding up his hand. 'Don't start, please. Don't worry, we're going in.'

He pushed open the door and she went before him with an odd decorum, hurrying on tiptoe. 'Oh, it *is* nice,' she breathed as if she had viewed a dozen apartments that day. Her bone-like fingers bit into the scarf still under her chin. 'Very posh. I bet you like it here.'

'I do,' he replied. 'When I'm quiet.'

Quickly she went to the big window and to his astonishment familiarly flicked the curtains aside. 'Cor, look at that,' she said surveying the rainy night. 'I bet some of my mates could see me if I waved.'

'Your mates are *not* coming in here,' he warned with a touch of panic. But she was already waving. She waved widely with both hands, then pulled the curtains firmly and revolved to face him. 'Nobody there,' she said. She unwound her soaked scarf revealing her thin head and damp, dank hair. 'You're a good bloke,' she said as if he needed reassurance. 'I want to say thanks.'

'That's all right,' he said solemnly. Her face was narrow, so narrow it made her nose big and her eyes long. Her hair was tangled. Her lips were bloodless and her nose running. 'Snotty me,' she sniffed wiping it with the end of the football scarf.

'Take your coat off,' he suggested nodding at the dripping nylon fur. 'My Paddington,' she smiled slightly. 'All right. I call it after Paddington Bear. You know, the one from Peru.' She took it off and eyed it unhappily as it hung from her hands. 'It looks quite good when it's clean.' Underneath she had a thin, checked dress. 'It niffs a bit.' She handed him the coat and he took it into the kitchen where he draped it across a stool.

When he returned she was standing with mock meekness. Her fragile dress was creased, the hem three inches clear of her knees. 'Sit down, will you,' invited Savage awkwardly. 'Would you like something to drink?' He glanced at her. 'Tea or coffee?'

Demurely she sat on the edge of the sofa. 'I didn't think you meant champagne,' she giggled quietly. 'Anyway, I've gone off champagne. I'll have a cup of tea though. Three sugars.'

With relief he returned to the kitchen, put the kettle on, and put his head through the door. 'Are you hungry?'

'As a rule, yes. Always. But I've just scoffed about three tons of chips. You saw Charley with the chips, didn't you. He nicked them from some drunk. So I'm not that hungry. What's your name, by the way?'

He merely said: 'Savage.'

'Not just Savage,' she objected. 'Can't be. That's something you *are*. Savage.'

'It's Frank Savage,' he said.

'Don't like Frank,' she ruminated. 'That sounds like something you *are* again. You can *be* Frank or you can *be* Savage. I think I'll call you Savage.' She quickly caught the alarm in his eyes at the suggestion that this was to be a longer relationship. 'Just for now,' she reassured him. 'One night only. I *said* I'm off tomorrow and I'll *be* off tomorrow. Always keep my promises I do. That's one thing about me.'

'What is your name?' he asked. The kettle began to whistle.

'I'll tell you after you've made the tea,' she said. 'We can sit down and have a good natter.' She drew together her skinny shoulders. 'I've not felt so warm for weeks.'

Sure that the situation was slipping away from him he hesitated before going to the kettle. 'Go on,' encouraged the girl. 'I won't nick the family treasures.'

He returned embarrassed to the kitchen and poured the water into the teapot. She began singing tunelessly and moving around the room. He peered around the door. She was standing examining his typewriter, her thin back to him, the dress hardly curved over her buttocks, her white legs carelessly knock-kneed. As though she had an acute sense of being watched she turned abruptly. 'What have you got this thing for?' she asked.

'I'm a writer,' he hesitated. 'A sort of writer.'

'What sort?' She pointed at the machine. 'This came out of the Ark, didn't it.'

'I'm putting together an encyclopaedia,' he responded solidly from the kitchen doorway.

'On that?'

'Yes, on that.'

'You ought to get a word processor.'

'I don't want a word processor. I can't use one. Was it two sugars?'

'Three,' she corrected. 'Please. I've got to build myself up. I'm vanishing. Look at me.' She spread her legs and threw her arms sideways. 'Like a skellington.'

He carried in the teapot with two mugs, each with milk, and the sugar on a tray. He had put some chocolate biscuits on a plate. Her eyes went instantly to them and she reached out eagerly. 'I hope they mix with the chips. I don't want to throw up, not now. Not on your nice carpet. I was hot at school on computers. You ought to get one.'

Patiently he poured the tea and she smiled as she studied him. 'You're like some old lady doing that.'

'I'm not used to guests,' he told her defensively. 'Especially not at this time of night.'

'What time *is* it?' she asked without much interest. Ignoring the clock, she caught hold of his wrist and blinked at his watch. 'Late,' she said. 'Quarter past two.' Her thin eyes rose to him as they sat almost formally on the sofa. 'You was asking about my name,' she reminded him. 'You know the name of my coat, Paddington, but you don't know mine.'

'Well, yes. What is it?'

'Korky,' she said bluntly like someone laying their cards on the table. 'Korky Wilson.'

She waited for his blink. 'My father called me after a cat in a comic. Korky the Cat.'

'In the *Dandy*,' he agreed solemnly.

'You remember it?'

'I used to read it,' he nodded. 'But it's not your real name.'

She giggled, spluttering out some biscuit crumbs. Her teeth were small and white and neat, the only visibly cared-for thing about her. 'Korky?' she repeated. ' 'Course not. Nobody's called Korky, are they. No, it was my old man. It amused him, I suppose. My name's Kathleen. I'd rather be called Korky. It's like you being called Frank and me calling you Savage.'

She saw he again detected the insinuation of permanence. 'But don't worry about it. After tomorrow we won't know each other. Can I have a bath? That's one thing I could do with, a good bath.' She grimaced. 'Smell me. I'm mildew.'

He backed away from the invitation. 'I need a bath,' she repeated, her voice dropping confidingly. 'I really do.

I've been out in the streets. Baths are difficult to get out there.' Abruptly she held out her arms like wings and rising from the sofa, capered around the room pretending to be an aeroplane. She landed on her knees almost in front of him. He sat motionless, speechless. She still had her arms at the horizontal. 'I need a bath.'

'The bathroom's in there,' he pointed almost sullenly. He started to get up. 'I'll run it for you.'

'Don't, don't.' She pushed him briskly and with surprising force back onto the sofa. 'Don't you dare. I know how to turn the taps even if I don't get much of a chance doing it.' She stood and looked quizzically towards the kitchen. 'Maybe I could take old pongy Paddington with me,' she suggested. She giggled and turned quickly to meet his concerned expression. 'Don't get manic, I won't. The gunge that would ooze out of Paddington would block up the drains of these flats for weeks. I'll give him a scrub soon. He likes a good scrub.'

She went towards the bathroom and began singing thinly and apparently aimlessly, as she turned on the taps. Savage remained seated and unsure.

'Talking about scrubbing,' she called through the thickening steam. 'I bet you think I'm a scrubber, don't you?'

'I don't at all,' he said relieved to find something he could say.

Her straggling hair hung around the door. 'But I bet you think it.' She paused impishly. 'What are you going to do while I'm in the bath? Peep through the keyhole?'

Solemnly Savage rose from the sofa. 'I was just thinking of going to bed,' he muttered. Her head and one bare shoulder reappeared. 'Don't,' she said with genuine urgency. 'Don't go to bed yet. I'll have to put all the lights off and stuff. I've only just got in here. It's *your* flat.'

Grimacing, Savage took the cups to the kitchen. 'All right, I'll wait,' he called. He glanced at the cupboard, opened it and almost roughly took out the whisky bottle. He poured a short measure and added some water. Then he walked back into the room, to the curtains which he tugged open. He stood framed in the dim light gazing out at the puddled reflections on the Kensington roofs. Behind him Korky was singing tunelessly in the steam. He remained there, taking only a single sip at the whisky, until she opened the door and came back into the room. Her vague reflection was caught in the dark window before him. He could see she was standing still and observing him. 'You look all by yourself,' she said from the far end of the room. 'With nobody.'

'That's how I am,' he said still facing the night window. 'That's how I want to be. For now anyway. That's why I came to live . . .' He turned. She was wearing his blue dressing gown, slightly stooped as though under its weight; she looked white and vulnerable. 'I borrowed this,' she shrugged in a diminished voice. 'Is that all right? Otherwise I'll have to wear smelly Paddington.'

Savage turned and sat carefully on one of the armchairs. 'Do you want anything to eat?' he repeated.

'No, not now, thanks. Like I said I'm stuffed with chips. I could feel them coming up when I was in the bath.' She surveyed the room as though appreciating it over again. 'It's a good place this,' she decided. Once more she noted his alarm. 'Don't worry. I'm not staying. I wouldn't even if you wanted me to.'

'Would you like anything else to drink?' he asked.

She walked towards him holding the dressing gown together and sniffed over his glass while he sat rigid. 'I got myself clean.' He did not know what to do with her. 'What's in that?' she asked.

'Scotch,' he answered stonily. 'But you're not having Scotch. I meant some more tea or cocoa.'

She grinned mockingly. 'Bedtime cocoa for a little girl.'

'Do you want some?'

'No, thanks. It won't mix. Can't I have some of that . . . that Scotch . . . to keep me warm? Only a smidgen.'

Savage inhaled deeply. He went into the kitchen and reappeared with a second tumbler. He poured a splash of his whisky into the glass and handed it to her. She examined it minutely. 'Shit,' she muttered, 'that much is not going to warm my little toe.'

'That's all you're getting. And it's not shit, it's Scotch.'

'Sorry I swore,' she said airily. She sat on the sofa again, opposite him. Her bony knee came through the folds of the dressing gown and she covered it, with genuine modesty. 'Oops,' she chided herself. Taking her time she looked up and smiled at his expression. Her darkened hair was lank, framing the sharp colourless features. Her eyes remained lively. 'You don't know what to make of me, do you?' she said.

'It's difficult,' admitted Savage. 'Why are you homeless anyway?'

'It's no life for a young girl,' she said as though completing the thought for him. 'I just cleared out. But I'm not a tart and I'm not a junkie. I couldn't afford drugs anyway and I can't stand the smell of glue. Yuk. I've been scared, I can tell you. Shitless I've been. I was scared for weeks after I ran away.' Her expression cleared. 'Mind, it was all right last summer, great in fact, great, except for the fleas. Then I went off with this bloke from a band. A real trash band. But I hung out with them, travelling about doing gigs, when the weather got colder. But then he wanted to pass me around among his mates, like sharing a joint, and I didn't go a lot on that. So I scarpered and I haven't had anywhere since.'

'What are you doing away from home in the first place? What about your parents?' he repeated.

'My dad died when I was twelve. Accident at work. He worked in a slaughterhouse.'

'That was bad luck.'

'A bummer,' she said thinking about it for a moment. 'He was all right. Until then. We moved from London to Swindon, for the open air or something. Then Minnie, that's my mum, turned all funny. Sexy, you know, flirting about and there's nothing worse than someone like that getting flirty. Her age and fat legs. She ended up living with this man, and then marrying him, and then last year she just disappeared, vanished. I don't know where she went. Didn't leave a note or anything. And that left me with Merlin.' Her eyes challenged him.

'Merlin?'

'That was his name, Merlin. Like the wizard in the stories, except he was no wizard. Ugh, he was creepy. Told me he had only married my mum because he wanted me. I had to keep out of his way, I can tell you. One night he got pissed and that was a really bad scene. He broke down the door and I had to climb out of the window. After that I made myself scarce. And I've been scarce ever since. What about you?'

'Me?' Savage was surprised by the enquiry. 'Well, nothing much really. I was in the army.'

'What for?'

'What do you mean, what for?'

'What I said. Didn't you have anywhere to go?' She leaned forward with renewed interest, the dressing gown dividing at the top and baring her thin throat and chest. 'Did you ever kill anybody?'

He did not answer. Instead he said: 'The army is for . . . well, it's for protection, defence.' He felt ridiculous saying it.

'Oh, for *that*,' she said as if it had never occurred to her. Her eyes lit and once more she leaned towards him. 'I bet you shot 'undreds.'

'I was a soldier,' he reiterated doggedly. 'Then I was injured and in hospital and then I left the army and now I'm here.'

'You don't look like a soldier,' she said studying him quizzically. 'Not with hair like that.'

'I'm not now.'

'But it's funny, you talk a bit like one. I can hear it.'

She regarded him shrewdly and sideways. 'What about your wife?'

'How did you know I had . . . have one?'

'Oh, come on. A bloke like you don't get away with not being married, even if he is in the army and all over the place. What happened?'

Savage shrugged. 'When I came out we found we just couldn't get on, so we parted. That's it, just about.'

For almost the first time since she had entered the apartment there was silence. She had sipped the dregs of whisky away and now she studied the clouded bottom of the glass. She inserted her finger and licked it. 'Do you want to see my body?' she asked casually examining her fingertip. 'I have got one.'

He almost choked. 'No . . . thanks very much . . . no, thanks . . .'

Her tone became teasing: 'Oh, come on, soldier, 'ave a look. It's not bad considering I'm half-bloody starved.'

'Look,' he said. 'There's no need. I don't want you to.'

'Aw, come on,' she said. With a mock expression of seduction, moving her hips and rolling her eyes, she began to rise from the sofa. He tried to protest again and stop her but knocked his whisky glass on to the floor. It rolled softly on the carpet. 'Now look what you've done,' she said still tantalising, her voice low.

He was rooted. She was still rising as she spoke and now, stepping back with a parody of a dance, her face fixed in a wide, thin smile, her body moving skinnily, she let his outsized dressing gown drop to her waist. Savage stared at her apologetic breasts, little and pink-budded, her saucered shoulders, her narrow waist and jutting hip bones. 'Stop it,' he asked her softly, as he sat. 'It's wrong. It's not right for a young kid ... You don't have to ...'

'Yes, I do,' she answered quietly but stoutly. 'I want to.'

She performed another mock dance movement and let the robe fall to the carpet. Then, grinning over her shoulder as she revolved, she turned her back on him displaying her white, pinched bottom and the other side of her angled hips. Then slowly she pirouetted, as though to silent music, pushing out her stomach and the postage-stamp of hair between her legs. 'Not bad, eh?' she suggested.

'Stop it,' he repeated hoarsely. His decency was being strained. 'Korky, stop it.'

'Watch this, then,' she boasted brazenly. Before his astonished face she put her hands down and did a naked cartwheel across the carpet. Then she cartwheeled back again, displaying everything she had.

'Don't,' he said angrily. 'Now pack this in.'

'You called me Korky just now,' she said standing upright, white and thin. Her hands dropped with belated modesty across her pubis. 'That's the first time, the very first.'

'Put that dressing gown on,' ordered Savage. His tone lowered. 'Please put it on.'

'All right, sergeant major,' she mimicked.

'Put it on at once,' he repeated. Her eyes remained vivid for another moment, but then the brightness drained from them and she sulkily shrugged her skeletal shoulders. 'All right, I don't care. I thought you'd like it, that's all.'

'I don't want you to do it,' he said, his lips tight. 'You're a young kid.'

'Seventeen,' she said, then caustically: 'Merlin used to say he liked a bit of veal.'

Savage put his head in his hands and hid it there. When he looked up again she had her backside to him, had regained the dressing gown and was starting to pull it on. 'You're sure?' she enquired looking around.

He could hardly breathe, he felt oddly afraid. 'Quite sure,' he muttered. 'Very nice, thank you.'

Advancing carefully on him she stood in front of him as he again covered his face. She let the robe fall apart again and reaching out caught his hands and led them away from his eyes. She pushed her belly against his nose.

'I've got to tell you something,' he mumbled. She retreated and examined his face.

'What? Don't tell me you're queer,' she said. 'Not a queer soldier.'

'I've been mentally ill,' he said. 'Sometimes I don't know properly what I'm doing. So don't do this, please don't do it.'

'You could be dangerous?' she said looking interested.

'I hope not. But I don't want you to do this sort of thing. I don't need it. You don't need to do it.'

She could see his distress was real. 'You poor bugger,' said Korky. Her eyes were damp. 'You poor man. You need somebody to look after you.'

Seven

When he awoke he found that she had emptied his refrigerator and gone. Her single bed was neatly made and the curtains in the second room were open. All that was left in the refrigerator was a pot of Marmite. She had left a note in neat capital letters clinging to the shelf: 'I can't stand Marmite. Love Korky.'

Savage surveyed the apartment unhappily. He pulled the main curtains back revealing the misty morning fresco. It was nine o'clock. He had slept late. He returned to the smaller bedroom, studied it again and wondered what time she had left. Thoughtfully he made some coffee and toast. Sometimes he turned on the radio at this time but now he did not bother. She had been very strange.

In his chosen solitude he sometimes forgot which day of the week it was; very often he could not remember the date. Time had rolled itself into a long, meaningless mist like that outside the window. With scant enthusiasm he walked to his typewriter. On the paper slotted in she had left another block-letter note. It said: 'Thank you for being nice to a poor homeless girl.' He grinned. He sat at the desk and stared from the window for several minutes, but then made himself start to type: *Andaman Islands. There are five main islands of the group situated in the Bay of Bengal. North, Middle and South Andaman with Baratang and Rutland*

Island lying across the Diligent Strait from Ritchie's Archipelago, while on the Duncan Passage is Little Andaman . . .'

The doorbell rang. He tightened his lips and teeth. The summons was repeated. Irritably he strode across the room and pulled the door open. The old lady called Wilhelmina was there with a scattering of talcum powder around her and on her shoes. 'I've come to warn you,' she said.

Savage regarded her bleakly. She appeared to notice the falling talcum for the first time. 'Oh dear,' she remarked in a mild way. 'Where has that come from?' She raised her face as it broke into a smile. 'May I come in please?'

As politely as he could Savage answered: 'I'm working at the moment.'

'Don't you worry,' she responded understandingly as though it were he interrupting her, and pushing by him with surprising robustness. She scrutinised the apartment before speaking. 'We won't be long about this business. But I thought I must warn you.'

Savage had left the door half-open, an invitation for her to leave as soon as she liked. The talcum trailed faintly across the carpet. She still appeared puzzled by it but she said nothing.

She sat on the sofa. Savage pointedly remained standing. 'I couldn't discuss it with you when the other residents were here present,' she began. Again she was distracted by the room. 'That Mr Kostelanetz,' she remarked after her survey. 'A shady one, don't you think. I understand he was involved in all sorts of things. People with names like Kostelanetz quite often are, you know.'

'You wanted to warn me about something.'

'Indeed I did,' she said seriously. Her wrinkled eyelids

dropped and then rose like those of an ancient bird. 'You must beware.'

'Of what?'

'I had better remind you of my full name. Mr Maddison forgets everyone's name. Even his wife's, although that is understandable. I am Wilhelmina Blenkinsop. Mrs although I am widowed. My husband is buried in the basement, you know.'

Savage remembered. 'Oh,' he said inadequately. 'He is?'

'And a number of others also. It was a conspiracy and it became necessary. Would you like to see the exact grave?'

'Well ... no, not right now.'

'You're busy, I know,' she said flapping an understanding hand. 'And I promised not to keep you. But perhaps when the weather gets better you'd like to accompany me down to the basement and I'll show you.'

Savage became aware that someone was standing outside the half-open door. He looked up. You never knew in this place. There was a firm knock and Tomelty entered, his face puckered. 'Ah, I thought you might be here, Mrs Blenkinsop,' he said.

'I was just warning this gentleman,' the lady said primly, 'what to expect.'

Tomelty rolled his eyes towards Savage. 'Yes, well you said you were going to. Now you've done it. I think you ought to be off now and let Mr Savage get on with his work.'

She looked disconcertingly interested. 'Is it important work?' she whispered.

'I think so,' answered Savage.

'Of profound national importance?'

'Important to Mr Savage,' put in Tomelty firmly. He

touched her withered hand as she obediently rose. She then offered the same hand to Savage who shook it gravely. 'Be careful,' she said after squinting quickly towards the porter. 'Be warned.'

'Yes, thank you, I will,' promised Savage.

Tomelty led the slow woman towards the door. She had one more piece of news. 'Mr Belfont,' her eyes rose like those of an inquisitor. 'You met Mr Percy Belfont?'

Savage agreed that he had.

'He has left, you know,' she continued. 'He has gone to die in Antwerp.' She continued her exit, a faint snowfall of talcum following her. Tomelty spotted it with professional eye and glanced apologetically at Savage. 'She always leaves a trail,' he said.

'Hello, Jean. This is Frank Savage.'

'Frank. Well, well. How's the encyclopaedia? Finished?'

'Not quite. Another couple of years or so.'

'Where have you got to?'

'The Andaman Islands. In the Indian Ocean. Bay of Bengal. I thought I would let you know that I'm settling down now. I wanted to tell you again I was very grateful for your help when I had that black-out in London.'

'You must tell me about it some time. I only got the basic details from the nick over there. It sounds interesting.'

'I just had a brainstorm. I'll tell you some time. I went back to see the doctor at Marshfield Manor, Dr Fenwick. He says I'll be all right.'

'All I saw was a message about you getting into some sort of fight with some down-and-outs on the Embankment.'

'That's right. It wasn't quite as straightforward as that. Apparently I attacked a whole bunch of them.'

He heard her professional pause. 'Apparently?' she queried.

'It's a long story. Someone was throwing a baby about on a train and I . . .'

'Throwing a baby about?'

'Yes. Some yobs.'

'Are you serious?'

'I am. Perhaps I ought to tell you the whole story.'

'Would you like to come around to my place for supper?' she asked.

Savage took a long breath. 'Well . . . yes. Thanks. When?'

'Could you make it tonight? I'm off duty tonight.'

In the afternoon he went for a walk. He had intended to go later but at two o'clock the room seemed to gather round him. He went to the window. The familiar low, late, winter light and landscape were waiting.

Outside the damp of the day touched his face and he felt it on his hands. He pulled the collar of his overcoat higher and headed along the upward sloping pavement towards Notting Hill. At the top he turned right and eventually right again into the wintry park. A group of shambling young people came up the broad path under the wet trees, shouting extravagantly, defiantly, to each other, rough laughs and half-intelligible shouts, loud, spiteful, aggressive, as though they were warding off demons. He wondered if they knew Korky. Would they know where she had gone? He continued walking. At the bottom of the path, where it joined the main road through the park, a squad of soldiers marched towards him. He sat on a clammy bench to see them go past, their backs straight, their chins jutting as if each expected a punch. He almost felt an urge to stand to attention. 'Left, right, left, right, left, right,' he muttered. Their boots sounded in his brain. When they had marched by he opened his eyes and saw Mr Kostelanetz stationary on the opposite grass verge.

Mr Kostelanetz was wearing an expensive tweed overcoat. His moustache was lengthy but carefully tended, his hair silvery in the diminishing afternoon light. His whorled eyes went left and right as though expecting more troops, then he crossed the park road unhurriedly. Arranging his overcoat he sat down. 'Would you like a Mintoe?' he enquired.

Savage thanked him but declined. Mr Kostelanetz minutely unwrapped a Mintoe and opening his big mouth tossed it in. He seemed pleased with the trick and disappointed that Savage did not appear to have noticed it. He worked the sweet around. 'How is your life?' he asked.

'It is working quite well.'

'It is quiet at the Kensington Heights, like you wanted?'

'There have been interruptions.'

'The old people,' sighed Mr Kostelanetz understandingly. 'They are crazy.'

Silently he renewed his offer of a Mintoe. Savage again politely refused and said: 'Three men came calling for you the other night, in the early hours actually. One had a cricket bat.'

'I do not play,' said Mr Kostelanetz with an apparently genuine regret. 'I am a foreigner, you know.'

'I don't think they wanted you to bowl to them,' continued Savage. 'I think they were intending to sort you out.'

Mr Kostelanetz gave a quiet, unafraid snort. 'Those men are incompetent,' he said. 'Fools.'

'You know them then?'

Mr Kostelanetz sighed again. 'I have experience of them. They are going to work for me now. I am sorry they disturbed you. I understand you have a gun.'

'They told you about it.'

The overcoated arm came heavily up and the hand patted him comfortingly on the shoulder. 'I know about a lot of things, my boy. But do not worry. I know about the gun but nobody else knows, except those three, and they won't tell. They have made a sincere promise to me. And a soldier, even if he is not a soldier now, should have a gun.'

Savage asked cautiously: 'Mr Kostelanetz, what do you do? As a business?'

The moustache wobbled as the big man transferred the Mintoe around his gums. 'A business?' he queried. 'Well, now I am more or less retired. There is not so much work. I was a spy.'

Savage glanced sideways at him. Kostelanetz was looking straight ahead as if he were reconnoitring the distance.

'Who did you spy for?'

'Sometimes the Americans, sometimes the Germans, East and West, and on occasions for the Russians, although they were mean. I did not do much spying for them because they wouldn't pay. It's all gone now, of course, espionage. Nobody spies like they used to. It is a shame. We all knew each other and, if you were clever and kept to the rules, it was a good life, sometimes very good.'

His face had become reminiscent. 'I took after my father,' he revealed eventually still surveying the gloomy park. 'My father was also a spy. He operated in Lisbon during the war, where all the spies were. It was like a club. They all knew each other, they even had a football team.' He emitted a massive sigh evaporating the air around him as he breathed it out. 'Lisbon,' he said shaking his head. 'That must have been something, Mr Savage. My father enjoyed it, the city, the danger. And he died quietly in a bed. Not his own.'

'And now you've retired.'

'Semi,' corrected Mr Kostelanetz. 'I do some business. A bit. Removals mostly.' He turned towards Savage, his gaze profound from below the dark, overhung eyes. 'Moving things.' He paused. 'From one place to another.'

He rose ponderously as though his overcoat was bearing him down. 'And I have to go now, to do some removals. Keep well, Mr Savage.' He bent confidingly. 'And safe, of course. Keep safe.'

From the tweed sleeve projected a hand, the colour and texture of pine. Savage shook it. Mr Kostelanetz restrained him from getting up, walked a few paces of his departure but then stopped and turned. 'You must get better,' he called, holding up a finger as though for silence. 'Get entirely better.'

He continued on his journey, shuffling down through the park towards the main road. Savage could see his large coat as far as the gate and then he spotted it plodding along the pavement outside the railings. He got up from the seat and began his walk back through the dimming afternoon towards Kensington Heights. There were few people left in the park at that time. Its air was echoing and misty, and from the distance he could hear the soldiers who had gone by. They had halted at the top of the park and the shouted orders sounded across the abandoned grass and the empty trees. Glancing around guiltily he began to march, as he had once done, shoulders square, back upright, eyes ahead, arms swinging. No one saw him and after a few yards he stopped, slumped almost.

'What a ruddy life,' he said to himself.

Unspeaking they lay against each other, her breasts against his ribs. One bedside light was on. It was one o'clock and the street in Westbourne Grove was silent as a rural lane outside the dimly glowing window. She moved her head against him and laid one hand over his groin. 'Would you like me to tell you about the fascinating day-to-day life of a London policewoman?' she enquired moving her gaze up to his face.

Savage shifted. He saw her uncertain smile in the periphery of the lamp. Jean leaned up and kissed his chin. 'I thought it would help towards conversation,' she said.

'I'm sorry,' Savage said. 'I was enjoying the quiet.'

He rolled towards her again. 'It's a long time since I did this,' he said. 'It's one of the things that seemed to go away. I'd forgotten what it was like.'

'Do you want to do it again?'

'Yes. I'm looking forward to it.'

'I'd like to take my stockings off. They belong to the Metropolitan Police.'

'Take them off,' he said. She did without getting from the bed.

'And how do I look?' she asked as if she really needed to know. She kicked back the duvet and stretched her body, naked and now rosy in the lamplight. Savage eased himself up on his elbow. She closed her eyes privately. Her dark hair framed her troubled face and lolled over her shoulders. Her breasts were unassuming, lying as though separately asleep, slightly parted, the nipples like her own shut eyes. She had a flat stomach, easing to her breathing, and hips only a little wider than her indented waist. He began to stroke her between her legs.

'This is the first time I have felt completely human in a long time,' she said.

'I'm glad,' he told her.

'Kiss me down there.' He lowered his head as she opened herself to him. The low scent of her engulfed him. He kissed her. She wriggled and eventually raised his face from the crevice. 'No more,' she asked quite firmly. 'I want you to be there when that happens.'

He lay alongside while her fingers caressed him. 'I can't tell you how much I have needed this,' she muttered. 'I have to have a man.'

He eased himself above and slid into her. They moved against each other with slow luxury. But at the end she clung to his neck, almost throttling him with her slim hard arms. Then, cooling, they lay against each other, his hard body and arms about her thin but disciplined form.

'It's not necessary to be in love,' she whispered. 'Sometimes it is better if you aren't.'

'I know,' he said.

He left her at three. He was content to go. 'I'm on the early shift,' she said as though she had put aside everything else. She got into a robe, went to the kitchen and made coffee which they drank in silence while they waited for his taxi. He walked into the confined kitchen, and put his arm around her waist.

'I've not had many satisfactory relationships since my husband died,' she said.

'I see. You haven't told me about it. I was waiting for you to tell me.'

'He was beaten over the head outside a pub in

Shepherd's Bush,' she said staring into her cup. 'Nothing newsworthy like foiling a bank raid. He wasn't even on duty. Some coppers wouldn't have wanted to know. He hung on for two days in Charing Cross Hospital, then he died without regaining consciousness.'

When the taxi arrived Savage went out into the icy air. He climbed in and looked up at the uppermost window in the three-storeyed conversion. As he did so the light was extinguished. She had gone back to bed quickly. The early shift was the next bit of her life. He felt sorry for her in her loneliness and he sensed even then that there was little they would be able to do for each other.

The streets were empty, spectral sodium light splodged over the wet roads, and the journey took only five minutes. He paid the cab and walked introspectively towards the open yard of Kensington Heights. There were no illuminated windows, not even Miss Bombazine's. He turned into the entry and stepped quickly towards the main door, feeling for his key. As he did so there was a cry and a scuffle of movement in the low-lying darkness almost under his feet. Startled, he staggered backwards out on to the lit pavement.

'Where've you been?' she demanded. 'What sort of time do you call this?'

His hands went out into the almost black space and she caught hold of them and weakly drew herself to her feet. She began coughing, shaking violently, putting her face in his hands. 'Wait, wait a minute,' he pleaded. She leaned back against the brickwork, her face like a quarter moon, staring at him with real fear. Savage put the key in the door and opened it. Warm air rushed out. Korky staggered towards it as though she believed it would save her life. Savage helped her into the lower passage. He supported her against the wall and looked at her. He saw she was very ill, her face smudged, ragged, her eyes closing and opening wildly. He thought she might be drugged.

'Where have you been?' he asked wildly.

Korky held up a dripping plastic bag. 'I just went to get my things.'

She could not walk; her legs dragged as he helped her into the lift. He held her upright, her body like old wire, her exhausted chin hooked across his shoulder. 'Where've you been?' she mumbled again.

'Out,' he muttered. He kept her on her feet. Her squalid pink fake fur was hung with rain. She dropped the plastic bag on the floor of the lift. Her face felt hot against him. 'Where out?' she demanded scarcely able to say the words. 'I looked for you in the launderette.'

He held on to her while the lift clanked up. They reached the landing and he got her out. She had picked up her bag. Below them he heard a door open and a querulous and croaky female voice call up the stairs. 'It's very late you know, Mr Savage.'

'Bollocks,' he answered below his breath. He held Korky up while he got his key from his pocket. There were carpeted footfalls on the stairs. An old woman in a tasselled dressing gown reached the landing and took in the scene. 'Who is it?' she asked. He realised she was the one called Miss Weiz.

'It's an albatross,' replied Savage.

'And hanging on your neck,' observed Miss Weiz. 'Is this albatross drunk?'

'She's ill,' corrected Savage. 'Can't you see?' He had opened the door and now manoeuvred Korky inside. The girl tried to say something to the old woman but she could not get it out. Her coughs beat against his ribs. He turned her and closed the door in Miss Weiz's face.

'Casual women are not permitted!' his neighbour called thickly through the door.

Savage eased Korky into the chair. Her carrier bag fell sideways, tipping some jumbled scraps of clothes, a cheap plastic radio and some food cartons which had been in his fridge, on to the carpet. Ignoring it, Savage strode back to the door and flung it open. Miss Weiz, unable to straighten up from her position against the letter-box, almost tumbled into the room. 'Go away!' he snapped, frightening her. Still bent from the waist she backed away towards the stairs but remained unblinkingly watching him. 'Clear off,' he ordered. 'Go on back to bed.'

He shut the door loudly. She continued to reverse across the landing, then changed direction like an ancient figure on a weather vane and began to descend the stairs. 'Go away . . . clear off,' she muttered to herself. 'Orders, orders. Go back to the bed . . .' At the next landing she revolved again and projected her voice upwards, using her worn hands as a funnel. 'Casual women not permitted!' she bawled.

Another door opened and out came Miss Cotton wearing a tablecloth around her shoulders. 'Where are the casual women?' she enquired. 'Who has them?'

'That Mr Savage. I knew he was up to something. He was much too quiet.'

Half-bent she strutted towards her own door, opened it, and went in bad-temperedly. 'It is always the quiet ones,' commented Miss Cotton wagging her face as she returned to bed.

In the apartment above Savage was attempting to get the soaked fun fur from Korky's back.

'Poor old Paddington,' she moaned. 'He'll get pneumonia.'

'You look like you've *got* it,' grunted Savage. 'We'll sort out Paddington later.'

He manoeuvred the wretched coat, chewed and hung with dirt and damp, from her back. 'Poor Paddington,' she mumbled again. 'He's done no harm.' Tight-faced she sat down again. Under the coat she was wearing layers of old clammy cardigans, the stitches sagging, and the same skimpy dress as she had worn days before. Savage made up his mind. 'Take everything off,' he said. 'I'll get you some pyjamas.'

'Help me,' she pleaded holding out the woollen arms like a bird drying its wings. 'Help me then.'

He went towards the bedroom, returning with a pair of pyjamas he had ironed the day before. 'Can't you manage?' he asked her.

Korky gave him a pitying look. 'I can't bloody stand up.'

'Right. All right. I'll do it.'

'Don't look,' she muttered.

With difficulty, holding her, seating her, he took the ragged clothes away from her, the cardigans and the thin dress, fetid and clinging to her bony body. 'My pants are clean,' she said attempting to flutter her eyelashes.

He said nothing but unbuttoned the dirty dress and pulled it down her stark body.

'Ever seen a sight like this?' she croaked looking down wretchedly. 'Like a skellington.'

'Skeleton,' he said. She was sitting in the chair naked but for her pants, her narrow body pimpled and pale, her chest as flat as a child's, her nipples raspberries. 'I say skellington,' she argued. She regarded him with wet eyes. 'What a fucking mess, eh?'

Her apparently empty plastic carrier bag began to move across the floor. Savage heard it and swivelled. It had stopped. He turned back to Korky. 'We'll get you into bed,' he said uncomfortably. 'And I'll get you a drink. You ought to have the doctor.'

'I'll have the whisky,' she accepted.

He heard the carrier bag move again and this time saw it edging away. He began to go after it, then turned back and helped Korky into the voluminous pyjamas. 'Great,' she approved weakly. 'Warm as toast.' She began to wheeze again and he held her upright. 'John is in the bag,' she said. 'He's my only friend. Apart from you, Savage.'

The carrier bag restarted its progress across the floor. 'What is it?' Savage asked. He tried to help her to her feet; she was so fragile she could not manage a step. Easily he picked her up and took her in his arms towards the single room. 'John's a gerbil,' she mumbled. Her eyes were almost closed. Savage opened the duvet and eased her into the bed. She sighed deeply and lay back on the pillow as though she were dead. 'I *must* get the doctor,' he said.

'I'd rather have that whisky.'

Going into the kitchen he poured a prudent measure of Scotch into a glass. Then he reached up into the cupboard and took down a tin of Bovril. Quickly he boiled the kettle and made a cup full of the extract. He poured the whisky into it and took it into the bedroom. She was lying very still, ashen, with her eyes closed. Alarmed, he blurted: 'Korky . . .'

'I'm still here,' she said drowsily. He took the cup to her. 'Whisky and Bovril,' he said.

'Great,' she nodded. He could hear her chest creaking. She sipped at the cup and drank half of it. 'I can't

manage any more, Savage,' she told him helplessly.
'What a bummer.' Like a child she slipped under the
cover, her head scarcely denting the pillow. She coughed
and groaned again. He heard the carrier bag shuffling
into the room. It came to the edge of the bed and he had
to step quickly out of the way for fear of treading on it.
He picked it up and with an anxious glance towards the
girl, took it with him as he went out.

He knew he ought to call a doctor. Now. Early hours
or not. He sat on the chair trying to decide. The carrier
bag was continuing its rustling progress over the carpet.
He could be decisive about that. Lifting it and balancing
it in his hands, he detected the warm animal. Carefully
he took it out, rounded, short-furred, suspicious-eyed. It
seemed content, now it was out of the bag, to sit on his
carpet as if waiting to see what would happen next. It
gave its face a token wash. A harsh, low, voice came from
the second bedroom.

'Savage . . . Savage.'

Swiftly he got to the door. It was an effort for her to
move her lips. Her eyes remained shut. 'Give John some
milk and bread. Put him out for a shit.'

'Don't worry,' he said anxiously watching her slight
shape scarcely breathing enough to lift the bedcover.
'You get some rest.' He lied: 'I know about gerbils.'

Leaving the door an inch open he returned to the
gerbil which regarded him with sleepy nonchalance but,
at the moment he crouched to pick it up, darted away
from his hand. Creeping in pursuit he finally cornered it
behind the television. It felt fat and warm. He carried it
to the kitchen and, closing the door, put it on the floor.
Recognising the situation it made no attempt to evade
him again but squatted in anticipation watching him with
tight, bright eyes. He put some bread on a saucer on the

kitchen worktop and added milk almost to the rim. The gerbil stood on its hind paws and sniffed industriously. Even before he had balanced the saucer to the floor it had its sniffling nose over the edge. As he set it down the animal threw its paws across the rim and spilled the bread and milk. He left the kitchen and going carefully to the half-open door of the second bedroom he listened. She was still awake. She sensed he was there and called to him and he went in and sat on the side of the small bed. Her frail, old lady's hand came from the sheets and he held it. 'Savage,' she said, her eyes still closed and her voice grating and weak. 'Savage,' she repeated. He answered her. 'Don't worry, Savage,' she breathed. 'I'll look after you.'

Eight

At seven in the morning he went down to Tomelty's door. The caretaker and his wife, apparently anticipating some news or explanation, came out together, holding identical cups of tea before them, sheltering the cups with their hands as if hiding the contents from each other. 'I need a doctor,' said Savage.

'It's that girl,' nodded Mrs Tomelty dressed in a flowered overall and with her hair cramped into curlers. 'I knew she'd be trouble.'

'She's no trouble,' Savage said so uncompromisingly that they both looked alarmed. He softened his tone. 'She's very ill, that's all.'

'They get ill,' Mrs Tomelty gave a grave nod. 'Out on those damp streets.'

'In all weathers,' agreed her husband. He looked sideways at his wife. 'Donovan,' he said.

'I don't like Donovan's eyes,' she objected. 'Prassad.'

'Donovan,' said the caretaker decisively. 'Prassad takes his time. Being Indian. Donovan will come right away. Remember Mrs Golightly.'

'He came,' confirmed Mrs Tomelty sombrely. 'Too late.'

'Get Donovan then,' put in Savage to curtail the debate. 'She's very ill.'

'I'll come and look at her,' said Mrs Tomelty as though

127

offering an expert diagnosis. 'You get Donovan, Tomelty, and tell him it's urgent. Life and death.'

She pushed her husband inside so positively that he spilled his tea. Carrying her own cup before her, she led the way up the stairs. She wore carpet slippers that might have been made out of carpet. She bustled ahead of Savage. 'Donovan's quicker,' she conceded. 'It's just his eyes.'

He had left his front door unlocked. Mrs Tomelty entered in a businesslike way. She sniffed the air in the flat from habit and quickly turned to Savage. 'There's a funny smell,' she noted. 'It's her gerbil,' he said.

'Where is she, the girl? She's been reported by the other residents, you know.'

'I thought it wouldn't take long. She's in the small bedroom.'

'Yes, she would be.'

Mrs Tomelty shuffled towards the half-open door and pushed it quietly. Korky was asleep, her frail ribcage heaving below the cover. The caretaker's wife stood watching, still holding the teacup. 'I don't care for the way her lungs are rattling,' she intoned morbidly. She leaned over and held her free hand against the white forehead. 'Hot as toast,' she sniffed. She turned. 'Last time he was too late.'

They went back into the main room. 'I should have got a doctor hours ago,' said Savage bitterly.

'You weren't to know,' she said. Her body had dropped forward in thought but now she straightened. 'He *is* quick, don't worry. He only missed Mrs Golightly by minutes. I'll make some tea.'

She was still waiting for the kettle to boil when her husband appeared at the door. 'Donovan's on his way,' he said. He nodded towards Savage reassuringly. 'He's very quick,' he said. 'A clever man,' recommended Mrs Tomelty from the kitchen. She made the tea and poured three cups. 'How was it you took her in?' she asked Savage obliquely.

'She followed me back the other night,' said Savage. 'Early hours in fact. From the launderette. I let her stay . . .' He quickly glanced at them. 'Not . . .'

'Not in *that* way,' Mr Tomelty completed. 'No, we understand. You're a decent man.'

'I don't know about that,' sighed Savage. 'The next morning she had disappeared and then when I came back last night, again early hours, she was lying downstairs, outside.'

'You can't turn a young soul away like that,' nodded Mrs Tomelty. 'Whatever the residents say.' As though the possessor of acute sense she went to the window and pulled back the curtain. 'He's here,' she announced peering down. 'That's his new green car.'

Like someone conscious of their duty she went out of the door and down the stairs. They heard her returning with the doctor in the lift. She showed him into the apartment. He was a haggard man with a kindly manner, a deep blue chin and a fierce squint. 'Haven't had time to get near a razor this morning,' he said rubbing the chin. Mr and Mrs Tomelty edged towards the door. She reverted to formality. 'I'll be back later to see if you need me, doctor.'

'The Irish,' said Donovan as though they were beyond understanding. 'Now, where is the patient?'

Savage showed him the room. 'Korky,' he said as he went in. 'The doctor's here.'

She roused herself weakly and muttered: 'I dreamt I was dead.'

She looked like a ghost in bed, her young features

gaunt and damp, her eyes opaque. Dr Donovan put his bag on the floor and motioned Savage out of the room. With a sudden feeling of dread Savage walked to the window where Mrs Tomelty had pushed aside the curtains. He stared out, looking nowhere. A scraggy pigeon bounced on the narrow balcony and strutted along the parapet. Savage remembered the gerbil and turned inside to look for it. It had been in the kitchen nosing around the stain that the bread and milk had left on the floor. Now he could not find it. He searched, whispering: 'John, John, John.'

Eventually the doctor emerged, his face lower hung, it seemed, than previously. 'She's a very poorly girl,' he said folding his stethoscope and putting it into his worn bag. 'She ought to be in hospital.'

'No hospital!' It was almost a screech. They both went to the door. She was dragging herself up in the bed, trying to support herself on her elbows. Dr Donovan moved with professional alacrity and eased her back on to the pillow. 'You've no strength for shouting,' he said, his voice remaining mild.

Korky's eyes went to Savage. 'No hospital,' she repeated doggedly. 'I'll walk out, I promise you. I'll drop dead in the bloody street and then you'll be sorry.'

Savage said to her quietly: 'The doctor says you ought to be in hospital.' He turned to Donovan. 'It's essential is it?' He heard Korky croak. She began to cough and shake.

Donovan said: 'If you keep her here you'll have to have a nurse.'

'A nurse,' put in the girl with strange vigour. 'I'll have the nurse.'

'If you think it will be all right,' said Savage to the doctor. 'She could have a nurse.'

Donovan turned and walked back into the main room. He leaned back and closed the door behind Savage. 'No hospital!' called Korky from inside.

'You're not her father, I take it,' said the doctor. He too had walked to the window. It was strange how everyone did. The scruffy pigeon was still there and he regarded it with medical interest. 'Those creatures,' he said. 'They spread half the ailments in London.'

Savage said: 'You're right, I'm not her father. I hardly know her. Last night I found her lying outside the front door. She's been living rough.'

The doctor frowned. His blue chin folded and his eyes converged. 'She's got bronchitis. She's got no resistance by the shape of her. She's in a serious way.'

'If it's that bad then . . .'

'She won't go,' said the doctor putting his hand on Savage's sleeve. 'I've seen these kids, I've had dealings with them. I'm a police doctor. They roam the streets in packs. I've seen a girl like her dead in a rubbish skip.'

Savage felt his face drain. 'I hardly know her,' he repeated in a mumble. 'She followed me home the other night and I gave her a bed . . .' He glanced up. 'Not mine.'

'I would not have imagined so,' responded the doctor in his mild way. 'And so she turned up again.'

'The early hours of this morning. I had to take her in.'

'Of course you did. She'll be all right. But she'll need looking after. She's lucky she knew somewhere to come. You'll have to have a more or less full time, paid for, nurse for a while.'

Savage said: 'That's all right. It's no problem.'

'Good then.' He looked at Savage's clock. 'But I don't know how quickly I can get one. It might not be until this evening.'

'Perhaps Mrs Tomelty can help,' said Savage.

Dr Donovan nodded. He took out a prescription pad and began to write swiftly. 'Get Mrs Tomelty to go and get these things as soon as you can,' he said. 'Don't let the patient get out of bed . . . or try, although I doubt if she's really capable of it. I'll come back this afternoon. I can get all her details then. What did I hear you call her?'

'Korky,' said Savage resolutely. 'She's called Kathleen Wilson but that's her nickname.'

'Korky,' mused Donovan picking up his bag. 'That was a cat in my younger days.'

'Mine too.'

'Was it the *Beano*?'

Savage smiled seriously. 'The *Dandy*,' he said. 'I think.'

Thoughtfully the doctor went out. On the landing he turned and said: 'She'd be better in hospital, you know.'

'She's afraid,' said Savage. 'She has a sort of . . . general fear.'

'Yes, I can see. It's difficult. All right. I'll be back later on. Get the antibiotics down her as soon as you can. And keep her quiet. She should be as still as she can be. I'll get the nurse in as soon as possible. For the next few days she needs somebody here all the time.'

Savage thanked him and slowly closed the door on him. He heard the doctor passing Mrs Tomelty on the stairs. She knocked almost immediately. 'I'll go and get the prescriptions for you,' she offered. 'She's quite bad, isn't she? I'll get anything else she needs. I'll get a couple of nightdresses. Those pyjamas make her look drowned.'

Savage caught her eye. 'She had nothing else,' he said defensively. 'All she had was a few scraps of clothes . . . and the gerbil.'

When the porter's wife had gone he turned reflectively

into the room. He went to the door of the second bedroom and looked in at her. She was awake. 'No hospital,' she breathed.

Savage sat on the edge of the bed. Her fragile hand was lying on top of the sheet. He picked it up and put it below. 'You're not going to hospital,' he assured her. He could smell something. 'There'll be a nurse here some time today.'

It seemed to take all her strength to keep her eyes open. He could hear her chest creaking. Her face was luminous. 'Savage,' she whispered. 'I've wet myself.'

He stared at her then said slowly: 'Oh, don't worry. It will be all right. Mrs Tomelty will be . . .'

'Not Mrs Tomelty . . .'

Even then, he thought, there was a trace of mischief in her paled eyes. 'You do it.'

Savage looked about him as if hoping for help. He got up from the side of the bed, his eyes returning to her face. 'You,' she repeated. 'Please.'

'All right.' She closed her eyes. He lifted the duvet and the sheet. The undersheet and the pyjama legs were wet. Her shins and thighs were like sticks inside the pyjamas. 'I'll get a bowl,' he mumbled.

He almost panicked as he went into the kitchen. His hands moved haplessly. God, how had this happened? Perhaps he should ring Jean Deepe. No. No, he could not do that. She might not understand. When he returned to Korky's bed, carrying the bowl, she seemed to be sleeping. She hardly stirred; her face was damp, her breathing laboured.

Once more he eased back the duvet. He took away his wet pyjama trousers from her spindly legs and, with difficulty, the soaked sheet from below them. 'Just lift up,' he said. He might have been speaking to himself. Gently he lifted her legs and put a towel beneath them. The lower part of her was thin and wasted, the flesh tight under the white skin of her stomach. Timidly he washed her, hardly looking. He wiped the warm flannel across her stomach and between her legs. He levered them up again and washed her bottom. Then he took the towel and dried her, barely touching her as he did so. He still felt helpless. Going into his own bedroom he took another pair of pyjama trousers from the chest and went back with them. She roused and mumbled something. 'It's all right,' he said. He put her feet into the pyjamas and worked them carefully up to her narrow waist.

Korky hardly stirred. When he had finished he stood watching her fevered face. His was full of fear. What if she died? Tentatively he rearranged the duvet over her. The undersheet could wait till later. When the nurse came. When.

He had left the apartment door open and heard Mrs Tomelty come in. She put her head around the bedroom door and saw the bowl and the towel. 'I've got them,' was all she said. 'And I got her some nightdresses. And a toothbrush.'

She looked at the breathing shape in the bed. 'She don't look very well at all, does she,' she said sombrely.

More firmly than he felt Savage said: 'She'll be all right. The doctor is coming back this afternoon. The nurse should be here soon.'

'That'll be a great burden taken from you,' said Mrs Tomelty, her eyes again going to the bowl and towel. Savage picked up the wet pyjamas which were almost under the bed. He rolled them carefully. Mrs Tomelty put out her hand. 'I'll see to those,' she said. 'You won't do them properly.'

Between them they sat the girl up long enough for her

to swallow the first antibiotics. She had trouble keeping her eyes open and when she looked at them it was as though they were strangers. They eased her back on to the pillow and she slept again immediately. Mrs Tomelty went as far as the door and crossed herself. 'I don't like the look of her,' she said. 'Not one bit.'

Dr Donovan returned at three o'clock. He found Savage sitting on a stool beside the girl's bed. 'The nurse is on her way,' he said. He looked at Korky, her eyes closed, her face blank, and took her temperature, then held her wrist for her pulse.

They walked back into the main room together. 'She's got to be watched,' he said almost secretly. 'All the time. If anything worries you then telephone me. It doesn't matter what time. You've taken on a big responsibility.'

Savage said: 'What else could I do? She won't go to hospital, and she's a determined person even if she is ill.'

'But you don't know her well, you say.'

Savage's shoulders sagged. 'As I told you, this is the second time she's turned up here. Previously I'd seen her around the streets. She's got an old pink coat. Her mother disappeared and she ran away because of her stepfather.'

Donovan looked unsurprised. 'Keeping one step ahead. Some stepfathers have a lot to answer for,' he murmured pensively. He waited, then added: 'So do some mothers.' Breathing deeply he shut his bag. 'But that is how it is these days.' He glanced at Savage. 'Have you been married?' It was like asking for a reference.

Savage nodded. 'I still am,' he said. 'We've parted. I was in the army and I was invalided out. After that it never worked.'

'So you live here by yourself?'

'Up until now,' Savage answered wryly. 'I was trying to shut myself away. I thought I'd be . . . well, safe up here.'

'It's difficult to hide,' agreed the doctor as though he had tried it.

They heard the lift ascending and the clank as the doors were opened. The apartment door had remained ajar and through it came a cubic, brusquely striding woman carrying a small suitcase. She looked irritated.

'Nurse Bentley,' said the doctor with satisfaction. 'I'm glad they got you.'

'Out of bed,' responded the woman tartly. 'I was up all night.'

Donovan introduced Savage. Her handshake was as heavy as a man's. She examined the room as though checking the exits. Then she sniffed once and went directly into the second bedroom. The doctor smiled and eyed Savage before following her. Savage remained in the sitting room. He put his hands to his face. He had sat up all night also and now he realised how weary he was.

'Hello . . . Frank?'

'Oh, yes, hello Jean. I was going to call you.'

'But you didn't.'

'No. I'm sorry. I . . . I got back last night and . . . well, I have a problem.'

Her voice immediately became concerned. 'You haven't had another. . . ?'

'Turn?' he completed. 'No. That's all right.'

'What isn't?'

'When I got back there was a young woman . . . a girl really . . . lying outside. She's got bronchitis. The doctor's just gone. There's a nurse here.'

He heard her deep inhalation. It was a moment before she answered. 'You're incredible,' she said eventually.

'Absolutely bloody incredible. How . . . did this happen? You don't know her? She just happened to be lying there?'

Savage replied carefully. 'I *do* know her slightly. Her name is Korky . . . that's what she's called anyway.'

'Korky? And how do you know this Korky?' It was her police voice.

'She spent the night here a few nights ago. She followed me back from the launderette and she slept here. Don't misunderstand. Not with me. In the other room. Then she disappeared and now she's here again, very ill.'

Her voice was disbelieving. 'You didn't mention her last night.'

'I know. But there was nothing in it. I never thought I'd see her again. I didn't think it was worth telling you.'

'No, I don't imagine you did. For someone who is supposed to be a hermit you mix with a lot of people.'

'I've met a few,' he said flatly, adding: 'Including you.' He was sorry he had said it.

'All right. Including me,' she muttered. 'Is this Por-ky . . .'

'Korky.'

'Oh, for Christ's sake, *Korky*. What a bloody silly name anyway. Is she going to hospital?'

'No. She doesn't want to. She's staying here.'

'With you.'

'Yes, with me.'

Nine

It was two weeks before Nurse Bentley decided it was safe to go home at night. She had brought in a camp bed which she called 'My truckle', and she lay on it outside Korky's door, listening even when her eyes were closed. She had a morbid manner; she relished recalling patients she had nursed, the stories often ending sombrely. 'He very nearly lost her,' Savage heard her whisper to Mrs Tomelty on the stairs, the voice echoing up through the lift shaft.

Dr Donovan came in twice a day for the first week and every day after that. Korky said that she could sense when it was him in the lift. 'I love him looking at me with his crossed eyes,' she murmured. 'She's going to come through now,' he said to Savage after the first week.

'You thought she wouldn't?' asked Savage feeling shocked.

'Well . . . she will now. What are you going to do with her?'

Savage blinked at the question. 'I hadn't thought a lot about it,' he confessed. 'I've been more concerned with her getting better. What happens next I don't know.'

'You can't just let her out on the streets again.' The doctor's squint fixed him. 'Her physical condition is really poor for someone of that age. Seventeen.'

'I know. She looks terrible.'

Donovan swung his bag thoughtfully. 'You'll have to think of something. Talk it out with her when she's well. But she can't go back.' He pointed out of the window. 'Not out there, Mr Savage.'

They had been standing on the landing outside the apartment, the door propped open by Savage's back. He turned pensively into the room once Donovan had left. Nurse Bentley had gone home to feed her cat. John, the gerbil, was nowhere to be seen. Knocking first, Savage went into the girl's room.

'Where's John?' she asked. She was sitting up, her face as pale as her pillow. She wore a pink cotton nightdress that Mrs Tomelty had brought in. Her plastic, battery radio was by the bedside, playing distantly.

'I can't see him,' answered Savage. 'I looked.'

'I keep being afraid he might do a runner,' she said. 'It could be he might not like it here. He's not used to heights.' Concern creased her thin face. 'There's no way he could jump from the balcony is there?'

'I don't think so.'

'I'd hate to think of my gerbil splattered over somebody's car.' She smiled narrowly at him. 'I'm nearly better now, aren't I? I'll be up and away soon.'

'Away to where?' he asked. She made room for him to sit on the side of her small bed and he wondered if she had overheard his exchange with the doctor at the door.

'Where I came from I suppose.' She pointed towards the window.

He patted her veined hand. 'Let's not make any plans,' he said inadequately. 'You've got to be fully all right. That's going to take another couple of weeks.'

'What have you been doing? You've still got that old typewriter thing? Did I muck up your work moving in on you, being ill?'

He shook his head. 'It needed mucking up. Some of it is so dull. Islands are only lumps of land surrounded by water, after all. Once you start listing them, putting in figures about them, population and so forth, they all begin to sound very much the same.'

'Have you been to many of them?'

'None,' he admitted. 'That's the funny thing. I just became interested when I was in hospital but now I'm beginning to wonder why I started.'

'It's a dream,' she decided like an expert. She rolled her eyes. 'One of those things you have fantasies about.' Her ringed eyes went around the room. 'Being up here is a bit like being on an island. It's an island over London.' Her lips tightened. 'I'm sorry, Savage, for all this. You've been good to me,' she said. 'Better than a father.'

They regarded each other and both turned off in embarrassment. 'Go and find John,' she suggested quickly. 'He must be somewhere.'

Savage said he would and went into the other room. The apartment was soon searched. 'I can't find him,' he called. 'He's not gone out. I'm almost sure of that.'

Korky appeared at the bedroom door, holding on to the jamb, leaning forward with weakness, her straight nightdress trailing on the floor with one fragile foot projecting. Her arms were like driftwood, her face drained. Savage turned and saw her. 'You can't get up,' he said sharply. 'Not yet, Korky.'

She began to cough, held her chest and said: 'I want to look for John.'

'He's not here. I can't find him.'

The girl's smile became ghostly. 'I bet I know where the bugger's gone,' she said. She staggered forward a step. Quickly Savage stepped to her and caught her. 'You've got to go back to bed,' he pleaded.

'All right, I will,' she said holding on to him. 'Let me just look in one place.' Supported by him she staggered into the room. 'So this is how it is,' she said stopping and looking around. 'I forgot. I could hear you moving in here and I heard you typing but I couldn't quite picture what it was like except I knew you had a balcony.' She gave a snigger. 'I even thought of climbing from the roof on to that, on your balcony, and spying on you through the window.' She looked away from him and then moved further across the carpet. 'I bet he's down in the sofa. Down among the springs and stuff. He did it once before. When I was living with that Jasper.'

Savage helped her to the sofa. She sat down gratefully, her knees projecting like points through the nightdress, leaned towards the back of the cushions and pushed her hand into the crevice. 'John,' she called weakly, hoarsely. 'Are you in there?'

She glanced towards Savage for help. 'If you can get your hands down the back and sort of make the opening a bit bigger, I'll call down to him. He might hear me then.'

Kneeling on the carpet Savage put his hands in the aperture of the sofa and pulled it apart. 'That's it,' she whispered. 'Thanks.' She bent, the angles of her body showing through the nightdress, and called softly: 'John ... John ... are you down there?' There was an immediate scraping movement within the sofa. A spring echoed. Savage was astonished, Korky delighted. 'There,' she said. 'He's got in there. Like I told you.' With difficulty she lowered her face to the crevice. 'John ... John boy.' There came another distinct sound of frenzied clawing. Korky straightened weakly. 'He'll be all right. He's safe, that's the thing.' She began to cough but stopped herself.

'How long is he likely to be in there?' asked Savage calmly.

Korky gave a pleased shrug. 'God knows. When he wants to, he'll come out. Next summer even.'

'He'll come out when he's hungry?'

'He might not. We'll have to push food down to him.'

'But he can't . . .'

'He *might* come out,' she repeated like someone abrogating responsibility. 'But if he doesn't he doesn't. I can keep calling him until I'm blue in the face but there's no way he's obedient. They're hard to train.'

'I think you had better go back to bed,' suggested Savage hollowly. 'Before the nurse comes back.'

Korky nodded and straightened up. 'Carry me back, will you?' she asked. 'Like you did before.'

Savage regarded her uncertainly.

'Don't be cruel. I'm a sick girl,' she said.

He stepped to her and and picked up her feathery body; she smiled into his serious face. 'Misery,' she said putting her arms about his neck. He eased her into the bed and she waited for him to pull the bedclothes around her. With a sigh he did.

Savage went from the room and made the tea. He brought it back to her and watched her drink like a child unspeaking from the cup. Her eyes, outsized in her narrow face, lifted: 'He wouldn't come out when he got into Jasper's sofa.'

'Who was Jasper?'

'You *know*. I told you. He was the one with the band. I stayed with him. When John wouldn't come out he got very uptight about it. One day he got a chopper and chopped the sofa up. Trashed it completely. We were high, mind, and it was a rented place. Then he threatened to chop John up as well. That is when I decided I really wanted out. Apart from the other things.'

Tentatively she returned the cup to him. 'That *was* a *good* cup of tea,' she approved like an old prim lady. 'I've never liked tea all that much before.' She lay against the pillow. 'I feel shagged out, Savage.'

Her eyes closed. Her eyelids were almost transparent. She breathed regularly. He eased her skimpy body down into the bed. With the cup he went to the door, looking back at her once before going out. He took the cup into the kitchen and washed it under the tap. Whatever was he going to do with her?

After almost a month Dr Donovan said she could go outside. 'If it's a half-decent day, no rain, no wind, and you don't venture far,' he warned.

'I won't do a runner,' she said briefly eyeing Savage. 'I want just to see a few things out there. Buildings and shops and cars. It's strange how you get to miss them. I've seen masses of sky.' She nodded towards the window. 'I can't use any more sky.'

'Get a taxi,' suggested the doctor to Savage. 'Have a cruise around. Look at the world. Then come back.'

'Can I have the window down?' she enquired mischievously. 'To wave to people.'

'No,' he reproved. 'It's best that the window stays up.'

As he went the doctor patted her lightly on her flat hair. 'You saved my life,' she responded soberly. Her eyes dipped from one man to the other. 'You both did.'

'Keep it saved,' advised Dr Donovan without emphasis. 'Until you're ninety.' He picked up his bag and went.

'He did,' repeated Korky when the lift had descended. 'Him and you between you.' They were sitting opposite each other in the room. She was wearing a red high-necked sweater and jeans bought by Mrs Tomelty which were too baggy.

Savage had gone out the day before to have his hair cut. 'You do look like a soldier again,' she had said. 'I can see how you were.' Now she regarded him quizzically.

'What's going to happen now?' she asked. The uncertainty was genuine. 'Now I'm better, almost?'

'I don't know.'

'Nor me, either. No idea.'

She rescued him from the silence which followed. 'Let's go out,' she said formally. 'Get the taxi, like he said. Take a cruise around. Will that be all right?'

'Of course.'

'I bet I've cost you a fortune. The nurse for one. All the other things as well.' Her expression was low but he laughed and said: 'Don't let's worry about that.'

'What you *are* worried about is what next. Like I'm worried.'

'We can sort it out later,' he hedged. 'Let's get the taxi.'

'When later?'

'Later.'

He telephoned for the taxi and it was there in ten minutes. Korky was wrapped heavily, her chalky, thin face projecting from layers of clothes. She wore her fake fur which had been washed by Mrs Tomelty. 'Paddington is going to enjoy this too,' she said. 'It's his first time out as well.'

Savage rang for the lift. 'Is this how we got up here?' she asked. 'On that night. Or did you carry me?'

'We came up in the lift,' he said. 'I don't know how but we did.' The lift arrived. 'When I was in bed I used to hear this thing banging up and down,' she said as he closed the gates. 'I used to play a game trying to imagine who was in it. I had a sort of dream that my dad, my real dad was coming up in it. He came into the room. But when I opened my eyes it was you.'

'Only me,' Savage smiled. At the bottom he helped her from the lift. She sniffed the sharp air. 'God, that's how it smells,' she said. She held his arm. 'Yes, it was only you.'

The driver left his seat when he saw how unsteadily the girl emerged from the door of the apartment block. 'Been taken bad, has she?' he asked Savage solicitously.

'I was,' Korky answered. 'But I'm all right now. We're going to have a bit of a tour.'

The driver glanced towards Savage. 'Just drive around for half an hour, will you,' said Savage. 'This is her first time out. Like she says, a tour.'

'What is it you want to see?' asked the driver when he had regained his seat. 'I can show you some traffic jams. There's a lovely one in Earl's Court Road.' He half-turned: 'But I expect you'd like a spin around the park, wouldn't you?'

'Anywhere,' said Korky leaning forward in her bulky, clean pink coat. 'Surprise us.'

The driver appeared to enjoy the challenge and give it some thought. 'Notting Hill,' he decided like an announcement. 'Bayswater Road, Marble Arch, up to Baker Street Station and then through the Park. We could go to the Zoo.'

As they drove they dropped to silence. The driver, looking at them in his mirror, saw the girl staring, almost searching, from the window, and the man was expressionless, looking ahead. Then the driver saw the girl move closer to him and he put his arm around her.

'I've kipped over there,' she said to Savage as they turned into Gloucester Place. 'See that doorway. Paddington and me. There's a sort of bit going back, like a cupboard without a door. I slept in there a couple of nights in the warm weather. It was all right. And he was saying about the Zoo. I had a place near the Zoo as well. Right across from it. The lions woke me up in the night, roaring.'

The driver was enjoying himself. He took them around some Victorian streets almost concealed behind buildings lining the main road. 'Look at them houses,' said Korky caustically. 'Who wants to live in a house like that?'

Savage grinned but the driver's eyebrows went up. They halted at lights. 'Those blue things,' she said directly to the taxi man. 'Like dinner plates on the walls. What are they for?'

'The blue plaques, miss? They put them up on the houses where famous people lived. It gives a little bit of history, telling you what they've done.'

'Just because they're famous?'

Savage saw the driver's frown in his mirror. 'Some people like being famous, miss.' He started off from the lights. 'That one there on the corner. That's a famous actor. I forget who. Sir Somebody Something.'

'What does he act in?'

'Nothing now. He's dead. But that's where he lived.'

Turning her pasty face to Savage, she enquired: 'Would you like one of them?'

'A plaque?' He grinned again. 'It wouldn't matter if I did. I wouldn't get one.'

'You might. You could.' She made a circular sign with her finger. 'Sir Frank Inigo Savage,' she recited. Then, very slowly: 'Who helped poor, sick, homeless, girls.'

The driver choked and Savage felt himself colour. Korky was enlarging on the theme. 'Or me. Me, I could have one. "Here lived Korky the Cat." ' She paused. 'The cat who walked by herself.'

They were back in Upper Regent Street, going towards Oxford Circus. 'All these people,' she sighed. 'I wouldn't want to be crowded up like that. Working in offices and going into shops. I can't stand shops.'

They reached a corner where two youths were squatting. Each had a notice on the front of his box and there was a begging dish in front of them. Korky looked interested. 'Working together,' she said knowledgeably. 'Fair shares afterwards.' Her voice had dropped. Tiredly she turned to Savage. 'I think I've had enough now,' she said. 'I've seen the lot. Please, I want to go back home.'

With the early days of March there came some tentative sunshine. On most afternoons during the first week they went for a walk in Kensington Gardens. She was well by now; there was some warmth in her skin and depth to her eyes, her hair thicker, her hands more calm. She had put on weight. He had given her money to buy clothes. 'I'll pay you back when I'm working,' she said.

Winter was backing out; there was mild sun ruffling the coloured backs of the waterbirds on the big park pond. The trees were becoming broad, brimming with green buds; crocuses were bright and daffodils opening. People walked in a new way.

'Why don't we take up jogging,' suggested Korky. 'We can both jog. Walking's not the same.'

'I did enough jogging in the army,' he answered. 'Quite a lot of it on the spot. I think I'd rather walk.'

'Why did you have to jog on the spot? You don't go anywhere.'

'It was the army way of doing it.'

Korky had gone towards the edge of the pond and was pretending to berate the geese who, accustomed to more sympathetic human sounds, turned their beaks towards her like fingers pointing her out. She returned to Savage. 'Everybody's so nice to them,' she said. 'They don't even know when they're being shouted at.' Their eyes were ahead as they continued to walk separately. 'You'll soon be able to get shot of me,' she asserted.

'It's not a case of getting shot of you,' he said eventually. 'But we'll have to sort it out at some time.'

'I know! I've got it! I could get a job.' She clutched his elbow. 'And I could pay you rent for my room.'

Savage halted and faced her. 'You know that's not going to work, Korky. I moved into that flat so . . .' Her mimicking voice cut him short: '. . . That I could be all on my own. So that I could be quiet.' They continued to walk a yard further apart and both again looking ahead. Slyly she added: 'So that I could have my own little world.'

Again he stopped and this time turned her to him. There was no one near and from a distance they could have been lovers of different sizes about to embrace in the emptiness of the park. 'Yes,' he responded firmly. 'So that I could be alone, be quiet, and have my own little world.' He continued walking; she caught him up.

'Excuse me for putting you out,' she sniffed sulkily. 'Excuse me for being ill and nearly dying on your doorstep.'

'Don't mention it,' he replied evenly. 'It was no trouble.' He was learning to deal with her. 'But now you're recovered, we've got to sort things out.' He looked at her unconvincingly. 'Korky, I want to get back to my work.'

'You *are* working. You've been working all the time. Writing down all those dull island things.'

'They're not dull,' he said defensively.

'They're bloody dull,' she reaffirmed. 'Why don't you

make them a bit interesting?' She drew an outline in the afternoon air with her finger. 'This is the island of Plonky-Poo,' she announced in a tight squawk. 'The natives here fuck each other every three weeks. The rest of the time they're fucking . . .'

He caught her arm firmly. 'Pack it in,' he said.

She gave him a hard look. 'All right. I'll move out as soon as I can find my gerbil.'

'You *know* where he is. He's in the guts of the sofa.'

Disarmingly she giggled. 'We'll put a trap down for him. When he comes out for his food at night. Bang! We'll grab him. I'll stick him in a bag and off we'll go.'

'Right. Fine.'

Walking at his side she moved her nose slowly towards him. 'Don't you want to know what I plan to do?'

'All right. What are your plans?'

'I'm going to get a place and go on the game,' she announced flatly.

He did not believe her for a moment. He drew a deep, ill-tempered, breath. 'Very nice. What makes you think you'll make a living doing that?'

'Thanks very much. Thanks for the vote of confidence.' She moved away from him and pantomimed a seductive walk along the grey pond's edge. 'Oooh, look at me,' she cooed brazenly. 'A hundred quid for a short time. Yes sir, come on up to my flat for a quickie. We'll have some dirty fun.' She performed a blatant pirouette and shouted towards a puzzled mallard: 'Hello duck, want a fuck?'

The duck glanced her way as if considering the offer but then floated on. 'That duck wouldn't know a fuck if it was free,' she said determined to aggravate him. 'A quickie for a quacky.' She watched the effect. Savage's face had gone dark. 'Don't . . .' he managed to say. 'Don't you . . .' He raised an abrupt hand. 'Don't . . .'

'Don't you hit me,' the girl concluded for him. 'Hit me and I'll tell Mr Kostelanetz.'

'All right then. How do you know Mr Kostelanetz?' he asked an hour later when they were back in the apartment.

Airily she wagged her head. 'Oh, I've seen him around, before you ever found me, Savage. And a couple of days ago he came up here.'

Savage was astonished. 'You didn't tell me,' he said.

'I *am* telling you. He came up when you were at the library. Just to see that his pad was all right, I suppose. He didn't get heavy or anything, but he was interested in me. He said he was and I could see. He just said that if I wanted a job . . . a *position*, he called it . . .'

'A position, more like it.'

'Don't be shitty, Savage. He was only being friendly. He said he would like to help me.'

Savage sat down. 'All right, take up his offer,' he said fractiously. 'Go for this *position*.'

'I didn't say I *would*,' she pointed out. 'You're only saying that because it suits you, because it lets you off the hook. When I go I'll make my own arrangements, thank you. Mr Kostelanetz is only one of my options.'

'Tell me the others.'

Korky pouted, hardly expanding her cheeks. 'Mind your own business,' she said. 'As long as I'm not bothering you, disturbing you in your little ivy tower . . .'

'Ivory tower,' he said.

'That's it, go on, put me right. Tell me I'm just a nerd come in from the cold. I know that already.' Her face suddenly collapsed and she began to weep copiously. 'Oh, Savage,' she said stumbling dramatically towards him, dropping on to her knees and putting her head on his lap. Her now shining hair fell over his trousers. 'Oh, don't send me away.'

He was getting to know her by now. Gently he lifted her head, the hair now growing touches of dark auburn falling over his hands. 'Korky,' he said just as gently. 'We can't live together like this. It's not going to work.'

'Because *you* don't want it to work.' The wet cheeks, upturned to him, reflected the light of the reading lamp beside the sofa.

'It's not going to work,' he repeated flatly. 'There are reasons.'

'You want to be on your own.'

'That's one of them. That's why I came here.'

Her expression became more interested. 'You're afraid you'll have one of your mad turns,' she surmised. 'You're afraid you'll attack me. Jump up and down on me.'

'It could happen,' he said seriously.

'You haven't gone mad since I've been here.'

'Perhaps I've had too much to think about,' he said.

'There! That shows I'm good for you.'

'Korky, you're not staying.'

Her features creased to sullenness. From within the sofa came the mutterings of the gerbil. It often protested if anyone continued to sit above it. 'All right,' she said with finality. 'I'll go.'

'I will help you to find somewhere to live,' he promised firmly. 'I'm not just throwing you out like that.'

'I might turn up on your doorstep again. Dying.'

He studied her patiently. 'I will make sure that you have somewhere to live,' he repeated. 'And a job.'

'The same as Mr Kostelanetz?' she shrugged mischievously. She saw his reaction and went on hurriedly. 'I'll go, don't worry. I'll make arrangements...'

'I don't think you should take Mr Kostelanetz too seriously.'

'Well, I'm just saying what he told me. I could have a good place. Like Miss Bombazine.'

'Korky, you're talking crap. And you know it.'

She wriggled her body. 'Don't you think men would like me?'

'No,' he said with desperation. 'You're not the type.'

'How would you know?' she enquired hotly. 'Miss Bombazine's got a bum like a horse. I've seen it.'

'How? Oh, I know. She left her curtains open.'

'And I've been in that room for a month. It was all I had to look at. Her bum and the sky.' Her eyes lit. 'Savage, I've seen her operating. *At* it. The back view is unbelievable.'

Savage struggled. 'Men like big women like her,' he tried.

'So I'm too skinny. Listen, mate, men are not all the same. I could dress up as a schoolgirl.'

'Shut up!' he shouted at her. 'Don't talk like a scrubber!'

'But you won't have me staying here.'

'No. It's not good for either of us. You don't have to move right away. First we must get you a job.'

'There's lots of *them* around,' she said caustically.

'There are in London.'

'I could go home to my stepfather,' she said, again with a little taunt. 'Good old Merlin. He'll have me back.'

'Korky, shut up.' He studied her sweater and jeans. 'You'll need some more clothes.'

'You'll buy me some and I'll pay you back when I'm

earning,' she forecast without enthusiasm. 'All right. Thanks. I'll have to look decent.'

She sighed and rose from her kneeling position. 'You'll miss me,' she forecast like a threat.

'I know. But we can't duck this now. We'll end up fighting.'

'All right,' she sighed with a further onset of finality. 'I'll take my gerbil and go.'

As if it recognised the mention the animal began to squeak more insistently from the echoing interior of the sofa. 'There,' said Korky. 'He heard.' Her expression suddenly froze. 'Oh, Savage, get up! Get up! You're sitting right on him. You're squashing him!'

She tugged him from his sitting position. The gerbil appeared in a hurry, thrusting its nose from the crevice between the seat and the back of the sofa. It flailed its feet in panic. In pulling Savage upright the girl had brought him against her. They were touching. Their arms went about each other. They were laughing, almost weeping. John the gerbil, free from his hideaway, ran across the sofa down to the floor and swerved between their legs. Laughing, they held their faces together. Korky's cheeks were wet again. They drew back and regarded each other silent and still. She studied his expression and then her shoulders slumped. 'I'm still going, am I?' she said.

'Yes, Korky, you have to go. It's not right. We're different.'

'We're the same,' she argued. 'I think we are.'

'It's not just the matter of our ages.' He hesitated. 'It's all sorts of things. We shouldn't live under the same roof. It's too difficult. We can't go on like this.'

Ten

She went, as she had done before, early in the morning while he was asleep. Her bed was neatly made and the contents of the refrigerator were missing. He picked up the note on the bedside table. She had taken her last two bottles of medicine with her as well. 'Dear Savage,' he read aloud as though he were not alone. 'All right. I've gone. As you can see. Don't worry I won't end up dressed in a gymslip. Thanks for saving my life. Love, Korky.'

He muttered: 'Shit,' and sat down on her bed. From there he had the view across to Miss Bombazine's apartment. He studied it more carefully than usual. Surely Korky wasn't over there. Like an answer the curtains were energetically flung back and the window opened. Miss Bombazine, in a black nightdress, stood breathing in the March morning air as though in relief, her majestic bust projecting over the sill. Savage stood up and took the step towards his own window. She saw him immediately and waved cheerily like a housewife. He half-lifted his hand to return the wave but instead opened his own window.

'Good morning,' he called across the divide. He had never spoken to her before, only passing within nodding distance outside the block or in the corridor. Once he had seen her puffing up Kensington Church Street with three bags from British Home Stores.

'Hello there!' she called in an assumed voice, accentuating the aspirate. She dropped the tone at once. Perhaps she used it professionally. 'I'm doing some spring cleaning,' she cooed. 'It gets a bit dirty in here.'

He prevented himself saying that he imagined it did and instead asked, trying to sound casual: 'You haven't seen Kathleen, have you? Kathleen Wilson. She's been staying here.'

'That Korky, you mean?' responded Miss Bombazine unhesitatingly. 'No, I haven't. Has she done a runner? Silly girl.' Savage took time to absorb the familiarity in the reference. 'Well, she's . . . gone,' he answered.

'Listen,' Miss Bombazine confided, her bulging, black, silken-held breast thrusting from the window as she clung on to the handle. 'It's no use us talking like this. Why don't you come over? It's only down the passage. I'll make us a cup of coffee.'

Without waiting for an answer she closed the window and retreated. Savage hesitated. Another rampart of his privacy was about to tumble. He swore silently. Inside his own door he again paused but then opened it, closed it behind him, and went with a furtive step past the lift and on down the carpeted corridor where Mr Tomelty was mysteriously cleaning a fire extinguisher fixed to the wall.

'Ah now, sir,' he said with a hint of triumph. 'You've missed the lift. Taken the wrong turning.'

Savage decided against subterfuge. 'I'm going to see Miss Bombazine,' he told the caretaker doggedly.

'Number six-o-one, sir,' provided Tomelty. He looked at his watch as though thinking the visit was on the early side. 'As you probably know.'

'I don't actually,' denied Savage primly. 'I'm going to have a cup of coffee.'

'And why not?' said Tomelty lifting his duster. 'A civilised occupation.'

'Kathleen has gone,' he told the porter. 'Korky. I thought this lady might have some idea where she went.'

'Gone? Korky?' said Tomelty genuinely surprised. 'Now there's a thing. You'd have thought she would have been comfortable there.'

'Well, she had to go some time,' said Savage awkwardly.

'But now you're looking worried for her.'

'I didn't expect her to just vanish. I thought she'd get a job and then find a place to live.'

'Ah, I see now why you're heading for six-o-one,' nodded the Irishman. 'Well, that makes sense. For some sin is a safe refuge.'

Savage scrutinised him in a hurt fashion. This was lost on the porter who recommenced polishing. 'I just thought Miss Bombazine might know,' Savage said over his shoulder as he continued down the corridor. Tomelty began to hum as he polished but Savage heard the tune halt as he went around the corner and rang the bell.

Miss Bombazine came to the door. She now wore an airy pink negligee over her black nightdress. The folds and flutes ran down her body. She was a tall, large, apparently handsome woman with a massive smile of welcome. To Savage, seeing her at close quarters offered a quick relief. Korky could never be like that. 'Please do come in,' breathed Miss Bombazine. 'I have the coffee bubbling.' Tentatively Savage stepped through the doorway into a room of uncertain taste.

'It's nice and warm in here,' he said fumbling for something to say and prodding the thickness of the carpet with his feet.

'Some of them only come in from the cold,' said Miss

Bombazine frankly. 'I try to keep it comfortable. They want a good home more than a good . . . intercourse.'

Fussily she sat him on a damask sofa with oriental antimacassars protecting the back. She saw he had noticed. 'Some men still wear hair oil,' she revealed. 'The older ones.' She went toward the coffee percolator and returned with two cups, a milk jug and a sugar bowl on a tray covered with a doily. 'This is cosy,' she enthused genuinely. 'Very neighbourly.'

She treated him to a swift, professional survey. 'Didn't you have long hair once? Was it you? I've only seen you in the distance.'

Savage said simply: 'I had it cut.'

'I should have mine cut,' she mused. 'It would be more comfortable. But they like it long, most of them.'

He could see now how worn her face was, the pouches below the eyes, the folds at the edges of the lips. 'What is your proper name?' he asked.

'Geraldine,' she responded as if glad he had asked. 'I've had some funny surnames including Madbladder, because I've been married a few times. Miss Bombazine is just a professional name, you understand.'

Savage said he did and she added: 'It's because I always wear black. I even had a black bed at one time but it depressed me.'

'You know everybody in the block?' he asked.

'Almost. I've been here six years and you get to know them all in time, more or less. Even the people who are out all day at business. They're all very neighbourly, although some of them are a bit doolally. And I'm very discreet, or I try to be, although I do sometimes forget to draw the curtains, as you might have noticed. And I'm quite particular. I work from a couple of clubs in the West End and I advertise privately, and I tell everybody in the flats I'm a chanteuse, although nobody actually believes it. I can't squawk let alone sing, not now, since I had my throat done.' Her expression altered. 'Why have you got a gun under your bed?' she enquired.

Savage choked and spilled his coffee. Like a mother she leaned across and dutifully mopped him with a lace handkerchief. 'How do you know I have?' he said.

Miss Bombazine laughed. 'That Korky, she told me.'

'It's only an old one,' he admitted lamely. 'It's only a sort of souvenir. It doesn't work and there's no ammunition. I was in the army once.'

'So I heard.' She appraised him again. 'What rank? My father was a soldier.'

'I got to the dizzy height of Staff Sergeant,' he said.

'I can't remember my old man's rank. But he did something brave. He got a medal. He's dead now. I wouldn't do this if he wasn't.' She was silent, almost embarrassed for a moment. 'Not that I blame you, having a gun,' she said. 'I've got a big tin of pepper under my bed although up to now I haven't had to throw it in anybody's gob. But you never know.'

'I can't get over Korky telling you that,' he muttered shaking his head.

Miss Bombazine shrugged. 'Well, she found it when she was poking about I expect, having a look. Kids like that always search around, see what's what. When you live on the edge, like I do for that matter, you always have a little nose into anything you can. It's a sort of defence, being prepared.'

He sighed. 'Do you have any idea where she might be?'

Miss Bombazine pursed her big, crimson lips. 'Any number of places,' she said. 'But *you* told her she had to leave, didn't you. What are you worried about? She told me you wanted her out.'

'But not like that. Not immediately. I thought she would get a job and then somewhere to live.'

'To make you feel better,' she said bluntly.

Savage drank his coffee to screen his discomfiture. He put the cup back on the saucer. 'I came here to these flats to get some privacy,' he said. 'I've got my problems too. I don't want anybody living with me.'

'God knows where she's gone,' sighed Miss Bombazine. She regarded him shrewdly. 'She won't go on the game if that's what's worrying you, I can tell you that. She asked me about it but she's not the type. Too strong, too self-willed. She'd spit in a man's eye. Doing this you've got to put all your own feelings under the bed. It pays well and once you've learned to pace yourself the work isn't hard, but it don't do a lot for your self-respect. Korky would argue. And that's no good.'

He had finished his coffee and he stood up and then solemnly shook hands. Hers were big and soft. As he reached the door he asked: 'What about Mr Kostelanetz?'

'What about him?' she shrugged. 'That old wanker, pretends to be this, pretends he's done that. According to him he could have married the Queen Mother, he's got the Victoria Cross and he swam the Channel. He's brimming with shit. He's got his fingers in a few pies but I reckon he's harmless. All talk.'

He thanked her for her information. 'What are you going to do now?' she asked as he left and went down the corridor.

'I'll have to go and look for her,' he called back. 'I can't leave her on the streets.'

He spent the morning touring West London in a taxi. He instructed the driver to go slowly and he searched the pavements and the doorways. The man was keen to take part. 'Who is it you're looking for?' he asked soon after they set out. He claimed to have been a sailor and to have acute eyes.

'A girl. She's thin with long darkish hair. She'll be wearing one of those fun-fur coats. Pink.'

'What's her name?' asked the man as if it were an important recognition factor. 'Korky,' Savage told him with a hint of embarrassment. 'Kathleen actually.' His driver's eyes searched the mobile streets on one side as Savage scanned them on the other. They saw no sign of her and the bill came to forty-five pounds with the tip. 'Hope you find her,' said the driver.

In the middle of the day he went into a pub, something which even a few weeks earlier he would have avoided. It was only two corners away from Kensington Heights, the Balmoral Castle, and sitting in a corner, with the three dull men he recognised as the trio he had ejected from the apartment at gunpoint, was Mr Kostelanetz. The smile was broad and thick as the overcoat. 'Mr Savage,' he said. 'Frank, come and sit down. These gentlemen will buy you a drink on their way out.'

The three men looked disconcerted at the news that they were leaving but rose with ponderous obedience. The one who had carried the cricket bat asked Savage solicitously what he would have. He asked for a whisky. 'Make this whisky a double for Mr Savage,' purred Mr Kostelanetz as the man shuffled towards the bar. Savage made to protest but the smooth overcoated arm came across like a barrier to deter him. 'Have a double, Frank,' said Mr Kostelanetz quietly. 'He owes you.'

While the others loitered uncomfortably near the door

the man, half-looking over his shoulder as though he hoped for a change of mind, went to the bar. He did not have enough money, he protested, for a double. One of the others came forward with the offer of a loan. The whisky was borne almost ceremoniously back by all three men before they backed away and went outside. 'Good chappies,' murmured Mr Kostelanetz. 'But short of brains, and courage. And almost everything.'

Savage took one sip of the Scotch. 'Has your young lady gone?' enquired Mr Kostelanetz looking deeply into his own whisky as though he might find her there.

'You know?'

The grey man heaved his shoulders as if there were many things he knew but for which he could not be responsible. 'I knew she was going,' he said. 'She told me that you had said she would have to. I offered to help her in any way I could. I am a helpful man, Frank.'

'She told me.'

The overcoat sighed. 'But she is a free spirit. And now she has gone, that little Kathleen.'

'Korky,' mentioned Savage. 'She's called Korky.'

'Ah, I don't understand you English and your nicknames. You give some person a name and then you change it. What sense is there in that? To me she was Kathleen. And now she has gone.'

'I'm trying to find her. I've been everywhere.'

Mr Kostelanetz raised his solemn eyebrows. 'But you wanted her to leave, to be off.'

'Yes, all right. I didn't intend her to just *go* like that. Walk out. I wanted to help her get sorted out first...'

'A nice job, a nice home,' intoned Mr Kostelanetz as though reciting some poem from his homeland.

'Yes,' said Savage regarding him firmly. 'That was more or less the idea.'

'And now she's out there in the cold.'

'Yes,' he responded like an admission of guilt but then adding: 'It's not all that cold.'

'At night,' nodded the big man. 'It *is* cold. If you're outside it is cold.' He continued the sigh. 'I like this girl,' he said. 'She's got, you know, balls. Character. She'll be around somewhere. She won't have gone away very far.' He glanced furtively around the bar as if fearing he might be overheard. 'I'll have my people search for her,' he whispered. 'Everywhere.'

Savage returned to the apartment and opened a tin of soup. He half-warmed it and ate it. Then he went out again to look for her, this time on foot. He went through Holland Park and Kensington Gardens. He asked nomadic groups of young people. Nobody had seen her although some knew her. His legs ached; he had not realised he was so out of condition.

At the dark end of the afternoon he gave up and went back to Kensington Heights. He made himself some tea and stood at the window, peering out dismally on the moving dusk as though in hope he might spot her from that height. As he was returning to the kitchen with the cup the telephone caught his eye; he waited, regarding it as if he had never noticed it before. He put the cup in the kitchen and returning to the phone picked it up. His fingers went to the buttons. He began to tap out Jean Deepe's number. His hesitation offered him time to think again and he put the receiver down, slowly, in three stages. What could he have said to her after all this time?

Still looking at the phone as if daring it to ring, he sat down again. It did not. He wandered around the room, lost in his own home.

He decided to have a final search. Pulling on his long

overcoat, he went out again, down the stairs and out into the drab evening. Drizzle smeared the streets; in Kensington Church Street the shop lights reflected sadly silver on the pavement, the traffic sizzled cheerlessly. He walked around the streets, along the ranks of parked cars, into a mews, around the railings of the park, and down into a church crypt where fifty homeless people watched him walk in and quietly moved their meagre personal belongings closer to them on the benches. Someone was achingly playing a flute and someone else was shouting at them to shut up. There was little light down there and the limited illumination incised the shadows on faces; eyes moved towards him. There were old people at one end of the crypt and young people at the other, a recognisable frontier between them. There was no one he could see of middle age; perhaps the old ones were really middle-aged. When he surveyed the expressions again, trying to pick someone he could ask, he saw that even the young looked old. Old, defeated, fierce.

No one had seen her. 'Don't know what you're rabbiting on about,' said one youth truculently. 'Coming down 'ere asking questions.'

'Makin' inquiries,' objected another. He took in Savage's shape and the haircut. 'Are you the fuzz?'

Savage said: 'No, I'm not.'

A blanket in a corner moved and hollow eyes appeared. 'Interferin',' complained the ghostly voice. 'Piss off.'

Savage retreated towards the door. Sitting on a bench reading the *Evening Standard* was a fat youth with a ring through his nose. 'Who was it?' he asked.

'I'm looking for a girl called Korky,' asked Savage carefully. 'Have you seen her?'

'Don't know her,' said the plump boy peering back to the newspaper as though she might be mentioned there.

'I do. I know that Korky.'

It was a girl wearing two coats and a woollen hat with a bobble that dangled to her mouth. She blew it aside. 'Skinny bit. She was down around World's End today.'

Savage stared as if he did not believe her. 'World's End . . .' he began stupidly.

The girl grinned like a spectre. ' 'Course not the *real* World's End.' She laughed harshly. 'This is the *real* one down here, mate. World's End in Chelsea I mean.'

'Right. Yes. Of course. Thank you very much.' He became cautious in case she changed her mind. 'Where-abouts was she?'

'Just World's End,' repeated the girl. Her face was puffy, her eyes uncaring. She followed him to the door. 'That info's got to be worth something,' she said putting her hand out.

He gave her ten pounds. She gasped and thrust the note swiftly into her top overcoat pocket. Looking cagily behind her she followed him out from the crypt. 'Got any more?' she demanded. He gave her another five pounds. She snatched the money and treated him to a sharp stab of defiance before turning and running off into the Kensington night. He saw her in the distance dodging among people on the pavement and wondered where she was running with the money.

Savage hailed a taxi and told the driver to go to World's End. He scanned the pavements as they travelled on towards Stamford Bridge. It was a windy night and people bent their heads as though each had a secret or a sorrow. 'Chelsea are playing tonight,' mentioned the driver over his shoulder. 'They'll be just about finishing now. It's going to be murder along there.'

It was. The football watchers disgorging from the floodlit stadium trooped along the King's Road. Chelsea had lost. 'Piss off,' snarled one as he tried to get out of the taxi. 'What d'you think you're fucking on?' demanded another. The taxi driver shouted to Savage. 'Sure you want to get out 'ere, mate?'

'I'll risk it,' Savage called back.

'Animals, this lot,' called the driver. 'I'm a Millwall man myself.'

Savage got out of the cab and eased his way through the crowd. The men were trudging like a defeated army, those going into the wind with their faces scowling down at the pavement. There were other vehement groups, hostile, arguing, cursing among themselves and with anyone else they could. Suddenly he found himself pushed and pinned against a shop front by four youths. 'You're bloody Newcastle, you are,' accused one.

Savage, feeling the glass pane at his back, shook his head. 'Chelsea,' he managed to say.

'All right, then,' challenged another, hooded below an anorak like an ugly monk. 'Who's the reserve keeper for Chelsea?'

'Yeah, that's right,' growled one of the others glancing admiringly at the interrogator and adding his hand to the clutch holding Savage against the window. ' 'E was on the bleeding bench tonight.'

'Look,' Savage said, his voice rising. 'I haven't been to the match. I'm looking for a girl.'

All four appeared astonished once they had collectively grasped the information. 'Looking for what?' demanded the quickest one.

'A young kid,' he said stoutly. 'She's lost.'

The information seemed to knock the aggression from them. One after the other they took their hands away, releasing him from the plate glass. 'If we see 'er we'll let you know, mate,' said one utterly mollified.

'Yeah, we'll do that,' promised the cowled face.

They turned from him, continued the way they had been trudging and within yards had joined with another group of lamenting Chelsea supporters. 'It's this fucking wind what done it!' wailed one. They put comradely arms about each other, sad and vanquished, and stumbled into the dim disconsolate throng.

Seeking an escape Savage swiftly turned down a side street away from the indignant human river. There were terraced houses down there, one door was ajar with half a face projecting like a reluctant moon. 'Want to come in?' enquired a rough but motherly voice. 'Keep you out of the way for a bit. Only two quid.'

He was about to decline but immediately saw another rowdy gang wheeling into the street. 'Yes, all right,' he said. Eagerly she admitted him and he found himself in a smelly passage with a dozen other anxious men. The woman shut the door with finality and her tiny eyes surveyed the line. 'Two quid,' she repeated to Savage. He produced the coins and she took them with a hand like a crab. She was only slight but she had no difficulty in bustling in ragged slippers along the crowded passage. Savage realised there were more men in the adjoining room.

'What's this?' he asked the man standing next to him.

'Ma Pelling's,' grunted the man as though he was surprised Savage did not know. He listened to the sounds outside and alarm grew on his face. The rowdy gang were moving along the street in the wind, crying their wild slogans. Another mob could be heard approaching. When the first party had moved along the street and the second were still in the distance, the man standing opposite him in the passage, an Asian, whispered: 'It is called a safe house.'

As the second hooligan group strode nearer, silence dropped over the cowering men around him. 'Shush,' warned Savage's Asian neighbour urgently. 'No talking please.'

Eventually they heard the clamouring threat move away. The relief was tangible. Ma Pelling shuffled to the front door and opened it gingerly. 'Nearly all clear,' she croaked.

For a further ten minutes the men waited, hardly shifting, in their dim sanctuary. Eventually Ma Pelling made another chary inspection and, having done so, dragged the door open. 'All clear,' she announced. The men began to sidle into the street, not without first looking each way as they reached the door; some went on tiptoe. They shifted past Savage and he realised that there must have been twenty hiding in the house, two with young boys and one, mysteriously, with a dog.

Savage lingered. 'It's like the air raids,' Ma Pelling reminisced. 'Waiting for the Germans to go over.' She grinned gummily. 'Mind you, it's a good earner.'

'Do you know any of the young people who hang around here?' asked Savage still in the corridor. The final man apart from himself, a large, apprehensive-eyed Black man, was scrutinising the street. He crept out heavily.

Ma Pelling sniffed at the enquiry. 'I see them,' she said. 'They come and pee in my entry. Them and their drugs. At least in the war you knew where you was.' She could see he really wanted to know. 'Somebody gone missing?' she asked shrewdly.

'Yes.'

'Boy or girl?'

'Girl.'

Further creases joined her face. 'Girls is trouble,' she acknowledged pursing her lips. The statement appeared to prompt her to deeper thought. 'There's a gang 'angs about at the back of the supermarket,' she said eventually. 'Where it's warm from the pipes and they can eat any stuff what's chucked out.'

'Where's that, the supermarket?' said Savage.

'Safeways. Right up this street, turn left and it's ten minutes along on the other side. There's a yard at the back.'

He thanked her for the shelter. 'Come back any time,' she invited genially. She added a harsh laugh. 'I ought to call *this* place Safeways, didn't I? When Chelsea're at home, I always do it then. A quid a time. Two if they lose.'

Following the pattern of his predecessors he glanced each way before going up the street towards the main road. At the junction the wind seemed to be blowing in three directions at once. The lights remained emptily flooding over the football ground. The crowd had cleared except for stragglers but the World's End was crowded and so were the other pubs along the King's Road, their windows thick with silhouettes.

He followed Ma Pelling's directions and at the shuttered supermarket turned down a service road into the yard behind. There were two unattended trucks and, standing apart, a jacked-up trailer, almost against the back wall of the supermarket, near an outlet issuing steam. Below the trailer was a huddle of bodies. He could see other lying forms in boxes along the wall next to the steam pipe.

With caution he approached the trailer and slowly bent to look under it. The huddle remained unmoving, except for deep collective breathing. He stooped further.

A face, long and pale and disturbed, peered out at him. 'Oh, fuck,' murmured the boy. 'Not the fucking fuzz again.'

There was a stirring and a grumbling from the pile of bodies. 'They been 'ere once,' complained another voice.

Savage asked distinctly: 'Anyone seen a girl called Korky?'

'Piss off,' came an echo from a box marked Daz.

'Korky Wilson, Kathleen Wilson,' Savage insisted. 'I'll pay.'

A white hand was projected from below the truck followed by a riven face. 'I see'd her.' Until she spoke he could not tell the sex of the figure. He leaned eagerly towards her. 'Where was that?'

'Around today. Up till the match started.'

The hand poked towards him insistently like a hungry fledgling's head from a nest. He pushed five pounds towards it. The note was grasped voraciously. Nobody else shifted, only breathing moved them. 'Then what?' he asked gently.

'There was some bloke what 'ad no ticket. He'd lost it or something. She went off with him to 'ave a drink.'

Each pub he entered was blocked to the door; there were men still pathetically brimming with venom, cursing the goalkeeper, the referee and the wind. Once he had got in he had to push his way into the crowd. There were few protests; far worse things had happened that night. A frightened man was pinned over a pool table by two others. 'It's only a game,' he was pleading. 'It's only a bloody game.'

He went into six bars desperate in his search; he listened for her voice in the drone of the drinkers. He could not hear her. Once he tried asking a feckless-faced bartender if he had seen a long-haired young girl. 'Wish I 'ad,' grunted the youth moodily tugging the beer handle. 'I'd 'ave 'ad 'er out the back.'

Savage made a comment between his teeth and went again into the blustering night. The pubs were beginning to empty. Shoulders hunched, he trudged along the King's Road. Where was she? What was she doing?

He had walked a mile when, at last, a cruising taxi stopped at his wave. He asked to be taken to Kensington Heights but then changed his mind. 'West London Police Station,' he said. The wind banged around the cab. The streets were emptying, some already deserted, left to the weather and the night.

A beleaguered gleam came from the police station. He settled the taxi fare and walked up the steps. A Black woman was mesmerised by a book in the waiting room; there was a youth curled up like a snail on one of the benches. Savage went to the desk. The sergeant shouted to the youth: 'Hey, lad. I told you if you want to wait for him you've got to keep awake.' The boy uncurled. 'It's not a ruddy doss house,' the sergeant said to Savage.

Savage had some vague notion of reporting a missing person. The sergeant saw his hesitation and asked what he wanted. Savage made up his mind: 'I don't suppose Miss Deepe is on duty, is she?'

'PC Deepe,' said the sergeant correctly. 'She was here. She probably still is. She's off at midnight.'

As though she had heard her name Jean appeared from a door behind him. She looked tired. 'Well,' she breathed. 'Look what the night's blown in.'

'Oh, hello,' Savage said uncomfortably. Her uniform looked creased.

'I wondered if I could have a word.'

'Have a word if you like,' she said off-handedly. The

sergeant came from behind the desk and going over to the youth, again curled up, picked him up by one arm and led him to the door. 'Have a kip out there,' he said. The Black woman put down her book to watch but reopened the page and continued to read. 'Harry,' Jean called to the sergeant who had gone through the door behind her. 'I'll go in the interview room.'

She said nothing to Savage but he followed her. Turning on a light switch in a side annexe she walked in ahead of him. She straightened a sagging plant which immediately sagged again. There was a table and three chairs. She sat on the edge of the table, her legs tucked one behind the other. 'Sit down,' she invited flatly. 'What was it?'

Savage sat on the wooden chair. 'I've been looking for Korky,' he said.

Jean's slim eyebrows rose. 'Oh dear, oh dear, oh shit,' she said. 'Poor little Korky's gone missing. There's a surprise.'

'I've come to report a missing person,' he said, his tone and his eyes hardening. 'If that's all right with you.'

'Of course it is, that's the only reason we're here. To find kids who will only sod off again the next day. It's all part of the thrill of this job.'

'Can I report her missing?'

'All right,' she said with barely contained scorn. 'One minute.'

She left him in the room, sitting in the grim light, miserable, angry. She returned quickly holding a form and a pen and sat behind the table not looking towards him but staring at the form as though she had never seen anything like it. 'Name?' she muttered.

'Mine or hers?'

'Both. Yours first.'

'Frank Inigo Savage,' he said.

'Address.'

He recited the address. She wrote it deliberately.

'Name of Person Reported Missing.'

'Kathleen Wilson.'

'Of?'

'Same address.'

'Age?'

'Seventeen.'

'Vulnerable,' she said flatly. She turned her eyes up to him. He could see she was holding back tears. 'I don't know how you could have done that,' she said controlling herself. 'You come around to my flat, we have dinner and I let you screw me . . .'

'Jean,' he pointed out. 'We screwed each other.'

'But, for Christ's sake, I'm a human woman. Underneath this fancy dress, I hurt like anybody else.'

'There's *nothing* between Korky and myself,' he informed her firmly. 'Nor has there ever been.'

'So why did you never call?'

'When I got back that night, just as I told you, she was lying on the doorstep. She was very ill. Bronchial pneumonia. She's taken more than a month to get over it. What was I supposed to do, kick her out? She could have died. I couldn't think òf anything else.'

'And there's nothing between you?'

'Nothing. God almighty, she's a kid. Not a very stable one either.'

'You make a good pair.'

He tightened his mouth. 'Perhaps we do,' he said.

His shoulders pulled together against the darkness and the rain sweeping the streets, he trudged up towards the pattern of lit windows at Kensington Heights. It was a gradual slope but tonight it seemed a long way. Savage was angry with himself, with Korky, and with Jean Deepe. What the hell was he doing stumbling around looking for some wandering girl at midnight? He growled the question aloud. The coat-and-plastic-draped tramp who slept on the bench outside the library grunted.

He let himself into the lower lobby. The lift was standing there open-mouthed, so, uncaring about the noise, he took it up. On the top landing Miss Bombazine was supporting a discoloured young man against the wallpaper. His head and his hair lolled. 'He's been sick,' she complained but mildly. Savage stood aside as she manoeuvred her client into the lift. 'The excitement proved too much for him,' she muttered as she closed the grille.

Savage watched the conveyance disappear and went towards his own door. It seemed a long time since he had been away. The wind was shrieking somewhere in the culverts of the building, whirling around the top of the lift shaft, howling in hidden holes. She would get bronchitis again.

He went into the flat and without taking off his overcoat turned in the direction of the bathroom, unzipping his fly as he did so. Sharply he opened the door. Sitting in the bath, foaming with soap suds, was Korky. She was very drunk and a half-empty whisky bottle was standing on the floor. 'I couldn't get a job,' she bleated. 'So I came home.'

'Jesus,' he breathed. Then: 'How did you get in?'

'I've got a key. I had one made.'

He attempted to sort out his reactions; gladness at seeing her, annoyance that she had run away, anger that she was smashed. Her fake fur was in the bath with her, pink and grotesquely half-floating like a drowned animal.

The girl gave him no opportunity to add anything. Like a soapy, swaying mermaid she rose from the bath, the suds running down her pallid skin, her nipples like small red spots, her pupils rolling. She staggered as she made to step out of the bath, and involuntarily he moved to catch her. She clasped him and hung nakedly on to him, soaping his overcoat and the front of his sweater, and dangling against him as he endeavoured to prevent her sliding to the floor. 'Stop it,' he heard himself pleading. 'Stop it, for God's sake.'

His foot caught the whisky bottle and it clattered over the tiled floor, spilling Scotch as it rolled. 'Oh, Savage, don't waste it,' she howled. She made to rescue the bottle but slid through his arms. He grabbed at her slipping body but she flopped like a fish on to the floor. She got her fingers around the neck of the bottle. 'Put it down,' he ordered angrily. 'Put the damn thing down.'

'But you *spilt* it,' she argued drunkenly. She could not focus him. 'It's good drink. Waste not, want not.'

Savage almost wrenched his overcoat from his back and threw it behind him into the sitting room. 'Paddington!' she suddenly screamed pointing towards the bath. 'Don't let Paddington get drowned!' She lolled forward and caught the side of the bath with her soapy hand.

'Paddington will be fine,' he told her desperately. 'He can swim.' She appeared to believe him.

'That horrible man, that Monty, or whatever-he-was-called, was sick on him,' she moaned.

'Come on,' he said, more softly, encouragingly. He bent and put his arms below her wet, bare, armpits. Firmly he pulled her upright. She tried to kiss him but he turned her around, backside to him, and, his arms still locked below hers, attempted to ease her forward into the sitting room. At that moment a plastic bag came around the corner. Her gerbil emerged and headed for the spilt whisky. Savage tried to put his foot in the way. 'Don't,' she howled. 'You'll step on him. He won't drink much.' She was half-sitting on the edge of the bath now. 'He's my family,' she said pointing vaguely at the sniffing gerbil. 'Him and Paddington.' She began to cry dramatically. 'I'm a poor, lost girl.' Not for the first time he picked her up bodily and carried her into the bedroom. 'Dry me, Savage,' she moaned swaying as he attempted to stand her upright. 'I'm all wet. I'll get cold. I'll be ill again!'

Desperately he rolled her on to the bed. She was still hung with suds. She made a weak attempt to scrape them from her breasts. 'My chest, my chest is getting cold,' she complained. Savage with a muted oath left her and ran back to the bathroom. He picked up two towels. When he returned she had collapsed on to the bed, nude and soapy, her eyes closed, her legs spread out. He closed them briskly then rubbed her with the towel, her feet, her legs and her body. 'Take it easy, Savage,' she protested dreamily. 'You're skinning me.'

He dried her and helped her get into her nightdress. He pulled the bedclothes back and coaxed her between the sheets. Her hair was still dangling lankly. He dried it as best he could. He thought that she had gone to sleep by that time. Breathing hard he stood back and surveyed her calm face. Once more she half-opened her eyes. 'Thanks, Savage,' she said lucidly. 'I'll look after you. And you'll look after me.' Her pink eyelids drooped. 'We'll look after each other.'

Eleven

Real spring came to Kensington, timidly at the start but with increasing confidence and resolve, greening the trees and prompting flowers in the pots and parks of the neighbourhood. Widening spaces of blue spread over the roofs and sunlight warmed windows. People tried sitting outside pubs and cafés. Traffic fumes increased, ducks were to be seen strutting among the cars in the streets, itinerants began to gravitate from their shelters.

In Kensington Heights people stood at their windows to observe the spring, some of the elder inhabitants marking off another winter survived. Casement windows and the doors of narrow balconies were opened a few inches so that the residents could sample the warmer air; some even decided to venture out into it. The business people went and came, morning and evening, as they did whatever the month. Miss Bombazine ordered a new mattress.

The gerbil, sensing the shifting season, scrambled from the guts of the sofa to the floor where he squatted preening himself as though expecting a guest.

'Even night-time animals know about the spring,' said Korky observing the detailed ablutions. 'He needs a mate. He's getting all clean for nothing.' She turned to Savage. 'You think I need a boyfriend, don't you?'

He made a face. She continued: 'Then *you*'ll be the one

who's sorry.' She put on his stern voice: 'Where've you been? Who you been with? What have you been doing?'

'I wouldn't say any of those things,' responded Savage calmly. He returned to the upright typewriter on the desk near the window. He had reached the Cayman Islands. *'West Indian group, 150 miles west-north-west of Jamaica. Formerly salt panning, and the hunting of turtles, now banking and offshore finances. Some tourism . . .'*

Korky watched over his shoulder and said: 'Salt panning.' She gave another sniff. 'You'd be jealous as hell.'

They laughed. Their domesticity was more settled; they had solemnly shaken hands and made a pact, a bargain. She would remain in the apartment until she had an assured job and could make her own arrangements for accommodation. 'And we'll always be friends,' she said stoutly.

'Always friends,' Savage said.

She had closed her slim hand on his. They had faced each other for a moment and then turned away. 'I'm going to buy a paper,' she had told him resolutely. 'I am going to find a . . . position.'

She put on her earphones and left. He had brought the Walkman for her. She wore them like a bonnet out of doors, the repetitive thump, thump of the base sounding as she went along the pavements, although she never discussed the music, she barely mentioned it, and when she sang it was in the aimless way she had always done. No tune, no song, was recognisable. Even when they went out together she sometimes wore the earphones. They would march a yard apart, eyes ahead, her long skinny legs striding to the pop beat. But she never listened to it indoors. 'I don't need it here,' she had explained. 'There's nothing else to do when you're walking or sitting on the Tube.' Her young face turned to him. 'You never mind if I sing though, do you, Savage?'

'It depends how much you sing.'

'Not all that much. I've got a terrible voice.'

'I know,' he said.

She insisted that he go with her to purchase the new clothes she needed. He sat with his habitual unease in shops while she tried on dresses, skirts, tops and shoes. Under the scrutiny of shop staff and the sniff of manageresses he nodded as she displayed her acquisitions.

'Him and a kid like that,' grunted a cash-desk woman when they had gone from the shop.

'He's a bit dishy,' muttered a young assistant. 'I wish I had him.'

Her attempts at finding work were more successful than retaining it. 'That poofy Percy!' she raged returning from her third day at Percival's Divine Hair, Kensington High Street. 'I've had enough!'

'You left?' He was unsurprised.

'Left? No, hell, the bugger threw me out. Physically. Me! Out of the door. Him and that lard-faced Angela. It took two of them.'

'What happened?' He was mildly making tea. It was five o'clock and springtime bright outside their window.

'That grungy dye stuff they use.' She sulked. 'It gets everywhere.'

'Where did it get?'

'Over some old dear's legs.' Her eyes warmed at the memory, her face began to quiver, her hand went to her mouth. 'She had *purple* legs, Savage. Accidentally I tipped it over and she went screaming around the shop with purple legs.' She could not subdue her laughter. 'Christ, you should have seen her.'

'*That*,' said Savage handing her a cup of tea, 'I imagine is *that*.'

'You imagine right.' She drank some tea and going into the kitchen, returned with a handful of chocolate biscuits. She piled them precisely, one on top of the other, and bit into them simultaneously. 'But something good came out of it.' Her mouth was full. Her eyes went to him. 'I got myself a boyfriend.'

He looked up from his tea. 'Who?' he asked. 'Who is it?'

She regarded him carefully over the edge of her cup. 'You *know* him, Savage. He's called Freddie. He works at the estate agent's at the bottom of the hill.' She had one of her moments of mimicry. 'Oh, come Easter then the entire house market will be booming, my love.' Her voice reverted to normal. 'He rented this flat to you.'

'How,' sighed Savage, 'can you say he's your boyfriend? You've only just met.'

'Half an hour ago. For me, that's all it takes. He was coming out of his office when I was charging up the street effing and blinding about the old woman and her purple legs and getting the push. We more or less collided.'

'You think he was attracted to you?' Now he regarded her teasingly.

'Attracted? Aw, come on, Savage. His eyes were *burning*, mate. He's good looking.' An edge of doubt entered her voice. 'Isn't he?'

Savage surveyed her. She was taking off her new red coat. Her fake fur had become a bed for the gerbil, out on the balcony of the side window. 'Fancy,' she had said happily. 'Paddington and John sleeping together.' She unbuttoned the coat. Under it she was wearing a denim skirt and an inky blue top which displayed the shape of her small, pushy breasts. Her face remained slim but her skin had become soft and her eyes lively. 'I wouldn't have thought he was your type,' he mentioned. 'But if you think so . . .'

'My *type*? Savage, I thought you'd be over the *moon*. He's got a car. Well, he *did* have a car. He's been disqualified but he'll get his licence back in a year. At the moment he rides a bike. And he's got a flat.'

'A flat tyre?'

They laughed. 'A flat flat,' she answered cuffing him. 'Oh, Savage, he's a bit of a posho but he's quite nice really. I might give him a whirl. I've never been out with a bloke who has a suit.'

'And a bike,' he said.

She sat frowning at his typewriter. 'This old thing,' she said. 'It's cruel to keep banging away at it.'

'It hasn't complained to me.'

'It's probably too scared,' she observed. She pressed her middle finger against the embossed letter of one of the keys and withdrew it to examine the inky imprint. 'It's an X,' she reported. 'A cry for help.'

'I've never used anything else,' said Savage. 'It took me long enough to learn how to type.'

'You'll never get through to the end of your islands,' she forecast. 'This'll be a pile of old metal before then.' She eyed him. 'I've told you before. You ought to have a word processor.'

'I don't want a word processor. I couldn't fathom a word processor.'

'I can. I was brilliant at school. I could teach you.' Her enthusiasm seemed excessive. Then he knew the reason. 'I've got this man coming around to demonstrate one to you. He's . . .'

Savage stared at her. 'Go on. Take over my work now. You're trying to take over my whole life.'

Korky returned the challenge stoutly. 'I'm not. I just want to bring you into the computer age, Savage.' She caught hold of both his hands and examined the middle fingers. 'And to stop you wearing out your fingers.' Sadly she turned to the typewriter. 'And this poor old bugger.'

'When,' he asked, 'is this man coming?'

Korky checked the clock. 'In five minutes.'

Immediately the lift sounded and the doorbell rang. 'He's desperate,' grunted Savage.

'Businesslike,' sniffed Korky. She went to the door. The man, compact, neat, with a disconcerting blink, came in carrying two packages. 'Hello,' he said, his lids flickering. 'Have I got something to show you.'

'Good,' said Savage flatly. Korky directed smiles of encouragement, first at the salesman and then at Savage. 'Over here,' she said. She led the way to the desk and the upright typewriter. 'Oh dear, oh dear,' said the visitor. 'What do we have here?'

'A typewriter,' said Savage stiffly.

'Yes, of course. I remember,' said the man.

'Let's see what you've brought,' put in Korky hurriedly.

The man began to open his packing, the cardboard first, then the polystyrene. He brought out a grey, flat case, which he laid on the desk. Korky approved: 'No bigger than a sandwich. You could take that anywhere, Savage.'

'I don't go anywhere,' replied Savage moodily. He tapped the typewriter as though reassuring it.

'It's pretty though, isn't it,' insisted the salesman. He eyed Korky who got his message and moved the typewriter to one side. 'Just for the time being,' she said gently, patting it also.

The salesman sat at the desk, like someone about to play a prim tune on the harmonium. He flexed his fingers and opened the lid. He pressed a button and a slow flash appeared on the screen accompanied by a metallic but musical sound. 'Battery power,' he said. A robotic face appeared. 'He's smiling at you,' pointed Korky.

Doubt creasing his forehead, Savage stood bending over the demonstrator's left shoulder; Korky smiling serenly stood behind his right. Now he was in front of the screen the man no longer blinked. He tapped the slight grey keys and images appeared, small notes sounded, the vision cleared and a grid occupied the screen. Lightly he tapped out a phrase which ran silently across the opal space: 'Today is my birthday. I am thirty-four years of age. I live in Peckham.'

'Is it really?' asked Korky with a touch of kindness.

'No,' admitted the salesman. 'I always write that. It makes people more receptive.' He turned towards her and began to blink furiously again. 'And I'm only twenty-nine. This is a hard job.'

He returned his attention to the screen.

Rough winds do shake the darling buds of May, he wrote.

'That's nice,' said Korky. 'It was on television.'

'I learned it at school,' he shrugged.

He tapped again. *Go lovely Rose! Tell her that wastes her time and me.*

'Very romantic.' She smiled at Savage who remained impassive.

'I learned that at school as well,' said the salesman. 'And what about this one: *It was the schooner Hesperus that sailed on wintry sea.*'

'He knows a lot, doesn't he, Savage?' said Korky encouragingly.

'But only odd lines,' confessed the man. 'That's all I know.' He appeared despondent. 'I keep meaning to look them up, learn the rest, but I don't get any time. I'm lucky if I get twenty minutes for lunch.'

'Let me try,' suggested Korky. 'I was a whizz at computer studies.' The salesman moved over and stood. Korky had to move the chair close. 'Insert page break,' she said. She worked the cursor around the screen. 'Under *Document*,' said the saleman. He smiled nervously at the watching Savage. 'Really, it's quite simple,' he said.

Korky drew a dotted line across the screen. 'Now what shall I write?' she asked herself. Neither man helped. She turned winsomely to the salesman. 'How do you spell *incey*?' she enquired.

'*Incey*. I don't know.' He recovered. 'There's a spell-check on it.'

'Do you know, Savage?' She revolved in the other direction.

'In what context?'

'Oh, it doesn't matter. I'll spell it like it sounds.' With her long, light fingertips she began to tap the keys. The obedient letters danced onto the screen:

Incey, wincey, spider,
Climbing up the spout.

The salesman glanced at Savage who smiled seriously.

Down came the rain
And washed poor Incey out . . .

Korky turned. 'There,' she said. 'Do you know the rest, Savage?'

'I believe I remember.'

'Go on, then. Write it.' She rose from the chair and waved her hand at the seat. 'It's easy,' she said.

Slowly he took his place in front of the screen. They stood behind him, Korky pleased, the salesman uncertain, puzzling about their relationship.

Savage poised his broad middle fingers over the keyboard. He found the letter *o* and touched it. The salesman said: 'Touch this one first, for a capital.' Korky glared at him. 'There's no need to be technical,' she said. 'I thought you were on my side.'

'Oh, sorry, I am. You're right.'

Savage said: 'I might as well do it properly.'

Korky took his finger and guided it to *Delete*. She pressed it on to the key. The *o* vanished.

'Which one now?' enquired Savage.

She took his other wide middle finger between her frail finger and thumb. The salesman's bemused eyes followed the movement. 'This,' Korky said softly. She placed her finger on the *Shift* key and said: 'Now on the *o*. It's the same as your old typewriter.' Savage pressed down and a small smile of triumph creased his face. 'You've done it,' she said.

'I have too.'

'Next lower case *u*,' offered the salesman not wanting to be left out. Savage did it and followed it with *t*.

'You've written *out*,' said Korky happily. 'Now save it.'

'Save *one* word?' queried the salesman.

'Just that one,' said Korky frowning at him again. 'It's his first word.'

'My baby said her first word the other day,' said the salesman. 'Dog.' He beamed at them finishing on Savage. 'And now you've done yours.'

They pushed and edged and guided him through the

sentence, deleting, inserting and correcting until it was
finished:

Out came the sunshine
And dried up all the rain.
Incey wincey spider
Went up the spout again.

Savage leaned back and, as though his fingers needed
rest, placed them on his lap. Korky smiled and the
salesman blinked furiously. 'I bet your baby couldn't
manage that,' she remarked.

The device's presumption, its mechanical brashness, had
irritated him at first; the smug chime, the square smiling
robot. Even in the army he had shied away from
computer innovations, preferring the simplicity of a gun.
But the characteristics of the word processor screen
quickly became familiar. He found himself acknowledg-
ing the empty greeting.

Korky kept the flat clean, did the shopping, and was
what she called a good take-away cook. Each evening
they ate pizza, Chinese or Indian take-away or fish and
chips which she warmed in the oven. Mrs Tomelty's
initial scepticism dissolved. 'It just shows, you can never
tell,' she said. 'Deep down inside she's a domesticated
creature.'

She went out with Freddie Spencer-Hughes and
Savage remained in the flat; an odd, selfish, loneliness
came over him. On the first evening he watched her from
the window walking youthfully away beneath the dimming trees. He could see her bright coat below the
branches. She stopped and for a moment he thought she
was going to turn back but then she strutted on. He

poured himself a Scotch and put a steak and kidney pie she had bought from Marks & Spencer into the oven. He ate it moodily. Then he turned on the word processor. The telephone rang. It was his wife.

'Frank, how are you?' The concern was genuine.

'Irene, I'm really fine thanks. And you?'

'I'm all right. I'm telephoning from my mother's so I don't want to be long. She still listens. You sound fine.'

'I am. I've had no real worries, no setbacks. It's begun to work out very well.'

Her voice softened. 'Are you still by yourself?'

'If you mean do I have a romantic relationship,' he answered cautiously, 'I don't.'

'I see.' There was an interval. 'Frank, I've met someone.'

'Oh . . . good. That's very good.'

'I'd like to meet up with you some time, if it's all right. About a divorce.'

'Yes, I see. Well, why don't we?'

'There's no news about the house, I suppose?'

'I've heard nothing. But down there in the middle of winter I don't suppose much was selling at all. Now the weather's changing it might be better. Come Easter then the whole house market will be booming.'

She laughed in a puzzled way. 'You sound like an estate agent,' she said.

Twelve

Irene was already sitting watchfully at the restaurant table when he arrived early. She was drinking a Campari, the glass just against her lips, when she saw him at the door. She lowered it to the cloth and smiled, but with a shadow of anxiety. He walked towards her and they kissed awkwardly. Sitting down he ordered whisky. 'You've changed your drink,' he said nodding towards her glass.

'I've been trying to change a lot.'

'Have you been here long? Sorry I was late.'

'No,' said Irene hurriedly. 'It took less time than I thought. There's a through-train.'

Her fingers reached for the back of his hand. 'Frank, I'm very pleased you're so much better. You look really well.'

The waiter returned and they ordered their meal. They were both grateful for his interruption. 'It's a nice place,' she said looking about her.

'I've not been here before,' he said. 'I'd noticed it.'

'Do you go out much?'

'Not much. But more than I used to.'

'It doesn't bother you now?'

'No, not now.' He smiled encouragement. 'Is he nice?'

'Oh, Graham. Yes, very nice. I think so. He's an architect. He's forty. His wife died.' Her expression was intense. 'I'm not living with him. We see each other. He's happy to wait. Do you *want* me to marry him, Frank?'

He could only say: 'Well ... yes. Whatever you want.'

She regarded him with real sadness. 'It was such a damned pity, wasn't it. But perhaps it would never have worked out. We weren't meant.'

Savage returned the touch. 'It's too late anyway,' he replied quietly. 'You can never go back.'

Slowly Irene took her hand away. 'You're right, of course. I'm just so glad that you've got better.'

'There have been one or two bad ... difficult ... moments,' he admitted. 'But I've had plenty to occupy me ... I ...'

He was intending then to tell her about Korky when he saw Korky peering deeply at them from outside the window. She saw him and waved impishly beyond Irene's back. Then she strolled the few paces to the door and stepped into the restaurant. Savage groaned inwardly. He saw her attract the waiter's attention. 'Can I have that place, please,' he heard her ask winsomely. She pointed. His heart descended. 'I am all by myself.'

Irene glanced around as the girl, in a mini skirt and tiny jacket, came across the restaurant. Savage was preparing himself to introduce her but she went angularly past with no recognition, her stalky legs projecting bare from the lampshade skirt. She sat at the table only three feet away, and gazed directly and deeply at Irene. Picking up the menu she peered over the top at her. 'I'd like a red-coloured drink, please,' she whispered loudly, her eyes only going to the waiter as he arrived. 'Like that lady's got there.'

Savage felt his teeth clamp. Irene smiled towards him and pretended she had not heard. Korky's whisper rose again. 'With ice, please. Just like hers.'

'Soda, miss?' asked the waiter.

'Soda? Oh yes, *please*. Soda as well.'

She squinted intently at the menu as if she urgently needed glasses and Irene, a little puzzled by their pause in the conversation, said to Savage: 'It's a shame about the house not selling.'

'They'll be selling soon,' interjected Korky blatantly from her table. 'Don't you worry. My boyfriend's an estate agent and *he* says that when Easter comes the market will . . .' Her voice altered in an attempt at refinement: '. . . Just buck up no end.'

Savage winced and kept his eyes away. Irene grinned slightly and nodded across the aisle. 'Thank you very much.'

'Very reassuring,' added Savage turning and surveying Korky grimly. Now he could not tell Irene who she was. It was too late. Triumphantly Korky knew it too. She returned the expression with coyness. 'That's all right,' she almost whispered. 'So glad to be of help.'

Savage leaned across towards his wife. 'Perhaps we ought to move,' he grunted. 'To another table.'

Irene shook her head. 'Don't worry. She's only chatty.'

'We have things to talk about,' he said more loudly intending it as a warning to Korky.

'Yes,' Irene responded, lowering her voice. 'We have.'

The waiter arrived with their food. Korky watched him approach. He also had her Campari. She grimaced as she sipped it. 'What have you got?' she enquired leaning over archly as he set the dishes down. Savage tightened his teeth. Irene remained patient.

'I have mushrooms,' she said touching hers with her fork. 'And . . . my husband has smoked trout.'

Korky's young eyes gleamed across to them. 'That looks nice, really, *really* nice,' she sighed. She had poured the Campari into the flowers on her table. 'What are you having next?' Savage did not dare lift his eyes from his plate. He sliced the smoked trout fiercely and bit just as unequivocally through a piece of brown bread. He would not allow himself to look towards her.

'We've both ordered the lamb,' Irene told Korky kindly.

'Both *together*,' sighed Korky. 'You two look really nice with each other. Have you been married long?'

Savage muttered murderously: 'Years.'

Korky had ordered a salad. The waiter brought it with a glass of white house wine. She sorted the salad around her plate. It appeared that she had withdrawn from the exchange but then she confided: 'I'd like to get married. My boyfriend, the estate agent, he would like a shot, tomorrow, if I wanted, but there's this man I know who's quite a bit older than me.'

'Married?' guessed Irene still politely.

'Y . . . yes married,' stammered Korky. To Savage's chagrin and Irene's concern she began to cry. He wanted to order her to stop but the situation had gone too far. 'Do you want to move to another table?' he repeated to his wife. Irene handed her handkerchief across the gap between the tables. 'Don't be so mean, Frank,' she whispered. 'She's only a kid.'

'Sorry,' sobbed Korky blatantly. 'I shouldn't have come here really. I was hoping to see *him*, my older lover. He's with his wife, I *know* he is.' She stood and drank the wine at three gulps rubbing her cheeks with Irene's handkerchief. 'I'll have to go,' she sniffled. 'I've made myself miserable and I'll only make you happy married people miserable too.'

'Let me settle your bill,' offered Savage hurriedly. The sooner she went the better.

'Oooo, *thank* you. What a nice thought,' said Korky smiling across her wet face. 'My name's Samantha, by the way. Sam Percival.' She offered her skinny hand. 'What's yours?'

'Frank and Irene Savage,' provided Savage resolutely. He saw the waiter approach. Korky was on her feet. 'I'll get this young lady's bill,' Savage said.

'Thanks ever so much,' breathed Korky. She solemnly shook hands with both of them. 'And goodbye,' she concluded tragically. 'Have a happy, happy life.'

Like a corkscrew she revolved and went towards the door, her hurrying bottom throwing the unsuitable mini skirt from side to side. They watched her leave. At the door she paused and for a moment Savage, heart descending, thought she was going to return. But all she did was make a little wave to them before going out into the sunny street.

'That was very good of you, Frank,' observed Irene.

'Picking up her bill?' said Savage. She studied him from her side of the table. 'I just wanted to get rid of her. After all we came here to have a private talk.'

'Poor kid,' she said. 'She seems very disturbed. I imagine she causes someone a lot of trouble.'

'You can bet on that,' agreed Savage.

'All right, Korky,' demanded Savage. 'Why did you do it?'

'Spur of the moment,' she answered as if she hoped that might satisfy him. She smirked but uncertainly, holding the gerbil in front of her like a protection. It lay there in her hands rolling its eyes as if it knew.

'For God's sake,' he said angrily. 'Can't I have lunch with my own wife without you rearing your . . .' He saw her expression fall. '. . . Popping up and making a drama?'

'I thought you didn't love each other any more. That's why you don't live together.'

'That is not the damned point. It's none of your business. You are not involved.'

Korky sat subdued on the sofa, stroking the gerbil who still regarded Savage with caution and visibly cringed at his raised voice. 'Why?' Savage repeated standing before her.

'Don't sound like a sergeant, or whatever. I only wanted to see what she was *like*,' sighed Korky looking towards the other end of the room. 'It's a woman's instinct. To see how her rival looks.'

He stamped on the carpet, conscious that the movement came from the parade ground. 'She is *not* your rival! I am *not*, repeat *not*, involved in a relationship with you. Here you are merely a lodger.'

Korky put her narrow nose in the air. 'Here you are *meeerely* a lodger,' she mimicked. 'All right, then, why didn't you tell her who I was? At the beginning, as soon as I came in. I'll tell you why, because you were scared to tell her. And after that it was too late.'

He sat down. 'We were meeting to discuss our eventual divorce,' he told her trying to be patient.

At once her face glowed. 'Oh, *that's* good,' she enthused. 'That's a *lot* better news, that is. There was me thinking you were going to get together again. I knew you were going to meet up because you wrote "Irene" and the restaurant and the date and the time on your telephone pad. But I thought it was all going to be patched up. But . . . divorce . . . that's a bit different.'

'It's *not* different,' he told her truculently. 'So you can forget that for a start.'

'*I* wouldn't have you,' she returned haughtily. 'Not if you was giving yourself free. Anyway I got in the sack with Freehold Freddie yesterday.'

'Oh, did you.' He tried not to sound shocked.

'Yes, and it was all your *fault*.'

'How could it be *my* fault, for Christ's sake?'

'Don't swear. Jesus doesn't like it. I did it for *revenge*.'

Sitting wearily down beside her, he lowered his head into his hands. 'Revenge? What are you talking about now? Revenge.'

'Revenging myself on you because I thought that you and your Irene would be making it up, getting together. I did it to spite you.' She paused. 'Freddie kept his tie on in bed.'

'Why would he want to do that?' Savage asked dully. He felt defeated.

'In case he got a call. To go and sell a house. He's very keen. He's on commission. I thought your Irene was nice.'

'She's *not* my Irene,' responded Savage.

'All right, your ex-Irene then, your former Irene. Has she got somebody else?'

'Yes. She wants to marry him.'

'Everybody meets somebody but me,' she complained.

'You haven't done badly for someone not yet eighteen.'

'Anyway, then you'll be free,' she said thoughtfully. 'After your divorce.'

'And I intend to stay free.'

'A soldier of fortune. That's what you want to be.' It was a hint of mockery. 'What about Jean Thing. Jean Whatsit.'

'Jean Deepe?' he said, surprised. 'That's finished. It hardly started. *You* put the kibosh on that.'

'Being seriously ill,' lamented Korky. 'I've buggered up your big romance.'

'It was not a big romance.'

'I don't like her anyway, that Jean Whatever-she's-called. I prefer your wife.'

It took a moment for Savage to realise. 'How do you know what Jean's like?' he asked slowly, eventually. 'You've never even seen her.'

Korky emitted a small yawn. 'That Jean. I have. She was here the other day.'

'Here! You didn't tell me.'

'Forgot,' she lied easily. 'She was here in this flat. Standing right there. Said she was doing the regular security whatever-it-is. Something to do with shooting down Prince Charles's helicopter. I told her to get on with it.'

'Where was I?'

'At the library.'

'But you didn't tell me. Don't make out you forgot. You wouldn't forget something like that.'

Korky made a face. 'She's not for you,' she asserted as though that were sufficient answer. 'She's a copper lady but she's a tiny bit sly. Maybe that's why she's a copper lady. She's a bit tarty too, I think.'

'Oh, for God's sake. I can't get over you not telling me.'

'I'm doing it now. I'm telling you, aren't I? It was only a couple of days ago. Anyway, I knew you were going to meet Irene and I didn't want anyone to spoil it for the two of you.'

'You certainly come out with some beauties.'

Korky shrugged. 'Really that Jean only came to get a butcher's at me,' she said. 'Same thing as me wanting to see what your wife looked like. Women are like that. They get curious about other women.'

'Did Jean leave a message?' asked Savage in a spent voice.

Korky hesitated and he knew she was going to lie. 'Did she?' he insisted.

'All right, she did. But I wouldn't bother about her, if I was you, Savage. She's trouble.'

He had kept the policewoman's telephone number but now he could not find it. Korky helped him to search but with such unconvincing conviction that he guessed what had happened to it. She went out to do the Saturday shopping and said she was going to Shepherd's Bush market. These days she always told him where she was going; at least where she *said* she was going, and she came back.

He got a taxi to Westbourne Grove. He rang the bell of Jean's flat and realised there was an eye scrutinising him through the security spy-hole. 'You got my message,' she said when she had opened the door. 'I'm amazed.'

'Slightly delayed,' he admitted. He walked into her sitting room, feeling a sense of surprise that it looked the same. So many things had happened to him in the few weeks since he was last there.

'I'm amazed she passed it on,' said Jean. She was slight in jeans and a cream sweater. Her hair was tied behind her head and with no make-up her face looked stark and thin. Cigarette ends were mangled in the ashtray. She was smoking nervously.

Uncertainly Savage sat down and she went at her businesslike pace into the kitchen and made some coffee. She returned more slowly. 'It took a couple of days for her to tell me,' he said. 'But she came out with it in the end. Korky has a conscience. It gets the better of her eventually. But then I'd mislaid your phone number and I didn't want to call you at the station.'

, They faced each other over the low ceramic table. 'Well, I'm glad you came over, Frank,' she said looking down at her cup. She picked up the cigarette she had put on the edge of the ashtray but then stubbed it out. 'I ought to apologise for the hard time I gave you that night you were looking for her. She turned up anyway.'

'She was at home,' he nodded.

'She's a funny thing, isn't she,' said the policewoman thoughtfully. 'Streetwise as hell, watch her eyes. But she doesn't look as though she wants to be out in the streets.'

'Korky's unusual,' he conceded.

'You've been good to her.'

'She's been good *for* me, I think. She's given me something different to think about. God, if you could have seen her when I found her that first night. She wasn't far off being dead. It was a month before she got over it.'

'What are you going to do with her?' The eyes rose professionally.

'Do with her? Well, we have an arrangement. As soon as she gets settled into a job then she's going to fix herself up with somewhere to live.' He looked abashed. 'We've shaken hands on it.' Jean was still studying him. He added lamely: 'We're sort of . . . well, like father and daughter.'

She laughed knowingly. 'I bet that young lady doesn't see it quite like that.'

'Well, that's how it is,' he said firmly.

She put her cup on the table and he put his down also. She stretched forward over the cups and he leaned forward too and they kissed. 'I've had problems,' she said quietly. 'Big ones.'

'In what way?'

She stood up and went to the window and seemed to be searching the street. 'I'm glad you came,' she said without turning around. 'I need a bit of moral support.'

'What's it about?'

'A man called Brendan Brownlow,' she said turning towards him. She looked shaky even mentioning the name. 'He's a bastard, a right villain. He's inside just now but he'll be out soon. He's applied for parole and the way they dish it out these days he'll probably get it.'

'What's the connection?'

'Him and me.' She sat at the table again, her fingertips together. 'I had a bit of a fling with him once, Frank. Not long after my husband died. I was very low when I met him. He had a record and I knew about that, but I picked him up. I must have been mad but I needed somebody. The Met had not been particularly helpful or even sympathetic over Malcolm. They made the right noises and that was about it. A copper inconveniently dying after a pub brawl is not like a copper killed by a terrorist bomb. Different sympathy category altogether.'

Her fingertips tapped. Once more he thought how slight, how furtive, she was. She breathed confessionally. 'Anyway, our Brendan then did a jewellery job. He got shopped and put away.'

'And now he's about to reappear.'

'It's worse than that. He thinks *I* shopped him, or I was in on it with the bloke who did.'

'You weren't.'

She quickly avoided his face. 'There was a reward,' she said. 'The informant picked it up. Twenty-five thousand.'

Apprehension floated in her eyes. 'He's just sent me a letter. Well, just one sentence. It said: "See you soon." '

'And that's a threat?'

'I think it could be.'

Rising she went to the window again. 'Frank,' she said. 'Be a friend. Just keep an eye on me, will you. Keep in touch. Just for the next few months. They might even let him out earlier. They do sometimes if there's a special reason. He could say it was his dear old mother's birthday. Anyway, he'll be back. There's nothing more certain.'

Again she was smoking, drawing quickly on the cigarette.

'And you can't tell anyone?' he said.

'The police? Obviously there's no way I want to get them involved. I'd get protection but there would be a lot of difficult questions asked.'

'What about the man who got the reward?'

'He's inside now as well.' She looked directly at him. 'I haven't been too particular with my friends.'

'I've got a gun you could have,' he said.

'I know all about your gun,' she replied flatly. 'Your Korky told me.'

'She tells everybody.'

'It's useless anyway,' shrugged Jean. 'No ammo either. I had a look at it. She took it from under your bed for me.' She waited then went on: 'The gun is not a problem. I've got one. But that doesn't stop me being scared.' She glanced up. 'Can I give you a key?' she asked. 'Then you can get in any time. If I call you.'

Savage looked at her more steadily than he felt. 'All right,' he decided. 'Give me a key.'

'Come and see me,' she smiled tightly. She kissed him

on the mouth but her lips were like a beak. 'Whenever you like.'

Thirteen

Fine weather moved across the London sky by the end of the first week in May. The gerbil was installed in a hutch on the tight balcony of the side window which faced east and received the sun until almost afternoon. He stayed in the dark away from it. Korky had triumphantly carried the wooden rodent house from Portobello Road; she bought it with her only week's wages as a child minder. 'It's meant for rabbits. It's antique,' she claimed happily as she manoeuvred the box on to the balcony. The gerbil, sensing an involvement in the excitement, sniffed around her feet. 'There's even old droppings in the bottom.'

After some wariness the animal was persuaded to enter. 'There, John,' said Korky. 'Now *you've* got a home as well.'

She was not easily employed. Hopefully they read the Situations Vacant in the *Evening Standard* but it was Mr Tomelty who provided the most promising opening.

'Child minder,' said Korky. She glanced for support towards Savage. He said doubtfully: 'Excellent.'

'The people live in the next block,' said Tomelty. 'Out all day like a lot of them are. Two mites. They had a girl to help, from the East by the look of her, but she's gone. Back to the Orient maybe.'

Korky was not exact with the children's ages. 'The boy

can walk but he can't talk much,' she reported after her first day. 'The baby can't do anything. Except the usual.'

'What are the parents like?' asked Savage still peering at the word processor. He was accustomed to it now; he could write and correct and print. He had no need to attempt anything more ambitious.

Korky was not impressed with the parents. After three days she reported: 'They come in shagged out and they talk in numbers — all they talk about is money and numbers and who's having it away with who. She makes sure I change the baby's bum before I leave because she almost goes into a faint doing it. They want me to move in there full-time.'

They were eating Chinese take-away; Savage's eyes came up to fix hers, noodles hanging from his fork. 'But I'm not going to,' she forestalled him, biting into a spring roll. 'You never know how long I might last.'

She found it humdrum pushing a pram in the park. On her final afternoon, she propelled it along the Kensington Gardens path and, in an attempt to ease her boredom, let it go. It rolled away from her with the boy and the baby, both aboard, shouting with the fun of it. Playfully Korky waved them off but she mistimed her pursuit. Gathering pace, the pram rumbled into the chilly shallows of the Round Pond, scattering ducks, and halted, fortunately upright, with the grey water lapping its wheels. Korky ran shouting, but as she caught the handle the vehicle toppled and the boy tipped into the shallows. People passing rushed to help. Korky hoisted the soaked and howling child clear of the water and the bystanders tugged the perambulator with its excited baby to the bank.

She might have got away with it; since neither child could speak she could have got back to Kensington

Heights in time to change their clothes, but one of the rescuers was a neighbour. She was given immediate notice even though the parents had a big business lunch the following day. 'I rescued him,' she complained to Savage. 'He could have drowned.'

Her attempt at being a waitress in a Fulham bistro was similarly brief. 'There were collisions,' she shrugged. 'I could never remember which door you went into the kitchen and which you went out.' Moved by her tears the manager said she could stay and load the dishwasher but that lasted only an afternoon.

'I'm not cut out for the catering trade,' she said.

Her lack of servility did not suit her for employment in the big stores of Knightsbridge and Kensington. Eventually, and surprisingly, however, she did find a job in a second-hand bookshop in Bloomsbury and there she stayed.

'It's all dirt and dust and books,' she related with satisfaction. 'Been on the shelves for years, some of them. Nobody buying them, nobody even opening them up, poor things. I've told Mr Furtwangler I'm going to have a good clear-up. He wasn't that keen because he said he knows where to find everything. He doesn't even seem worried whether we sell any. There were only five people in today but he doesn't mind. He went off for a couple of hours this afternoon, to a gallery or somewhere, and left me in charge. It was lovely, really, Savage, and cosy.'

She knew Savage had Jean Deepe's key in his bedside drawer. It was a strange key. Mr Kostelanetz said it was specially made, the sort of key which was very difficult to copy although he knew a man who did that sort of work.

When she had the duplicate Korky telephoned West London police and asked to speak to PC Deepe on a private matter. They said the officer would not be on duty until eight o'clock the following morning. Korky went and loitered near the flat in Westbourne Grove and watched her leave. Quickly she was inside the apartment. She was frightened but she wanted to see the place where this woman lived, where Savage went.

It was ordered and dim. The blinds were down. She sniffed the cigarette smoke and went towards the bedroom touching the door open with one fingertip. There was the *bed*. There were stubs in the ashtray beside it. She curled her nose at the quilt and the two embroidered cushions propped against the bedhead. Her heart sounding she stepped forward, turned back the covers to the sheet, and gave a little spiteful spit at it.

As she went back into the diffuse sitting room there was a sound outside the front door. She felt her eyes widen. Stepping back into the bedroom she peered through the thin aperture of the door. Through the letterbox dropped two letters. They bounced on the carpet. Korky took her hands from her chest and, after a full minute, went towards the letters and picked them up. 'Bills,' she said with a satisfied sniff. 'I hope they're big ones.' She dropped them back on to the carpet and then, with another guilty glance around the room as if she suspected some hidden witness, she let herself out of the apartment.

She stood behind him as he worked at the word processor. 'You're nearly getting the feel of it now,' she approved. 'Don't hammer it so much.' He could feel the front of her sweatshirt slightly touching his shoulder. He had reached the Dodecanese. 'What's the most out-of-this-world island then?' she asked. 'The furthest, I mean. From anywhere else. Where nobody goes?'

Savage clumsily worked the pages back. She leaned over and deftly did it for him. 'Tell me when to stop.' she said.

He reclined in the chair. 'Bouvet,' he said. 'That's it. Miles from anywhere.' She stopped at the correct place. '*Bouvet*. Fancy that,' she sniffed. 'You went to see *her* this afternoon, didn't you?' she said without looking away from the screen.

'Who? Jean? Yes.'

'Tea and muffins?'

'Just for tea,' he responded calmly. 'How are you getting on with Freddie?'

'Freddie is just someone to see.' She was staring at the screen without seeing it. But then with a conscious effort she recited: '*Longitude 54.23 north . . . latitude 6.52 east . . .*'

He felt her withdraw slightly from his shoulder. He remained facing the screen. 'It's not very interesting. Nobody lives there. It's just a rock in the ocean.'

Her sniff sounded again. 'One thousand five hundred miles from anywhere,' she put in pensively. 'A bit like you really. And me.' Without waiting for his response, she turned towards her bedroom. 'I nicked a book from work today,' she called back. 'Well, borrowed it. Mr Furtwangler won't mind. It will be years before he'll realise it's gone anyway.' She returned with the thick, scuffed book. 'It's about islands and other remote places. It's not like yours. There's mountains and lakes and rivers and stuff like that as well as some islands.' Clumsily she turned the pages. 'Here it is, Bouvet. Not much about it.'

'I told you there wouldn't be.'

'It says . . .' She read slowly and with exaggerated care as if auditioning: '*Early mariners wondered if Bouvet really existed. It was lost for years only to reappear again. Thick ocean fogs have always engulfed it. The explorer Sir James Clark Ross called it "Bouvet, that child of the mists".'*

She closed the book as if closing an argument. He rose from the desk. 'I'll go and get some take-away in a minute,' she said moodily. 'What sort?'

'Burgers,' he said. 'We've had every other sort this week. Chinese, Indian, fish and chips.' He looked at her and she giggled, the small tension going; he went into the kitchen. 'Drink?' he called to her.

'Wine, please, little glass.' Leaning over the word processor her fingers began to work adroitly. He came back and saw her.

'I was just putting some of this interesting stuff from the book in,' she said hurriedly. 'I've changed the words so nobody will know. I'll try and find some more out tomorrow.'

He stood behind her whilst she continued. *'There were fogs and massive storms in this part of the ocean,'* she recited when she had finished. *'And the old sailors were frightened because they thought Bouvet was a ghost island. It vanished for years and appeared back out of the mist.'* She half-turned, waiting for his reaction. 'That cheers it up a bit.'

Silently Savage read through her words. To her pleasure he nodded. 'A couple of paragraphs,' he said thoughtfully, 'of legends.'

'Well, it's more interesting than just saying the size of the place, how many people live there, and saying that they grow beans.' She rose from the keyboard. Picking up the white wine she swallowed it. 'I'll go and get the McDonalds.'

She left briskly and he went to the window and watched her hurrying across the street below. He shook his head and returned to the word processor and, gradually smiling, he read again the few lines she had added. Then he shut it down and poured himself a drink.

She returned clutching the paper bag like a prize. 'I didn't tell you at the time,' she confessed as she distributed the hamburgers and chips on two plates. Thoughtfully she transferred a single chip from one plate to the other. 'But I dropped the lot last week. These bags are ever so thin. Went straight through the bottom and on to the road.'

'And. . . ?'

'We ate it.' She stood and grinned.

'Thank you for telling me.'

She went to the kitchen and returned with the ketchup and the remaining white wine. They ate and drank in their customary, uncomplicated silence. They were easy with each other now. Eventually Korky said: 'When I'm an old lady I'm going to get my rail pass and go all over the place on the train. In the winter I'll even live on the train. I'll sleep in it and eat sandwiches and go from one end of the country to the other, Cornwall up to Scotland and back. What will you do?' She wiped the grease and the ketchup from her mouth. Her eyes moved to him.

'I hope not to be an old lady,' he said.

She shoved him lightly.

'Pack it in. You know what I mean.' He picked up the same paper napkin as she had used and wiped his chin. 'I've never thought about it,' he admitted. 'Thinking about today and tomorrow is difficult enough.'

'When you're in the army you don't have to think, do you?' she continued mildly.

'What makes you say that?'

'I've met squaddies. I once stayed in Aldershot, working in the Naafi.'

As she said it she went into the kitchen and returned

with two chocolate ice creams from the refrigerator. 'You didn't tell me that,' he said.

'I haven't told you everything, Savage,' she teased.

'You haven't told *me* everything. In fact you've hardly told me anything. You never talk about the army.'

'I've not wanted to talk about it,' he said. 'After the way I ended up.'

'Have you told that Jean about it?'

'I've told that Jean about some of it,' he replied.

'Were you really mental?' She tapped her forehead. 'Had you lost it?'

'As close as I've wanted to be. It still scares the hell out of me.'

'It's a bummer,' she said without emphasis. 'But there's mad and there's mad. There was an old mad bloke used to be around here. Mad as a drainpipe. Old Crony they called him because he was always going on about his old cronies. That must have been army too. Some nights he used to sit with us, when we had a fire, and blather on about yonks ago. He was really mad. One night I came across him all frozen and stiff and he asked me if I'd hold his willie because he was dying.'

'He did what!'

'Hold his willie,' she repeated as though he might not have heard. She shrugged: 'Because he was on his last puff, see. Just to give him a bit of pleasure. So I did.'

Eventually he said: 'You would.'

'Well, who cared? I took it out for him. I had a job finding the poor old thing, believe me, and when I did, God, it was like my thumb. I squeezed it in my hand until it had warmed up a bit. And then an ambulance came what somebody had called. I put his willie away and they carted him off. He didn't die, though, the old fraud. A couple of weeks later I saw him creeping down Church Street.'

She munched the chocolate ice cream oblivious of his expression. 'I'll tell you something else funny,' she rambled. She was in a confessional mood. 'You know that old dear, Mrs Blenkinsop, Wilhelmina, who reckons her husband is murdered and buried in the cellar? I went down there with her to have a look and . . .'

'You actually went. . . ?'

'Down in the cellar,' she insisted. 'But she couldn't find the place. She's well gone, you know. God it was horrible down there. All dark and ratty.'

'How,' Savage asked attempting to appear patient, 'did you get into that situation? You seem to know half the people in these flats.'

'A lot of them,' she shrugged. 'Wrinklies enjoy having somebody a bit younger to talk to. They're all into death, you know, well into it. Like that old geezer who went to Antwerp specially to die. They go on about the past a bit but more often it's the future . . . when they're going to snuff it. None of them seem that interested in what's happening right now.'

She regarded him narrowly as if to ascertain that he was still receptive. 'Mrs Blenkinsop, that Wilhelmina, had a seance, you know,' she told him with care. 'She had in this geezer who could bring back loved ones.'

Savage looked alarmed. 'You didn't go . . .'

'Course I went,' retorted Korky airily. 'It was a bit of a hoot really, but sad. This bloke was a right con artist, I had him sussed. He had a way of getting information, you know, about people that were dead and gone and then mixing it all up and telling the same stuff back to them. And they took it all in. They believed him.' She looked pensive. 'They wanted to really. One woman brought along some pictures of her husband's funeral and she showed them to me. She wouldn't show them to anybody else, even this medium man. Only me. She seemed to think I would understand.' She leaned and caught Savage by the shirt cuff. Her voice became throaty. 'And, Savage, there was her old man's *ghost* standing up in the middle of *his own funeral.* You could *see* him, Savage. It was a shock, I can tell you. But then I saw he was wearing *shorts.*'

Beyond words, Savage raised his eyebrows.

'Shorts,' she repeated. 'Honest. There was this photo, all these miserable people sitting after the funeral, eating cold pies and drinking sherry or whatever, and there was the dead bloke standing in the middle of them. I didn't tell her but it was . . . you know . . . what do they call it? A double exposure. She said she'd used the camera last summer at the seaside. They'd left the film in and somehow it got filmed over again. In his beach shorts. At his own funeral.'

One afternoon she arrived at the flat with Freddie, the estate agent. Her hair was in rows of tight plaits. 'I begged her not to, Mr Savage,' Freddie said in a tone he used when a sale had fallen through. 'It's too ethnic.'

'I wanted to,' said Korky stoutly. Challengingly she revolved to Savage. 'I thought you'd like it. Anyway, it's my hair and it's my birthday.'

'When is?' enquired Savage suspiciously. He knew her too well.

She raised her nose. 'Tomorrow. I'm eighteen tomorrow. I can do what I like then.'

'You do what you like now.'

'We're going out to dinner tonight,' Freddie said. 'My

209

treat.' His teeth dropped over his lip. 'How about coming with us?'

'I want you to,' pleaded Korky anxiously. 'For my birthday.'

He still doubted it but he said: 'All right.'

Unconvincingly Freddie said: 'Great.'

'Ask Jean,' suggested Korky brazenly. She did not meet his eyes. 'Make a foursome.' Freddie went pale. Savage said: 'That's a good idea. I'll ring her.'

At the conclusion of the meal Korky said cheerfully: 'I might as well confess.' She regarded each of the three variably expectant faces in turn. Freddie leaned his pale, moon countenance forward, a tongue of his black hair lolling over his forehead. The quartet had consumed four bottles of wine. 'It's not your birthday,' guessed Savage.

Korky pouted. 'Lousy spoilsport, Savage.'

Everyone, except Jean Deepe, laughed. Jean had observed Korky throughout the evening and now she only wearily closed her eyes. 'When is it?' she asked. She lit a cigarette. No one else smoked.

'October,' said Korky, looking squarely at her. She then made a face at Savage. She was quite drunk. Her expression changed again and she smiled extravagantly around the table. 'But it was great, anyway, wasn't it.'

They agreed it was, Freddie by a bowing of his head which continued until it descended to the tablecloth, where it remained. Korky regarded him with a small scorn. 'I think I'd better take him home,' she said.

'My treat,' mumbled Freddie. 'My treat.'

'We'll split it,' said Korky beaming towards the older pair. 'Won't we?'

'I've got money . . . somewhere,' insisted the mumbling Freddie. He could not find his inside pocket. Korky slapped his hand lightly. 'Pay up tomorrow,' she decided casting a glance at Savage. 'We could, couldn't we, Frank?'

She had never called him Frank and he blinked before agreeing. He helped Freddie to his feet with the assistance of Jean who, with professional facility, eased him from behind the table. Jean knew where to put her hands. 'Thanks ... thanks ... thanks so much,' the youth kept saying. 'Very sporting.' Korky gave token support and sighed: 'He soon gets pissed.' Savage asked the waiter to call a taxi and they got the sagging Freddie to the door. 'It's you she loves, Frank Savage, not me,' he moaned as he hung between them. He attempted to raise his head. 'You can't fool me. I'm an estate agent.'

Once the pair had gone Savage and Jean remained sitting silently.

'It's you she loves,' Jean eventually repeated with a smile.

'She loves me like her father,' Savage said. The waiter came and he settled the bill. They went out into the light spring night. 'How long ago did her father die?' asked Jean. 'You did say he was dead?'

'Years ago,' answered Savage. 'Then there was a stepfather and then her mother went off leaving her to fend for herself.'

'And fend off the stepfather.'

'That's what happened.'

'The usual,' she shrugged. She smiled tightly and privately, looking at the pavement as they walked. The night-time roofs were shaped against the pale sky, lights like coloured banners shone square in a few upper windows. 'That story she told tonight, about the old man who asked her to hold his willie because he was dying.'

Savage laughed quietly. 'She's told me that before.'

'The old bugger asked me to do the same thing,' Jean mentioned almost casually. 'A couple of weeks ago. He was flat out in the ambulance and he took his penis out.'

'What did you do?'

'I told him to put it away or I'd nick him for indecent exposure.'

'And he said he was dying?'

'Right. And this time he was spot on. He snuffed it before we reached the hospital.' They got to her door. 'Do you want to come up?' she asked.

'If you're going to invite me.'

She unlocked the door. 'I thought you might not want to tonight.'

'I want to.'

They went into the warm room and drank a brandy each.

They were sitting opposite each other, their conversation dwindling. Eventually she blew smoke toward the ceiling and leaned over and kissed him. Her face was taut. 'Are you going to take me to bed?' she said.

'I hope so.'

'You've never been in bed with her, have you Frank?'

'Korky? No, I haven't. I've told you that.' He kept his voice low. 'It hasn't happened and it won't. All that's sorted.'

'Sorted? You sound like her,' she said drily.

They remained where they were and she began to take her clothes off. She did it quickly, almost proficiently. 'Pardon the hurry,' she said. She lay against him wearing only her slip. 'Put your hands against me, Frank,' she demanded. 'Let me feel them feeling me.'

First he stroked her waist and then ran his touch up to her breasts. As they stood against each other she pulled his right hand down between her legs. She rubbed herself blatantly against it and they kissed. 'I don't want to wait any more,' she said. Still holding each other, almost like a slow dance, they went into the shaded bedroom. She pulled back the duvet. 'You know I prefer to do it under the covers. It gives me a feeling of being domesticated.'

They made love. They were familiar now. 'I wouldn't like you to think I was jealous of Korky,' she told him. 'I'm a bit afraid of her, that's all.'

Fourteen

He walked for ten minutes along Notting Hill, the shops like dimly lit caves, his footfalls sounding from the pavement. It had become cold but the sky was pale, peaceful, and the air unmoving. The spring leaves on the beeches shuffled indistinctly above his head. In Kensington Church Street a black taxi loitered like a ghost; traffic lights signalled each other.

His stride was slow, his mind crowded but he was no longer nervous. He wondered about Korky, if she would be home yet. He smiled as he remembered how she had enjoyed the evening. He quietly thought of his wife, Irene: was she lying, still awake perhaps, in the arms of her dependable lover? His mind went back along the night-time streets to Jean, her lone life and her fears. Finally, he wondered about himself. What was he to do?

Kensington Heights was solidly dark apart from Miss Bombazine's window displayed like a large orange ticket. He let himself in and climbed the stairs on his toes. Korky had not come in. Her bed looked neat but lost as it always did when she was not there. John the gerbil was in his night-time box at its foot, engaged in a sleepy wash.

Savage poured himself another drink. He felt safe to do it now. He had drunk a lot that night. Out of habit he wandered to the window with the brandy glass. London was lying low, a blink of moon, appearing, disappearing, reappearing among unhurrying clouds, briefly silver on the roofs and small towers. He turned and pulled the curtains and then, prompted by another, newer, habit, switched on the word processor. The reassuring glow and childish chime greeted him. It was strange how infantile much of it was, the elementary diagrams and their short, basic labels: *Getting Started, Tools, Read Me.* He moved the cursor to *Book,* clicked on it twice and his encyclopaedia appeared on the screen.

At once he saw that Korky had been at work. Often he found her sitting there adding her own fanciful contribution to his basic entries, her poetic additions purloined, occasionally word for word, from travel and topographical books which she obtained from the shop. 'Nobody is going to recognise a few words they wrote years ago,' she had argued.

By now he had reached Flinders. *'Island group, north-east of Tasmania. Named after the explorer Matthew Flinders.'* Korky had added: *'Home of the Cape Barren goose and two hundred people. In 1914–18 they were so cut off the islanders used to club together and pay for a telegram to be sent to them telling them who was winning the First World War.'*

Savage smiled now and, shaking his head, again thought about her. 'You can turn it into a bit better English if you want,' she had insisted. 'But I'll pick out the interesting stuff and put it in after. Those shits in the Cayman Islands, by the way, used to nail live turtles to the decks of their boats to keep them fresh.'

It was two thirty. He finished the brandy, took the glass into the kitchen and washed it under the tap. The extra drink had made him unsteady. He admonished himself as he fumbled with his shoes in the bedroom. His clothes seemed heavy, difficult and oddly shaped, and he pulled on his pyjama jacket inside out. After thinking about changing it he decided not to but, grumbling again, climbed into bed and slept at once and deeply.

Half an hour later Korky returned. She stumbled and grumbled. 'Fucking Freddie,' she told the lift gates at the bottom. 'Or *not*, more like it.' Noisily she opened them and then, realising the hour, hushed herself, and without getting into the lift, closed them again with inebriated softness. Leaning against the wall assisted her ascent of the stairs and the exposed lift shaft was the recipient of her soliloquy. 'Oooh, Lord Plonker, this is a most desirable residence,' she mimicked. 'And, Lady Plonker, so convenient for 'Arrod's.' She made a face on the landing but then carefully steadied herself and smiled knowingly as she went towards the apartment.

She opened the door with excessive caution. It scarcely breathed as it brushed the carpet. She allowed herself a stifled giggle and went on her toes to Savage's bedroom door. It was ajar and, even without applying her ear to the aperture, which she did anyway, his regular breathing could be heard plainly. Good. He was home.

Korky retreated to her own room. She patted the gerbil with her foot which made it snuffle with pleasure. It began to inspect her shoes, continuing to do so when she had taken them off. She went to her window and peered out speculatively. Miss Bombazine had neglected to pull her curtains again. With an anticipatory sigh Korky sat on her bed and watched.

A set of buttocks were in full view, a young man's athletic bum. He was standing legs hard apart in the attitude of a soldier and Miss Bombazine was kneeling in front of him. As Korky watched, jaw slackening, her breath almost arrested, she saw the woman's arms move in a clasping circle around the man, hanging on to him. 'That's it, girl. Give it to him,' muttered Korky. She studied the strong male back then, on the thought, pulled her own pants down, keeping her eyes on the scene, and tapped herself with her thin fingers, quietly at first but with more and more energy. The client opposite half-turned away from Miss Bombazine towards the window. 'Blimey,' Korky sighed aloud. 'What a beauty. And she's getting paid.'

As if the pair had detected her, they both looked towards the window. Miss Bombazine's cheery breasts were lolling from the top of her negligee like enthusiasts hanging over a balcony. Unceremoniously scooping in her bosom Miss Bombazine went to the window and briskly drew the curtains. Korky sighed: 'Spoil sport.'

Suddenly sad in the darkness of her room, she took off the rest of her clothes, dropping them on the floor, at first on top of the gerbil who scuttled from beneath. 'Sorry, John,' she murmured. She sniffed at him. 'If I give you a kiss will you turn into a prince, or a bloke like the one over there?' Something was stopping her getting into bed and decent sleep. Freddie could not handle his drink at the table let alone after, that was certain. So much for him and his desirable properties.

She heard Savage stir in the other room. She sat up attentively, briefly lapsed into her drooping pose, but then straightened with a daring smile. He could only throw her out.

She put a finger to her lips as a warning to herself. She was naked. At first she thought she would go like that but halted and pulled on her long cotton nightdress. She could always say she had been sleepwalking.

Tapping the gerbil with her toe as she left the room she wished him: 'Nighty night.' Then unsteadily she crossed the shadowy floor and, an inch at a time, pushed Savage's door. He was lying on his side facing outwards.

Heart pumping, she eased herself into the opposite side of the bed. Beneath the sheet she could feel his maleness, sense the solid, warm workings of his body, his heart, his breath. She wanted to crush herself into his backside but she stopped, instead lying close but barely touching him. She was near enough. Happily she closed her eyes for sleep.

Both were awakened by the ringing of the apartment doorbell. Savage swiftly sat up in bed as he felt the girl beside him. The bell sounded again. Korky stirred. 'Oh, Savage,' she mumbled. 'What are you doing here?'

He glared and snapped: 'That's it.'

'The doorbell, you mean?'

Muttering he rolled from the bed, pulling his dressing gown over his pyjamas. 'Would you mind going back to your own room,' he said harshly.

She stared around her. 'I must have lost my way.'

'For Christ's sake,' he grunted. The bell ring was repeated. He turned on her. 'Come on, I mean it,' he said.

'You don't want anybody to see,' she suggested with a wry expression. She put her feet on the carpet. 'It might be your Jean.'

Firmly he pushed her out and towards her own room. There were two more sharp spasms from the bell. He shut the door on her and opened the front door. Standing supportively close together on the landing were a nervous-faced man and a woman with a determined stare. Their expressions apart, they were a picture of ordinariness. He was short and stout, half-strangled by his collar. His eyes flapped behind his spectacles. The woman adjusted her hat, her face moving grimly below it.

'Yes?' asked Savage.

The pair looked briefly at each other; then the man, taking responsibility, said: 'We've come for our daughter.'

'Our girl,' reinforced the woman. 'Kathleen. Kathleen Wilson.'

Savage almost fell down on the mat. 'Your . . .'

'Daughter,' finished the man. 'We know she's here.'

'She's only sixteen,' the woman snapped.

Savage could scarcely get the name out. 'Korky?' he whispered.

The man's mouth sagged, his glasses filled with bewilderment.

'Korky?' he managed to enquire. 'Who is Korky?'

Fifteen

'She even made up a new name,' he said to Jean. Again he shook his head. 'Korky.'

'So she wanted a new life.' Jean did not care. 'They all do. That's why they scarper. Kill off dad, dispose of mum, bring in wicked stepfather, call yourself Korky.'

He fingered through the magazine spread on her ceramic table. 'And they get all the attention,' she added still bitterly. She blew a think skein of smoke then doused the cigarette. 'All those kids take the easy road. They don't need to work, they don't have to get up in the morning, they chuck all responsibility.' She looked straight at him. 'They *use* people.'

'It's not exactly a comfortable life,' he pointed out. He pictured the back yard of Safeways, with the lumped figures under the trailer on that windy night but she dismissed the objection. 'Not for you and me it wouldn't be,' she said. She had been pouring drinks. 'But they can put up with a bit of cold and hardship. They're young. The old ones, the tramps and the bagwomen, they've got it worked out. They hunt alone. You get better pickings like that. And some privacy. But the kids all stick together in packs. You've seen them. Slinking around together or shouting at each other as if they've got a sort of madness.'

She faced him as though she had decided she might as

well tell him. 'Her parents came to the nick,' she said. 'They'd been searching.'

'And somebody told them where they could find her.'

'Yes, me.' Her tone became crisp. 'I'm a copper. Remember? I couldn't not tell them. They brought a photograph of her. The desk sergeant knew she'd been around. I propelled them in your direction. I couldn't do anything else.'

'No,' said Savage in a dull voice. 'I suppose not.'

She put the drinks on the table. They were both drinking Scotch. 'Anyway, now she's gone home sweet home with mummy and daddy,' she said. Her eyes came up acusingly. 'Do you want to hear about *my* problems?'

Savage turned his glance sharply. 'Brendan?' he said.

'Yes, Brendan,' she retorted. 'Are you interested?'

'Of course I'm interested.'

'That's one thing with your little Korky gone. At least I can come around to see you.'

'She wasn't my Korky. She was her own person.'

Jean said sharply: 'I don't want to talk about her any longer if you don't mind.'

'All right. She's gone. Finished, as far as I'm concerned.'

'You wanted to get shot of her.' She got up and took short strides about the carpet holding her drink at her waist. 'There's been an objection to Brendan's parole,' she said. 'I'm hoping to God it's sustained. Keep that bugger inside for a while.'

'Who objected?'

'I don't know. It wasn't me although, shit, I'd have done it like a flash. There are plenty of people who would rather he was the other side of the bars. Someone has put their spoke in.' She gave a grim smile. 'Whoever it is, is going to have to watch out when he does get out. I know how they feel.'

He telephoned her three times over the next few days but there was no answer. Then he walked to Westbourne Grove in the late afternoon thinking he might call at the flat. As he approached he saw her coming from the lower door accompanied by a man. They were quarrelling. They walked to a car and were still arguing across the roof as the man unlocked it. They got in. She slammed her door and the car drove jerkily away into the traffic. Savage went home.

'But Korky was going to teach us to cheat at cards,' complained Wilhelmina. 'And help me at the seances.'

The eyes of the snow-haired Miss Weiz and the thin-necked Miss Cotton trembled. 'And now she's gone,' they said together.

The trio were ranged in his doorway. Already a dusting of talcum powder was lying on the doormat. Mr Prentice, of the metallic teeth, appeared on the stairway as if late for a rendezvous. 'We said eleven,' Wilhelmina admonished him. They then entered the flat without invitation, almost hustling Savage aside, Wilhelmina in the van, fanning out as soon as they were within as though performing a reconnoitre raid. With no further words they surveyed the apartment, one looking one way one another, and Miss Cotton tottering across and bending like a bird to peer into what had been Korky's room. Mr Prentice remained standing awkwardly and silently. 'She's gone,' concluded Wilhelmina when they had clustered again. 'There's little doubt about that.'

'There's *no* doubt at all,' Savage pointed out patiently. He realised they were regarding him accusingly. 'Her parents turned up and she went back home with them.'

'Not without a fight I imagine,' said Miss Weiz stoutly. 'She wouldn't.'

'How do you *know* they were her parents?' demanded Miss Cotton. 'They could have been imposters.'

'She *had* no parents,' put in Wilhelmina loftily. 'Only a naughty stepfather.'

'She told us,' confirmed Miss Cotton folding her arms in front of him. 'And we believe her.'

'Implicitly,' said Miss Weiz.

'Implicitly,' said Wilhelmina, last for once. Mr Prentice showed his silent teeth.

'Ladies,' responded Savage patiently. He spread his hands. 'I can assure you that nobody *could* abduct Korky. Nobody would take her away without her consent. It's not possible.' As though they thought he might be speaking for an extended time, the trio, one after another, sat down to listen. All three fitted easily on the sofa. They remained upright, still interrogative. Mr Prentice stood at ease behind them. Wilhelmina, in the centre, shifted her legs and loosed another shower of talc. None of the ladies seemed to believe him.

'She put up no resistance?' asked Wilhelmina.

'No resistance?' echoed Miss Cotton and Miss Weiz as one.

Savage sighed. 'She did not want to go at first,' he said. 'But she knew very well that these people were her mother and father, they had done her no harm . . .'

'Why then did she leave home in the first place?' demanded Wilhelmina. She seemed pleased with the interruption and further stiffened her back. Miss Cotton clapped her hands and Miss Weiz joined in. Mr Prentice nodded as if it were getting beyond him.

'Yes, why?' asked Miss Cotton.

'I don't know,' Savage admitted. 'It seems it was not

for the reasons she originally gave. She made a lot of things up, I'm afraid.' His eyes travelled along the three implacable expressions. He ignored Mr Prentice. 'It seems that her name is not even Korky,' he told them helplessly.

'Nonsense!' they hooted together.

'What *utter* rubbish,' added Wilhelmina vehemently. 'Of course her name is Korky. We *all* know that.'

Miss Cotton and Miss Weiz agreed so vigorously he had a momentary horror of their heads falling off.

'All right, all right,' said Savage spreading his hands. 'She'll always be Korky to me as well.'

'Are you sad?' asked Miss Weiz a little timidly.

'Yes, I am.'

'You wanted her to go,' pointed out Miss Cotton but with no aggression. Wilhelmina, taking a respite, only nodded. Miss Cotton pursued: 'You *wanted* to be by yourself. But it's miserable by yourself. We know.'

The trio of heads wagged. Mr Prentice joined them belatedly. Savage sighed. 'I felt that it was not right that she should live here, that's all. In the first place I came here because I needed the privacy, the isolation.'

'You went potty at one time, didn't you?' enquired Wilhelmina.

'Potty,' echoed the others.

Savage swallowed. 'I was psychologically ill,' he pointed out as calmly as he could. 'I had been wounded in the army and some other men had been killed and it upset me. That was all.' He glanced at Mr Prentice who nodded understandingly.

'Did it hurt?' asked Miss Weiz with new interest. 'Being shot?'

'It always hurts,' said Mr Prentice, the first words he had spoken.

224

Savage had to smile. 'It did a bit,' he said. 'And later I wanted time to be by myself and to write. Then Korky arrived. She was very ill, as you know, but when she recovered and got a job and more or less sorted herself out we had an agreement that she would find somewhere else to live.'

'You were not in love then?' Disbelief strained Wilhelmina's face.

Savage dropped his head in his hands. He was walking up and down in front of them like a losing lawyer with a jury. 'No, there was nothing, I promise you,' he said. 'My God, I'm forty-three, she's seventeen, or sixteen, I'm not sure. We had nothing in common like that. I was like her father.'

'Korky already had a father,' pointed out Miss Cotton. She glanced at the others for approval of her astuteness and they nodded.

'I didn't know that. No one knew, except Korky.'

'Fancy her father refusing to call her Korky,' mused Miss Weiz sadly. 'It's such a jovial name.'

'It suited her,' asserted Wilhelmina.

'It did,' confirmed the others.

They appeared to be in danger of running out of words. Wilhemina recovered. 'So she went of her own free will?' Her friends regarded her gratefully.

'Absolutely. Her father pleaded with her and her mother cried buckets. I had to tell her that I thought she should go.'

'Which is what you wanted in the first place,' accused Miss Cotton. She picked out Wilhelmina who looked at Miss Weiz who completed the circuit.

'I had such plans for her,' mumbled Wilhelmina privately. 'Her skin was quite ethereal.'

'Whatever. She's gone home to Swindon and I think

it's the right thing,' said Savage. 'I am sad, as I told you. I was very fond of her. But, in the long run, I don't think she should have lived here indefinitely. Perhaps in a couple of years she'll come back and live in London. Properly.'

Miss Weiz asked: 'Will you marry her *then*?' She giggled and the others, after a moment's proprietary sternness, giggled too.

'Ladies,' he said retaining his patience. 'It's very good of you to be so concerned but I think that is unlikely. Now, if you'll excuse me, I have work to do.'

They knew an ultimatum when they heard it and together they rose. Wilhelmina banged at her skirt and a small avalanche of white descended on to the carpet. None of them noticed. 'You *do* have another lady,' mentioned Wilhelmina.

'We've seen her,' said Miss Weiz tightly.

Miss Cotton appeared put out that she had been left behind. 'Several times,' she said sulkily. 'Since Korky's been gone.'

'Yes, yes,' nodded Savage. He was ushering them towards the door. 'She's a police lady I know.'

'Does she know you've got a gun?' said Wilhelmina. Savage was speechless. Mr Prentice appeared to be awaiting a cue.

'*We* were quite shocked and afraid,' said Miss Cotton primly.

'Afraid,' confirmed Miss Weiz. 'And shocked.'

Savage tried to recover. 'There's no need,' he said his shoulders drooping. 'It doesn't work. It's a souvenir.'

'There,' said Mr Prentice.

Wilhelmina pushed him forward. 'We'd like to see it,' she suggested sombrely. 'That's why we brought Mr Prentice. He was a soldier.'

'Royal Engineers,' Mr Prentice confirmed as if he thought Savage might have forgotten. 'Explosives.'

'We've never seen a gun,' said Miss Cotton.

'Never,' said Miss Weiz in a deprived way.

Grimly he turned and went towards his bedroom. They followed him and stood clutched together apprehensively around the door. Mr Prentice came to attention, his chin rose expectantly. Savage took the submachine gun from below the bed and held it in a professional grip which made them back away. They hesitated, regarding him unsurely. 'Here,' he said holding it out. 'It's harmless. The magazine . . .' He tapped it. '. . . Is empty.' He handed the weapon to Mr Prentice who pretended to look at it professionally. Timidly Wilhelmina put out her hands to take it from him. 'It's jolly weighty,' she said trying to hold it. She handed it first to Miss Cotton who made a strained face. Miss Weiz almost dropped it. 'We've never seen a gun,' repeated Wilhelmina.

'Only on television,' said Miss Weiz.

'And then they don't look real,' said Miss Cotton.

'Nor do the people being shot,' objected Miss Weiz. 'Except on the news.'

'I saw enough guns,' said Mr Prentice sombrely. He glanced at Savage as if for support.

'So did Mr Belfont,' put in Wilhelmina with a frown. 'Before he went to Antwerp. To die.' She blinked and made an effort to say something. 'I hope Korky is still alive.'

Savage opened his mouth to protest. Then, to his huge relief the telephone rang. They politely moved towards the main door and went out twittering farewells. Mr Prentice gave him a comradely look. He closed the door on them. Still with the gun in his grasp, he answered the telephone. 'Please, hello,' said an old man's voice. 'Is Rosamunde at home please?'

'Rosamunde,' said Savage flatly. It was not a question.

'Yes, this is right? Rosamunde Von Fokker.'

Savage sighed. 'She has gone away,' he answered.

The dim-windowed shop was in a Bloomsbury alleyway where the sun marked slowly mobile triangles on the paving slabs. There was a mauve-tiled Victorian public house on one corner and a patisserie opposite. Mr Furtwangler was awaiting him. He appeared nervous but Savage thought he probably always was. He had a bookshop stoop and a swathe of speckled baldness running over his head between two tufted growths of grey springy hair which he kept attempting to push flat; he beamed apprehensively over his glasses and thrust his hands deep, as though he were hiding them, into the pockets of a collapsed cardigan. His white knuckles showed through the sagging wool.

'Thank you sir, so much,' he enthused taking the pile of books from Savage. 'I did not know so many she had borrowed.' He shuffled around as though hoping to put the volumes in some spare place in the chaotically piled shop but he failed to find one. Instead he lowered them to the dusty floor among other piles placed about like the footings on a building site. 'But she was so hard studying for her degree.'

Mr Furtwangler's handshake was soft and warm. Once more he peered with mild impatience around the cluttered shop. There were narrow trenches between the deep shelves. 'I must ask you to sit,' he fussed. There was a chair, low, wide, round-backed, dusty and worn, like Mr Furtwangler himself, laden with old catalogues. The bookseller swept them to the floor with an abrupt aggression, as if he had long wanted to do it, then regarded the scattered heap shamefacedly and tried to make amends by gathering them gently together with the side of his foot. 'Please sit,' he invited spreading his hand towards the chair.

'I could have stood,' said Savage taking it. The old man, now himself marooned, hovered without a seat. Abandoning all restraint he flung another pile of grime-clogged papers from a second, upright chair and after testing its safety with both hands, sat down.

'I hope they are not important,' said Savage nodding at the scattered journals, their dust rising like a mild protest.

'Old things only,' said Mr Furtwangler disdainfully but treating the debris to a glance, again touched with regret, before abandoning sentiment and thrusting his pale hands once more deep down into his cardigan. He could leave the question no longer. 'Where is Rosamunde gone?' he asked. His bespectacled eyes moved like two fish through two bowls towards Savage. '*Why* is she gone?'

Savage needed to proceed carefully. 'You knew her as Rosamunde Von Fokker?'

'Yes, yes, of course. That is her name but she maybe did not use the Von. She was a modest girl.'

'You were happy with her working here?'

'Oh, indeed, sir. She brought the sunbeams into this dark hole.' He peered about him as though trying to pierce the gloom. Then he added sadly: 'I am alone without her.'

Savage nodded. 'I understand. Unfortunately she has had to go away.'

'Back to Germany?'

'Yes, home. Her mother is ill and she has to nurse her.'

'She is a saintly girl. And her English is so excellent.'

'Yes, I suppose it is.'

Mr Furtwangler sighed. 'All I could find was the telephone number. You are ... a ...' He studied Savage's age. 'A ... friend?'

'Yes. She rented a room from me.'

'I did not pay her much money. I am ashamed. But she seemed to like to be here. It is not so busy and she could study for her PhD.'

'Yes,' agreed Savage solidly.

'*The Fantasy and Reality of Islands*,' recited Mr Furtwangler with a nostalgic sigh. *'Their literature, in fact and fiction, their peoples and communications and economies and the erosion of their isolation in the twentieth century.'*

'Yes.'

'She is so clever. I hope her mother will be well.'

'It's going to be a long illness, I'm sorry to say.'

'Ah, that is sad.' He brightened a fraction. 'But maybe she will die and then Rosamunde can come back. Your poor Prince Edward? He will miss her.'

'Oh ... will he?' Savage attempted to gather some words. 'Oh yes, Prince Edward. *That* Prince Edward. He certainly will. He probably has already.'

'Well, there is nothing to be done.' Sighing, the old man took his hands from his cardigan and folded them primly in his lap. 'But it is unhappy for me.' He leaned forward confidentially. 'It is crazy, I know, to say this because I am almost eighty and I was married for forty years before my wife passed away. But I was jealous of your Prince Edward.' His voice became a shy whisper. 'I was a little in love with her.'

'I understand,' said Savage.

He walked over to the window and the view as ever made

him pause, his familiar but changing prospect of London. Below him now were the full, summer heads of the trees, the sky was pale and still, the sun opaque. Airliners dropped in their unending crocodile towards Heathrow. Below him he could see Tomelty in a green pullover sweeping the pavement outside the main entrance, his grey hair like a button. As Savage watched, a man walked across the street and approached him. Tomelty straightened and pointed upwards. The visitor turned and made for the side entrance. Savage waited and two minutes later his doorbell rang. Stonily he opened it. It was a youngish, strained-looking man, rimless glasses glistening. His ginger sports jacket was too small although he was slight except for a pot stomach under a pullover of mixed colours. His wrists projected inches from the sleeves. 'Is this the address for Anna Zubber?' he enquired. 'It's the flat number she left.'

'Who,' asked Savage although he already knew, 'is Anna Zubber?'

The young man seemed astonished. 'The wife of Charlie Zubber,' he said as though everyone must know Charlie Zubber. He detected that Savage did not. 'Of Excess Energy ... the band.'

'And. . . ?'

'I work for Brutton's, the publishers. It's about the encyclopaedia she is compiling.'

'You'd better come in,' groaned Savage opening the door and stepping aside. The young man looked at him oddly and said an uncertain 'Thank you,' as he went into the apartment.

'So *this* is where Anne Zubber lives,' he said deeply when he had sat down. He blinked about as though trying to detect some trace of her. 'When she's in London.'

'Lived,' corrected Savage.

'Oh, she's gone away?' said the man. Disappointment creased his face. 'I wondered why she never turned up any more.'

'What is your name?' asked Savage attempting to get something straight. 'Mine's Frank Savage.'

With a little confusion the visitor rose and his bony arm emerged, almost hydraulically from his threadbare sleeve. 'I'm Stephen Stevens,' he said, then with an automatic apology: 'It really is. One with a *ph*, the second with a *v*. My father thought he was clever.'

'Well, Mr Stevens, I have to tell you that if you're looking for the young lady I think you're looking for her name is not Anna . . . what-was-it?'

'Zubber,' provided Mr Stevens. Disbelief now filled his spectacles. 'It's not?'

'She's Kathleen Wilson, otherwise known as Korky, otherwise known as Rosamunde Von Fokker . . .'

'. . . Otherwise known as Anna Zubber,' mumbled Stephen Stevens. 'Just my luck.'

'She told you she lived here?'

Embarrassment caused hesitation. Then he said: 'Well, quite truthfully, not actually. You see we met in a coffee bar near the British Museum, near my office. I was chatting to another chap in publishing and she . . . well . . .'

'Picked you up.'

'Well, I wouldn't like to claim that. She joined in the conversation.' He looked timidly at Savage but bravely enquired: 'May I ask what your relationship to Miss . . . Wilson, wasn't it . . . ?'

'I'm her uncle.' He realised how adeptly he had taken to romancing. 'Her mother is my sister.'

'And she stayed here with you.' Again he surveyed the

apartment, dwelling a moment on the half-open doors to the bedrooms.

'Temporarily. She's gone home to Swindon.'

'Swindon?' Disillusion congested the changing face. 'Swindon? She said she lived in New York.'

'Perhaps you misheard her.'

'I didn't mishear her saying that she was Anna Zubber, wife of Charlie Zubber . . .' His voice trailed.

'Of Excess Charges,' provided Savage.

'Energy. The band is called Excess Energy,' corrected Stevens. 'Charlie Zubber is a pop icon.' He looked up as if hopeful of salvaging something, anything, some small genuine item. 'And she is *not* writing a thesis on islands, I take it, nor planning to publish an encyclopaedia?' His sleeves retreated up his arms as thought backing away from the truth. 'I even suggested a title for her thesis. *The Fantasy and Reality of Islands: Their literature, in fact and fiction, their peoples and communications and economies and the erosion of their isolation in the twentieth century.*'

'I wondered who came up with that,' said Savage.

The visitor was pleased. 'She told you about it?'

'No, someone else did. But she was partly correct. She was, in fact, putting together an encyclopaedia concerned with islands. In fact, we were both working on it.'

'Ah, co-authors.'

'For the moment I am carrying on alone.'

'I told her the firm I'm with might be interested in publishing it,' related the young man, his eyes low but rising guardedly. 'Which is true. We are. No one has ever done a book like that.'

'I know. Well, perhaps I can send it to you when it's ready in a few years.'

'Please do,' said Stevens only a little taken aback. 'I do

quite a lot of research at the British Museum Reading Room and I introduced Anna ... well ...'

'Korky,' provided Savage. 'Or Anna if you prefer.'

A small blush provided a dab of colour to the pallid skin. 'Korky?' He seemed to have to rouse himself from the resultant reverie. 'I introduced her to the Museum Reading Room and I have to confess that I noted her address on the application form.' The blush spread. There was moisture on the upper lip. 'And I kept ... stole ... the spare copy of her application photograph.'

Savage said nothing. Rising, Stevens felt in his pocket and took out a prim wallet. 'This is it,' he said. He produced a black and white picture of a straight-faced Korky. 'That's her,' confirmed Savage. 'Anna Zubber.'

The young man remained standing, and embarrassed. 'Well, I'd better be off,' he said with real sadness. 'If she's not here, I can't think that I shall ever see her again.'

His hydraulic arm shot out fiercely and they shook hands. 'She won't be back, will she?' he asked forlornly. 'In London.'

'I doubt it. She's gone home to marry,' lied Savage easily again. 'A tax inspector.'

He thought Stephen Stevens was going to cry. The young man sniffed so hard his nostrils squeezed. Savage could not resist patting his shoulder as he made towards the door. 'I'll be in touch with you at ...'

'Brutton's,' prompted Stevens.

Savage let him out and followed him on to the landing. 'The encyclopaedia should be finished in a few years. The first draft.'

'Please do,' sniffed Stevens. He ignored the lift and went to the top of the stairs. He looked down the stairwell and Savage thought he might be considering a final jump but he then rushed down out of sight around the bend in the stairs. Savage heard him trip at the bottom and pick himself up with a sob.

Savage returned to the room. He sat on the sofa and put his head in his hands. 'Anna Zubber,' he murmured. 'Where are you now?' He allowed himself a small smile. '*Who* are you now?'

Sixteen

Day after day, like a willing dog, he continued with his work. Who, he asked himself increasingly, would want to read it? He had to make himself sit down before the word processor and it took a distinct effort to open it; its chimed greeting sounded tinny and the laughing automatic face became a mocking caricature. The keys fixed him with their banked blank stares, daring him to touch them with a come-and-get-us insolence; put your fingers on us if you dare, you poor solitary sap. Stone-faced, he went through the everyday geographical motions, lost for words, wondering what she was doing, who she was with.

'*Formosa*,' he tapped. '*Large island off the mainland of China also known as Taiwan and as Nationalist China following the retreat there in 1949 of the Chiang Kai-shek government during the war with the Communists. . .*'

He regarded the screen with distaste. Who needed islands anyway? Perhaps the distraught Stephen Stevens would get it published in the hope that somehow it would bring Anna Zubber back to him.

After only a few minutes Savage got up from the word processor and made coffee, the succour sought by word-bound writers. Studying its liquid swirling muddily in the mug he was tempted to reach for the Scotch and pour a measure into it. The telephone rang. It was his wife.

'Frank,' she said. 'Good news.'

'I could use some.'

'What's the matter?'

'Nothing that won't right itself.' He wished he had sounded softer. He could sense her back off. 'I'm sorry,' he said quietly. She said: 'You sound lonely, Frank.'

'That's what I wanted to be, remember?'

'Now you're sorry.' She waited, then made the offer: 'Do you want me to come to London?'

He knew she meant it. 'Thanks, Irene,' he said. 'You're lovely.'

'I will if you like.'

'No. I wouldn't drag you here. What was the good news?'

He sensed her hurt but she gathered herself. 'Yesterday,' she said. 'I went down to our house.' She amended it. 'The house. I was in Southampton with Graham and I went in on the way back. Just to see if the place was all right and to pick up any letters.'

'That's . . . your fiancé.'

'Yes. Fiancé sounds a bit odd, doesn't it, second time around. But that's him. It's going to be more than a year, anyway.'

'Oh, right,' he said vaguely. 'Yes, it will be, I suppose.'

'The point was I went into Askard's, the estate agents, and they said they thought they had a buyer. It's a couple of chaps, Jehovah's Witnesses.'

Savage blinked. 'I saw them.'

'You did?' He detected her concern. She still thought he hallucinated.

'That day when you and I were both there, in January. When you had gone this pair – it has to be them – turned up and wanted me to help them change the world. I didn't have time just then.'

She laughed but cautiously. 'How strange. Anyway

they want the house.' There was a silence before she said: 'I really enjoyed our lunch, Frank. It was nice to be together again, even for a while. And what about the odd-bod girl who arrived. The one at the next table. Telling us all her troubles. Remember her?'

'I'll never forget her,' he said.

He thought she was going to make a comment or ask him a question but instead, after another pause, she said: 'According to the agents they're not quibbling about the price. They'll pay the full ninety thousand.' Her voice became subdued. 'Once it's all done and the house is sold there won't be anything else remaining. Nothing left of us. Except a few certificates in a file somewhere.'

'I'm sorry, Irene.'

'So am I. It's terrible when something just vanishes, disappears.'

They said goodbye and he walked a few moody paces to the window and looked out on the summer day, dull and dozy. There was the regular airliner in the background sky. When he opened the window a puff of warm air came in; the summer thickness of the trees muted the traffic sounds.

How odd that the apartment and its silence should be getting to him now. For two weeks, since Korky had gone, he had taken to walking, morning and afternoon, in between his spasms of forced work. Once he had seen a girl squatting with a small tribe of aimless youths on the grass of Holland Park, shouting bad advice to a class of amazed infants crocodiling with a teacher up the straight path. At a distance she had looked like Korky, lean, long-haired and ash-skinned, but as he neared he saw, to his relief and his disappointment, that it was not.

Now, as he went out, he locked the apartment door with a peevish turn of the key. As he tugged it out he turned and saw Miss Bombazine coming along the corridor from her flat. For someone in a young woman's business she waddled in a strangely old-fashioned way. 'She's taken off, I hear,' she said.

'Yes, her parents turned up. She's gone home with them.'

'Just like you wanted.'

She was going to take the lift but instead they walked down the stairs together. 'My poor hip's been giving me murder,' Miss Bombazine grumbled. She was in her customary black but summer-style with a flowered scarf and hat. Her hair looked as if it had been hurriedly crammed into the hat. 'In this job an achy hip is bad news,' she said.

They walked out of the apartments and down Kensington Church Street. 'Still, I'm off to an easy one now,' she told him with a change of tone. 'I go and see him a couple of times a month, poor old bugger. He's eighty so it's not physical except I have to take my clothes off. He likes me to read him children's stories. *Peter Rabbit* is his favourite. He sits in bed like a little boy, me sitting there starkers. It's a funny life.'

At the junction with the High Street they met Freddie Spencer-Hughes wheeling his red racing bicycle. Savage realised he did not know Miss Bombazine's real surname but she was accustomed to saving people embarrassment and she waved a big arm which hailed a taxi and bid them farewell in the same pole-axe movement. The taxi halted twenty yards along the road and she puffed after it.

'She's a lady of the night,' Freddie informed him as they watched her formidable backside fill the doorway of the cab. 'Did you know that?'

'She's quiet about it,' said Savage.

'Ideal neighbour,' observed Freddie professionally. He

pushed his bicycle pensively and then his voice altered, rising to a poetic flurry. '*The night is silent when you have gone,*' he recited.

'Who said that?'

'I did,' responded Freddie with a pleased sadness. 'I made it up. I do, you know.'

Together they began to walk towards the park. 'I've got a minute,' the youth told him as he wheeled the bike. 'I needed to get out of the office to cool down. I might just ride off into the bloody sunset. Some people treat us as if we were racketeers. I actually told one couple to . . . well, piss off.' He glanced gingerly at Savage as though he did not expect to be believed. 'I'm not sure they heard me,' he admitted. 'But I think they got the gist of it because that's exactly what they did. I've become quite down-market.'

'You've changed,' Savage told him.

'Since Korky,' conceded Freddie. He shoved his bike testily. 'I certainly have. I used to wring my hands and bow and scrape with the best of them. Now, I'm different. I feel like wringing their necks.' He stopped pushing and regarded Savage. 'Do you think she'll ever come back?' he asked.

Savage shrugged but did not answer. 'It seems she knew everybody,' was all he said. 'People keep turning up and asking for her. All the time I'm amazed.'

'She was different. To anybody,' said Freddie.

'Different,' agreed Savage. 'Altogether.'

'That's why I've started writing verse.' He looked at his watch. 'Cooling-off time over,' he sniffed. 'I'll have to go back to the nerds.' They shook hands at the park gate and Freddie turned. He halted after a few paces. 'Your six months is up soon, I think, Mr Savage,' he called. 'End of next month.'

'That's right,' returned Savage. 'I don't think I'll be staying.'

Freddie was astonished. 'You won't? Where will you go?'

'Formosa,' Savage answered but without turning. He walked on. 'Or somewhere.'

He was certain that Jean had a new lover. Their times together dwindled and then stopped. She told him she was working. Dutifully he telephoned her but often he could get no reply. Once she answered but she was laughing drunk and there were voices in the room. Twice a man answered almost angrily. Savage put the phone down. According to Mr Kostelanetz her new man – perhaps the man he had seen her quarrelling with – was a solicitor, married but free most nights. Savage wondered how a married solicitor got nights off. It did not worry him. There were no regrets. It never had been right.

Now he was as alone as he ever had been, as much as he had required to be. He worked relentlessly as the summer continued outside his window and every day he went for two long walks. He had reached: '*Georgia (South), Antarctic Dependency of the Falkland Islands, Capital Grytviken Population: seasonal. . .*'

Grytviken, even South Georgia, could scarcely be emptier, more silent, than his lofty room. Scientists, sailors and whalers went to South Georgia; the winds blew, the snow shifted, there were months of night followed by months of day. Here everything was the same, every morning, every noonday, every night. Just as he had planned it. His island. Nowhere was more remote than Kensington Heights.

'Good morning, Crusoe,' he greeted himself caustically

in the shaving mirror. 'How is Friday today?' But there was no Friday. He almost crept up on the word processor; sometimes when he opened it he felt he would scarcely care if it had all gone, been wiped away, vanished.

Bertie Maddison invited him to go to the Wigmore Hall. 'Cello recital,' he said. He had intended to remain at the door of the apartment because he did not want to interrupt Savage's work. 'Interrupt all you like,' invited Savage beckoning him in. 'I'm desperate for interruption, believe me. Anything.'

'It won't be much good,' forecast Bertie glumly. 'They're giving the tickets away. Some Chilean git who thinks he can scrape out a bit of Debussy.' He eyed Savage with a sort of warning. 'Mrs Maddison will be accompanying us but she will not, I hope, cause any trouble. The management have given her a last chance.'

On the evening they went to the recital Mrs Maddison had been at the sherry and her husband eyed her warily. 'One can only hope for the best,' he whispered to Savage as his wife stumbled over the entrance steps.

They sat two-thirds of the way to the back. Despite the free distribution of tickets the hall was scarcely half-full. By his downcast manner and shabby aspect the soloist appeared not to expect much more. His black, brimming eyes cowered between overhung eyebrows and sagging moustache. Furtively they searched the room as though hoping to fix on a sympathetic face. There was no introduction. He sat down and after a few coughs began to play.

'I don't know why he needs to cough,' Mrs Maddison boomed almost as soon as the recital had commenced. 'It's not as if he's sodding singing.'

'Watch it,' warned her husband leaning over Savage to

whisper. Savage was seated between them, an arrangement insisted upon by both Maddisons so that he represented a frontier, which still did not preclude sudden and sharp exchanges.

'Watch what?' she responded staring belligerently around Savage's neck as he kept his face solidly to the front.

'Watch your tongue,' whispered Maddison but not so softly as before. 'You know what they said.'

'See if I care,' she sniffed. 'They can stuff this place, and this bloke.' The sniff was profound; even the soloist looked up. Stoically he played on but as if he had just arrived by air and had travelled a long distance, economy. The opening piece was acknowledged with cautious applause, but his second item, which he announced in contorted English, made the audience restive. The instrument droned on. 'He's nodding off,' announced Mrs Maddison with a sort of triumph. 'Look, he's going to kip.' The musician certainly appeared to be lolling over his instrument, holding on to the notes as though every movement of the bow might be his last.

People began to shift and to mutter and, knowing what might follow, Maddison leaned behind Savage in an attempt to soothe his wife. 'It's bollocks,' she complained. Unable to restrain herself, she bawled: 'It's bollocks!'

Two attendants of forceful demeanour, who had been lurking, appeared on tiptoe, shifted some flustered members of the audience and bodily lifted Mrs Maddison from the seat as she bawled.

'I suppose we'd better go with her,' sighed Maddison. 'They might drop her on her head.'

Savage rose with him. The soloist continued to dream and drone; Maddison directed an oddly apologetic bow towards him and reprised it for the benefit of those sitting near. Savage, shuffling out, found himself bowing also. When they got to the back of the hall Mrs Maddison had already been ejected and as they were going out she was attempting to claw her way through into the foyer bellowing: 'I'll sue this fucking tuneless place!'

A policeman arrived and she swung her fist at him. He retreated prudently and called for help on his radio. 'Another night in the pokey,' forecast Maddison gloomily.

They went to Marylebone police station with her. Her husband privately suggested that she should be placed in a cell until she had quietened. She was. 'It would be murder trying to get her home,' he groaned to Savage. 'A couple of hours and she may have run out of steam. Let's have a drink somewhere.'

In silence they walked to the nearest corner. 'The Hope Abandoned,' read Maddison surveying the pub sign.

'How often does she get like that?' enquired Savage when they were at the bar.

'Now and again,' sighed Maddison. 'When the sherry bottle's full.' He reached behind him for a stool, pulled it up and levered himself upon it. 'I'm afraid she's always a risk. And musically she's very critical, as you can appreciate.'

'Yes, she seems to be.'

Maddison became pensive. 'You see she could *play* once,' he said. 'Piano, violin, oboe. Multi-talented. Sang a bit too. But there was no money. Her father even sold her drums. Understandably she became bitter.' He regarded Savage with curiosity. 'I envy your peace and quiet,' he said.

Savage grimaced. 'I've got too much of it at the moment.'

'Can't get used to the girl being gone, I expect. She was lively, there's no doubting that. Will she come back?'

'I doubt it. Even if she did I don't think I ought to let her stay. It wasn't right, the situation, and now she's gone it's better it should remain like that.'

'Are you going to continue in the flat?' asked Maddison with a hint of mansion-block intuition.

'I think I'll be moving out,' Savage said. 'I've got to go somewhere else.'

'Where's that?'

'No idea. I'll find a place.' He laughed quietly. 'I thought I could sit silent and safe up there on the top of Kensington Heights. I wanted isolation. But the world came in under the door.'

'It's apt to,' nodded Maddison as if it were stating the obvious. 'There's no hiding place. I used to be a purser, you know, in the days when they had pursers on aeroplanes. The old propellor jobs. I had lady friends in half the countries of the world. And, what do I do? I end up with my wife.' He glanced at the clock above the bar. 'We'd better go and see when they'll be ready to bail her,' he said. He made an embarrassed grimace. 'She's all I've got.'

Standing again at the window he saw Mr Kostelanetz crossing the street. Even from six floors up Mr Kostelanetz was readily recognisable. The word processor was still smugly whirring. He had reached Guadeloupe. He turned if off and waited. The lift coughed and rattled as it ascended. The gates scraped open and crashed closed. His doorbell rang.

As it was June Mr Kostelanetz had replaced his powerful overcoat with a fawn jacket that was faintly luminous and gave a darker intensity to his skin. He came in and his voluminous eyes scanned the apartment as if to make sure it was the same place. 'So you are going somewhere away,' he said falling back bulkily on the sofa. His brow was glistening. As if acting on information he put his hand between the cushion and the arm and brought out a morsel of biscuit, balanced it on the end of his finger and appeared about to eat it. 'That's gerbil food,' said Savage.

Mr Kostelanetz did not seem incommoded but lowered the finger. 'It is because I have been poor,' he said, his doleful eyes clouding further at the memory. 'A refugee. Nothing to eat. We never wasted one scrap even something like ... where does this gerbil grow? It is like corn?'

'Something like that,' nodded Savage not inclined to correct him. 'Would you like a drink or some coffee?'

The large man studied the watch on his hairy wrist. It was strapped to the widest extent. 'Too early for one, too late for the other,' he decided. 'But nearer to a drink, maybe.'

Savage went into the kitchen. 'I've got whisky,' he called. 'And some wine, red or white . . .'

'Whisky is good,' returned Kostelanetz. 'How long is she gone now? One month?'

'Five weeks,' corrected Savage from the kitchen. He brought in the glasses. 'I'm getting accustomed to some calm again.'

'But you're leaving; the agent boy, Freddie, tells me you want to go. End of the month.' As if to wish him well on his journey Mr Kostelanetz raised his glass a centimetre. 'And where is the place you are going to?'

Savage responded with a tip of his glass. 'I'm not sure yet.'

'But anyway you will go?'

'Yes. I'm grateful to you for letting me live here. It was just what I needed. It's given me time to pull myself together.'

'After your wounding,' said Mr Kostelanetz. 'For your country.' Sadly he shook his head. 'I would not like to be a soldier now. I would not like to be a spy. It is all right, fair enough, when you know why you are fighting or spying, but now everything is different. No soldier and no spy can be sure any more.'

Savage said: 'I think I ought to go. I feel all right now.'

Mr Kostelanetz nodded his large head. The ends of his moustache bounced. 'She gave you help, this Korky.'

'She helped,' admitted Savage carefully. 'We helped each other.'

'So now you will go off to see the world.'

Savage said: 'I've been writing about islands, as you know, and I think it would not be a bad idea if I went to visit some of them. Maybe I'll go on a cruise.'

'A cruise? Ah, that would be nice. Dancing with all the grey ladies, doing the bingo. No, it is the *tango*. And playing the bingo. And floating on the wet sea. Very nice.' Again he nodded heavily.

'It was just an idea,' answered Savage defensively.

'But you must be doing something,' advised Mr Kostelanetz. 'A man must. That is why I operate, Mr Savage. I am always operating on some operation, having some interest in some thing.' He brightened. 'You could go to Tahiti and see the girls dancing with the tits.' To Savage's surprise he rose from the sofa and performed a clumsy sway, cupping his hands across his chest. 'La, la, la,' he half-sang. 'Like that, you know, showing all they got.'

Savage laughed. 'You have some good ideas, Mr

Kostelanetz,' he said. His guest had fallen, a little short of breath, back on to the sofa.

'I am always big on some ideas,' he agreed. His eyebrows, his eyes, his nose, his mousache and his chin all rose. 'What is with your police lady?' he asked.

'Jean?' said Savage unsurprised now by any turn of conversation. 'She's all right, I think. We are just friends. She helped me.'

'So many women to help you,' murmured his visitor. 'But she is now with this wanker. He is a lawyer. He is a wanker-lawyer.'

'We were only friends,' repeated Savage.

'Like with Korky.'

'Not quite. But there was nothing deeply serious.'

'No big love with the police lady,' nodded Mr Kostelanetz understandingly. 'Just some bed. And now you are getting used to your own self again. You can carry on with all your plans, writing, travelling, maybe cruising to Tahiti for the . . . you know.' His hands cupped across his chest again. 'All this adventure. And you don't need somebody about.'

'No. I think I've managed to get through. My wife and I will be divorced as soon as we can. We have sold our house to some Jehovah's Witnesses.'

'They pay,' nodded Mr Kostelanetz sagely. 'They are good payers.'

'I'll be completely without ties. I can take off.'

It all seemed too much for the big man to digest. He sat thoughtfully, morosely, for a while.

Savage collected his glass after he had refused another drink with a gruff shake of his head. Eventually he made to rise. 'Okay, okay,' he said extending his heavy paw to shake hands. 'So you go.' He held on to Savage's hand and gave it another dip. 'So everybody lives happy ever and ever. The police lady marries her wanker, after he is divorced. And then you are divorced. And what about the Korky? What will she do?'

'She'll live with her parents in Swindon,' Savage told him firmly. 'And she'll get a good job because she is very bright and capable. And one day, when she is twenty-two or three she will meet a nice chap . . .'

Kostelanetz broke in tetchily. 'So she meets this nice chap at the fucken Swindon dancing and they go off holding their hands and get married and have children . . .'

'More or less,' said Savage with a serious smile.

Mr Kostelanetz, eyes rolling, leaned towards him. 'I know where she is.'

Seventeen

'She's inside there,' said Mr Kostelanetz. He indicated the row of damaged houses. 'Somewhere.'

'In there,' agreed Nod. He was the one who had come armed with the cricket bat into Savage's bedroom. As they were travelling to the place he had given Savage a bashful smile. 'Haven't had no chance to play this season.'

The squat was in a line of ghostly Victorian houses, dripping and grey, in Balham. At one end of the terrace a painted sign, depicting fresh green trees, happy, confident people and open windows, by far the brightest item in the street, announced that Endersby Court was about to be transformed into luxury dwellings, although the only sign of the coming rehabilitation was that the doors had been nailed up and the windows blocked with corrugated iron.

There was indeed a tree in the street, a sorrowful plane, and the raw stump of another, recently and savagely felled.

'Firewood,' indicated Nod knowledgeably. 'For fires.'

Mr Kostelanetz paused on the pavement, shuffling his crocodile shoes on the grit, and surveyed the wretched scene. The wet summer's day gave it a deeper pall. He apparently wanted to give Nod some kudos or confidence because he looped his tweedy arm around the fatty shoulder and said: 'So you are the contact man, okay?'

'Yeah, I'm the contact man,' agreed Nod filling the words with importance and pleasure. 'I contact.'

'Then now begin to contact,' urged Mr Kostelanetz less gently. He gave the bulging shoulder a push. Savage, surveying the terrace, said: 'Where do we get in?'

'*They* got in,' pointed out Mr Kostelanetz. 'So we get in.' He regarded Nod as a field marshal might regard an unskilled scout. 'Which place?'

'The middle one,' said Nod with no confidence. 'I reckon . . . or the one next to the middle. One of them.'

He advanced heftily. A gate with an aching creak led them to a flight of six outside steps scarred and carpeted with debris. Nod surveyed the door, gathered his shoulders and strode the two paces like an odds-on boxer entering the ring. But he then paused, glanced uneasily at Savage and Mr Kostelanetz, and knocked daintily.

'Kick it,' ordered Mr Kostelanetz.

Nod was troubled. 'They get upset,' he said.

'It is not *their* door. This door is stolen by them. Also all of the house. Kick it.'

Nod complied. He only did it once. To their surprise they heard it being hurriedly unbolted. The door scraped open, revealing the head of a nervous-eyed youth whose sallowness was accentuated by his vivid ginger hair. 'Who is it?' he enquired.

'Police,' answered Mr Kostelanetz with no hesitation. 'CDI.'

'CID,' corrected Nod in a whisper. Mr Kostelanetz curled a dismissive lip towards him.

'Any dogs?' enquired the occupant endeavouring to peer beyond them.

'They're eating their breakfast,' replied Mr Kostelanetz.

'Oh, all right then,' said the youth in a surrendering

voice. He did not appear to have the strength to pull open the door fully. Mr Kostelanetz eyed Nod who put his foot to it and pushed it. They went into a hall sagging with damp. Behind the door was a barrier of leaves, rags, dusty junk mail, and khaki-coloured newspapers. Ginger appeared apologetic. 'We were going to have a sweep-up today,' he muttered. He gathered himself. 'We're quite legal,' he asserted looking from face to face and adding: 'Officers.'

Nod, who liked being cast in the role of a policeman, was trying to think of some likely remarks. 'We'll see about that, chummy,' he growled eventually, flipping an approval-seeking look first towards Savage and then Mr Kostelanetz. 'Won't we, guv'nors . . .?'

Mr Kostelanetz seemed inclined to give Nod a push and he backed prudently against the mildewed wall. He withdrew his hand from the damp surface, sniffed it and made a face. Mr Kostelanetz began striding down the grim hall, Ginger reluctantly hurrying before him, half-turned, asking who they wanted.

'Kathleen Wilson,' put in Savage.

'Don't know her,' said the youth with some relief. 'What's she done?'

'Known as Korky,' added Mr Kostelanetz holding and fully revolving Ginger with his large hand.

'Korky,' nodded Nod.

'Ah, now I know,' said the youth. Savage felt his own expression change. 'Where is she?' he asked.

'She lives two down,' said Ginger. 'Along the street.' He pointed sideways at the passage wall. 'Woodbine Villa it's called. Number four.'

'How long has she been there?' put in Savage.

'I don't know, not for sure. I never take much notice of the neighbours. About a week or so. Nobody stays long.'

Ponderously the three men turned in the confinement of the corridor and began to go back towards the open door. The bleakest of summer daylight was pushing through the aperture like bright sunshine. Ginger let them almost get there before saying: 'You can't get in from the front. They're all nailed up.'

'Tell us how we *do* get in there?' suggested Savage. Ginger appeared to be trying to work out who was in charge. 'You have to crawl underneath,' he replied making a dipping motion with his head.

'Show us,' said Mr Kostelanetz.

'Yeah, show us,' echoed Nod.

Again the trio turned in the narrow space. 'This way please,' said Ginger with a butler's bow. 'Along here.' He paused and pointed: 'Don't fall over the rat.'

He pushed the huge dead rodent aside with the edge of a ragged slipper.

Mr Kostelanetz tutted and remarked to Savage: 'How some peoples live.'

Ginger led them down a stretch of rotten wooden stairs, again warning them to take care where they trod. Nod tested each stair before he consigned his weight to it. All around was airless, dim and damp as a vault. 'Soon they're going to start the alterations,' said Ginger conversationally and with a perverse pride. 'Windows, everything. They're going to build trees.'

They went into a room where the dull June daylight seeped through a grille sending a band of insipid illumination over four forms lying curled under rugs and blankets and piles of newspapers. 'Why don't they get up?' demanded Mr Kostlanetz like an aggrieved employer. 'It is now eleven.'

'Eleven-o-three,' corrected Nod putting his watch close to his eyes in the dimness.

'What for?' asked Ginger. Warily he trod between the figures. 'It's not Giro day. They're all up and about on Giro day. That's tomorrow. In the winter some of them only move once a week.'

'Shut up,' grumbled a voice from beneath the mounds.

The intruders eyed each other and curiously fell to silence as though appreciating that they were trespassing. 'Along here,' whispered Ginger.

'All right,' whispered Nod as Mr Kostelanetz studied him caustically through the gloom.

They went through another room where a boy was propped against the wall in the corner. His head came up and he regarded them moodily. 'I'm going 'ome soon,' he said as if he needed a reference. Another figure materialised in a doorless doorway. 'Any dogs?' he asked.

'No dogs,' Ginger assured him. 'They're eating their breakfast.'

'Bit late for breakfast,' sniffed the new arrival. His face was an ashen triangle between long filthy hair. Savage stared at him, wanting to ask him why. But Mr Kostelanetz tugged his sleeve and advised: 'Don't get mixing.'

There was another passage followed by another room, what had been a kitchen with a gas cooker, the only fitting now remaining.

Ginger pointed casually: 'It was there if anybody wanted to cook. The last one put his 'ead in it but he didn't know this gas won't kill you. They've cut it off now, anyway.' He appeared offended. 'They've even cut the phone off.'

He had reached a pantry in the corner of the kitchen. The door remained and he scraped it open. 'This way, please,' he intoned like a guide in a catacomb. He stopped and went through a hole in the plaster and the wall. The three bending men followed him. Savage went first, Mr Kostelanetz followed grunting and brushing his jacket, and Nod afterwards, bringing down bits of mortar and plaster as he forced himself through the burrow.

As if getting through the wall had created a new familiarity, Ginger turned to them on the other side and, wiping his hands on his jeaned hips, held the right out to each of the trio in turn. 'My name is Jock Paradise,' he announced.

Savage mumbled his, Nod just shook hands as if reluctant to divulge anything, and Mr Kostelanetz said: 'I'm Mr Winston Churchill.' There was no reaction from the youth. He was occupied with being cautious in the house like someone who had crossed a border and needed to be polite to the natives. He led them guardedly through debris on the opposite side of the cupboard and into a room slushy with mud. 'They had a bit of a burst,' he explained. 'Nobody knew how to cut the water off. Then the council came and cut it off for them and they've never come back to put it on again. Diabolical liberty.'

There was a flight of wooden stairs, so obviously rotten that there was no need of Ginger's warning. Each of the three men went up tentatively and separately. The wood yielded like sponge under Savage's feet. Ginger, stooping in front of them, had reached a room where, surprisingly, a young, filthy man was seated at a desk staring at an old typewriter. 'S'cuse me, Wordsworth,' the ginger youth said seriously. 'Where's that girl? The nutty one.'

'I'm writing,' objected Wordsworth. He looked up and saw the other three. 'Who wants to know?' he asked suspiciously.

'Police,' Mr Kostelanetz told him swiftly.

Wordsworth peered around the corner of his desk. 'No dogs?' he said.

'They're in the dog show – at Crust's,' said Mr Kostelanetz.

Wordsworth addressed Ginger directly. 'Number five she is now,' he said. 'She was in bed with that vicar.'

Savage swallowed heavily and Mr Kostelanetz rolled his eyes with alarm.

'What vicar?' asked Savage quietly.

Wordsworth sighed. 'Oh, he's some sort of reverend who comes around here. Says he's a missionary, but he's not, he's a dickhead.' Without taking his hands from the keys he nodded fiercely at the typewriter. 'But he got this for me. To write my life story.'

His eyes dropped again. Savage observed that there was nothing written on the paper in the typewriter. The author grunted: 'I haven't started yet.'

They moved away and he called after them: 'I've got eight O levels.' The claim resounded through the stagnant house.

'Sleeping with a priest can't be so terrible,' observed Mr Kostelanetz in a comforting way to Savage. They now had to climb through a hole halfway up a wall, standing on a wet armchair which sighed soddenly under each one's weight. Short of breath, Nod became jammed in the hole, and they had to pull him through. Mr Kostelanetz needed to rest, grumbling: 'Even spying was not like this.'

'One more,' reassured Ginger. 'Then we're there.'

He took them through what seemed to be an entirely empty house and then, like a game-show host revealing another test, pointed to a trapdoor in the floor. 'Down there,' he said. 'And up the other side.'

'No better way?' asked Mr Kostelanetz. He was trying

to get the grit from his jacket. Nod brushed him like a valet.

Ginger smiled cannily. 'There *are* other ways, but nobody can tell them.' He cocked his head. 'The front doors are all locked up and barred and the windows boarded over.'

Ginger bent and lifted the trapdoor. It was dark and narrow below. 'It is like a testicle course,' sighed Mr Kostelanetz.

'Obstacle,' corrected Nod proudly. 'Obstacle course. And it's Cruft's not Crust's.'

'You are going to hurt your balls,' insisted Mr Kostelanetz.

'Do I get paid something for this?' suggested Ginger as though the idea had just occurred to him. He held open the trap. 'Expenses?'

Silently Savage handed him five pounds. Nod watched the transfer enviously. The youth checked the note, thanked Savage politely and clambered down the hole. Savage went next. Mr Kostelanetz peered with doubt into the depths but eventually followed, and Nod, after once more becoming wedged, managed to descend also. There was an iron ladder bolted to the wall below and a strong stench in the darkness. 'We've reported it,' said Ginger, his voice echoing in the tunnel.

It was only a few dark yards. They could see the faintly lit outline of another door ahead and, to Savage's relief, the ginger youth pushed this open without resistance. 'This is it,' he announced. 'Number five.' He paused and, as if he now appreciated the drama of the situation, added: 'She'll be in here.'

There was a bent form in the corner, two thin, pale fingers rolling a thin, pale cigarette. 'Where's the priest?' Ginger asked. The cigarette was pointed at the ceiling like an indication of heaven. They went from the room and into a hall where the wallpaper was hanging in tongues; an oil lamp stood unlit on a box. Like a raiding party they went swiftly up the stairs. Ginger turned into a room, took a look, and came out again. 'Not in there,' he said as though he would rather they did not see what was. 'In this one.' He moved towards the adjoining bedroom. 'In here.'

They went in after him, Savage first. To his astonishment there was a decent double bed piled with an assortment of rugs and blankets. Two figures were below the coverings with a distinct curved valley between them. One of them was snoring. 'Reverend!' bellowed Ginger. He needed to gather strength to raise his voice. 'It's the police!'

'Christ!' The howl came from below the bedclothes, the lump rose like a whale from the sea and a rounded man with a scarlet face appeared. He was wearing a dingy singlet and a guilty expression; a crucifix swung jerkily on his neck as he pulled himself up in the bed. Bad-temperedly he flung it around to his back. The mound next to him groaned and moved. His consternation went from them to it.

Savage was transfixed. First the top of her hair appeared, then her white forehead, and deep, startled eyes. Her narrow face and her body, engulfed in a shell suit of orange and blue, eased itself up. His instinct was to rush and pick her up and run with her from the room; to take her somewhere safe. Her initial dismay was followed by delight as she realised who was standing there. 'Oh, Savage darling!' she breathed. 'You've found me!'

'You're getting out of here,' he ordered. 'At the bloody double.' His face was set, his eyes determined.

The priest sat pop-eyed beside her in the bed and looked at her. 'Who the hell are you?' he croaked.

'John's here somewhere,' said Korky clambering vigorously from the bed, giving Savage a swift but decisive kiss, and then leading them through the holes and labyrinths of the terraced squat. She seemed utterly at home. Savage was relieved that she was fully covered by the terrible Day-Glo shell suit that illuminated their progress through the darkened apertures and unofficial entrances, but reason told him that few of the denizens of that place changed for bed.

'John! John!' Korky shouted urgently before her as she led the short procession around and up and down again like a sergeant of sappers through military earthworks. She appeared unflustered that Savage had discovered her, only glad to see him. He followed closely behind her illuminated orange backside and they went from house to house with Mr Kostelanetz a flagging third, brushing his clothes and pursuing them with the waning agility of a one-time man of action. Nod came at the rear, grumbling and stumbling.

'John!' called Korky as they burrowed into the final decayed house. Along the terrace various occupants had merged with, or emerged from, the shadows but in the last habitation a solitary youth wearing a blanket over some sort of sailor suit squatted over a meagre fire on top of which was a metal bucket. He was sluggishly stirring the contents, like a bored sorcerer. Korky's eyes flared in the shadows; she pointed soundlessly at the figure who continued stirring with a metal rod and showed no sign that he had noted their arrival. Her accusing finger was followed by a chicken-like squawk. 'You!' she accused as she staggered towards the form hunched rancidly over the fire and bucket. 'You! Benedict . . . you bastard!'

Benedict looked up mildly but continued stirring. He had the face of someone between twenty and fifty. It filtered into a private smile.

Korky halted as if afraid to advance. Her nose twitched towards the steam from the pot. 'He's had him,' she growled sorrowfully. She whirled on Savage. 'The bugger's eaten my John.'

Movement seemed beyond her. Feeling odd, Savage moved tentatively towards the youth and his dire bucket. 'Have you cooked her gerbil?' he asked. He peered into the bucket. Swirling in the grey water were some ominous lumps. The cooker shook his head. 'Not yet.'

Now Mr Kostelanetz moved forward. Menacingly he approached Benedict. His face moved over the steam to confront that of the youth. 'Which ear do you want me to take off?' he enquired in his villain's voice.

'Either one,' offered Benedict blandly. 'Can I keep it as a souvenir?'

Nonplussed Mr Kostelanetz began to fumble for an imaginary knife. Korky intervened. 'Benedict,' she demanded. 'Where's my John?'

Breathing an ancient sigh Benedict gave his bucket a parting mix and retreated into the folding shadows. He returned with a shoebox and opened the lid to reveal the curled and sleeping animal. 'I was going to make a nice gerbil curry,' he said.

Korky snatched the container from the youth causing the pet to wake uncomfortably. She thrust her nose into the box and made intimate sounds. Benedict, giving no one another glance returned to his bucket.

Eighteen

'Straight, Savage,' she said facing him adamantly. 'How was I to know there was a bloody vicar in the bed? All I know is that it was a bed and I crawled in. Either he was in there already and I didn't notice or he climbed in later. Take my word, a bed is a bed in a squat.' They had reached Kensington Heights. Korky looked around happily. 'It's so nice to be home,' she sighed.

Savage said: 'How did you get there anyway, in that dump? The last time I saw you your new parents were taking you home to good old Swindon.'

Korky was immediately downcast. 'I know,' she admitted avoiding his eyes. She sat down and asked for a drink. He brought a Coca Cola from the refrigerator. She studied him over the rim of the tin. She lifted it. 'You knew I'd be back then? Some time.'

'I bought a supply in case I met up with some other wandering waif,' he said, then repeated: 'What were you doing in that hole?'

'Living,' she shrugged. 'Being. Until I could find more suitable accommodation.' She choked on the Coke.

'How long did you stay in Swindon?'

'Three weeks,' she answered. 'Nearly.' Her expression became pleading.

'They're your mother and father,' he said steadily. 'Don't you love them?'

The enquiry appeared to astonish her. 'Of course I love them. But I love them like mother and father. I don't want to be *with* them.'

Stone-faced he went to the window. 'I never know why you always go to the window,' she complained lowering the Coke tin from her lips. 'It's always the same out there, give or take a bit of sky or a few more leaves. There's bugger-all to see but you stare out like you're trying to see the future.'

'Maybe I am,' he said continuing to gaze outwards.

She put on her small girl voice. 'It was hell in Swindon,' she pleaded. 'I had my own room back and God I hated that room. When I was thirteen I used to climb out of the window and go and muck around with the boy next door. He was sixteen and he wore glasses in bed so he could see what he was doing. But he's moved now. Oh, they fussed over me, you know what I mean. But I had to do a runner. They fixed me a job in a *boutique* . . .'

'What was wrong with that?'

'What *passed* as a boutique,' she grumbled. 'In any case you know clothes bore the pants off me. One of the neighbours who came from the country introduced me to a . . .' She mimicked a Wessex burr: '. . . A suitable young man.' The imitation pleased her and she continued with it. 'Aaah, my lover, 'ow be you then . . .?' She sighed. 'Winnie Wilts shit.'

'So you cleared out.'

'While I was still sane.'

'Did you tell your parents you were going?'

'No, I didn't mention it.'

'Well, you've *got* to tell them where you are,' he ordered her. 'Phone them. Now.'

It was one of the few times he had seen the confidence

drain from her. 'Now?' she asked. He nodded. She walked slowly to the telephone and dialled the number. Savage heard a woman's voice answer. 'Hello, Mum,' said Korky. 'It's me.'

A squeak of delight and relief sounded and some gabbled words. Korky apologised for leaving. Her mother sounded concilitatory and tearful. Savage heard her say: 'Where are you?'

'Where am I, Savage?' Korky challenged looking round at him. 'Where shall I be?'

He avoided her face. 'Here, I suppose,' he said defeated. 'You're here. I'm taking the flat for another six months.'

She let the phone drop. It swung on its cord, the voice of her mother hanging with it.

'Oh, Savage!' she shouted joyously. 'Oh, Savage. I'm back! I'm back!'

Savage retrieved the receiver and handed it pointedly to her.

'Sorry, Mum,' she said into it. 'I've just had some good news. Yes, yes, I'll tell you later. I'll ring you, I'll write to you. Promise on my life. I'll keep in touch.'

She replaced the phone and turned, then jumped to him, flinging her thin arms about him, hugging him close and kissing him deeply on the mouth.

'Oh, Savage ... Savage,' she sighed putting her forehead against his face.

'Stop it, stop it,' he said holding her to him. 'Don't.'

'It's for you,' said Savage. He held the telephone towards her. A skein of rain lay across the window. It was evening and they had been watching television in domestic silence. She had carried the remains of the take-away pizza to the kitchen.

Korky took the phone. Savage went into the kitchen to make coffee. He eavesdropped expectantly. 'Hello . . . oh, hello, Mr Furtwangler. Yes, yes . . . it's me . . .' Her eyes anxiously swivelled towards the kitchen. Her voice fell to a whisper: 'Rosamunde.'

'Von Fokker,' added Savage his head coming around the door.

She went pink and shook her head irritably at him. He remained where he was and watched her sit with the telephone, her neat knees and long straight thighs exposed by the shortness of her skirt. The call had made her leave the remnants of the meal on the kitchen table. He went back and scraped them into the waste bin and put the kettle on. 'Yes, Mr Furtwangler. I really would love to come back. My mother . . .?' Her eyes travelled towards the kitchen door again. 'Yes, well I'm afraid she passed away. Yes, Mr Furtwangler. Oh, don't cry, Mr Furtwangler. I didn't really know her all that well.'

Savage reappeared and lolled against the door jamb; she tried to avoid looking in his direction. 'We must look on the bright side . . . Yes, of course. Right, I'll be there on Monday. Yes, I'm glad too. I'll be there at ten, Monday morning.'

Guiltily she replaced the receiver and revolved towards him. 'My mother was ill, right?' she enquired. 'Very ill.'

'Quite ill,' he replied. 'I had to give him some reason for your disappearance.'

'I hope my real mum doesn't go and die because of what you made me say,' she threatened. 'I'd never forgive you. Did Mr Furtwangler telephone?'

'He did. And I went to see him. I took the books back. The ones you borrowed.'

Alarm altered her face. 'You went to the shop? All that way? By yourself?'

He ignored her astonishment. 'He's a nice old man,' he said. 'He thinks a lot of you ... Rosamunde.'

'Stop being so shitty. His wife's name was Rosamunde and she's been dead for yonks and he says I remind him of her. That's nice. It makes me feel a bit happier. There's nothing wrong with making people happy by telling a few porkies.'

'Another of your friends called around,' mentioned Savage. He walked to the chair and sat opposite her looking directly into her face. The evening coming in from the window was adding a light patina to her skin. 'He knows you as Anna something. Wife of a pop star.'

'Anna Zubber,' she provided. 'Stephen. Well, he's helping me as well.'

'Towards a PhD, I gather.'

'In that direction,' she shrugged avoiding his gaze. 'He works for a publishers and he said they may be interested in your encyclopaedia of islands.' She flicked her eyelashes at him. 'He's deeply, deeply in love with me,' she intoned. 'Really deeply.'

'I got that impression,' agreed Savage.

'He's a scream to look at, isn't he,' she grinned. 'Poor bloke. Everything about him is wrong. But he loves me, that's one good thing in his favour.'

'And you've certainly become popular here, in Kensington Heights,' he told her. 'All the neighbours wanted to know what had happened to you, where you'd gone. Wilhelmina Blenkinsop thought I had done you in.'

Korky squeaked and put her hand to her mouth. Her eyes shone above her fingers. 'Done me in!' she exclaimed joyfully. 'She said that?'

'She suggested it.'

'That's bloody priceless! She said that!' She halted. 'She wants me to help her with her spirit meetings.' Her grin spread thoughtfully. 'It might have been better if you *had* done me in. Then I could come back and really help her out.'

'What does she want you to do?'

'Give her a hand knocking on tables and stuff. Being a spirit guide. A sort of medium's general help. She's going to tell me.'

'Do you think that's a good idea?'

'Don't know. But she only does it to help people out. She only takes two quid fifty plus expenses for the gas and electricity and that doesn't come to much, the lights are out most of the time. Like I said, Savage, telling a few porkies to make people happy is all right. She gives them a cup of tea afterwards and they go away feeling a bit better because they've had a natter with their dead gran.'

They changed the television channel and sat, reunited and silent, against each other on the sofa. The quiet was interrupted by the doorbell. Korky rose quickly and answered it. Over her slight shoulder Savage saw the beam spread over the face outside the door. 'Ah, you're back!' exclaimed Mr Maddison. 'We've all missed you.'

She invited him in. He shook hands fiercely with Savage as though congratulating him on winning an award. 'Wonderful, wonderful, wonderful,' he enthused. Dandruff bounced on his shoulders.

He gladly accepted a glass of wine. 'Tickets,' he said. 'I have some tickets for the Albert Hall.' He winked. 'It pays to know people. Thursday. Beethoven. If you come *she'll* probably behave.' His expression shaded. 'They're doing the Pastoral, unfortunately, and she's inclined to join in the cuckoo bit. But generally she keeps it quite soft so there probably won't be any trouble.' He beamed at them. 'I hope you can both make it,' he said.

Korky said: 'It will be lovely. Oh we love our Beethoven, don't we, Frank.'

There were some hot days in August; London, unsuited to heat, lay below haze. From Savage's window the prospect was of dusky skies and soupy streets. The trees stood lifelessly. Drivers, far below, could be heard shouting. There were ice-cream men in Kensington High Street and people queued for the coolness of cinemas.

Korky, getting up on Sunday, saw Miss Bombazine facing the hot, gritty air from her half-open window. She went to her own window and waved.

'Can't breathe,' complained Miss Bombazine across the gap. 'It's like the East.'

'Never been East,' Korky called back cheerfully.

'It's no good for your chest, this weather,' warned Miss Bombazine. Her pink-chemised bosom was lolling from the window as though separately gasping for air. 'Especially one like mine.'

'They're important to you, I expect,' sympathised Korky.

'I have to look after them,' responded Miss Bombazine seriously. 'I can't be wheezing. Somehow I'll have to get some air today.'

'Let's go out,' suggested Korky. 'The three of us. We'll go somewhere nice – where it's clear.'

An hour later the trio boarded the bus at Notting Hill Gate and another at Chiswick. By one o'clock they were beside the Thames at Windsor. There was scarcely room to move along the towpath or in the town but they found a riverside place for lunch and sat down gratefully.

Miss Bombazine was in a light print dress. It was the first time that either Savage or Korky had seen her when she was not wearing black. 'I don't care,' she said panting and pink from the dusty walking. 'It's lovely. Look at the water. I haven't been here for years.' Her face softened. 'It's funny now I come to think about it, I used to come to Windsor with this man.'

Korky fixed on her intently. 'Were you in love?' she asked.

'Yes, I was,' she said reflectively. 'But I never fall in love now. It only makes you miserable.' Her expression changed again. 'Thank you so much for bringing me,' she said.

There was a moment of embarrassment. Miss Bombazine broke it herself. 'Generally on a Sunday I go for a walk,' she said. 'Anywhere.' She laughed almost shyly. 'I swore I'd never walk the streets,' she said. 'And now I do it in my time off.'

'Let's go on a boat,' suggested Korky, her eyes going quickly to the window.

'Who'll do the rowing?' said Savage.

'You,' she returned. 'Come on, we'll probably have to queue.'

They waited in the line for half an hour and Miss Bombazine bought them all ice-cream cones. It was very hot. Korky purchased cloth sun hats for herself and Savage. Miss Bombazine had a straw hat with a chiffon scarf tied around its crown. When it came to their turn they climbed giggling into the agitated rowing boat. Savage, attempting to look in control, took the oars and pulled out into the river with stiff, military movements. They rocked and Korky and Miss Bombazine squealed.

He succeeded in guiding the craft into the main stream where they joined the other boats bouncing on the thick green water. Pleasure steamers sent up heavy rolling waves that rocked them alarmingly and Savage's inexpert rowing soaked everyone. 'It's a dead cert you weren't in the navy,' howled Miss Bombazine. They laughed wildly. The river sun shone. Savage perspired, Korky was getting red and Miss Bombazine's straw hat kept slipping over her ears.

Ashore again they had a cup of tea. Then a Polaroid photographer badgered them and Korky insisted that they have their pictures taken. They posed, smiling in the bright light, Korky at the centre. When the photograph appeared the man beamed at it. 'Look at that, Mum,' he said to Miss Bombazine, handing her the still damp and curved exposure. 'Best little family group you'll ever see.'

A thin, long person, probably a man, was standing at the door of the pub in Portobello Road, dressed as a clown and with a collecting box. He was giving off low noises, a mix of moans and appeals, and occasionally people on their way out put a few coins in his box.

It had been raining again but the sun was beginning to show, there was steam on the windows and a thickening humidity in the bar. 'Why have you suddenly started calling me Frank?' he asked.

Korky seemed surprised he had noticed. 'That's your proper name,' she whispered as if telling him something he did not know. '*I'm* going to keep calling you Savage – but only between ourselves. When it's somebody else then it's Frank. It's part of our new relationship.'

'What new relationship?' he asked deliberately casually. 'Nothing's changed.'

'Inside me I feel it's a new relationship,' she insisted leaning confidingly towards him. 'And today I'm going to buy you a present for your birthday.'

'My birthday is not for another four months.'

She withdrew her face. 'Yes, but that's only four months away.'

They left the bar. Korky put some change into the clown's collecting box. 'What's he collecting for?' Savage asked.

'Clowns,' she said. 'Probably.'

The stewy market street was crowded, made narrow by the press of people. There were stalls down both sides, their canopies like the roofs of poorly erected tents; there were shouts and offers, vendors trading junk and insults; people moved unhurriedly and thickly down both pavements and in the road itself. Vapour hung casually, the sun fingering through it. Three dark girls leaned over the parapet of a flat roof making Cockney catcalls to a group of Asian youths below. One of the youths shouted: 'Piss orf.' The stalls were cluttered with faded bygones and brassy trinkets, leather and glasswork, holed books and cheap-framed prints. A grim man sizzled hot dogs. On a corner, the pavements drying below his boots, a young man was playing a Spanish guitar.

He looked wild, wearing tight jeans and leather boots and a tasselled shirt with a hat slung over his back. His expression was intense but distant, as though he had something on his mind, and his fingers picked out a deep tune which drew people to him. The youth began to sing in some sort of Spanish, low and howling like a dog. Savage and Korky paused with the crowd. Savage believed by then that nothing she ever did would surprise him. But he felt her go from his side and in a moment she was occupying the damp space in front of the guitar player and fluently whirling into a Spanish dance. Savage watched amazed. She could *do* it. Her chin dropped to her shoulder, her slim arms reached above her head and she snapped her fingers. Sharply her heels clicked on the pavement. The watchers joined in, clapping in triple time. The guitarist played on fiercely, vividly, not even looking at her, as though he had fully expected her to appear and the dance to happen.

Savage gazed. Sometimes he could not believe her. Her narrow face had become beautiful, rapt; her eyes were almost shut, her mouth barely open; the slim shoulders dipped and swayed, the head rose, the slight waist rocked, the arms curled, the fingers were flung out, as if she had been born to it.

At the final chord the crowd, by then so swollen that the police had become interested, applauded appreciatively. Korky performed a dramatically humble curtsey and flagrantly kissed the guitarist on his dark cheek. The youth's remote expression did not alter and, after a quick, formal, but careless bow, he began to play another distant tune. The police and most of the crowd moved on.

'I learned it in Benidorm,' she explained in her cursory way when they continued along the street.

She led Savage in through one of the side doors to where there were stalls along interior walls and there were fewer people. He was still thinking of her dancing. The stallholders regarded them hopefully but Korky knew where she was going. The man she was seeking saw her and said: 'I've still got it.'

'I hope you have,' she answered. 'I just wanted to bring him . . .' She gave Savage a light dig with her elbow. 'To have a look. It's his birthday.'

'Happy birthday,' said the vendor, a man with eyes of sharp blue and a bald head but a mass of gingery hair displayed under his open shirt. Savage did not argue. Korky pointed to the back wall. 'There, that's it,' she said. The man was already unhooking the map.

'Isle of Wight,' he announced handing it across most

reverently. 'John Speed . . . well, after John Speed to be honest, as I always am. It's a print. But it's a nice one.'

Savage felt himself smile deeply. He studied the coloured map in its small wooden frame and then turned softly to Korky. 'Do you like it, Savage?' she asked.

'It's a print,' repeated the stallholder fairly. 'But it's sound enough.'

'Yes, I know,' said Korky. She regarded Savage hopefully. 'What d'you think?'

'It's very nice, Korky,' he answered. The vendor, listening to their private names, looked from the young girl to the square-shouldered, middle-aged man. All he said was: 'Fifteen pounds. It *was* twenty. And it's a nice little frame.'

'All right,' said Korky impetuously. 'Done.' Her eyes went to Savage's face again. 'You do like it?'

'Of course.' He kissed her on the cheek while the stallholder wondered more about them. 'But it's not my birthday.'

A frown shaded the vendor's face. 'When is it then?' he enquired.

'Four months,' provided Korky. She brightened. 'But then it will be even older. More antique.'

'Like me,' laughed Savage. The stall man watched as he rubbed her upper arm under the flimsy sleeve. 'Thank you,' he said. 'I love it.'

They took it home, Korky carrying it in its newspaper wrapping as though it were some discovered treasure. She held it in both hands and when they were in the apartment laid it almost reverently on the table. 'Savage,' she said. 'It's the first thing we've bought together, apart from my clothes.'

He grimaced mildly and went into the kitchen to pour

some wine. She folded back the newspaper and surveyed her purchase intently as if she feared it might have deteriorated. She picked it up, touched it and smelled it.

Savage poured two glasses of white wine and they raised them over the map. 'Look at it,' breathed Korky. 'The *colours*. And look at *this*. It says "Wight Island" and "The British Sea".' He leaned over her, one of their moments of accidental intimacy. 'And here,' he pointed.

'Part of England,' Korky read slowly. 'That makes it sound really *abroad*, just like a foreign country.' She studied it, then turning back to him, breathed deeply and caught his arm. 'Savage,' she said like a conspirator directing her finger at the map. 'The Isle of Wight. It could be *your* . . . *our* island. Savage, some time let's go there. Soon.' Then looking up at the long wall she said: 'We'll put it up there. Take down that picture that Mr Kostelanetz left. It's 'orrible anyway.'

Smiling Savage removed the Levantine print from its hook. Korky put the miniature map in its place. 'It's a bit lost there,' he pointed out.

'No, it isn't. It gives it . . . space.'

Usually she was home by six thirty; seven if she had to shop.

At seven thirty she had not arrived, at eight he was half-anxious, half-resigned that she had gone off again. You never knew with Korky. At ten past eight Mr Prentice arrived. 'The police have got your young lady,' he reported.

Savage almost pulled him into the room. Mr Prentice nervously bared his metallic teeth. 'I'd have come before but I was on my way to the British Legion. We had a meeting.'

'Where?' demanded Savage. 'Where was it?'

'At the club,' said Mr Prentice.

'No. Where did the police arrest her?'

'Oh, I see. Sorry. In Holland Park. I was just sitting down on a bench because I was early and it was quite nice this evening and I saw it all. There were some youngsters, you know the ones who hang about around here, and they had some cider or something. They were getting rowdy and the police turned up and there was a bit of a struggle and they got taken off in vans.'

'And Korky was with them?'

'She'd only just turned up. She was telling them something, warning them. She'd probably seen the police vans. Anyway then they turned up, the police, and carted them off, your girl as well.'

Savage swore quietly. Mr Prentice was worried. 'I'd have come right away but I had the meeting.'

'It's all right,' said Savage patting him on the shoulder. 'Thanks anyway. Was it much of a scene with the police?'

'Quite a bit.' Mr Prentice hesitated. 'She was right in it, I'm afraid. A lot of shouting went on and I saw the policewoman hit her and she hit the policewoman.'

'A policewoman?'

'Yes, and dogs. In the middle of it all your little lady and the policewoman were having a right tussle I can tell you.'

'Christ,' breathed Savage. He moved towards the telephone. 'Thanks anyway, Mr Prentice.'

'Glad to help,' smiled Mr Prentice snapping his trap teeth. 'I hope it's all right.' He went to the door. 'I'll be in if you need me.'

Savage had already picked up the telephone. 'I'll let myself out,' said his visitor doing so. Savage was speaking: 'Do you have a young girl, Kathleen Wilson, there?'

There was an interval while the police decided they

had. 'Right,' said Savage sharply. 'I'm coming to fetch her.'

Korky had a bruised cheek and a black eye. 'That cow-in-uniform, your former Jean, did this,' she announced. It hurt her to grin but she did. 'But I got a souvenir.' Curled in her palm was a tuft of hair.

He put his arms out to her and she fell against him and began to cry. 'It wasn't my fault, honest Savage. It wasn't.'

'I know,' he replied.

'She can go now,' said a calm-looking sergeant appearing at the door. 'She's bailed to appear in court tomorrow. Ten thirty.'

'On what charge?'

The man appeared surprised and had to consult a piece of paper. 'Assault on police,' he said eventually. 'It says here. As she's got an address she can go. The others have to stay inside.'

'At least they'll have a roof,' retorted Korky. The sergeant did not seem to want to get further involved and merely said: 'That's one way of looking at it.'

Savage took her out, put her in a taxi and said: 'I'm staying.' She smirked at him tearfully. The bruise under her eye shone in the police station lights. 'You're going to see her,' she said. She opened her hand again. 'Give her this back if you like.'

He took the hair and put it in his pocket, then walked back into the police station and asked to see PC Deepe. 'She's on dinner,' said the same placid sergeant giving no sign of recognition. 'I know she is.'

'I'll wait.'

'I'll let her know. What name is it?'

Savage told him. 'I'll tell her,' confirmed the officer.

'Sit yourself in the waiting room. There's some magazines in there.'

Savage did not have to wait long. Jean appeared at the door. 'Why did you arrest her?' he demanded.

'I'm not on the parade ground,' she retorted. 'Even if you are, sergeant.'

'Staff,' he corrected meanly. 'Staff Sergeant.' His lips and eyes were tight. He repeated: 'Why did you arrest her?'

'Kathleen Wilson, also known as Korky?' she asked. 'Assault on police.' He decided not to return her scrap of hair. He thought how furtive and unattractive she looked. She purposefully turned her eyes away to study the blank wall. 'I've got a witness,' he said.

'To what?'

'To the fact that Korky had only just arrived on the scene, she hadn't been part of that group and she hadn't been drinking with them.'

'She pulled my hair out,' said Jean, suddenly petulant. 'And she called me a uniformed cow. Christ, have you got trouble with that . . .'

'*I've* had no trouble with her,' he said quietly. 'My witness, a man who saw everything that happened, will say it was *you* who attacked her. She's the one with the black eye.' He leaned a little forward his eyes hard. There was something like a sneer on her lips. It was amazing that they had been lovers.

'And please get this straight,' he continued. 'If this gets to court then you'll be the one who needs to do some explaining. You picked on her. I'll make sure she's legally represented.'

'She's a back-street trollop.'

'You'll have to give your reasons in the witness box.'

He could see that he had got her. To his amazement

he realised she was going to crumble. Her body sagged, her eyes filled, her face began to tremble. Sadly he put his hand halfway out to her but she did not accept it. 'I bloody hate her,' she muttered. She faced him from behind the tears. 'You don't know how much.'

'There's no need for you to hate her,' he said steadily.

'You were going to help *me*.'

'I've rung you,' Savage answered. His voice remained firm. 'Once you put the phone down on me and another time it sounded as though there was a binge going on and you hung up then as well. And twice after that a man answered. He wasn't that friendly.'

'Adam,' she said and as though it mattered added: 'He's a solicitor. But I've elbowed him.'

'What about Brendan Brownlow?'

She shrugged. 'Now he writes to me with love and kisses. I don't know what to think. It may be all right.' She looked up. 'I don't think he knows as much as I thought he knew.'

'I've brought your key,' he said. He took it from his pocket and placed it on the table. She picked it up and turned it over in her palm. 'You don't know what my life is like,' she muttered still contemplating the key.

'I have some idea.'

Slowly but starkly she turned her face up to him. 'You love her, don't you.'

Savage said: 'I care for her.'

Nineteen

Mr and Mrs Maddison arrived precisely. 'It's difficult to be late when you live under the same roof,' he observed jovially. His wife was staring at Korky's bruised eye and shiny cheekbone. Maddison followed her direction and transferred his glance unhappily to Savage.

'The police did it,' Korky informed them. 'For fun.'

Breathing sherry Mrs Maddison moved in for a closer survey. 'Any charges?' she asked expertly.

'They tried,' sniffed Korky.

'Then decided not to proceed,' put in Savage.

Mrs Maddison sighed feelingly. 'The trouble I've had with the buggers,' she complained.

Her husband frowned. 'I don't suppose this young lady did what you did – called a distinguished orchestral conductor Bollock Chops,' he pointed out. He eyed the others without conviction and promised: 'Tonight she has assured me that she will not make bird noises during the "Pastoral" Symphony.'

'I think it's so nice when the audience can join in,' sniffed Mrs Maddison. There was a whiff of sherry as she spoke. 'Especially at the Albert Hall.'

Bertie Maddison regarded the other two soberly. 'I try to avoid the "Pastoral" if I can, and Delius, and the others who put birds in, especially cuckoos.' His face returned, filled with doubt, to his wife. 'With her there are no guarantees.'

They walked together down Church Street hill. The evening was dove grey, warm and quite quiet. Korky wore dark glasses to cover her bruise. They turned the corner and went alongside the park railings; there were walkers, joggers and people exercising dogs. 'I'd like a dog,' mentioned Korky. 'It's hard to take a gerbil for a walk. One day . . .' She gave Savage a sideways look. 'When I get my own place.'

When they were in their seats she sat transfixed, her astonished gaze travelling around the great bowl of the Albert Hall. 'How did they get it so round?' she said. She sat upright when the orchestra came on to the platform, her face stretching over the heads in front, and remained in the same, eager, position as the musicians took their places and began to tune their instruments. When the conductor came to the rostrum she applauded as if she knew him personally.

When the music began she sat beside Savage and held his hand, settling beside his broad frame, face lifted to the great domed roof as though she were trying to see the rising music. Mrs Maddison loudly sucked boiled sweets. Her husband watched her cagily. When the orchestra reached the springtime passage in the "Pastoral", Mrs Maddison, unable to resist it, leaned forward and began to call softly: 'Cuckoo . . . cuckoo . . .' adding a trilling sound from her throat. Bertie put an alarmed finger to his lips and some nearby people peered towards her but the theme was short and she was soon subdued, silent and attentive again.

'We have laid on a little repast,' said Mrs Maddison as they left. Korky was walking silently. She had scarcely moved during the concert. Savage nudged her out of her quiet and she smiled. 'Wasn't it great, Savage,' she said. 'That ceiling. It was like being inside an egg.'

They called in at a wine bar. 'At the Albert Hall do they play Spanish music?' Korky asked. 'With the whole bit, like tonight?'

'Of course,' said Mrs Maddison. 'Granados, de Falla, Rodrigues.' She performed a plump turn and snapped her fingers above her head. Korky laughed and did the same.

'That's good,' said Mr Maddison.

'Ever so,' agreed his wife.

'I learned,' said Korky. She performed the movement again. 'In Spain, Benidorm.'

'I've seen her,' confirmed Savage.

'I learned every day, from some Spanish girls,' Korky told them. 'I used to buy them hamburgers and pizzas and they showed me how to do it. One of them had a grandfather with no legs because he was in a war they had, and he used to balance on a stool and play the guitar.'

They went to the Maddisons' big and old-fashioned apartment. The furniture had been in place for years, castors buried in the carpet. On the walls were framed music scores and photographs of conductors, soloists and singers, some of them sere with age and seasons of filtered London sunlight. 'This,' pointed Mrs Maddison leaving the table where she had spread the cold supper, 'is Dr Ralph Vaughan Williams. I was at a performance of his Sixth Symphony. Nearly fifty years ago now. I was just a girl. He conducted and afterwards I got this autographed photograph. They were selling them for sixpence.'

'It must have been a brilliant night,' said Korky.

'Saturday afternoon,' remembered Mrs Maddison. 'It was a toss-up between Vaughan Williams and Queen's

Park Rangers. My Uncle Bob used to take me to see the Rangers and the two things clashed. Afterwards I was glad I went to the Albert Hall because they lost two goals to nil.'

She knew how to prepare a cold supper. There was a glistening chicken and ham pie and cold lamb and salad and small potatoes. They drank two bottles of German wine.

'The composer Granados, the Spaniard, drowned in the English Channel,' mentioned Mrs Maddison helping herself to the pie.

'Right, so he did,' Mr Maddison nodded into his napkin. 'Ship sunk by the Germans. First World War.'

'He was coming back from his opera in New York,' added his wife. '*Goyescas*, wasn't it, dear? About Goya.'

'Yes, *Goyescas*,' nodded Mr Maddison. 'And Spain wasn't even in the war.' He turned to Korky, a pickled onion speared on his fork. 'We have some Spanish music,' he said. She crossed her eyes at the pickled onion close to her face and said: 'Do you want me to dance?'

He left the table and opening a long cabinet revealed two racks of long-playing records. 'All ancient now, of course,' he said. 'But you can't beat them. Somehow Sir Thomas Beecham seems too big for one of these compact disc things. Ah ... here we are ... Rodrigues.'

He swung open the polished lid of an old-fashioned record player and switched it on. 'At least we don't have to wind it up,' he joked. He put the record on and watched for a few moments while it revolved before returning to the table and picking up his fork and the impaled pickled onion once more.

Their glasses were replenished and the four sat round the table in the solid, antiquated flat, the windows open, the lace curtains moving to the muted street sounds of the limpid London night, and listened while the rich Iberian music swelled through the room and filtered out into the air of Kensington. 'Please dance for us,' invited Mrs Maddison. Korky stood up, her face grave, and began to dance.

She was wearing a long lace dress, dark blue and old, which she had bought in a charity shop. Her shoes were modern, black and thickly wedged. She tapped them on the carpet and twirled the hem of her dress. Bertie Maddison got up mumbling: 'One moment,' and removed a square of rug to reveal a parquet floor. With no change of her set expression Korky moved to the wooden space and continued. She drummed her heels and swayed her body.

'They're stone deaf downstairs,' said Mrs Maddison.

Her husband, watching Korky, said: 'She's wonderful.'

Savage nodded. He could hardly take his eyes from her. The music had caught her and she moved her hands and body as if in a dream; her feet drummed. Her eyes were almost closed, her hair jerked with her head, her arms and fingers were pale and there was a soft sheen of sweat on a face so intense that she looked old as well as beautiful.

He knew too well how accustomed to each other they had become. He knew how happy they had been that day.

How long could it go on like this?

Mr Kostelanetz had become oddly emotional when Savage informed him that he would like to continue the rental for a further six months. His eyes, as big as an old dog's, had filled mistily and he had produced a significant red handkerchief to blow his nose. 'This is good,' he said copiously shaking Savage's hand. 'Very good. Not for me. For my rent, I am not thinking. The rent is good but what you tell me is better.'

Since that time he had become more involved with them, often arriving at the apartment, his face filled with friendship. In September he was there but looking uncomfortable.

'I'm moving out,' announced Korky casually. She said it as she idly rolled the pages of a magazine. She was sitting on the sofa. Savage revolved in astonishment. 'When?' he said. 'You've never told me.'

'I didn't know until now. I've just heard.'

Mr Kostelanetz stood bashfully. 'It was just an offer,' he shrugged and his eyes fell guiltily to Savage. 'While you were getting this good wine.' He raised the glass. 'Very welcome on a day so warm.'

Korky folded the magazine. She had only been browsing, but now, gaining time, she deliberately bent the corner of one page as if to mark a place. 'Mr Kostelanetz kindly told me that I can move into a little flat here,' she said avoiding Savage and looking directly at Mr Kostelanetz.

The sweeping moustache seemed to droop. 'I did not want to offend you,' he said awkwardly to Savage. 'Or that you would think I was stealing her away.' His damp eyes eventually moved up. 'But you have always wanted for her to move into somewhere.'

'And this will be just the job,' put in Korky without conviction. 'It's in the next block and it's just big . . . small enough and I'll be able to manage the rent because this Mrs Longbottom is going away for six months at least and wants somebody reliable to look after the flat. So she's giving me a good deal.'

Savage's eyes travelled from the girl to the large man

and back again. 'That seems a lot of information to get through while I was pouring a glass of wine,' he observed.

Mr Kostelanetz hunched his shoulders. 'Well, I did mention this matter before.'

'Very briefly,' put in Korky her eyes now fixed on her bare knees. 'I didn't take a lot of notice to tell you the truth.'

Savage said: 'But now, suddenly, you've made up your mind. You've just said: "I'm moving out." '

'Not just yet,' she corrected defensively. 'It might be weeks. This Mrs Longbottom doesn't know exactly when she'll be going off. It depends when her husband comes back. Then she'll go.'

'Well, thanks for telling me.'

'Don't sulk,' she said sulkily. 'I'll be here in Kensington Heights. I'll be a neighbour, so we can pop in and see each other. I bet we'll be in and out all the time. And that's what you wanted, you've always said.'

'All right,' sighed Savage. 'That's what I've always said.'

'Have you changed your mind?'

'Well, no. In principle it's a good thing. But this is a bit sudden, that's all.'

'All life is sudden,' shrugged Mr Kostelanetz as if quoting an Eastern proverb. He studied each of them in turn as if wondering if they comprehended. 'Life is.'

Savage returned the shrug. 'Well, that's it, then.' He turned to Korky. 'You'll let me know when you're ready to move out, won't you.'

'Don't be like that, Savage,' she pleaded. Her eyes pinned him. 'I won't go at all if you don't want me to.'

'No,' he argued, attempting to be lofty. 'It's the best thing. As you say, that's what I've always thought.' He regarded her ruefully. 'It's right you should go. Quite right.'

'Good, good,' said Mr Kostelanetz seeking to conclude the embarrassment. 'This Mrs Longbottom will be pleased. She trusts Korky.'

Savage said: 'I don't even know who *this* Mrs Longbottom is.'

'Number one-eleven,' said Korky. 'Next block.'

'Her husband,' Mr Kostelanetz explained anxiously, 'is in Australia. But he is coming back.'

'So Mrs Longbottom is going *to* Australia. They can't stand each other. They like to pass each other in mid-air,' said Korky.

'What happens when he finds you in the flat?' asked Savage.

'Nothing. It's her flat but she wants to have somebody there. Just in case. He's no problem.'

'She wants to keep out of his way though?'

'That's it. They want to avoid each other. When he goes back to Oz she'll come back here. It'll be at least six months. He likes our football.'

Mr Kostelanetz finished the last triangle of wine. 'I must now go,' he said. Gravely he shook hands with both and just as gravely moved towards the door.

Korky let him out leaving Savage to return to the kitchen and sit almost weakly on one of the stools.

'You seem to know everything that's going on,' he said when Korky returned. 'Everything in this big, dumb building.'

'I hear it all,' she agreed. 'You can't live in Kensington Heights without hearing bits and pieces. Well, *you* might, but I can't.'

Savage rubbed his hands across his eyes. She reached out and with cautious tenderness touched him on the shoulders. 'Anyway, it's not yet. It depends on this Mrs Longbottom.'

'And this *Mr* Longbottom,' he stressed. 'I wonder which of us is the craziest.' Perched on the stool he solemnly regarded her.

'Oh come on, Savage, mate,' she pleaded. 'You wouldn't want life to be dull would you.'

'That,' he said, 'was the object when I came here.'

'Ah, but that was before I turned up,' she said walking briskly into the sitting room. The miniature map she had bought in Portobello Road was now the sole adornment of the long wall, hanging at the centre like a small seal on a large letter. She reached and took the map down. Savage came slowly from the kitchen. 'You haven't forgotten,' she said holding it up triumphantly. 'That's where we are going. Our very own island.'

'When?' He felt defeated.

'When we like,' she told him. 'All sorted. Mr Furtwangler gave me a book.'

She passed the map to him and he stood holding it while she went into her room and returned with a dark, old, worn book. '*A Guide to the Isle of Wight,*' she announced formally. She squatted childlike on the sofa and began to rustle through the elderly pages. Gently he took it from her. He was glad of the diversion. 'Nineteen hundred and eleven,' he said.

'So what?' she exclaimed. 'It's still the Isle of Wight. It's in the same place in the sea and it can't have changed its shape. Look at this picture of the cliffs, Savage. High as anything. And the lighthouse and those massive rocks.' She peered closely at the small old print. 'The Needles. What will they think of next? And here, I was reading it in bed, there's a bit about smugglers and pirates and stuff.

And people who lured ships onto the rocks so they could nick the stuff.'

'Wreckers,' he said flatly.

'That's it, wreckers. See, you're getting in the mood now. It's going to be brill, so exciting, Savage.'

'Not half as exciting as living here,' he answered.

They were late leaving. As they were about to go from the flat Korky decided she needed a suitcase. They had agreed to share his but as his old army case lay open on his bed she had appeared at the door, her hands dangling with underwear and, surveying it briefly, announced that she had to have one of her own.

In half an hour she returned with a single piece of cheap luggage. 'Some man offered to carry it for me,' she giggled. She opened it alongside his on the bed. 'And I got myself a dress.'

It was long and black, the neck cut away low and with tails around the hem. She held it against her front. 'It's for when we dance in the evening.'

'It's the Isle of Wight,' he said studying her. 'And it's September. It's not Monte Carlo in the season.'

Korky looked determined. 'I *will* wear it and we *will* dance.'

'All right.'

'And I bought a red bikini.' She eyed him and held it up. 'Sexy, eh?'

'Very,' he said. 'You'll freeze.'

'So I freeze.' She piled her clothes into the suitcase and placed her purchases on top. 'A girl's got to have some kit.' She broke into a smirk. 'People will think we're on our honeymoon.'

'No they won't.'

'I don't care. It *is* in a way. We've never been away

together before. I bet we have a terrific time. We'll be like those people in the telly commercials running along the empty beach by the waves.'

'If we ever get there,' he said taking her wrist and looking at her watch.

She slammed the lid of her new case, mauve plastic, the locks and catches bright tin. 'That's my first suitcase too, come to think of it,' she said.

'What about your gerbil?' he asked.

'John!' Aghast she put her hand to her open mouth. 'Oh God, am I careless! It's because he's out on the balcony all the time. I forgot him. God forgive me.'

'I've asked Mrs Tomelty to come and feed him,' Savage told her. Her expression remained.

'She won't. She'll forget. You know what a daft old bat she can be.' She corrected herself: 'A nice, daft old bat.' Her hands went to her mouth. 'Oh, Savage, she won't look after him properly. She won't talk to him.'

'He's happy out on the balcony.'

'Not while I'm enjoying myself on holiday,' she retorted, her face crammed. 'Oh, I'm so selfish!'

Savage sat heavily on the bed. 'Are we going or not?'

'Going? Of course we're going. But ...' She spun around and dashed from the bedroom. There came the heavy metallic opening and closing of the balcony door and she returned carrying the sleepily sagging gerbil in one hand. 'John's coming with us.' Savage felt his face drop. 'You can't ...' he protested. 'You can't ... take a gerbil.'

Defiantly she dropped the animal in her suitcase. 'Why not?' she demanded. 'Just tell me why not.'

'We're going ... well, to a hotel.'

She picked the tattered guide-book from the bed and brandished it. 'Show me,' she challenged. 'Show me where it says: "No gerbils allowed." Go on, I dare you. Just show me.'

'Gerbils weren't invented when that was published,' he protested. 'Some hotels don't allow animals anyway.'

'We'll go to one that does,' she said. 'Anyway we don't have to *tell* them. John will be fine in this suitcase.'

'John will suffocate,' he forecast.

She threw her hands to her face again. 'Oh, Savage. Thanks. Thank you very much. He could too. I never thought of that.'

She whirled again and disappeared from the room. He peered into the case. The gerbil had already made a nest for itself on her new dress and was settling to sleep. She returned with the breadknife and, closing the lid of the suitcase, took a stab at it. The knife went straight through. 'Oh, no!' she screamed and tugged open the lid again. She had not pierced the gerbil although he had opened an anxious eye. She waved the knife uncertainly. Savage reached over and took it from her. Leaving the lid open he made half a dozen holes from the inside and handed the knife back to her. She blushed gratefully, returned the knife to the kitchen and called from there: 'He'll need food.' Savage, who was about to close the lid, sighed and opened it again. John blinked irritably. Korky returned and put in a bowl filled with cornflakes. 'That should do him until we get there.'

Savage studied her. She smiled primly. 'Shouldn't John go to the toilet first?' he suggested. 'It's a long way.'

'He went,' affirmed Korky. 'He went in his tray.' She surveyed the curled animal doubtfully. 'We'll have to take him somewhere when we're on the journey.' She glanced unsurely at Savage who said: 'Perhaps they'll have a gerbil toilet at the station.'

Korky closed the lid of the suitcase and turned it

carefully upright, listening as the animal slid slowly into position inside. 'John,' she called through the air holes. 'You're going to the Isle of Wight.'

Twenty

It was clear, early evening before they were on the local train to Lymington. Korky had insisted that they embark on the ferry there rather than sail from Portsmouth or Southampton. 'You're not so long at sea,' she pointed out. 'I've never been on the sea so I don't know if I'll be sick or not.'

'It only takes twenty minutes,' Savage told her.

'I don't want to be sick for twenty minutes.'

They drew into the single-track marine station at Lymington, the platform lying like a jetty against the water and the horizon full of masts. For most of the journey she had sat close against the window, engrossed in the transposing countryside. She remained childlike, carrying her mauve case; they went through the barrier and saw the ferry.

Korky halted. 'It looks safe.'

'I'd say she was seaworthy,' Savage responded with the same seriousness. She held his hand as they walked. 'Oh, Savage, what a terrific idea this was of mine. We're going to have such a great time.'

They climbed the gangway. The vessel was uncrowded. Korky eyed the lifeboats and emergency rafts and boldly tested the firmness of a suspended lifebelt, reading aloud the ship's name printed on its side. 'You can see the island from here,' he said. She followed him to the upper deck, below the bridge, and looked out over the quiet, dun evening to the smudged rising land on the near horizon.

'There it is,' she breathed. 'It looks close enough to walk.'

They went into the cafeteria and drank coffee. She was engrossed with the old guide-book, now falling apart with unaccustomed use. 'This must have been a cheap edition,' she grumbled. She said to Savage: 'It says Tennyson used to come across this way. We've got his books in the shop.'

She had a moment of apprehension when the ferry moved with a minor jolt away from the quay. They went out on to the foredeck again. The weighty movement of the ship passing through the low estuary was eddying the evening air. 'Sniff,' said Savage.

Korky sniffed: 'Salty.'

They passed the tinkling masts of the marina. 'I wouldn't want a yacht,' She sniffed again. 'Too noisy.' They went to the port side where the land was flat and grey-green down to the water's edge. A solitary large house faced the estuary. '*That's* where I want to live,' she decided. 'I want to look from bed and see the water and the ships. Will you buy it, Savage? Buy it for me.'

'I'll save up,' he promised.

She took the gerbil to the ladies' toilet. 'He did it,' she whispered triumphantly. 'He seemed to know.' She slid him into the case, locked it, and circumspectly returned it to the perpendicular. The ship had left the low banks of the estuary and they were heading across the open channel to the looming island.

Again Korky resorted to the ancient guide-book. '*Sunset and evening star*,' she recited loudly and doggedly. '*And one clear call for me.*' Several passengers stared at her; a woman muttered below a headscarf, another laughed. Korky turned to Savage. 'Tennyson was on this very ferry when he wrote that,' she said. 'Well, not this one but a hundred years ago.'

He smiled and took the book from her to read the words. She was standing close against him as though hiding herself from the late breeze. 'It's just like that old film we saw on the box,' she whispered. The woman with the headscarf was watching them. Korky smiled and gave her a small wave. 'Remember. That Gregory . . . what's his name? Gregory Bird?'

'Gregory Peck.'

'That's it. The film where America bought that place, where all the snow and ice are, from Russia for a couple of dollars. Alaska.'

He regarded her wryly. 'You know,' she urged. 'When they were on the ship and the wind was blowing and he had his arms around her from the back. God, it was bloody romantic. I got all moony.'

'It was ages ago. We saw that.'

'I know. But it's just like this.' She waited. 'Savage, stick your arm around me. We'll make out we're going to buy Alaska.'

He let his hand rest on her narrow waist; the evening calmness was spread all about them, the sun low and lemon. The land was growing dim behind them and taking shape ahead. They could pick out buildings, the square church, roofs. A few silent gulls cruised with them. There was a small cargo boat pushing west. The woman in the headscarf watched them close together, the young girl and the man in middle age. 'Disgusting,' she grunted.

According to the 1911 guide-book the Isle of Wight was of

sufficient area to accommodate the entire known population of the world without anyone treading on anyone's toes.

'I wish a few more of them would come here,' grumbled the taxi driver. He hunched low against the wheel as though prepared for the worst. 'Once the kids have gone the season's over more or less.' He rallied: 'Still, you'll have a nice time. We've got grottoes and walks and a waxworks. All sorts. Over at Ryde there's an exhibition of teapots.'

Savage had instructed him to take them to a hotel on the sea. It took only ten minutes. 'You'll like it here,' he forecast as they alighted and doubtfully examined the damp, cream building. The windows were salt-stained. A face appeared at one on the second floor, staring like a ghost, and like a ghost it vanished. 'It's cheerful but quiet you might say. The kids run a bit riot, do some damage, during the summer, but they've gone now.' The driver surveyed the semi-steamed bay windows. 'Anyway, you'll like it.'

Inside the hotel it seemed as though the winter heating should have been on. The rosy-faced woman at the reception desk was demonstratively glad at their unexpected arrival. 'Don't blame you not booking,' she said thrusting the hotel register towards them. 'You've got a choice then. Although Charlie the Taxi always brings people here. He should do, he's my father.'

Korky had wandered to the end of the lobby and was studiously selecting brochures from a rack. 'The paddle steamer trip's nice,' the receptionist called to her. 'If it's not too rough.' As though she needed to do it while the girl was at a distance she said to Savage in a low, conspiratorial, voice: 'Is it two rooms?'

Savage blinked. 'Yes. Yes, of course. If you have two.'

'You can have two *each* if you like,' the woman told him honestly. 'It's your daughter, is it? I thought it was your daughter. She looks like you.' She giggled primly. 'Not that I haven't made mistakes.' Savage signed the register and she put two keys on the desk. 'Norman's gone off for his break,' she said peering over the counter at their luggage.

'We can manage,' Savage said.

'Good. Very good of you. He has a long break sometimes.' She looked at the loud clock on the wall behind her. 'Dinner is on now,' she said. 'Last orders nine thirty. You've got plenty of time.' Savage took the keys and was about to pick up the cases when from Korky's came an urgent scratching. The receptionist backed away behind the counter, her eyes widening. 'What's it doing that for?'

'Korky,' he called.

She was peering into the open door of the dining room. 'Yes, Savage?'

'It's John. He's restless.'

The woman watched fascinated. 'The suitcase is called John?' she asked.

'No, no. It doesn't have a name,' said Savage soberly. 'John is inside.'

'He's fed up,' said Korky advancing on the case. She laid it gently flat. The receptionist was joined by a fragile man who appeared from the office behind the desk. They observed the sounding case intently.

Korky opened the hasps of the tin locks and revealed the gerbil as she lifted the lid. 'He hasn't even messed,' she announced proudly. She picked up the animal and squeezed it gently. 'Good man, John.'

'No animals,' announced the frail man in a thin voice. The receptionist swiftly nudged him. 'No *dogs*,' she corrected. 'Or *cats*. But the odd hamster's acceptable, Mr Penney.'

'John is a gerbil,' corrected Korky succinctly.

Mr Penney saw the receptionist's glance. 'Oh, a gerbil is it. Yes, gerbils are allowed.'

'He sleeps a lot of the time,' Korky assured them. She patted the animal. 'Although I may try him on the beach. He's never been on a beach.'

'It's all right then?' said Savage.

'Absolutely,' the woman almost enthused. She rolled her eyes at the man who obediently retreated to the back room. 'We've had hundreds of excruciating children through the summer. Little swines,' she continued. 'A quiet gerbil is most welcome.' She laughed, attempting to make it light. 'No extra charge.' Her expression became concerned. 'But you won't take him in to dinner, will you. We couldn't have him in the dining room.' She reached over and stroked the plump, warm, bent back. 'Nice as he is.'

The suitcase had remained open and Korky, with an anxious look at the woman peering at the otherwise sparse contents, slammed it and picked it up. 'I've left room for shopping,' she said.

'It's on the first floor,' pointed the receptionist. 'No need to use the lift. The lift is dodgy anyway due to the dear children.'

She decided she would see them to the rooms and led the way up the wide staircase. 'It's so lovely and peaceful now,' she continued. 'We like it like this, except we don't make any money.' They had reached the rooms, the doors only inches apart. 'Number twelve and number fourteen,' recited Korky. She glanced at the receptionist. 'What happened to thirteen?'

'We don't have one,' answered the woman. 'Superstitious people don't like it.'

'Which do you want, Savage?' asked Korky. He could see her hardly suppressed excitement.

The receptionist regarded them oddly because of their names. Savage said he would take number twelve. The woman unlocked both doors and they all walked into his room. 'Oh, it's great,' said Korky. 'Really big. Look at the windows.'

'The beach and the sea are just across the road,' said the receptionist. They followed her to the window. It had begun to drizzle. From window's edge to window's edge there was no sign of life, only the raindrops on the glass. 'I'll draw the curtains,' said the woman, deftly doing so as if to shut out the view.

Then they went into the other room. It was almost the same. The receptionist moved towards the curtains. 'Leave them,' said Korky. 'I like them open even if it's dark. I'll pretend I can see the sea.' She smiled without embarrassment. 'Maybe the moon will come out when I'm in bed.'

The woman delicately showed them the bathrooms and took their orders for morning tea. Then she left them and Savage went back to his room.

Korky followed him. She closed the door and ran across the room and threw herself backwards across the double bed, bare legs flying in the air. John, whom she had placed on the floor, began to scamper around matching her excitement. 'Oh, Savage,' she enthused. 'It's magic! I've never been in a hotel before.' She regarded him wickedly: 'Especially with a man.'

'Pack it in,' he warned. 'And get off my bed. Your room is next door.'

'It's terrific though, isn't it. I can't wait until morning so I can look out and see the waves.'

She embraced him and he held her with their contrived restricted physical closeness, arms about each other, brother-and-sister-kisses, he softly tugging her hair, both knowing the moment when to pull away. Now she drew from him smiling and bending, picking up the sniffing gerbil which had homed in on her feet. 'John and I are going to our room,' she announced loftily. 'To prepare ourselves for dinner.'

The tables in the sadly lit dining room were randomly occupied. Those eating at them spoke in mumbles as though they had food in their mouths. One section had been cordoned off.

'The no-go area,' explained the waiter lugubriously. He had a dried cascade of gravy on his waistcoat which he attempted to conceal with his arm while serving the soup. 'That was where we used to put the worse of the them.'

He spoke solemnly. There was little choice on the menu. 'You seem to have suffered,' observed Savage.

'Everybody has,' continued the man. He looked worn out. 'The parents don't care, and the kids get worse every year. I was personally struck by chips. Our longest-serving waitress was knocked cold by a tray.' He sighed at the remembrance. 'It went like a Frisbee.'

Outside the long, gaunt window the wind pushed; there was the regular blink of a lighthouse. The nearest occupied table seated three people, a piled-up old lady whose drooped eyelids swung with her jaw as she ate, a woman in her late thirties with blonde streaks who at intervals stared across at them and a vapid teenage girl who aimlessly spooned her dessert. Marshalled by the younger woman they rose at the end of their meal. She smiled fiercely and paused as they made for the door. 'Not too many guests around now,' she observed. Korky eyed her in silence.

'No. No, it certainly seems quiet,' agreed Savage. They had finished their main course. Korky took her wine glass and drank with a sophisticated lift of her fingers, watching the young girl from the edge of her eye.

'I *do* like a good bottle of wine,' gushed the woman. The fat lady had her eyes shut, apparently sleeping as she stood. 'The trouble is wine sends my mother to sleep. Wherever she happens to be.' She watched her mother nodding, and did so herself as though counting the nods. The girl gave the old lady a nudge and she woke, her eyelids lifting truculently.

'And Bianca here doesn't like it,' said the woman. 'Wine.'

'Yes, I do,' protested the girl. 'I like pina colada.'

Her mother surveyed her scathingly. 'We're not in Majorca.'

She returned her attention to the table. 'Well, I suppose I ought to introduce us,' she said as if settling everything for the next week. 'My name is Margo Bull.' She looked directly at them as though challenging a reaction. 'This is my mother Thelma and this is my daughter Bianca.'

Warily Savage said: 'My name is Frank Savage and this is Kathleen.'

With difficulty they all shook hands across the table. The old lady had to be prompted. 'I'd better take her up,' sighed Margo. 'Otherwise she'll just drop off where she is. That's what she does.' She smiled fully, attentively, at Savage, then reduced the size of the smile for Korky.

'Perhaps we could have a drink a little later. It can get quite jolly in the bar.'

Awkwardly Savage told her: 'I think we'll have to make it another night. We thought we might take a walk and then watch television. We're tired.'

'You've come a long way?' pried Margo.

'All the way from England,' answered Korky.

The night was dark with a slight glow around the edges and as they walked there was a wind brisk enough for Korky to have to shout against it. 'She's after you,' she warned.

'Who?' shouted Savage. They were pressing forward buttoned into anoraks. Not far away the invisible sea growled and the lighthouse beam flew around like a lost thing.

'That Margo. She's after you.'

'She won't catch me.'

'She'd better not! Couldn't you see it in her eyes?'

They walked for half a mile and then turned and, with the gusts behind them, went back to the grimly lit hotel. 'We can always move,' suggested Savage. 'We don't have to stay here.'

He detected her affronted movement in the dark. 'There's no way I'm moving,' she said, her voice lower now without the combat of the wind. 'Not for Margo.'

They went into the hotel lobby. The porter had returned from his prolonged break and was now resting stoically in his cubby-hole.

' 'Evening, sir, miss,' he greeted. 'Sorry I wasn't here to take up your bags. I've been having a bit more time off. Now they've gone.'

'What did they do to *you*?' asked Korky. Her interest was growing.

'Do? What *didn't* they do, miss?'

'What then?' insisted Korky. Savage was collecting the keys from the same receptionist. 'Poor soul,' the woman confided. 'He still hobbles.'

'I can't tell you,' said the porter. 'It upsets me too much. Baby vandals, four-year-old hooligans. And they bring them all here.'

Savage and Korky ascended the stairs, the faded goodnights of the porter and the receptionist following them. On the landing Korky put her hand over her mouth. 'He still hobbles,' she whispered.

Savage began to limp thumpingly along the carpet. 'What *didn't* they do, miss?' he mimicked.

She squealed and he put his finger to her lips in warning. They were at their doors now. Korky leaned against the side of hers as he was inserting his key in his door. 'Goodnight, Daddy,' she said mischievously.

'Don't start that,' he warned. She pushed her face towards him and they kissed lightly on the lips. She had her door open and then he opened his. 'Let's hope the sun shines tomorrow,' he said.

'I don't care,' she answered. She yawned. 'I'm having such a good time. Goodnight, Savage.'

'Goodnight, Korky.'

She went in, slowly closing the door behind her. The bed-head was against the wall which separated the two rooms and the wall was thin so she could hear him moving. She went to the bathroom and when she returned she heard the flush from his. She even heard his bed-springs creak. Grinning to herself she got on to her bed on her hands and knees and, putting her mouth close to the wall, called: 'Goodnight, Savage.' There was a pause and another creak from his bed-springs before the call was returned: 'Goodnight, Korky.' Her tentative smile remained as she leaned forward and briefly kissed the wall at the place opposite where she thought his head would be. Then she slid down into the bed and lay with her eyes open. 'You're bloody stupid, you are,' she told herself.

Twenty-One

They brought the hired car to the hotel the next morning and, sitting in the driving seat, Savage fumbled nervously. Taking his hands from the wheel he lowered them into his lap. 'It's three years since I drove anything,' he said.

'On the day you got shot,' she guessed.

'That was the last time.'

'In that case go slow,' she suggested practically. 'There's not much on the roads. Pretend you're a learner.'

'I feel I am,' Savage replied wryly. He turned the key; his head jolted back as the engine started. It was a manual gear change. He slotted the lever carefully remembering the clutch and the car moved forward nervously.

'Take it around this bit,' suggested Korky. The gravelled area in front of the hotel was limited but he said: 'All right. I'll practise.'

The hotel staff, alerted by the observant porter, gathered at the windows to see the car going around in a tight oval. It did so a dozen times in second gear. Then Savage stopped and gingerly attempted reversing.

'They're all looking at us,' warned Korky spotting the silent faces. 'Nosy lot.'

'I'm ready now anyway,' said Savage only briefly

examining the audience. 'I've driven an armoured car, so this shouldn't be any harder. Let's go!'

'Let's go!' she echoed. He bent the car in a tight circle and turning down her window, Korky raised a caustic finger to the observers. They drove on to the road. He felt more confident now and he increased speed and almost hit a corner. She hooted: 'It's not an armoured car.'

He slowed and apologised with a grin. 'Sorry, I forgot.'

The way took them along windy clifftops into clefts where there was sometimes a beach and some late, hopeful souvenir shops. They drove inland into the island countryside, into valleys and through villages where they could not even see the sea. 'Can't we stop for a while?' she asked.

'I'm not sure I *can* stop,' he laughed. They swung off the tight road into a lay-by, gravel flying as he hurriedly braked. He switched off the engine and they sat laughing. 'Oh, Savage, look at it!' she exclaimed swivelling to look through the rear window. He turned, towards her, and saw the English Channel like a blue hammock between two plunging green hills. 'Let's go and see,' he said. She climbed out of the car and he checked the handbrake and followed. She was running ahead, her hair and her jacket blowing in the salt breeze.

Animated as a child she began mounting a zigzag path. He followed and stood beside her at the top. 'Lovely,' she breathed. 'And to think it all belongs to us.' She corrected herself. 'It's England's.'

As if to prove the claim he pointed to the edge of a huge flag to the extreme right of their vision. She held his hand and they went to the top of the brief hill where they saw the immense Union Jack, flying flat out in the wind. 'That'll show them!' exclaimed Korky.

'Who?'

'Foreigners in boats,' she said as if it were obvious. 'They can see this is England.' She glanced at him. 'In case they're lost.'

They remained standing in the sunny wind for a few moments, then descended the way they had come. An odd, embarrassed silence fell over them. They got back into the car unspeaking and he continued driving along the coastal road, turning and bending before them in the September light.

They reached another tight beach with a harbour sheltering a few small boats in the lee of its wall; they walked along the sand and the tide mark. Korky took off her shoes and kicked at the water. Her feet and legs were as pale as her urban face. They sat against the wall, silently, feeling the sun.

Then Korky said: 'There's not a soul here.' She scanned the beach. There was only a distant dog. 'I like being lonely,' she said. 'As long as there's somebody near.'

'Weren't you lonely before?'

'Before you?' she said. 'Not all that much. Most people with no homes hang on to each other. We even used to sleep in piles.' She watched the waves. 'There's plenty of lonely people around. The world's full of people who haven't met. Look at Kensington Heights. Look at Freddie.'

'You think Freddie's lonely?'

'Everybody's lonely in some way. Freddie, Stephen Stevens, Mr Furtwangler, Mr Kostelanetz, even Miss Bombazine though she meets so many people. She goes for a walk by herself.'

The silence came to them again. The dog began to

bark remotely; otherwise only the sea sounded. 'You've never told me about getting wounded,' she mentioned.

'It's not something I like to think about.'

'I've often looked at that grey bit in your hair,' she said. 'It wasn't far off, was it?' She moved closer to him against the wall. 'Tell me what happened.'

'I don't know, really,' he said. 'Only what I've been told or read.'

'What happened?' she repeated.

'It sounds ridiculous,' he said wryly. 'But they got us on our tea break.' He shook his head. 'It was unbelievable. I'd told the section to stand down. There was a canteen wagon. It came to the same spot every day. Usually we checked the area but this day I didn't do it. There was an explosive device, a big one, planted in a telephone box. They'd put "Out of order" on the door and we believed it. It was detonated while the boys were lining up for tea. Three killed outright. Then we came under fire from a barn just opposite. That's when I was hit. That's when my friend Henry Barnard caught it as well. He died months after. I went and saw his grave once.'

'That's it?' she said.

'That's all there is to tell,' he told her.

They got to their feet. As they walked the way they had come, treading in their own footsteps, she asked quietly: 'What are we going to do, Savage?'

'You mean what's to become of us?'

'Yes. What are we going to do?'

They continued walking as though discussing someone else's problem. 'I don't know,' he said. 'I thought you were going to move.'

'Mrs Longbottom's not moved out yet,' said Korky. They began to walk up the inclined sand towards the car.

'It'll be better,' he forecast without conviction. 'Then we can still be friends and see each other . . .'

'Without getting in each other's way,' she finished.

'Right.'

Standing a little apart, they regarded the sea in silence, then, thoughtfully, they got into the car. On a whim, he drove away from the coast and up a climbing and winding way which became steep towards the top. 'It goes up and up,' she said looking high and ahead to where the road had become indistinct. The car was in second gear. 'I never realised islands could be high like this.'

Around the descending corner came a boisterous red bus. Savage made an exclamation and stopped the car's laboured climb. There was no room for both vehicles. The bus halted and they faced each other. Savage saw the bus driver flapping his hand from his window. 'Go back!' shouted the man. 'I *can't* go back up. You have to go down.'

'God,' muttered Savage fumbling for the gear lever. 'Go on, Savage,' encouraged Korky sternly. 'You can do it.'

He managed to put the car into reverse. Korky looked behind; there was nothing coming up the hill.

'It's all the same if there is,' he muttered. Twisting in his seat he began the tortuous journey down the bent road. The vehicle wavered from one side to the other and once hit the roadside bank and he had to go forward before reversing again. The bus driver, the conductor and several passengers had left their vehicle and stood in a watching group. 'Go on, have a good laugh,' grunted Korky.

He inched the car down the narrow road, around one bend, and then one in the opposite direction, descending a mercifully straight piece and then negotiating two more hairpins. The bus was now following them, big, red, threatening. Korky could see the driver sitting smugly. 'Arsehole,' she said.

At last there was space at the side of the road. He inched into it, his arms aching, his back stretched. The bus continued its heavy downward journey. As it passed the driver leaned benignly out of his cab. 'There ain't nothing up there anyway,' he called.

That evening there was to be a dance. 'Last of the season,' said the dining room waiter with a sigh of regret or relief. 'People come in from outside. Real, proper dancers. Strictly ballroom,' he said. 'And they always kept those kids out.' He clanked the dessert dishes together then laid them on the table lugubriously. 'The Punch and Judy man will never work again,' he said rolling his head.

Near the end of the meal they saw the streaky blonde making towards them followed at a sulky distance by her daughter and, some further way behind, by the ponderous mother, eyelids half-lowered, mouth munching as though she had not quite finished her dinner. Margo smiled winningly. 'Had a lovely day?' she enquired and without waiting for their report added: 'There's dancing this evening.' She eyed Savage speculatively. 'The band is rather good.'

'They come from Ryde,' put in her daughter. The contribution was determined, almost desperate, but she seemed at a loss to continue. Her mother stepped a couple of decisive paces in time to prevent the old lady toppling, taking her fat hand and wrapping it like sausage meat around the top rail of a dining chair.

Bianca tried again: 'If all the people in the world came

to the Isle of Wight, they could stand next to each other and not tread on each other's toes.'

'Excepting China,' put in Korky.

The girl appeared peeved. 'Well, yes, excepting them.'

'I knew Bianca and Kathleen would get on,' said Margo her face squeezed with enthusiasm. Keeping a fraction of an eye on her leaning mother, she said: 'There's a pop group performing in the town tonight.' She studied Korky unsurely. 'Perhaps you could both go.' She simpered. 'She's got no one to play with here. I can't let her go by herself. She's only fifteen.'

'They're called the Bay Watchers,' Bianca informed Korky.

Korky looked at Savage for an escape but he said: 'Why don't you go?' She bared her teeth and muttered: 'Well, later.' She produced a fulsome smile for Margo. 'There's dancing in the hotel, you say?'

'Ah, but not your sort of dancing,' argued the woman. She did not like the look of Korky. 'You'd be much better with the . . . the . . .'

'Bay Watchers,' reminded Bianca proudly.

The old mother interrupted the exchange by beginning to slip sideways. 'She's dozing off,' said Margo. 'I'll have to get her to bed.' She waved girlishly to them both and caught her mother heavily but with some deftness in the same movement.

The Ryde Romantics were warming to a waltz when Savage and Korky crept covertly downstairs. They had intended to escape to a pub by the harbour but Margo was lying in the shadows. 'You're here!' she exclaimed as though there had been a major search for them. 'Now come along. I will buy you a drink. Both.'

Bianca was sprawled, wan and moody, in a cane chair

near the bar. She wore a short skirt and thick black tights. In the background the lights were pink, lending an ethereal glow to the faces of the band. Margo indicated two chairs.

'It's not your sort of music, I know, Kathleen,' sympathised Margo as she turned to get the attention of the waiter. 'The . . . er . . . Bay . . .'

'Watchers,' provided Bianca sipping through a straw.

'Yes, the Bay Watchers. You'll be able to . . .'

'Rave it up,' muttered Korky transferring her dulled eyes to Savage.

'You'll enjoy it,' he said. He was aware of a strange contrary feeling of not wanting her to go. She looked unhappy.

'You will,' enthused Margo looking meaningfully at Savage. 'You younger set.'

The waiter came over. People had, Margo said, come from a distance to the dance. It was the only weekday dance left. The tables about the floor were full and twenty couples moved moonily now to a foxtrot. Korky grimly ordered a whisky. Margo hesitated and glanced at Savage. 'I'll have one too,' suggested Bianca. 'You will not!' retorted her mother like a scarcely controlled explosion. 'You're only fifteen.'

'That's my age, not my fault,' said the girl cheekily. She rose in Korky's estimation.

'Don't speak to me like that,' Margo warned incisively. 'Or off to bed you go. And no Bay Watchers.'

Her voice trailed a little as though she immediately regretted the threat. 'Just be reasonable,' she suggested with a stiff smile. 'For once. Please.'

Margo and Savage were dancing. He moved tentatively but the dance was slow and she helped and prompted, her full bosom supportively against him. From her distance Korky thought how good he looked now, his upright body, his head in profile, his smile. When they turned Margo pushed.

'My mum fancies your dad,' mentioned Bianca.

'He's not my dad,' muttered Korky fiercely. She took a breath. 'He's my lover.'

'He is!' Bianca was enthralled. She leaned eagerly. 'Christ, what's it like?'

Korky swallowed. 'Well . . . not properly. But he's not my dad either.'

'What is he then?'

'All right, he *is* my dad. I was only sending you up.'

'My mum fancies him,' repeated Bianca overcoming her disappointment. 'She doesn't get many chances. My father went off and she has to drag around my granny. But she's the one with the money.'

'Why is she always falling over?' enquired Korky. 'Your gran.'

'Because she's tired,' shrugged Bianca. They continued observing the close couple on the dance floor. Margo was laughing girlishly. 'Shit,' muttered Korky.

'My gran doesn't mind,' said Bianca mistaking the oath for an expression of sympathy. 'She still thinks it's years ago. She's eighty or ninety.'

The music finished. Korky watched grimly as Savage and Margo slowed and stopped. They remained on the floor for a moment as the other dancers dispersed, still close, their left hands held, their right arms about each other. Margo was chattering. Unhurriedly, reluctantly it seemed to Korky, they uncoupled and walked towards them.

'Was it a nice dance?' enquired Korky sourly.

'Heavenly,' said Margo with her lush smile. She turned to Savage. 'Wasn't it, Frank?'

'Oh, yes,' said Savage avoiding Korky's eyes. 'I'm afraid I am a bit rusty, that's all.'

'We'll have the next one,' said Korky decisively. She began to get to her feet. 'Come on, they're starting.'

'It's a cha-cha-cha,' warned Margo with a hint of foregone triumph. Bianca smirked towards Korky.

'We always dance the cha-cha-cha,' Korky returned with soft tartness. 'When we're at home.' Her eyes challenged Savage. 'Don't we, Frank?'

Savage responded weakly. 'All the time.' He took a desperate swallow of his Scotch and allowed Korky to tow him on to the dance floor.

He stood woodenly, his hands held out in front, solid as a big puppet. 'I can't dance this,' he protested hoarsely. 'Not the cha-cha-cha.' His worried eyes went to the feet of the dancers already primping into the steps, but Korky had fixed him with a small smile. ' 'Course you can,' she encouraged privately. 'You just plonk your legs up and down to the music.' She held out her thin arms to him and they got into position a foot apart. 'Plonkie, plonk, plonk, plonk, plonkie, plonk,' she encouraged. His eyes were still swivelling. 'Don't do that, you look like a scared bloody horse,' she told him softly. 'We'll do it our way. Plonk, plonk, plonk. That's right. Keep going.' Her smile grew and glowed as they pumped up and down on the same spot, his lumbering legs and her light limbs like different pistons. 'That's right, you've got it,' she breathed happily. She allowed herself a sharp scan towards Margo and was gratified to see her observing from behind a deep scowl; Bianca's head had dropped to one side, her expression envious.

Savage's anxiety began to ease. No one was laughing,

no one was even watching them. The dancers were too intent on their own intricate patterns. 'Plonk, plonk, plonk,' sang Korky to him. 'Now let's turn when we do it. This way. Plonk, plonk, plonkie, plonk.' He revolved slowly, nervously, still keeping his feet pumping, but no less ponderously, in time with the music. Korky pushed herself closer to him, her flimsy frame against his chest, their legs brushing.

'Oh, Savage,' she breathed happily. 'We're dancing, Savage, we're dancing.'

At the end of the tune he insisted that they should quit the floor. 'My knees have gone,' he whispered. She laughed and kept laughing so that Margo could see, as they returned to the table.

'That was good,' said Bianca with envious enthusiasm.

'It looked very difficult,' sniffed her mother. It was a time for decisions. She looked at her watch. 'It's almost ten. Do you two want to be off now?'

'It started at nine,' said Bianca her eyes going pleadingly towards Korky. 'Shall we?'

'Oh, all right,' responded Korky like someone now sure of their ground. 'We'll give it a go.' She sniffed airily. 'Watch out the Bay Watchers.'

'Gosport's top band,' quoted Bianca. Her face fell. 'Wherever Gosport is.' The girls picked up their handbags.

'Have you got enough money?' Margo asked her daughter. 'You had five pounds at the weekend.'

Korky looked embarrassed for Bianca. 'I've got some,' Bianca replied low-voiced. 'Enough to get in and for some coke.'

Margo seemed pleased but then became stern. 'Don't drink anything else,' she warned. Her eyes fixed her daughter and then transferred briefly to Korky. 'Understand?'

Bianca nodded and Korky said brazenly: 'You don't *drink* coke.'

'What then,' demanded Margo, 'do you do with it?'

'She's joking,' interrupted Savage. He scowled at Korky. 'Don't joke like that.' He rose. 'I'll take you into town. You'll have to get a taxi back.'

Margo lifted her full eyes to him. 'Don't be long, Frank,' she said. 'Don't you go in there with them.'

He laughed mildly and said he thought it was unlikely. 'I'll be here,' she promised.

Outside it was blowing wet. As they went towards the car Korky whispered against the wind: 'Watch out for that Margo. She's after you, Savage. Before you know it she'll have you.'

He grinned and patted her bottom and she kissed him on the cheek. 'It's blowing up my skirt,' complained Bianca waiting on the other side of the car.

He drove them the mile into the harbour town, across the bridge and around the cornered streets. 'You can hear it,' said Korky easing down the window. 'It's over there somewhere.'

Two more narrow bends and they saw the unmistakable venue. The front of the sober hall was gaudily lit and surrounded by a crowd, its heads illuminated. 'The greats of Gosport,' muttered Korky.

'I hope we can get in,' said Bianca. 'I'm not allowed usually.'

'Look after her,' said Savage to Korky. 'And yourself.'

'She's sound with me,' she answered. She kissed him on the cheek again and got from the car. 'If that Margo tries anything,' she whispered, 'say you've been wounded.' She regarded him as if she meant it and then turned and went with Bianca. He was pleased that she held the girl's hand as they approached the lights and the music thumping over the cut-out of the crowd. He waited in the car. They went through the figures at the fringe and did not re-emerge. He waited another three minutes hoping she would come back, and then drove off.

'You've been hours,' Margo complained winsomely. 'I missed you.'

Uneasily he sat down in the wicker chair. There were fewer people dancing now. 'I got another Scotch for you,' she said. 'Were the girls all right?'

'Yes, fine. There was a terrific din and a huge crowd of kids there, but they went in all right and I waited for a couple of minutes. It looked like my idea of hell.'

'It's all so uncivilised, it seems to me,' she sighed. She looked moodily into her gin. 'In my day ...' She coloured. 'And that was not *so* long ago. It all seemed so much gentler. What did she mean by coke? Not what I ...?'

'She was joking,' Savage told her quickly. 'It's typical of her.'

'She's very ... lively. What happened to your wife?'

'We're separated. We're divorcing.'

'Does ... Korky ... live with your wife?'

'No. She lives with me.'

'Oh. That's a responsibility, isn't it?' She wanted to pursue the questioning but she was also eyeing the possibilities of the dance floor. The band were winding into a waltz. 'Shall we dance?' she said. 'Before they pack up.'

'Yes ... yes, of course. I can manage this one.'

She laughed enticingly, girlishly, over her shoulder at him as they went towards the floor. The lights had dropped to purple. Some of the dancers were still engaged in dextrous ballroom steps but most were now lying close against each other as though exhausted. Margo stood, big and blonde, her arms held invitingly, her smile deep. He put his arms properly about her, about the roll of her waist, and began to plod the three-step movement.

'You don't have to count,' she reproved softly. 'I'll count for you. And relax. You're not marching.' She eased him closer to her lacy front, her perfume engulfed him. 'Why does she call you Savage?' she enquired into his ear.

'Korky?'

'Korky,' she confirmed.

'Oh, it's just habit,' he replied uneasily. 'I call her Korky and she usually calls me Savage, that's all.'

'It's very matey.'

'I suppose it is in a way.' He moved closer against her to try and prevent further questions. She did not ask any. Her full arms went around his neck and he felt the heat of her face. She pushed her stomach against him. He mentally counted: 'One, two, three. One, two, three . . .'

They danced in a romantic glow. He found it easier now. 'That's better, relax,' she said against his ear. 'You're more fun like this.'

The band played low, the lights gleamed pinkly. She moved her warm face and kissed him luxuriously on the lips. He returned the kiss. 'Let's go, shall we,' she suggested secretly.

Almost blindly he followed her from the floor. She was tall, her backside still swaying to the music as she went before him. 'Don't let's wait,' she whispered. 'They'll be playing the national anthem.'

Holding hands they left the lounge and crept by the

empty reception desk. 'Goodnight sir. Goodnight madam,' recited the half-concealed night porter. 'Would you like a morning paper?'

Dumbly they shook their heads at the single inference and released their hands. He retreated somewhere and they went up the stairs together arms about each other's waists. Then, round the bend, they saw her mother, wearing a tented nightdress of coloured stripes, sitting, legs horribly apart, on the top landing. Her eyes were closed, her toothless mouth agape. 'I want a drink,' she demanded cranking up her lids. 'And I want it now.'

'Oh Mother, oh God, oh shit,' itemised Margo fervently. Disappointment and embarrassment crammed her eyes. 'I'm so sorry,' she said to Savage with a pathetic politeness. 'She'll have to have a drink. She'll never settle down otherwise. She'll come looking for me.'

'I can see you've got a problem,' he said. He tried not to look at the old lady. His voice firmed. 'Let's sort it out.'

'Help me heave her up, will you,' pleaded Margo. 'If I can only get her upright, that's half the battle.'

Between them they caught hold of the woman like a heavy sack. He had a fleeting memory of instructing in casualty evacuation under fire. Margo knew what was required. It needed a complex manoeuvre to get her mother to her feet and to stagger with her along the landing to a substantial ornamental couch where they eased her down. The base of her body spread out as though in relief. 'She'll be all right there,' said Margo hopefully. 'Propped up.'

'I'll get her a drink,' suggested Savage. 'What does she want?'

'Guinness,' ordered the old lady in a businesslike way. 'Two bottles.'

'Right,' he said and retreated down the stairs. The bar

was just closing, the band had ceased and were packing their instruments, the dancers were leaving. 'Guinness,' he said to the barman. 'Two bottles please.'

The man, who had observed their coming together during the evening and their eventual clasped departure, raised his eyebrows a trifle and said: 'Really? Well, you never know, do you, with women . . .'

Savage regarded him levelly. 'It's for her mother.'

'Ah, so that's it,' said the barman. He produced two bottles from below the bar. 'Opened now?' he asked.

'Yes,' said Savage sulkily. 'You'd better.'

The barman eased the tops from the bottles and handed them across. Savage signed the bill. 'Have a nice night,' said the man blandly.

Savage grimaced and went towards the lobby. He could hear Margo's cajoling voice from the top of the stairs. 'Now, come on, Mummy, *promise* you'll go back. Your Guinness *is* coming. Here it comes now.'

'I had them take the tops off,' said Savage as he reached the scene and handed over the bottles.

'That's good,' approved Margo. 'She'll drink them both, one after the other. I'd better take her into her room. Come on, Mummy. We've got the Guinness. Two bottles.'

'Opened?' enquired the old lady pedantically.

'Yes, they're opened.' Margo raised her pencilled eyebrows at Savage then blew him a promising kiss.

The old lady missed nothing. 'You and your bloody men,' she complained.

'Come on, dear,' Margo ordered firmly. She made an aside to Savage. 'Dangle the bottles.'

He felt odd dangling a brace of Guinness bottles in front of the woman's big folded face but it was enough to encourage her slowly back to her room. At the door

Margo paused. 'She'll drop off soon. But I'll have to stay with her.' She blew another kiss. 'See you later.'

Gratefully Savage reached his room. After considering it, he locked the door. It was eleven thirty. He undressed and got into bed. Perhaps she had meant tomorrow. After half an hour he was drifting into a relieved sleep when there was a tap at the door. 'It's me,' she called through. 'Margo.' He opened the door. She looked sad and embarrassed. 'I'm sorry. It looks like it's off. She's got downstairs now. Will you help me retrieve her again? Please.'

Savage pulled on his dressing gown and rubbed his face. She waited on the landing looking over the stairwell. 'She's sitting at the bottom,' she reported. She clutched his arm. 'I'm so sorry, Frank,' she told him suddenly tearful. 'I wanted to come, really I did. But the moment I turned my back she was downstairs.' Her face curled. 'The old cow.'

'Let's see what we can do,' said Savage inadequately. 'She's not a small woman.'

'Sixteen stone,' muttered Margo like a curse. 'Deadweight.'

The old lady was snoring asleep when they reached her, her backside on the third stair, her head propped against the bannisters, in her striped nightdress like a beach tent toppled by the wind. 'Come on, Mummy,' cajoled Margo. 'Mr Savage is going to help you.'

The gnarled eyelids rose painfully. 'You again,' she sniffed at him. She heaved her face around to her daughter. 'You and your men, Margo. *I* never had the chance of men.'

'I'm not surprised,' responded Margo tartly. 'Come on, we're going to get you back to bed.'

'So he can whip you?' suggested her mother brazenly.

'Shut up and stand up.' Margo turned briefly to Savage. 'Don't take any notice of her,' she pleaded.

'I won't,' promised Savage desperately. 'Let's pull her to her feet.'

Between them they manoeuvred her upright, so that she was sitting on the stair with her face folded forward. 'You get one armpit and I'll take the other,' said Savage surveying the striped lump.

'Where's the bloody night porter?' grumbled Margo. 'He's used to lifting things.'

As though answering the porter appeared from the lounge where he had been dozing. He buttoned his shirt and straightened his tie. 'Left hand down a bit,' he suggested measuring the situation. He moved forward as if it had all been part of his training. 'If you get her upright, I'll make sure she don't topple.'

Savage decided to let him take charge. Neither he nor Margo had a clear idea of the plan but they hauled the slumped woman to her feet. She was a great weight. The porter kept moving his head from one side to the other, his eyes narrowed, as if overseeing some intricate stone-laying. Eventually he put his hand against the old lady's stomach to finely balance her. 'Right,' he muttered. 'Start hauling.'

They stumbled up one stair at the time, perspiring, winded, the old lady grunting each time her heels hit the edge of a step, and again when they set her down to rest. Like an experienced removals man the porter supervised.

They had almost reached the middle landing when there was an urgent hammering at the glass front door. It was raining and they could see a white oval pressed to the glass, a mouth shaped in a shout.

'Bianca.' Margo was panting on the top stair. 'They're locked out.'

'I'll open it,' offered the porter. He made a deft check on the grandmother now lying at an angle, straightened her a fraction, then descended to the door. Efficiently he unlocked and unbolted it. Bianca, her hair hanging, her clothes wet, her face stark, almost fell into the lobby. 'Mum, it's that Korky!' she howled.

Savage let go of the old lady, so did Margo, and she began bumping fatly down the staircase. 'What's happened?' demanded Margo almost tripping over her. Like an afterthought she propped her mother with her leg. Savage knew he had gone pale. With difficulty he stepped over the recumbent woman. In the lobby Bianca was shivering, soaked and crying. 'Oh, Mum, she's terrible, Mum!'

Her overwrought face flew to Savage. 'She's dropped some acid. She's gone mad.'

'Where?' demanded Savage so sharply the girl jumped. 'Where is she?'

'In the town, screaming around the streets,' She faced him dramatically. 'She thinks she can fly.'

He drove through the thick rain towards the limp lights of the harbour. As he crossed the bridge the wind howled around the car. He cursed as he drove. He was still wearing his pyjamas and dressing gown.

'Bloody Korky,' he cursed to himself. 'Silly bloody kid.'

The streets were blurred, wet and empty. The car slewed and shrieked as he cornered into the main square. He braked and looked frantically around. Then he saw her. She was standing on a roof. 'Oh, my God,' he whispered.

She saw him at once. 'Savage! Savage!' she shouted. 'Look, I can fly!' She began to flap her arms and bend her knees. He fell from the car.

'Korky! For God's sake don't!' he shouted picking himself up. 'You *can't* fly! You *can't* . . .' His voice grated and fell. 'Honestly.' Again he slipped on the cobbles as he stumbled forward. Now he was directly below her. The wind was throwing up her skirt and making her hair fly. 'Come on down, Korky. Please come on down.'

'I'm going to fly down. I can fly. Look!' She wagged her arms again. Her hair blew across her wild face.

'No! No!' he bawled. 'Korky, don't. You'd kill yourself. *You can't fly! Understand . . . You can't fly!*'

'You never think I can do *anything*,' she shouted in return. 'I'm taking off now . . .'

He rushed forward, his arms spread so that he could attempt to catch her. But once more she paused and then dropped her arms. 'You don't love me!' she called down.

'Love you? Of course I do.'

'Tell me then. Shout it to me.'

'I love you!'

'Will you marry me? Tell me you want to marry me. Go on! Ask me.'

'Korky . . . stop it . . .'

'Ask me.' She started flapping her arms again.

'All right. All right. For God's sake. Will you marry me?'

'I'll think about it.'

Then she vanished from the skyline. He heard her screeching. With a sick heart he ran to the side of the building thinking she might have jumped from there. It was an empty alley. He went frantically down it shouting: 'Korky! Korky! Don't!' He reached the rear of the buildings. She was not there either. He ran across a yard and completed the oblong. Then to the front again. To his huge relief he saw her coming out of a door. 'Korky! It's me. Don't be afraid.'

With a crazy laughing cry she was off. 'Catch me, Savage! I can fly! I can fly!'

He pounded after her. He kept running. God, where was she going?

She was making for the harbour; her thin legs stretched, her arms flapping, she ran like an ostrich. She kept going, running and squealing along the side. He could not catch her. 'Stop! Stop! Korky!'

She reached the rounded, projecting wall, at the mouth of the little port. He saw her clamber up the low parapet, spread her arms and, as he stood transfixed, horrified, a shout frozen in his mouth, plunge out of his sight with an ecstatic howl.

'Oh please, don't let her die,' Savage mouthed as he ran. He reached the wall. The tide was high. She had vanished. He bawled her name and stared at the water. Then he saw her being swept along into the harbour on the dark flow, a blur just caught by the shore lights. Spinning around he ran along the wall. He realised how unfit he had become. He panted but kept going. When he was ahead of her he climbed on the parapet, threw off his dressing gown, measured the distance and jumped in feet first.

The abrupt cold and salty water knocked the breath from his lungs. He spat out the water as he surfaced. Then he saw she was only yards away. Summoning every sinew, using every bit of strength, every moment of military training still in him, he swam madly towards her. He would have to grab her first time or she would be swept away. He managed it. She struggled but then went suddenly limp and he caught her around her thin waist. Half-swimming, half-dragging, his breaths reduced to sobs, he got her to a mud bank. It was like a combat experience. He had to think logically.

The mud was thick, foul and oozy but a few inches below the surface it was firm. Stumbling, gasping, spluttering, and trawling her with him, he levered them both on to the mud. It stank. They rolled on it. His face was full of it. He tried to keep hers clear. She had the bland expression of someone sleeping innocently. He felt her chest. She was breathing. He collapsed panting on to the mud and thanked God.

A probing torch found them. There were people on the harbour wall above. 'You all right?' He waved weakly. 'We'll soon get you out. There's a boat coming.'

It took almost half an hour. When they were back on the harbourside, thick with stinking mud, exhausted, and with Korky looking around fearfully but sanely, a policeman kneeled down by them and said: 'Well, I never did.'

Twenty-Two

'Heligoland: German island in the North Sea. In 1807 it was annexed by Great Britain. Stamps portraying the head of Queen Victoria were issued. It remained under British rule until 1890 when it was returned to Germany in exchange for the island of Zanzibar...'

'I've come to say goodbye.'

She had let herself in with her own key which she now placed pointedly on the table beside the word processor. Savage stood up. She leaned and surveyed the entry. 'Fancy that,' she said. 'Zanzibar. And I didn't realise.'

'Stop it,' he said taking her hands. 'And stop the "I've come to say goodbye" stuff. You're only going downstairs.'

'And in the next building,' she said. 'Miles.'

'It will be better,' he said.

'I'll get out of your hair,' she sniffed. Her long face seemed to become longer. 'You won't have to bother to save me from drowning or anything.'

'We'll see each other all the time.'

'Yeah, maybe we'll pass in the corridor or meet up in the launderette.' Her voice crumbled but he knew by now what she was like. 'Like we did before.'

'Korky love,' he said. He embraced her in the way he always did, affectionately.

She pushed herself against him. 'I'm ever so sad,' she said. 'I feel like crying.'

'Don't,' he ordered tenderly. 'We can't, Korky. I'm not going to let this go on. I've tried to be like a father. And you're a young girl.' He changed the subject gently. 'Is everything in the flat all right?'

'It's all right, I suppose,' she said morosely, still close to him. 'There's not much room. Hardly room to swing a gerbil around. And there's no balcony for John either.'

'Winter is coming on.' He eased her slight frame away from his chest.

'Oh, right. Glad you reminded me,' she sulked. 'I'll be warm and cosy down there. There's no room to be cold.'

'It's a good rent,' he reminded her.

'Fifty quid. Yes, I suppose. But it's only till she gets back from Australia. And I've also got the job of keeping her old man outside the door. Mind, that shouldn't be any bother. He's a weedy thing according to her.' She smiled mischievously. 'You should be able to deal with him.'

'Call me when you need me.'

'Oh right. I'll scream from the other building. You're sort of on tap as a rescuer anyway.'

'What does that mean?'

'Nothing.'

'It means something or you wouldn't have said it.'

Korky regarded him accusingly. 'You're keeping an eye on the police lady?'

'I was.'

'You phone her, don't you?'

'Not now. She's sorted out her situation, I think.'

She leaned forward with a gleam of expectancy. 'What about that dodgy solicitor she was tied up with?'

'You seem to know a lot about it.'

'I get to hear bits and pieces . . . things about people.'

'Mr Kostelanetz sometimes gets his information wrong. That's why he packed in being a spy. It's none of your business anyway.'

'All right,' she said with sharp finality. 'Here's your front-door key. Have it back. Don't mix it up with hers, if you've still got it. I just hope that when I'm screaming for help because Mr Longbottom has turned up from Australia and is raping me, she doesn't send out an SOS at the same time.' Turning briskly she made for the door.

He said: 'Korky, come on, that's a bit unlikely.'

'Goodbye,' she whispered at the door. She was wearing a black sweater and a short grey flannel skirt with black stockings and ungainly shoes. She smiled wanly. 'Forever.'

After a brief, bereft, wave she went out shutting the door sharply behind her. The bell rang immediately. He sighed and opened the door. 'Sorry,' she said stooping and poking her head halfway in. 'I didn't mean to bang your door.'

'I'm sure you didn't. Don't worry about it.'

'I'm going to a seance,' she started again. 'At Wilhelmina's. They're every week now. Freddie is coming.'

'Freddie? Ah, Freddie. Good. You're seeing Freddie again?'

'Just friends,' she shrugged. 'He's not as exciting as Wilhelmina's ghosts. Or Mr Prentice and his bangs. He does the explosions for her. He knows about bangs. And she has a big Chinese bloke who pops up in a sort of tablecloth. He's been dead two hundred . . .' She made a face. 'Sorry, you're working. I forgot. What was the place called?'

'Heligoland.'

'Yes. Heligoland. If I can think of anything to put in it I'll let you know. I'll come up.'

'Thanks.'

'And if anything goes wrong with the word processor just call me. Mrs Longbottom's left the phone on and I've promised not to ring Zanzibar or anywhere. I'd better give you the number.'

'You did yesterday.'

'Well, if you have trouble ring.'

'All right, Korky, I will.'

'Goodbye again. Savage, I love you.'

'Goodbye, Korky. I love you too.'

She moved to him again. He held her and patted her. 'But we've got to do this. It would be a disaster. It's not the thing for you. Or me. We've got to realise that.'

'Tell me again you love me.'

'I love you,' he repeated. He released her.

She gave a small sniff and went out.

He closed the door quietly but with a sense of finality. He heard her crashing the doors of the lift. By the time he was sitting in front of the screen again his smile had gone. 'Heligoland,' he muttered. Who the hell cared about Heligoland? Who would care that it was annexed by Britain in 1807 and returned to Germany in 1890 in exchange for Zanzibar? He grimaced at the screen. Good old Heligoland.

He could not imagine what it would be like without her. No more take-aways, no more disappearances, no more searching, no more finding, no more tuneless singing, no more oblique conversations, no more gerbil, no more explaining to the police why he was in his pyjamas floundering in a muddy harbour after midnight. As they had travelled home in the train she had grumbled: 'I don't get why they made such a bloody opera. Is there some law against swimming in your pyjamas?'

'There's probably some law against girls trying to fly,' he grunted. His backside was bruised where he had hit the water. She had only been sick.

'Anyone can make a mistake,' she complained. 'It's unbelievable what that acid does.'

'Good job the police didn't take it any further.'

She said: 'They couldn't prove anything.'

The train had gone through Basingstoke. 'I used to live near here,' he said.

'I know. You and Irene. You had a thatched house. That must have been good. I'd like to live in a house with a thatched roof.'

'They're difficult to fly from,' he said looking from the window.

'Shut up. I'm not going to do that again. Never. It could be dangerous.'

He was amazed at how quickly his life became monotonous again. The solitude, the privacy he had sought, the reason he had tried to barricade himself so loftily at Kensington Heights, seemed to get more protracted by the day. The fading autumn light hung around for hours and the evenings and nights were long. When it rained it rained all day. He even tried going to the cinema. He sat alone in the dark then bought a take-away on the way home, ate it in front of the late television news, then went moodily to bed. His encyclopaedia was slowly growing, the pile of printed pages thickened each dogged day; he began to make faces and gestures at the unresponding screen. He missed her in a way he had never missed anyone.

'I wondered,' he said to her when he went to Mr

Furtwangler's shop, 'if you would like to do some work for me.'

'What sort?' It was odd seeing her among the elderly books, the entrenched shelves, the pyramids of papers, the old man sitting obese and content in his background chair. She had a talent for making people happy.

'I would really like some more of those bits and pieces you used to add to the entries in the encyclopaedia,' Savage suggested.

'Like a sub-contractor.'

'Yes, I suppose so. We could agree a fee for each one.'

Korky said: 'What are you doing in these parts anyway? It's a long way from home.'

Defensively he said: 'I was just going to the British Museum. To the library.'

Mr Furtwangler stirred in his chair. He did not appear to have noticed Savage. 'Rosamunde,' he called between several coughs. 'Sir Gerald is coming. I see him crossing the street.'

She called back: 'I've got his books, Mr Furtwangler, I'll just get them.' She performed a small pirouette. 'Sir Gerald Gosling-Clarke,' she announced to Savage leaving him standing among the unkempt shelves. 'Yes, Sir Gerald. Glad to see you.' Her voice came over the shelves. 'Tennant, Central Africa. Burne on Tribal Rites and Ferrier, Louis Ferrier, that's the right one, isn't it? I thought so. It's the second volume. They're all ready.'

Savage moved sideways towards the door. A fair-haired, brown-faced man in a good tweed suit was standing inside it. Mr Furtwangler moved to greet him and seemed surprised that Savage was also there. He did not look at him closely and he did not seem to recognise him. 'I will come to you in a few moments,' he promised. 'Please look and see.' His hand, pale and podgy, indicated the shelves. He smiled towards his customer and Savage went out into the street.

He had nowhere to go and it was two hours before he saw Mr Furtwangler emerge from the shop and walk nodding away. Twenty minutes later Korky appeared and locked up. He strode quickly around a corner so that he almost collided with her coming in the opposite direction. 'Twice in one day!' she exclaimed. 'We can't go on meeting like this!'

'I just came out of the library,' Savage said lamely.

'Did you see the books you needed?'

'Oh, yes, fine.'

'How many?'

'Books?' He grimaced. 'Three ... or four. Four.'

She regarded him sagely. 'Do you want a cup of tea?'

'Yes, that's a good idea.'

She led him around another Bloomsbury corner to where there was an old fasioned café with marble-topped tables and thick china cups. 'I didn't think there were any places left like this,' said Savage.

'Stephen Stevens, you know, my friend from the publishers, I come in here with him sometimes. He daren't have a proper drink because his mother smells his breath when he gets home.' She looked directly at him. 'He's still interested in seeing your islands encyclopaedia.'

'It's coming on,' said Savage.

'You were lucky getting those books just like that, so quick, in the Reading Room,' she observed drily. 'You couldn't have been in there only a couple of hours. Normally it takes longer than that just to *get* the books, let alone read them. I didn't realise you were a member of the British Library.'

'Oh, yes. I joined weeks ago.'

'These books,' she pursued, 'must have just been sitting there waiting for you.'

'Probably.'

'Where are you up to? Which islands?' Her voice remained friendly but formal.

He groaned. 'Indonesia.' He regarded her across the table. 'Do you know how many islands there are in Indonesia, Korky? Thousands.'

'Why not skip them for a bit and go on to the next. What is it?'

'Iona,' he said. 'In the Hebrides.'

'One island? Small?'

'Yes, just one. Small.'

'Some time you could go back to Indonesia. Just stick the main ones in. There's no way you can do every island in the world or the book would be as big as the world.' She laughed over her tea. 'Anyway, you should let Stephen see it, as much as you've done. He's quite keen.'

'He's keen on you, I expect,' said Savage.

'He's lonely,' she shrugged. 'I attract lonely men. They think they can look after me.'

There were only two other people in the café apart from a waiter wearing a huge white apron. He studied the other couple. They were close and whispering over their cups on the marble table. 'I'd really like you to help me out,' said Savage. 'If you could get together some additional material it makes a difference, it really does.'

'It makes it a bit more interesting,' she agreed bluntly. He stirred his tea. 'And you're only a few yards away, just in the next building. You could bring the stuff to me, or I could come to your place.' He continued stirring. 'I've not been in your flat since you moved in.'

'It's too tight for a party,' she shrugged. She drank from the solid, white cup. 'There's no need to stir,' she pointed out. 'Unless you've started taking sugar.' He stopped stirring.

'Has Mr Longbottom turned up yet?'

'No. But he rang. He was all right. He sounded like a small man. I told him that his wife had gone to Australia. They could have waved to each other in mid-air. He just said: "Bloody good," and rang off.' She paused. 'But I may be moving out anyway.' She studied the whorls in the marble table top.

He took it in. 'Move? Where?'

'Mr Furtwangler wants me to go and live in his house.' She faced him, her cheeks beginning to pink. 'Not like *that*, for Christ's sake, he's about eighty. But he's there in this big house in Wimbledon all by himself. His wife's been dead years. He says there's a flat upstairs and I can have it if I like. He's not even going to charge me rent.' Her expression became challenging. 'He says he'll be quite happy to hear me singing and to hear my footsteps over his ceiling.'

'You can't sing,' he objected. 'You've got a terrible voice.'

'Mr Furtwangler won't mind,' she said patting the back of his hand as though to console him. 'It's better than silence. Anyway, even if I do go, I'll be coming back to Kensington Heights for Wilhelmina Blenkinsop's seances.'

'See you there,' Savage grunted.

Korky laughed. 'Don't be mean. They don't do any harm and they make people happy. I'm a brilliant spirit.'

'I don't want to hear about it,' he sighed.

'And I might come back to the party . . . the one Miss Harkness is having.'

'Who is Miss Harkness?'

'She hasn't been there long. It's a housewarming. I'll come down after the seance. You haven't been invited?'

'No.'

'They're afraid to invite you. They think you're too busy with your work and you don't want to be disturbed.'

'You make me sound like Miss Bombazine.'

He grinned uneasily at her but she laughed outright. The waiter seemed pleased. The other confiding couple glanced up with a hint of envy. 'They haven't asked her for the same reason,' she said. 'Funny, isn't it. Anyway, Miss Harkness is umpteen years old, stone deaf, and she's having this piss-up, whatever.' She paused and looked at him sideways. 'Do you want to be invited?'

'Well, I wouldn't mind,' he said avoiding her eyes. 'I'm not actually working all the time.'

'Right. I'll fix it. See you there.' Her look went to the waiter. 'I'll get the teas,' she said. 'I'll treat you, Savage.'

Korky was not at Miss Harkness's party. Freddie was. So was Percy Belfont who had gone to die in Antwerp. 'I found it was not suitable,' he said a little sadly.

'I got off early for her,' Freddie complained to Savage. 'I could have clinched a sale this evening. You've got to grab them these days. And instead I'm drinking sherry with a lot of crumblies.' He scanned Savage apologetically. 'And you.'

'She said she was coming after the spirit meeting she goes to,' Savage told him.

'She's into that,' frowned Freddie. 'It appeals to the crazy side of her.' He grimaced at the amber sherry in his glass and lowering his voice asked: 'Do you like this muck?'

'It's all there is,' said Savage sipping his diffidently. He surveyed the crowded room; the grey heads were like balls of wool. Easily looking above them he saw the salt-shouldered Bertie Maddison. Bertie eased himself towards Savage and whispered: 'She's on probation. Came up on Monday. She's at home sulking.'

'Festival Hall?'

'That's where it started.' Maddison ineffectually brushed his dandruff; a flake fluttered into his sherry glass where it floated. He extracted it daintily with his little fingertip. Freddie glanced at Savage. Maddison said: 'She took a strong exception to the Chinese violinist, the one with the odd name. Said he was squeaky. I managed to control her and they always have a couple of stewards lurking in her vicinity anyway, because of her reputation, just in case, but she was seething. "Tchaikovsky has died a second time," that sort of remark, and: "The death of a thousand cuts." She was muttering through the whole concert. It was eating at her all night. She couldn't sleep. Next morning she went out and flung a half-brick through the window of the ticket agency.'

Miss Harkness moved to them making her way with elderly aggression. 'Poor Minnie Weiz has syphilis,' she opened conversationally. She noted their surprise. Miss Weiz was standing near the ornamental fireplace. 'It was syphilis, wasn't it, Minnie?' she shouted.

Miss Weiz, struggling to hear, called back: 'A nasty dose this time.'

'It was *shingles*, Miss Harkness,' reproved Miss Cotton standing near. 'Shingles is quite a separate ailment.'

Miss Cotton muttered: 'Silly old woman.' She half-turned to Savage and coquettishly tugged at his lapel. 'I'd like to make you a proposition,' she said. She made a face towards the back of the hostess who had gone bleating towards Miss Weiz. Freddie had been eyeing the door and began to slide towards it.

'What is that, Miss Cotton?' asked Savage. She smiled winsomely and brushed her crinkly hair back from her forehead. 'Why don't you move in with me,' she suggested.

His face stiffened. 'Move in?' was all he could muster. 'In what way?'

'Move in,' she repeated resolutely. 'Live with me.'

Savage gathered himself inadequately. 'It's very kind of you but I'm settled in my place now.'

She pursed her lips and looked not very prudently around her. 'And at a fine rent, I must say.' She leaned closer so that her emerald necklace swung out suggestively and clinked on his glass. 'I won't *eat* you,' she confided. 'But it would be nice to have a man around, a younger man.' Her face hardened. 'That would show these old fools a thing or two.'

'But I can't,' he protested trying to whisper. 'I couldn't . . .' Then desperately: 'There's my work.'

'You could do your work undisturbed,' she offered calmly. She was not going to be put off. 'And I would buy you a car. Anything you wanted within reason. Clothes, anything.' She faced him knowingly. 'Now that you're on your own as well.'

'Well . . . that's really kind of you, Miss Cotton.'

'It's Penelope, by the way.'

'Yes. Well, thank you, Penelope.' He began to edge away.

'Think about it,' she suggested lightly. She leaned and the necklace tinkled against the glass again. 'We make music,' she tittered and more privately: 'There would be no rent involved of course.'

He managed to work his way over to the exiting Freddie and together they edged towards the door thanking Miss Harkness as they went. She exacted a kiss on the cheek from each.

In the corridor, they found Mr Tomelty padding along the carpet. 'They all shout,' he observed nodding in the direction of the party. 'No wonder they can't hear.' He took in Freddie. 'I've put your bicycle outside, sir.'

'Are you coming to the seance?' Freddie asked Savage doubtfully. 'I think I'll go.'

'No. No thanks.'

'Mrs Blenkinsop's. Right along this corridor, turn right,' directed Tomelty.

Freddie continued along the carpet and Savage went out of the building, crossed the yard, went through the side door and took the lift to the top floor.

As he opened his door the telephone began to ring. He picked it up and recited the number. She only said one word: 'Frank . . .' He heard a man tell her to put the phone down. It went dead. Savage pulled the handpiece away and stared at it. 'Jean,' he said, then raising his voice against the instrument: 'Jean, are you there? Jean, Jean!'

Swiftly he dialled her number. It rang but no one picked it up.

Savage stood staring at the receiver. Jesus Christ. What should he do? He spun around the room as though he expected to find some answer, some help. He had to go. He made himself move fast; groping below the bed he extracted the useless sub-machine gun. He pulled out the empty magazine and slammed it back. He ran towards the door. He would have to hide the gun. He rushed into the second bedroom, pulled his anorak from a peg, put it on to conceal the weapon, then bolted from the flat, almost falling down the stairs.

His mind was spinning. How could he get there? Taxi?

Run? With a gun? Korky. He had to get Korky. He ran around the building and along the corridor. There was a fat Chinese man wearing a white nightshirt outside the flat. 'No go in,' he said holding up a draped hand. He saw the gun hanging around Savage's neck under the unzipped anorak. His eyes dilated. 'Maybe can.'

An unworldly wail came from within the room. 'For me,' said the Chinese gratefully. He opened the door and hurried in shutting it behind him. Savage heard the bolt slot inside. Through the woodwork he heard a trumpet. He swore, turned and ran again up the corridor, swinging out of the outside door. Propped against the wall was Freddie's red and white striped racing bicycle.

He stopped, took it in, then grasped it, ran a few paces and mounted it, wobbling out through the enclosed courtyard and into street.

Wildly he turned left, head down, and went panting and pedalling furiously towards Westborne Grove. Pedestrians swung around to see him. The anorak broke open; the sub-machine gun swung from his neck, he went crazily through the Notting Hill traffic weaving and braking, almost falling, righting himself, skidding, pedalling, pedalling, furiously until he reached her street. He flung the bicycle against the outside wall of the small block of apartments and pounded up the outer steps like a street-fighting soldier.

'Somebody's shooting!' shouted a man from a window.

'Over there,' pointed an Indian on the oppsite side of the street. 'Where that geezer's going. That geezer wiv a gun!'

'A gun! He's got a gun!' bawled a woman ducking inside her door.

'Police, get the police!'

Savage plunged up the steps. He pounded her door

then, stepping back a pace, smashed the lock with the butt of the gun. He went in with the muzzle pointing. The room was wrecked, furniture overthrown, broken glass and china strewn, cigarette ends thrown from an ashtray, a window smashed.

'Jean!' he bawled. 'For God's sake, Jean!'

Jean was among the bedroom debris, almost posed on the floor by the foot of the bed. She sat with her hands spread out in an attitude of hopelessness. She had been shot through the neck and the chest and she was running with blood. There was no life in her.

Slowly Savage crouched beside her. He heard himself sob. Her head rolled to one side. The smell of blood rushed up his nostrils. His hands were covered with it. The front of her was soaked. He looked at his hands and felt the smell of the blood fill him. Blood! *Again*! His mind went. He felt it go. Screaming and screaming he rushed around the apartment jabbing about with his useless gun and flinging open doors. No one was there. It made him vomit to look down at his hands, one still grasping the gun. The horror, the terror, the awesome dream swept over him. He was mad again. Mad as he ever was. It was back! Howling he rushed from the fearful place, tipping down the stairs to the outside. Heads disappeared below window sills. His thick, red sticky hands somehow caught hold of the idiotic bicycle. He had to find Korky! Korky, where are you! Korky! Korky! Oh Christ, Korky . . .

He threw himself over the crossbar of the bicycle and pedalled crazily down the street, the sub-machine gun swinging wildly from his neck, his face crammed, his hands stuck by blood to the handlebars, his shouts wild. Two policemen at Notting Hill saw him charge by. 'That's interesting, Doug,' said one. 'Unusual.'

'He's got a gun,' mentioned the other. 'And riding a bike.' He lifted his radio to the side of his mouth.

Savage rode furiously among the traffic. He had to get to Korky. Nothing else mattered. Swerving he went head down across signals at red; drivers braked, skidded, collided. There were warnings, shouts and curses. He scattered pedestrians on a crossing, jumped another set of lights and rattled into Church Street, riding against the one-way traffic, sending vehicles swerving and bumping against each other. Police sirens began to sound.

Cars were waiting at another zebra crossing; bellowing he violently jerked the bicycle on to the pavement and zigzagged crazily under the shop awnings, strewing people and wrecking a china stall. There were cries and waving fists. None of it reached him. He had to get to Korky.

A final turn and he was there, throwing up the gravel in the courtyard of Kensington Heights. He threw the bicycle aside and flinging open the door, raced down the passage. The same Chinese man was waiting again in his white nightshirt outside the door. His face congealed when he saw Savage. He had no time to say anything; Savage thrust him aside, grasped the door and flung it open.

The room was dim, with the outlines of people sitting heads bowed. 'Korky! Korky!' he screamed. There were movements and exclamations. An expectant voice intoned: 'Who is it this time?'

'Korky!' he howled again. His breath was coming in sobs. He still had the blood in his nostrils, on his hands. He stared at it as though he could not believe it. Wilhelmina advanced waving her arms, berating him. Then he saw Korky. Christ, she was dead! She almost floated at the back of the darkened room, her face eerily shining, her body like muslin. 'Korky! Korky, help me!' he pleaded.

A spurt of white smoke shot up from the front of the room and there was a sheet of orange flame and a loud explosion. He flung himself flat. There were more shouts and screams. It was all happening to him again. His brain was on fire. Where was Henry? Where was Sergeant Barnard? All this smoke. Everywhere was smoke and blood. Where was Barnard? Somehow he got upright and in panic he whirled and ran out of the room colliding with the frightened Chinese who had just regained his feet. Savage, bawling, straddled him, got up and waving the sub-machine gun, plunged along the corridor and once more burst out into the yard.

Four policemen with guns were coming towards him. They scattered. Incoherently he shouted at them. There were police vehicles blocking the exit with officers and dogs. He halted on the steps. 'Stop!' a voice ordered hollowly through a megaphone. 'Stop! Armed police. Stay where you are.'

Savage turned sideways, bent almost double, and made to run along the wall of the flats. He was a soldier again. Nothing mattered. Nothing now. 'Stop. Or we fire!' echoed the voice. Miss Bombazine's window was flung open. 'Look out, Frank!' she screamed. He doubled up and kept running. Two shots sounded, resounding in the high and confined courtyard. Each one hit him and he stumbled, and slithered, and stopped, flat out against the wall. The useless sub-machine gun clattered along the gravel. A Black boy, who had been sheltering behind the wall with his brother, reached out and almost tenderly picked up the weapon. Wide-eyed and silent he handed it to the first policeman.

'You've shot him, you bastards!' Miss Bombazine

341

shouted out of her window. 'Stupid, bloody coppers. You've done it now!' Her face disappeared and a minute later she was out in the courtyard and racing towards the prone shape of Savage. She was wearing a black negligee. Her impetus took her through the policemen to Savage's side. Korky rushed from the block, wearing a muslin shift, her face painted luminous white. 'Fuck me,' commented one policeman to another.

'You've just killed a hero,' Miss Bombazine told him bluntly. Korky was crying against the bloodied chest.

Behind them, from the door of Kensington Heights, the residents were coming out. Slowly, as though entranced, they entered like players on a stage and formed a silent group. The Tomeltys were there, Wilhelmina Blenkinsop, Miss Weiz, the Maddisons, Miss Cotton, Percy Belfont fresh from Antwerp, and the others. Mr Prentice stood shocked and sooty-faced. Two young policemen attempted to usher the gathering back through the door. 'Go inside, please. There's nothing to see,' said one outstretching his arms.

'There's everything to see,' pointed out Tomelty hardly moving his eyes from Savage. His wife began to cry. 'Don't upset them,' she sniffed.

The remainder of the group stood motionless as a frieze. 'You have killed a good man,' said Bertie Maddison eventually.

His wife had brought her sherry glass. 'You really are . . .' she said in a low, shaky but outraged voice to the policemen: ' . . .the ultimate cunts.'

At her words the other residents broke into a ragged clapping. As they did so the senior police officer in a special cap arrived. He heard the rough applause as he left his car. 'This time, at least,' he grunted to his driver, 'it sounds as if we have done something right. We seem to have the full approval of the public.'

Twenty-Three

He was not dead. Not quite, the ambulance attendant assured Korky. A second ambulance arrived and took the soot-faced Mr Prentice and a policeman bitten by his own dog.

Korky got in with Savage. Miss Bombazine went to get dressed and said she would follow. As they were about to close the door Freddie breathlessly appeared and climbed in too. 'The sodding police have taken my bike,' he complained. 'They say it's evidence.'

'There's the evidence,' said Korky pointing to Savage stiff below the blankets. His ashen cheeks were streaked with red. 'He was frightened of blood.' The ambulance attendant seemed to notice her painted face and strange muslin dress for the first time. 'Party was it?' he guessed as though he had seen it all too many times. 'Got a bit out of hand.'

It took less than ten minutes to reach Charing Cross Hospital on Fulham Palace Road. Korky tried to hold Savage's hand as they carried him in. She and Freddie sat down to wait. Miss Bombazine arrived with one of her own coats which she put over the girl's shoulders. 'You go, both of you,' said Korky patting her hand. 'There's no use you staying here. I'll stay.'

Miss Bombazine said she understood but Freddie held Korky's hand and said he would stay with her. They sat unspeaking on the chairs in the waiting room until eventually she said: 'Please go, Freddie, it's going to be a long time.' She kissed him on the cheek. 'I'd rather be here by myself.'

He brought her a cup of tea and then left. A nurse appeared holding a piece of paper. 'Are you with the patient from Kensington Heights?' she enquired. Dumbly Korky nodded.

The nurse said: 'He seems to be all right. You can go in and see him.'

Astounded Korky stood and unbelievingly followed her from the waiting room. 'All right?' she managed to ask. 'Did you say he'll all right?'

'That's it,' said the nurse airily. 'It was only superficial.'

Stark-faced Korky followed her. They went into a room off the corridor marked: 'Casualty Department'. Sitting there, looking discomfited, was Mr Prentice. 'It was only my eyebrows,' he said.

Korky choked, turned without a word and went back to the waiting room. She sat for another hour, staring into the green space of the room, scarcely breathing, scarcely living. Her eyes only moved when someone appeared outside the glass panel of the door, framed like a picture. Once a man in a white coat stood there and she opened the door and said: 'How is Frank Savage?'

'Sorry, love,' he said softly. Her heart became ice. But he went on: 'I'm a dentist.'

After another fifty minutes a calm nursing sister opened the door and said: 'The surgeon will be in to see you.'

She would say nothing more. Korky sat praying tightly. The surgeon arrived quickly, a short man who looked as if he was normally cheerful.

'He's not dead. We're trying to save his life,' he said

solemnly. 'We've removed one bullet from his lung but the other is wedged in his spine.' He held up an X-ray photograph. 'See. There it is.' She saw the bullet, like a dead grub at the base of the backbone. The man seemed to be searching for something good to tell her. 'It's straight anyway,' he said eventually, squinting at the X-ray again. 'That makes it a bit easier. Sometimes they fly all over the shop.'

'They teach them to shoot straight,' Korky said dully. Full of pleading she looked at him again, tears welling. 'Just tell me he's going to be all right,' she whispered. She dropped her head and lay against the lapels of his white coat while she sobbed. Slightly embarrassed he put his arm around her shoulders, hardly touching her. 'We're going to try,' was all he would say.

She cried even more deeply and pounded his chest softly with her fists. 'You've got to make him live,' she said like a silly threat. 'He's all I've got.'

She eased herself away from him and apologised. 'You should go home,' he said kindly. 'Come in tomorrow morning.'

'What time?'

'About nine. He's in intensive care now but he'll need another operation.'

'And that's going to be difficult.'

'Not easy.' He opened the door for her and she almost stumbled out. 'I'll ask reception to get you a taxi,' he said kindly. 'It's pouring.'

'It's all right.' She shook her head. 'Thanks, it's not far. I need a walk.'

They went into the hospital lobby. A stretcher with a recumbent figure was coming through the door. 'I'll have to go,' said the surgeon.

'They keep you busy, don't they,' she mumbled.

346

It was raining coldly and it was almost one in the morning. She pulled Miss Bombazine's coat about her and thrust her hands into the pockets. From one she withdrew a packet of purple condoms and from the other a plastic crucifix. She looked at one object and then at the other and put them back. Instead of turning right in the main road, she turned left. The rain thickened and began to soak her hair and her face but she scarcely felt it. Like a sad reflection she walked slowly along the streaming pavement, in front of the dim shops, not noticing the cars, taxis and goods vehicles that passed her, throwing up the spray of Fulham Palace Road. A man shouted bawdily to her from a car but she kept walking. She turned left and eventually left again until she was in the King's Road. The rain poured. By the time she had reached the Safeway supermarket down beyond World's End, the coat hung on to her like blotting paper, the cold stream going down her neck and inside her clothes. She could feel it running down her legs from the top. Blindly fighting against it she turned into the yard at the rear of the supermarket. The trailer was still parked there, near the steam outlet, and beneath it was the group of waifs. Without a word she knelt down and edged herself in among them. Some groaned and grunted at the intrusion. A girl lying below layers of sacking against the inside of the wheel said: 'You're bloody wet, mate.'

'Sorry,' said Korky. 'It's pissing.'

'So it is,' said the other girl half-easing herself up. She glanced at Korky and reaching out pushing her soaked hair sideways. 'You're that . . .'

'Korky,' said Korky.

'Right. I remember you. Remember me? Bettina.'

Korky studied her in the damp dimness. 'Right, I remember.'

'You don't get so many down here now,' said the girl. 'A lot of them have chucked it. Gone home and that. There's not so many living out as there was.'

Bettina arranged herself around the big tyre of the trailer and pulling her covering about her prepared to return to sleep with a conventional: 'Goodnight then, Korky.'

Korky remained sitting, the wet coat clinging to her thin body. 'Want a puff?' Bettina suddenly asked. 'I've got some.' She sat up again and handed Korky a joint. 'Already rolled,' she said with a little boast. Korky took it and the other girl produced a match.

'Thanks,' said Korky. 'Sure you can spare it?'

'Tomorrow,' said the girl, 'I'm going to be lucky. I'm getting out of this bleeding lark anyway. There's got to be better ways of being by yourself.'

She did not smoke one herself but curled against the wheel again. Korky sat hunched, damp, dead of emotion, and smoked the joint. She took the crucifix from the coat pocket and clutched it. 'Save him, Jesus,' she threatened. 'Or I'm never going to bloody believe in you again. Ever.'

She pulled herself into the rain-soaked coat and curled against the others. She closed her eyes and began to cough.

'I've been in here three weeks.' His voice was slow as if he had to consider every word.

'It is three weeks yesterday that the policemen took shotpots at you.'

Mr Kostelanetz solemnly opened his overcoat. He had acquired a smooth-haired grey one for the changing of the seasons. It was warm in the ward. The window framed an afternoon sky more grey than the coat.

Savage said: 'Has Korky been?'

Mr Kostelanetz wriggled uncomfortably and opened the coat wider. His unease rose darkly to his face, his moustache bounced a little and his eyelids folded and unfolded. 'Before, no,' he admitted eventually. 'But today she will come. You understand, she is also in this Charing Cross. She is a little way only from here. In her own bed.'

Savage's head had remained upright on the pillow and his eyes had been fixed if not focused ahead with hardly a movement towards his visitor. At first, it had been too painful to move; now the gaze was dumbly, habitually in that direction. Mr Kostelanetz had understood. This time, very slowly, the eyes came around to face him with a hint of expression. 'In here? In this hospital?'

'You are correct,' muttered Mr Kostelanetz. 'Korky has been very sick.' His expression dropped to even further melancholy. 'We thought there would be two funerals in one week.'

Gradually, as if he wanted to avoid believing anything else, Savage returned his gaze to the front. 'What happened to her?'

The other man shrugged. 'It was the same as the first time. She was out in the rain all night. Next day, bronchitis. But this time it was bigger bronchitis. Worse, much worse. It was a race which one of you would die first.' He rolled his large head. 'It was not a good week.'

'God, I can't believe it.' Savage turned towards Mr Kostelanetz again. 'But she is all right now?'

'She is okay, recovered. She is coming to see you.'

Savage said: 'You have been a good friend.'

Mr Kostelanetz nodded lugubriously. 'I would like to say that it has been a pleasure . . . but I am afraid . . .' He tried to brighten. 'But maybe from now everything will be good. Soon you will be well.'

'Maybe.'

Savage's pale, creased face moved sideways on the pillow. 'I want you to help. You must tell her, Korky, that this is a break for good. I'm dragging her down with me. It's a wonder she isn't dead.'

Mr Kostelanetz puffed out his cheeks. 'It is sometimes seeming that way,' he agreed. 'That crazy policewoman, your friend. They have told you all about that?'

'I know. The police came. We're like bits of flotsam, some of us.'

'What is this floatsam?'

'Bits and pieces floating on the sea.'

'I see.' Mr Kostelanetz noted the word. 'And so they cannot help themselves.'

'Right.'

There was a movement at the door of the room and Savage caught it and saw Korky's long, pale head come around the jamb. She was trying to smile. Her hair was cut close. 'Hello, Savage,' she said. She attempted to make it cheerful but it emerged as a whisper. 'I'm here.'

He smiled towards her and lifted his hand. She came into the room in a quilted, flowered dressing gown that accentuated her washed-out skin. Miss Bombazine in her black shiny suit followed.

The older woman was holding Korky's arm but the girl gently broke away and stepped uncertainly towards the bed. Mr Kostelanetz, as if the sequence had been rehearsed, rose and she sat on the chair. She and Savage came face to face. She eased herself towards him and kissed him awkwardly, sideways on the mouth. He put his left arm around her neck. 'Oh, Savage,' she began to sob. 'What a bloody state we're in.'

'We will leave you,' said Mr Kostelanetz decorously. Miss Bombazine waved delicately with her gloved fingers but then halted. 'I just wanted you to see this,' she said nervously fumbling in her handbag. She brought out a single photograph and coming closer held it up so that Savage could see it. 'Remember.' It was the three of them, Savage, Korky and Miss Bombazine, laughing in the sunshine by the Thames. Savage nodded recognition. Miss Bombazine put the picture away. 'That was a lovely day,' she said in a hushed way. 'One of the best days of my life.' They turned and with Mr Kostelanetz holding her elbow, they went from the room.

'They've been so sweet,' said Korky still crying. 'Mr Kostelanetz is setting her up in proper business, a poodle parlour, where you take dogs to be . . .' The tears began to run again. 'Savage . . . I don't know what . . .'

He fought back his own tears, pushing her gently away from the bed. 'Sit down, Korky,' he said. She obeyed, moving back on to the chair, her face streaked grey with tears. She wiped her cheeks with the padded sleeves of her dressing gown. 'Let's pull ourselves together,' she told him.

He touched her wrist as it lay on the sheet. 'You won't want to talk about it, I suppose,' she said.

'None of it,' he said. 'How did you get bronchitis again?'

She looked abashed. 'I'm bloody mad,' she said. 'The night they brought you in here I just wandered around in the peeing rain. All night I was out. Down at World's End. It bloody nearly was the world's end for me too. It would have been a fine thing if we'd both snuffed it.'

A sadness more than a silence fell over them. 'I'm going to spend a long time in a wheelchair,' he said.

'I'll wheel you.'

'I think we've spent too much time wheeling each

other,' he told her with a slight smile. 'You've got to go out and get on with it alone, Korky. It's your life.'

'I can still wheel you,' she responded sulkily.

'They'll move me from here.'

'I'll follow you.' Her face was puffed. 'You're trying to give me the elbow.'

'Korky love, you've got to get yourself sorted out. We can't go on the way we have. I may never be out of hospital.'

'You're giving up, Savage. You mustn't.'

'Things have got to change. You've got to move into the top of Mr Furtwangler's house. You'll have a job and somewhere to live.' He regarded her wryly. 'And pack in the seances.'

Her hand went to her mouth. 'They're packed in.' Shakily she laughed. 'Mr Prentice, that old fart, blew his eyebrows off with the explosion. It was only supposed to be a puff of smoke. His moustache was jammed up his nose.' Her eyes deepened. 'When will they get you walking again?'

'I don't know.'

'You've *got* to want to walk again, Savage,' she warned. 'You've not got to give up, jack it all in just because of things going a bit wrong ... a few police bullets ... You've got the rest of your life.'

'And you've got the rest of yours.'

Twenty-Four

Still wearing her red headscarf the woman rammed her tea trolley into the waiting room at Marshfield Manor Hospital. The lower part of the door was dented and devoid of varnish. 'Never made this opening big enough,' she complained as she manhandled the vehicle into the room. 'Like some tea, dear?' she asked Korky.

Without waiting she carefully selected a thick cup from the pile on the top of the trolley. 'That's a nice one, no cracks,' she said. She smiled hugely, her rabbit teeth pointing down at Korky, who sat bemused. Korky said: 'Yes, please.'

'There's enough crackpots in this place,' giggled the woman. 'That's what Nurse Jones always says when I give her some tea in a nice cup with no cracks.' She seemed suddenly to become aware of Korky's youth. 'You've got lovely hair, dear,' she said. 'I used to have hair like you.'

Uncomfortably Korky watched as she removed her headscarf and revealed an almost bare scalp, its iodine baldness relieved by sparse tufted islands. 'When you lose your brains it rots your hair,' she explained. She replaced the headscarf and tied it carefully below her sagging chins. 'Now, tea,' she said.

'Yes, please,' repeated Korky unsurely.

She watched, puzzled and then astonished, as the

woman put the cup beneath the tap of the urn and apparently filled it with invisible tea. 'Just right,' she said as the cup was pedantically set on a saucer. 'Mustn't spill any,' she said. She looked brightly into the wondering face. 'Milk and sugar?'

'Oh . . . yes . . . please.'

'How many sugars?'

'Two . . . please.'

To Korky's immense relief the door opened again and a man walked in. 'Ah, tea-time,' he beamed. Once more her heart plummeted but the man winked at her. He carried a file.

'Nearly done, Dr Fenwick,' said the tea lady. 'Will you have some?'

'Thank you. I will.'

She directed another invisible squirt of tea from the urn and handed the cup to the doctor. 'I know it's only one lump,' she said adding the non-existent milk and sugar. He and Korky sat facing each other holding their empty cups on their knees. Dr Fenwick took a sup and hesitatingly Korky did likewise. 'Just right, thank you, Mrs Dines,' said the doctor.

'Yes, lovely,' agreed Korky.

With a massive clattering of the tea trolley the woman went out. Dr Fenwick introduced himself and they set aside their vacant cups and shook hands. 'It takes all sorts, I suppose,' said Korky inadequately.

'In here, it does,' he said. He smiled pleasantly. 'I'm sorry we haven't met before but I've been taking some leave. You are a friend of Frank Savage. You've been several times to visit him.'

'Yes, I have. I've been to see him just now.'

'How do you think he is?'

'I was going to ask *you* that,' said Korky surprised. 'But

since you ask I think he's in a diabolical state. He hardly speaks.'

He thinned his lips and nodded. 'When he was here at Marshfield Manor before, his wife used to come to see him.'

'Irene,' said Korky.

'Yes, Irene. She would come and stay for as long as she, they, could stand it then drive home in tears. He had nothing to say to her, he had blocked her out. He'd withdrawn.'

Korky sniffed. 'That's what he's like now,' she said. 'With me. He was all right at first in Charing Cross, after the shooting. I was ill myself so I didn't see him for three weeks but when I did he seemed to be all right, more or less, considering what had happened, but after that he just . . . sort of trailed off . . . shut me out. Now I come here and he doesn't seem to want to know.'

'It's not only you, he's shutting out the whole world,' he told her. 'Which is not all that surprising, considering what the world has done to him.'

'Shit on him,' she said bitterly.

'Exactly. He's scared stiff. He feels safe in here.'

'How long is he going to be here?'

'As long as he wants or as is necessary,' said the doctor firmly. 'In essence, he's a voluntary patient. He could in theory anyway discharge himself, although we would be very much against that. We've got to try, we are trying, to get him well. We almost did it once. The last time.' He regarded her sympathetically. 'You've been a great . . . help to him,' he said. 'I've read all the reports.'

'He helped me,' sighed Korky. 'We were helping each other. Maybe too much. We were trying to do without each other a bit, when this lot happened.'

Dr Fenwick opened the file on his lap. 'Did you ever know about the incident in the cemetery?'

'What was that?'

'Just after he had moved into the flat in London he went to the house in Hampshire, where he had lived with Irene. She was there, as it happened, although they had both moved out. That upset him, and believe me, in his sort of psychological state it would not take much, although he probably hardly realised it himself. Then some youths attacked him on the train . . .'

'He's never mentioned it.'

'It was incredible, farcical. He was trying to protect a mother and her baby from these characters and they left him covered in blood. He blacked out, which was not surprising either, and he ended up in the cemetery where Sergeant Barnard, his friend from army days, is buried. He died some time after the action in Northern Ireland. We had, reluctantly, allowed him to go there some months previously for the funeral, and in this amnesic state he returned there. The cemetery is in the Aldershot military area. That's how he came to get a house in the vicinity. It was near to his posting at that time.'

'And what happened?'

Dr Fenwick grimaced. 'Apparently he got locked in, although he did not remember that at all, and had to climb the cemetery wall. He went to a public house and drank a lot of Scotch and ended up in London attacking some tramps who were waiting at a soup canteen.'

'If I didn't know better, I'd say you were making it up,' she told him sadly. 'Poor Savage.'

'What about the woman police officer?' he asked.

'Jean Deepe,' she responded flatly. 'She was dodgy.'

'It seems so, from what I read in the newspapers, and

from the inquest report. But she helped him at the start, when he was on his own.'

'She wanted a man,' sniffed Korky. He could see her eyes had become opaque. 'Don't cry,' he said gently.

'I'll try not to,' she said rubbing her nose with her hand. 'I expect there's a lot worse to cry about in here.'

'Or laugh about. If you don't do one you do the other.'

Korky rallied herself. 'Everybody thought it was this ex-jailbird, Brendan Brownlow, who'd murdered her – except for the police, that is, who thought it was Savage. He had his gun with him and they shot him. They would.'

Fenwick sighed. 'I'm afraid the gun was my fault.'

'You knew about it?'

'I'm afraid so. When he was here as a patient the first time, they were assembling a military display at a museum and I allowed, in fact I suggested, that he should go and help set it up. I thought it might give him some temporary object, some interest in life. It seemed to work and he was there for about a week. One of the weapons in the display was found to be missing and it was not difficult to guess where it was. Frank had it. But it was harmless, there were bits missing, there was no ammunition, and I had a notion that it might even benefit him to have it.' He paused. 'A sort of prop, a crutch, a reassurance.'

'Like a teddy bear,' she nodded. 'Except it was a gun.'

He frowned. 'I took it on myself.'

'What you thought was right for him,' she said. 'That's what I was trying to do.'

'I made a statement to the police about the gun.' He paused again. 'I think I'll be hearing more about that. Imagine that getting in the newspapers.'

'Then, of course, it wasn't this Brendan bloke who did

it,' she said. 'It was that solicitor she'd been carrying on with. He went mad with jealousy.'

'Then he committed suicide.'

She said: 'There was a lot of shooting going on one way and another.' They fell silent. 'And now he's here,' she said eventually. 'Back where he was.' She stood up. 'How long will he be here?' It was like a demand.

'As long as it takes,' he told her firmly, also rising. 'I allowed him to be discharged last time against my better judgement, except that I thought he and Irene could work together to pull him through.'

'You don't think I could do it.'

'May I ask what your relationship was?'

'Pure,' she said simply. 'I love him. The ages don't matter.'

'You're how old?'

'Seventeen. I want to get him home, back to the flat. I can spend all day with him.'

He sighed and put his hand on her narrow arm. 'He's still in the wheelchair,' he said. 'We don't know how much of it is physical and how much psychological. We've got to make him *want* to walk. He doesn't seem to care at the moment.'

'I know. I've tried to make him see sense. He could be in here for the rest of his life.'

'I hope not. But for the time being this is where he's got to be. We're working on it, believe me, but we need his help. He's been kicked in the teeth, and not just kicked in the *teeth*, so many times, that he doesn't want to move. He feels safe here.'

'He'd be safe with me,' she said doggedly.

The taxi arrived just as the clock on the hospital tower sounded four. On the journey to the station the driver, as he always did, told her about his garden, his war against moles and aphids. It was always the same driver. She began to feel that these visits told her more about the life of this unknown gardener than they did about the life of Frank Savage.

At Marshfield Junction Korky went into the refreshment room which glowed in the dimness and damp. The woman behind the counter, a possible sister of Mrs Dines the dispenser of invisible tea, knew her by now. 'How is he then, dear?' she asked as she always did. 'Any change?'

She had no notion of whom she was enquiring, only that regular people went to and from the hospital. Korky lied, as usual, and said that her friend was showing improvement and the buffet woman recited her customary hope: 'Ah well, perhaps they'll be letting him out soon.'

There were only four tables, two on each side against the wintry windows with the counter occupying the back wall facing the door. A sheen of captive vapour caused a haze over the tubular light strips.

Moodily Korky sat with her cup, holding it like a warmer with both hands, on a table to the right of the counter. She tugged at the plastic wrapping of a packet of chocolate biscuits. There was a wall poster announcing a competition, with a prize of a holiday in Florida, sponsored by the same biscuit company, but she decided not to enter. The door creaked and a slim woman in a fawn coat came in. She and Korky smiled conventionally. At once Korky realised who she was. Irene.

'Just missed the two o'clock train, didn't you, dear,' sympathised the counter lady already preparing a cup and saucer. 'Could see you running.'

'The taxi from the hospital got stuck behind a farm

tractor,' confirmed Irene. She was at the counter, her back to Korky. 'And that means a three-hour wait.'

'There's not much to do here in three hours,' said the woman pouring the tea. 'Not this time of the year.'

'I walked down to the village,' said Irene. 'There's a café.'

'Mildred,' nodded the woman. 'My daughter works there. We're all in the refreshment business.' Irene turned and sat at one of the tables opposite Korky, the table nearest the door so that she was not immediately facing. She sipped her tea once and then glanced up. Her expression altered. Korky was looking directly at her. Irene said: 'I'm sure we've met before.'

Korky swallowed. 'Yes, we have.' The buffet woman paused, cleaning cloth draped like a damp flag. Not many coincidences happened there. 'Up at the hospital, would it be?' she suggested.

'It was in a restaurant in Kensington,' Korky went on ignoring the interruption. The damp cloth dropped and the woman nodded as though she had known all the time. Irene only said: 'Yes. You came in . . .'

'And I sat right next to you . . . and your . . . husband.'

'That's right. I knew I had seen you before. How strange.' She hesitated. 'So have you . . . been visiting someone at . . . at Marshfield?'

Looking down at her cup but then raising her eyes Korky said quietly: 'Yes. The same person as you. I didn't know you came to see him too.'

'Frank,' Irene almost whispered. The buffet woman had crammed the cleaning cloth to her mouth.

'Savage,' confirmed Korky.

In the almost dark afternoon they walked together to the end of the platform below the dripping trees. Framed in the light of the distant refreshment room window was a face straining to see, even to hear.

'I knew there was somebody,' said Irene. 'And it was you.'

'It was me all the time,' nodded Korky. 'And you came to see him this morning and I came this afternoon. And neither of us knew. He didn't mention it.'

'He wouldn't,' said Irene. 'And nobody else would. It's terrible, isn't it.'

'Terrible and sad,' agreed Korky slowly. She looked along the line. 'The London train is in five minutes.'

'Mine's in fifteen. There's hardly a train all day and then they have two close together.'

Korky said: 'You're getting married again, aren't you.'

Irene nodded. They had reached the end of the platform where there was a pile of gravel and a defunct signal box. Some wet pigeons sat in its window. Together the two women turned and walked back. The distant top of the buffet lady bobbed hopefully. An old couple arrived, swathed in coats, he wobbling with a stick, and stood wordlessly staring into the grey day.

Korky needed to tell her. 'We've never been . . . well, lovers,' she said. 'Savage wouldn't. But I love him.'

'Me too,' murmured Irene. 'I went to see him in Charing Cross Hospital. After it was all in the newspapers. It's as though these tragic things seek him out. It's so unfair.' Looking sideways at Korky she asked: 'How old are you?'

'Seventeen now. He took me in when I was sixteen and I had nowhere, although I told him I was older.'

'It's all strange, isn't it.' Irene gave a small laugh. 'You were really priceless that day in the restaurant. I can't believe how you carried it off.'

Korky smiled too and, almost by accident, they

touched hands. 'Nor me. Savage wanted to tell you, to say who I was, but I didn't give him a chance. He was livid.' Her eyes travelled along the misty track. 'Here's my train.'

They halted and stood by each other like mother and daughter as the train moved in. As it stopped they shook hands and then, impulsively but softly, kissed each other. The buffet woman almost fell from her stool. A few paces along the platform the elderly, silent, couple parted without contact. The man boarded the train and the woman stood immobile staring at him as if they would never be together again. It seemed a struggle for her to speak but eventually she said: 'Don't forget to tell her.'

'That's the only reason I'm going,' said the man without warmth.

Korky opened the door and got in. Her eyes were damp and when she turned she saw that Irene's were also. 'Thanks for looking after him,' said Irene quietly.

'You did too.'

'I don't think I'll come to see him again. I wanted to come this time but it didn't do much good. Not for either of us.'

Korky said: 'I know what you mean. He'd rather I didn't come.'

The train began to pull away. The elderly woman suddenly shouted vehemently: 'You *tell* her!'

Korky and Irene waved to each other almost shyly. 'You'll keep coming, won't you,' said Irene anxiously. She walked, keeping pace with the starting train.

'Nothing's going to stop me. But I'm going to get him out of there, Irene. And soon.'

Twenty-Five

Mr Kostelanetz balanced the big yellow tablet edgeways on his palm. 'See, this hand is still good,' he claimed. His big liquid eyes moved to Korky. The tablet toppled. 'We used them in the Balkans.'

'How long does it work for?' asked Korky.

'Up to three hours,' Mr Kostelanetz told her. She moved her nose near the pill.

'And it's the last one?'

'The last one.' he winked confidingly. 'I have needed to use them over the years.' He indicated Nod. 'And we tried one on his brother.'

Nod said: 'He went out for the count. But he was all right. He went down the pub after.'

Mr Kostelanetz was closing his olive fist over the tablet but Korky picked it up with two fingertips and wrapped it in a tissue. 'If it won't work we're buggered,' she said solemnly.

Mr Kostelanetz, unusually casual, was wearing an old green goalkeeping jersey. He kept running his fingers inside the collar. 'Once he is back here,' he said surveying the apartment sentimentally. 'In the place he knows. With his friends. He will want to stay.'

Nod said the van was outside. 'It's a bit of a banger but she's filled up.'

Mr Kostelanetz studied his watch as if it were a

complex piece of equipment. 'In ten minutes we must leave,' he announced. 'Everything is ready.'

Korky picked up the tissue containing the tablet. 'Let's hope it works,' she said.

Savage was in a room with two shelves of books which remained in the same order each time she went to visit, with a television set, a radio and a window over winter Wiltshire. The radio was always on but so low it was only a mumble. She always told him what she had been doing that week, how she enjoyed living at the top of Mr Furtwangler's house, and what was happening in the bookshop. He had little to tell her and there seemed nothing else to say. No small talk, no plans, no pieces of information. Invariably there was the tea ritual with Mrs Dines, her big empty cups, and her eccentric, relieving chatter.

Sometimes they watched television, sometimes they gazed out of the window, mentioning the birds, the bald earth and barren trees. There were no film shows now because there had been an upset and there were no funds for a replacement projector. With Irene he had been able to sit in the dark and silence. 'You don't have to come every week,' he said to Korky.

'I want to.'

'But it's a long way and . . .'

' . . .There's nothing much to say when I get here,' she provided bluntly. She leaned towards him determinedly. 'I know that, Savage, but I'm not letting you get away with this. I'm not giving up, just because we're out of small talk.'

He sat dismally in the wheelchair. 'Don't you know whether you *can* walk? Can't you *feel* whether you can?'

She had asked before and his answer was the same: 'I'm leaving it to the doctors. They'll know.'

She always consciously avoided checking her watch but they both knew the milestones, the signposts. After forty-five minutes she said she would go to the tea machine. By that time Mrs Dines and her phantom service had gone.

There was often a queue for the tea and coffee dispenser. She was ashamed at her relief that it used up a few more minutes. This time she did not have to wait long. An old woman in a flannel dressing gown was in front of her, talking to the machine as it squirted. She shuffled away, the dressing gown dragging on the floor; Korky took her turn and, with a sharp glance around, dropped Mr Kostelanetz's pill into Savage's plastic beaker.

'I think I ought to take you for a walk,' she suggested firmly when she returned. 'It's not raining or anything. You need some air.'

He always agreed; it gave them an escape from the tyranny of his room. They drank the tea. He did not detect the taste of the tablet. 'You're putting on weight,' she said watching him.

'No exercise,' he shrugged. 'Exercise is difficult.'

When he had finished the tea she helped him on with a heavy jacket, and wheeled him from the room and out of the building. Savage acknowledged a nurse who spoke to him but the patients seemed to be oblivious, perhaps ashamed, of each other.

It was a mild afternoon. Mr Kostelanetz had said that the drug would take at least twenty minutes to begin to work. She wheeled him as quickly as she could away from the hospital, making for the perimeter path against the screening trees, now an almost dark background. 'We

365

won't be out long, Savage,' she said to test his reaction. 'I don't want you getting cold.'

He remained silent and, her heart jumping, she thought she detected a sag in his shoulders. Then he slipped to one side in the wheeled chair. She stopped, glanced guiltily around, and went to the front. His eyes were closed, his mouth was open. She leaned forward and closed his mouth. Trying not to rush, she wheeled him to the rendezvous. 'You're coming home, Savage,' she told him over his slumped shoulder. 'Whether you like it or not.'

She rattled the wheelchair along the path, worried in case anyone came in the opposite direction. But no one appeared. The afternoon was dimming. Ahead she saw a clumsy movement among the bushes. Mr Kostelanetz was in place.

'It is like in the Balkans,' he enthused studying the unconscious Savage. Nod had been relieving himself among the shrubs and appeared sheepishly.

'Let's get him in,' urged Korky. 'The quicker the better.'

She opened the creaky rear doors of the van and kept a look-out along the road and inside the hospital grounds while the men positioned the wheelchair and in one hefty movement lifted it and its deadweight occupant into the back of the vehicle. Mr Kostelanetz climbed in and applied the brake to the chair. It was all done in two minutes.

'Planning,' said Mr Kostelanetz. 'Planning.' He whistled to Korky who appeared from the rough hedge. They climbed into the van. Korky put a blanket over Savage and, one each side, she and Mr Kostelanetz sat and silently held on to the chair. Nod started the rattling engine and they pulled away.

The wheelchair would only just fit into the confined lift at Kensington Heights. Mr Kostelanetz and Nod eyed each other with mutual apprehension and distrust as, with joint clumsiness, they manoeuvred the conveyance and the slumped Savage into the tight space. Savage had begun to rouse; he muttered and his head moved. Korky observed him anxiously.

Mr Kostelanetz said: 'Who will do the button?' Their faces drifted to Korky.

The chair occupied the entire lift space apart from a six-inch gap at one side. Korky eyed it. 'I could get in there,' she calculated. 'Sideways, standing on one leg.'

More mumbling from Savage spurred her. Deftly she climbed and wriggled into the aperture. She balanced on one stork-like leg. 'See you up there,' she whispered. She closed the doors and pressed the button.

The noise and upward movement further roused Savage. She watched him worriedly. The two bulky men were still panting up the stairs as the lift reached the sixth landing. Korky opened the door and waited for their arrival. They both leaned against the wall to recover. Then she said: 'Go easy. We don't want him waking up on the landing.'

Mr Kostelanetz unlocked the apartment door and they propelled Savage into it. He began to move more strongly. His arms went out as though searching for something to touch, he groaned and opened his eyes. They widened uncomprehendingly. His mouth opened. He screwed up his eyes and opened them again, his hands rubbed at his face.

Once more his eyes closed, wearily as though he could not take in what they saw. 'No, no,' he mumbled to himself. 'No. Not this.' He opened them again. They were full of disbelief, almost fear.

He turned his head around the apartment. 'What have you done?' he demanded thickly. 'What am I doing here?' Abruptly he realised and spluttered at the cautiously smiling Korky: 'Take me back! You're crazy.'

Mr Kostelanetz shifted his shoes on the spot. Nod looked frightened. Firmly Korky stood in front of the wheelchair. 'Why don't we all have a nice cup of tea,' she suggested. She made to turn towards the kitchen but Savage caught her arm. 'You don't know what you're doing,' he blurted angrily. 'You're crazy.'

'*I'm* crazy?' she exploded. She took in the others. '*We're* crazy?' She tugged her arm from him. 'Listen, mate, *you're* the one who was in the hospital. And you want to go back.'

His anger collapsed. He began to sob. 'Of course I've got to go back. Get me out of here. Don't you realise it's my only chance.'

Sternly she leaned towards him. 'It's your only chance of staying in that nut-house for the rest of your life.' She jabbed a finger at him. 'Or maybe that's what you *want*. You don't want to be a *person*, you want to be a bloody patient.'

'Don't you realise what has happened to me?' he said thrusting his head towards her.

'So you got shot,' she said. 'Twice. But you're still alive. Just a-bloody-bout.' She flung her hand towards Nod who backed to the wall. 'See that man? His parents were killed in the Blitz in London.' Nod, astonished at the news, attempted to agree. 'And Mr Kostelanetz,' she blazed on. 'His father was tortured by the Nazis. His mother died of a broken heart.' Her confidence dropped. 'In the Balkans.'

'Get me back,' Savage almost snarled at her through

gritted teeth. 'Get me back to the hospital.' He began to propel the chair towards the door.

'All right, all right,' Korky bellowed back at him. 'Go on back, you prat. Take the easy way.' She grabbed the handle of the vehicle. 'Listen, Savage.' Her harsh voice dropped to a plea. 'Listen. We've done this for *you*. They can't have you back unless *you* want to. Here you can at least live some *life*.' She studied his broken face. 'You can carry on with your islands. You've wasted all that. And I – me, Korky Wilson – I'm going to get you out of that chair and get you to walk again.'

'Korky,' he repeated gratingly. 'I want to go back.'

'All right! Sod you!' The telephone rang. Nod picked it up and handed it to Mr Kostelanetz who grunted and listened. He replaced the receiver and turned with slow drama. 'My contact,' he nodded at the phone. 'He informs that the police are coming around.'

For a moment nobody spoke. 'Maybe they just want the chair back,' suggested Nod.

Korky said: 'They can have it. And what's in it.' In a fury she turned on Savage. 'Go on, bugger off. Go back to the cosy loony bin. I'll never ... I'm never going to ...' She broke down sobbing, leaning across the wheelchair. Savage reached out and gently held both her forearms. She looked up into his face. They stared at each other. There was a tight silence. Then Savage sighed: 'All right. I'll stay.'

Korky whooped and kissed him through her tears. 'It's going to work!' she promised. 'We'll make it work.' Mr Kostelanetz, his eyes bubbling, reached over and sound-lessly shook hands with Savage. Nod stared with embarrassment out of the window and said: 'They're here. The coppers.'

'Christ!' exclaimed Korky. Her face went close to Savage again. 'Can they take you away?'

His shoulders sagged. 'At this point they'll do what the hospital tells them.'

'Hide . . . We've got to hide you,' dithered Korky. Her eyes went to each room, finally at the single glass door out on to the small balcony. 'Out there,' she decided. 'I'll get some blankets.' She nodded to Mr Kostelanetz who took hold of the chair and began to turn it.

Savage, words beyond him, hid his face in his hands. Nod opened the stiff glass door with difficulty. 'All of a sudden he has trouble with locks,' grumbled Mr Kostelanetz. The door pulled and the raw winter evening air blew in. 'Here,' said Korky appearing with two blankets. She wrapped them around Savage. 'Will it go through?'

'Just,' said Mr Kostelanetz.

'No, no. It's no good. All this is madness,' put in Savage hoarsely. 'Let them take me back . . . later we can . . .'

'Not bloody likely,' exclaimed Korky. 'Not now. You've promised.'

They heard the lift coming up. 'Quick,' urged Korky. They got the wheelchair outside on the narrow, dark balcony. Sideways it just fitted. Only Savage's head was projecting from the blankets. The doorbell rang. 'Stay with him,' said Korky giving Mr Kostelanetz a push. The startled man found himself out in the chill night with London's lights shining below. He pulled his collar up.

'Shush,' he warned Savage who huddled with eyes shut. 'Shush.'

From the inside Korky shut the door and locked it. She pulled the lace curtains across.

'Sit down there.' She pointed Nod to the sofa. 'We're in love, see.'

Nod was pleased. She opened the door to reveal two young and nervous-looking police officers. 'Good evening,' said one. 'Can we come in?'

'What for?'

'We're looking for a person called Savage, Frank Savage,' recited the other consulting a notebook.

'He's in an invalid chair,' put in the first.

Korky eased open the door. 'No one of that description here,' she said. She half-turned to Nod. 'We haven't seen a bloke in an invalid chair, have we, dear?'

Nod said: 'No, we haven't.' The policemen walked in cautiously. Nod added: 'Darling.' Korky sat beside him moving close. 'Just me and my fiancé,' she hummed. Nod blushed and wagged his head towards the policemen with a sort of triumph. Korky glanced down and saw wheel tracks across the carpet. 'Show the officers around, dear,' she said.

Nod blinked but led the policemen towards the main bedroom. Korky picked up a tufted mat and placed it across the wheel tracks. 'This place gets so untidy,' she explained as the visitors reappeared. 'Sorry about the bed.' She manufactured a blush. 'It's all over the place.' She looked meaningfully at Nod. 'Isn't it.'

Nod pinked with pleasure. 'Innit,' he agreed.

'He used to live here, that Mr Savage,' said Korky airily. 'But he got shot. By the police. By mistake.'

The officers looked discomfited. 'Right,' said one inadequately.

'Then the poor bloke went a bit funny and he's in a hospital somewhere.'

'That's the point,' said the second policeman as if relieved to confirm the background. 'He seems to have vanished from the hospital and they're worried about where he is. He's not dangerous or anything.'

'He couldn't have got far in a wheelchair,' said Korky archly.

'That's what we thought,' said the first policeman. He looked around. 'And up here on the top floor as well. There's no logic to it.'

'There's not,' said Korky. Nod and the second policeman both nodded agreement. The officers said they would be on their way. A sound came from the balcony window. 'Wind's getting up,' said Korky firmly moving towards the front door. 'It don't half blow up here.'

They were outside on the landing. One officer squinted towards the balcony but decided against saying anything. 'Goodnight then,' one said.

'Sleep tight,' said the other.

'We'll let you know if we see him,' said Korky putting her arms around Nod. She blinked. 'But I don't expect we will.'

They sat motionless for three minutes, her arms still loosely about his large, hot neck. Nod remained pleased. Then they heard the lift. 'I thought so,' muttered Korky. 'Quick.'

To his amazement she pulled off her sweater and the bra which she handed to him. 'Flash it,' she ordered. The doorbell sounded. Korky answered with the sweater held negligently across her chest.

'Sorry,' said the first policeman. He looked guiltily at his colleague.

'If he should turn up,' said the second, 'give us a call will you.'

Korky opened the door wider. Nod was standing dangling the bra. 'What number?' he asked.

'Same old number. Nine-nine-nine will find us.'

'Remember that,' Korky said to Nod who promised he would.

'Right,' said the second officer. ' 'Night then.'

'Yes, 'night,' said the first glaring at the other. They left. Nod demurely handed back the bra. She replaced her sweater.

Korky gave it another five minutes before she opened the balcony door. Mr Kostelanetz, purple-faced, stiff-moustached, watery-eyed, shivering, almost fell into the room. 'Whisky,' he said. 'I need whisky.'

He stumbled towards the kitchen. Nod went out on the narrow balcony and he and Korky manoeuvred Savage and the chair into the room. Savage let the blankets drop from his face. He blinked around at them. 'You all need treatment,' he said. 'You ought to be in there with me.'

Twenty-Six

Each morning they would get to the lift, Korky would open the old, crashing gates, and Mr Tomelty would appear to help her manoeuvre the chair into the confined space. Korky would hurry down the stairs to the ground floor and shout up when she was there. When he had closed the doors on Savage, Mr Tomelty would call down to Korky and she would press the outer button to summon the lift. Mr Tomelty would follow it down and be there to help extricate the chair. The routine went on for weeks.

With reluctance Dr Fenwick at Marshfield Manor had agreed that Savage could remain in the apartment. 'I'm not convinced,' he had said. 'But give it a try.' One of the conditions was daily attendance at a Kensington physiotherapy centre. In the exercise room there Korky cajoled and encouraged Savage while he progressed through a regime of exercises from his sitting position. When he flagged she would scold him. Sometimes she used the pulleys and weights herself, hanging on the wall while he laboured on. Weeks had gone by and he was still in the invalid chair.

'When's he going to stand up?' Korky asked.

The physiotherapist, a fragile-looking woman with big hands, shook her head. 'Nobody knows.'

'Can't we *try* and stand him?' insisted Korky. 'What would happen?'

The woman shrugged and said: 'He would probably fall over.'

When the daily session was complete she would push him along Kensington High Street. It was scarcely spring again although the trees were greening and there were odd times of tangible sunshine. Korky was learning to cook and they would do the shopping together when they were out, she wheedling him along the pavements. Then they would have coffee in a place that had made room for wheelchairs. There was another man who used to clatter into the café in a chair but he spoke no English. Later they would walk the width of the park to Bayswater Road, along with the traffic to Notting Hill Gate and then down the upper slope of Church Street to Kensington Heights.

She had learned to transfer him to the toilet seat and every day she helped him wash while he remained in the chair. A nurse bathed him at the physiotherapy centre. He shaved himself. Sometimes it took him half an hour. There was no hurry. One morning she found him, lather down half his face, staring at the mirror, helpless as a clown.

In the afternoons Mr Tomelty would come up, or sometimes Mr Maddison if it were Mr Tomelty's day off, and help him from the chair on to the bed. Mr Prentice, whose eyebrows had never grown again, took his turn with them in the evening assisting him into bed. Other residents would visit him, Wilhelmina Blenkinsop, Miss Cotton and Miss Weiz; Percy Belfont came and spoke about returning to Antwerp to die.

While Savage slept in the day Korky would sometimes

go out and walk, quite often without aim; sometimes she would watch an old afternoon film on television.

Savage had attempted some work on the islands encyclopaedia but his heart was not in it. The word processor stood with its lid shut like a closed mouth.

Once he had opened the window and pitched six random pages from his manuscript out into the London air. He had re-read them repeatedly and, despair folding over him, had sat staring through the panes before reaching and releasing the window catch. He fed them out one by one.

Wilhelmina Blenkinsop was returning from her weekly morning at Harrod's and one of the pages had fluttered down and struck her lightly on the hat. She lifted her lined face and narrowed eyes and observed the others descending. Mr Tomelty who was cleaning the courtyard watched too. 'Words from Heaven,' he said. Miss Cotton and Miss Weiz who had just emerged from the block followed their gazes.

'*Hawaii*,' read Wilhelmina aloud from the sheet which had landed on her hat. '*Pacific group formerly known as the Sandwich Islands . . .*'

'That *is* interesting,' put in Minnie Weiz. Mr Tomelty had dutifully gathered the other sheets. 'Here's another . . .' he said like someone given an unexpected pleasure. 'Now, that is most interesting. Fascinating that is . . .'

Mr Prentice joined the group, raising his non-existent eyebrows to peer up at the top window.

Miss Cotton, who prided herself that her eyesight was better than that of the others, thought she could see part of Savage's face behind the glass. 'Poor imprisoned man,' she said piously. Tomelty gave her a glance, then transferred it to the sheets of paper he had gathered.

'They must have slipped out,' he said. 'Accidentally. I'll take them back up to him.'

'I'm not getting any better, am I?'

Korky glanced at Savage apprehensively. 'They said we'd have to give it time,' she said.

'I don't think you ought to be here.' They were watching television and they kept their eyes on the screen.

'Where would I be if I wasn't?' she asked.

'Getting on with your life.'

'Oh, we're back on the old "getting on with your life" bit are we?'

He touched her from the chair. 'Yes, we are.'

Korky turned from the programme. 'As far as I am concerned I *am* getting on with my life,' she said firmly but softly. 'I'm taking care of you.'

'Do you know how long this is likely to go on? Me in this chair?'

'No idea.'

'Exactly. It could be years. The rest of my life.'

She said: 'You are not going to evict me again. We've been through all this more than once, Savage. You're always trying to throw me out, for Christ's sake.'

'I want you to have some life.'

'How much life did I have when you met me first? Do you call living rough with a load of kids with fleas having a life?'

'I want to go back to hospital.'

Rising angrily she strode towards the kitchen. 'Well, you're *not* going,' she almost snarled. 'You don't *need* to be in hospital. It's just a bloody let-out for you. You'd be taking up space they need for real patients.'

She put the kettle on. 'I need the space,' he insisted. 'Korky, I'm not just staying here. Hanging on. I'm not screwing up your life.' His voice fractured. 'I'm never going to be out of this fucking chair.'

Korky whirled around and charged back into the room. 'Bollocks!' she shouted at him. 'Bollocks, Savage!'

'Don't swear at me.'

'I'll swear if I like. You *need* somebody to swear at you.'

'Listen, those doctors *know* I'm not going to get any better. Can't you tell, they know.'

'What *do* they know, I'd like to know,' she said. 'Nothing. It's all bloody guesswork.'

'Exercise, exercise,' he said brokenly. 'Do this. Try that. Watching your face, Korky, as you realise how hopeless it is. I can't even stand — let alone walk.'

'It's not hopeless,' she said bluntly. The kettle was whistling. 'As for standing, how do you know? They haven't really tried, have they. They give you all that crap. They say you'll fall down.' She turned and shouted: 'Shut up, kettle.' It continued to whistle and she stalked in to turn it off. She strode back into the room. His face was to the television again. 'All right,' she said as calmly as she could. 'Let's see if you can.'

She took two paces and switched off the programme. Aghast Savage turned away from the blank screen. 'Can what?'

'Stand,' she said determinedly. 'Stand up on your feet.'

'But ... I ... they ...'

'Never mind about "I" and "they",' she retorted. 'It can't kill you. It can't set you back because you haven't gone forward anyway.'

Their eyes were locked. 'All right,' he said quietly. 'What do you think we should do?'

378

'Oh, Savage. Well done,' she breathed moving forward and stroking his hands on the arms of the wheelchair. 'Come on. Let's try it.'

'What should we do?' he repeated.

With suppressed eagerness, she turned the chair on its axis. 'If we get it at the side of the settee,' she said. 'Give yourself just enough room for your feet and hold on to the arm for support, then I'll try and lift you from the back.'

'Can you do that?' He was anxious to try now. 'Perhaps we should get Tomelty to help.'

'Let's just see if we can do it ourselves first. If you feel yourself falling try and flop yourself over the arm of the sofa. Tomelty will tell everybody.' She looked straight at him. 'I think this ought to be just the two of us. If it all goes wrong then there's nobody else to see. It's private.'

'Right,' he nodded solemnly. 'We'll do it between us.'

She kissed him on the cheek. 'First,' she decided, 'I'll push the sofa to the wall to steady it.' She did it as she spoke. Her gerbil rustled within the sofa. 'Shut up, John,' she said. When it was against the interior wall she glanced around. 'Ready?'

'I'm ready.' He propelled the carriage so that his projecting knees were touching the sofa. 'Let's go,' she almost whispered. 'Put your hands out on the arm.' He did so. 'Your knees will work. You've done plenty of exercises with them.'

'It's the rest of me I'm worried about.'

'We'll soon find out.' She climbed on to the sofa and after a single glance, began to pull his hands, gently but with increasing strength. 'Come on. Come on, Savage. You can do it.'

He almost did. His knees taking the strain he cranked himself out of the chair. His face sweated, he gritted his teeth. She was sweating too. 'It's coming. You're doing it,' she encouraged pulling on his arms. 'Wait, wait. Hold it there. I'm going to push.' She clambered quickly from the couch holding on to him and getting behind him, tried to add support to his back. The invalid chair was in her way. She kicked it backwards. 'There,' she panted. 'You've *got* to stand up *now*.'

Savage almost got there. But then the sofa shifted and he fell forward. She tried to save him but failed. With a shout of alarm he rolled sideways and fell heavily to the floor. Korky bent to him. She began to cry, he was cursing, his fist pounding in frustration. The gerbil emerged from the crack in the sofa and scampered to safety.

Savage and Korky lay together on the floor as though they had surrendered. She hugged him and he tried to pat her. They cried together, their tears seeping into Mr Kostelanetz's carpet.

'Oh, hello. This is Paul Fenwick. Is that . . . Kathleen?'

'It's me, doctor.'

'Is Frank there?'

'He's in the bathroom.'

'Good. I really wanted to talk to you. He has told you that he wants to be readmitted to hospital?'

'Yes, he told me,' she responded quietly. 'We talked it over. I'm really upset, doctor, but I'm trying to understand. He's not getting any better and it's playing on his nerves. And he thinks it's getting on my nerves.'

'Is it?'

'No, I can take it. I told him I can. But he wants to go back and that's all there is to it. We've tried; he's tried and I've tried. It's not been easy. It's been very hard for him. I tried to get him standing, just standing.'

'He didn't tell me that. What happened?'

'He fell over, that's what happened. And now he's scared stiff of trying anything. He doesn't even like me wheeling him out in the street any more. He's got some idea that people are laughing at him.'

'I can see that happening, the sort of person he is.'

'Well, he wants to go back to the hospital and there's nothing I can do about it. I'm just very upset, that's all. After everything. It makes me want to cry.'

'Don't cry,' he said gently. 'It may all come right in the end.'

'You don't really think that.'

'It could happen. But he has to do it himself. Without being afraid. People have walked again when every doctor had given up hope. When it happens it's like a miracle.' He paused. 'What will you do now?'

He could hear her sigh. 'I don't know,' she confessed. 'I haven't thought about it much. He's taken up all my time for the last few months. I suppose I'll have to get myself sorted out somehow. The usual things, get a job, get a roof.'

'You ... you won't go back to living ... like you were?'

'Rough? On the streets?' Her laugh was hard. 'Not likely. I know better now. There's better ways of being by yourself. I can always go back to Mr Furtwangler. I worked in his shop and he gave me somewhere to live.' She waited. 'When ... when will you come for Savage?'

'At the end of this week. We'll send an ambulance. You'll come and see him, won't you.'

'Yes, I'll come.'

'Even if it's difficult and he has nothing to say and the time drags while you're here?'

'I'll come.'

'You're a good girl, you know.'

'Thanks. I just wanted to help. He's a good man.'

He was in the chair looking from the window. If he sat upright he could get something of a view, plenty of sky and its moving aeroplanes, a fringe of treetops. Sadness filled him because he thought this would probably be the last time he would see it. It was spring again and evening. Tomorrow he was going back.

Korky was out shopping. She said she was going to cook them something special that night. She was brave and jokey but her eyes glistened. He watched the pigeon-coloured sky and the descending planes, his heart full.

They had talked, they had argued, they had shouted, they had quarrelled and cried together, but now it was settled. He was going back where it was best for him. They were sending the ambulance at eight thirty.

Savage swore to himself and turned the chair sharply away from the window. The word processor sat dumb. He did what he had so often done over those months; he swivelled in front of the television set and picking up the remote control switched it on. It was five thirty. The screen flickered; it was a very old film, a comedy in jerky black and white. Harold Lloyd, with his startled glasses and his unmovable straw boater, was being pursued by a vengeful gang. In silence the chase jolted across the screen. Savage watched dull-eyed. Soon Korky would be back. Soon he would never see her again. He would stop her coming to see him. His life would be without her. It would have to be.

Harold Lloyd opened a window and climbed out above a busy American street of seventy years before. Far below were moving people and traffic. There was a narrow ledge. The baddies were coming. To escape he would have to get along the ledge somehow, to a distant window. One poked his head out of the window but failed to see Harold, clutching his boater and pressed flat against the wall.

It came to Savage like a revelation. Harold Lloyd began to work his way along the ledge. It was only wide enough to accommodate his feet. Underneath, insect figures moved in the street. He slipped and recovered. His eyes squinted sideways from behind his glasses. Face to the wall he pushed himself tight and, arms flung out for balance, began to shuffle, inch by perilous inch, along the ledge. Two hands against the brickwork, two fore-arms, two elbows, two upper arms pressed flat; body tight against the surface, face turned to the side, legs splayed.

Savage found himself staring at the image, his face solid, his eyes unblinking. An intrusive commentator's voice joined in the drama: 'What will our hero do next?' Cut to the street below. 'It's a long, long, way down.'

Savage licked his lips. He moved away from the television set. Carefully he revolved the chair and pro-pelled it towards the kitchen. To the left of the door, the longest wall of the apartment extended to the bathroom. In the middle, alone, was their small map of the Isle of Wight. With an almost animal grunt he moved the chair so that it was as close as he could get it to the side of the kitchen entrance. His face worked, he felt himself sweat-ing. He wiped his palms on his shirt, calculated the distance between his hands and the jamb of the door. Then slowly, so slowly he feared for his resolve, he moved to grasp the door frame. He tested his grip as a climber might test a rope. Then he tightened his hold.

He began to do it. Alone, as he needed to be. He *made* himself do it. Slowly, agonisingly, he pulled and pulled himself away from the chair. His legs trembled, his stomach churned. God, it was working! It was happening! Desperately he wanted to fall back to the safety of the chair again but he would not let himself. His feet felt the ground and then stood on it. 'A . . . ttention . . .' he muttered. 'A . . . ttention.' He was bent like a bow but, sweating streams and keeping his terror just at bay, he pulled and pulled. He had purposefully not applied the brake of the chair and now, as though making a decision itself, it rolled back away from him. Now there was no going back.

But he was almost standing. Almost standing! Steadying his strength he gradually straightened his back; straight and straight and straight. It resisted, pain shot through his spine, but he ground his teeth and kept rising. Now he was standing to attention. God Almighty, he was *standing!* To attention! His face was soaked and his lips were working, almost blubbing; he tried to stop his body shaking. But he was *standing*, face and body against the wall, one hand still holding the door jamb and the other flat against the wall. Just like Harold Lloyd. The commentary still drifted from the direction of the television. If Harold Lloyd could do it, he could do it. Do it by *himself*. He swallowed his fear. His legs were quivering. 'Stop it, stop it, you bastards.'

He remained like that, like a police suspect being frisked, for a full thirty seconds. His legs were aching, weakening. Again he moved. Just like Harold Lloyd. He moved his left leg a couple of inches to the left. It did as he instructed. 'Not too much. Steady. Not too much.' Now he had made six inches sideways. Six inches! He had walked six inches! 'Left . . . right,' he grunted. 'Left . . . right.' Another six inches.

The door opened and in came Korky.

'Oh, my . . . God.' It began as an exclamation and finished in a whisper. 'Oh, Savage. Oh, Savage.' She dropped the shopping. 'Don't fall. Don't fall now, Savage. I'll help you.'

'I did it myself,' he almost choked. Then: 'Korky, I'm stuck.'

'Don't panic. Don't worry.' She was half-crying, half-laughing. She pushed herself against his back. 'Hang on, I'll keep you up. We'll do it together.' He swayed a little away from the wall but she was not going to let him fall now. With all her lean toughness she guided his body sideways. Reaching out she caught hold of an upright chair. 'Get to this chair,' she panted. 'You can do it. It's only inches.'

To the astonishment of both he was able to half-swing from the wall, so that he was only supporting himself with one side of his body and one arm and hand flat against it. With the other arm he fiercely grasped her shoulder. She almost squealed. Gritting her teeth she took his weight and they slowly revolved from the wall.

'You're *not* going to fall, Savage, no way.' It was an order. '*Not* this time, mate. You're just *not* going to fall.' She was babbling. She was trying to get some support from the wall herself and her hand knocked the map of the Isle of Wight askew. At that moment he was standing free of the wall held up only by his own legs and her failing strength. Korky held him up with her hands and shoulders. Her face was contorted with the effort. But he was *standing*, he was *moving!* She was holding him, shifting him towards the chair, revolving him. They were face to face, his hands on her slender shoulders, hers around his body. Their expressions were alight, alive, ecstatic. Together they were laughing hysterically.

'Oh, Savage,' she cried. 'We're dancing again. One, two, three. Plonkie, plonkie, plonk. Savage, we're *dancing!*'

*Also by Leslie Thomas
and available from Mandarin Paperbacks*

Dangerous By Moonlight

Lost, baffled, and alone in Willesden's mean streets, Detective Constable Dangerous Davies is up against the cream of criminality. Newspaper theft (the work of organised crime?), household robbery (including cheese from the fridge), it's all grist to his mill. When Dangerous is beaten up, yet again, at a European Friendship dinner dance he reluctantly takes some sick leave.

Recuperating in Bournemouth he is approached by a member of the local Widows' Luncheon Club. She wants him to find out the truth about her husband's disappearance. Dangerous declines. It's against the rules. Back in Willesden a further beating helps change his mind.

So starts a double life of regular casework and moonlighting as Dangerous lurches into a mystery fit to confuse the great Holmes himself . . .

'Not all detectives can be glamorous. Leslie Thomas makes a virtue of this with his ironically named Dangerous Davies, a Detective Constable who moves in a mysterious way his blunders to perform . . . Recommended to anyone who enjoys a good detective yarn with plenty of laughs'
Daily Express

Arrivals and Departures

Heathrow Airport is a bustling, stress-filled, ultra-modern world of international glamour and squalor. Scarcely beyond its runways lies the ancient, sleepy little village of Bedmansworth, where life goes on as it has done for centuries. Yet they are two interconnecting worlds.

Edward Richardson lives in Bedmansworth, but jets around the world faster than his marriage can tolerate. And when Mrs Pearl Collingwood and her daughter Rhona fly from Los Angeles, Edward little foresees the effect the two American women will have on his life . . .

'He inhabits that "bestselling author" territory that includes the likes of Jeffrey Archer, Jack Higgins and Ken Follett, but he is a far better writer than any of them'
Sunday Times

Running Away

Have you ever thought of running away?

Bestselling author Nicholas Boulting has always been a compulsive runner – from his parents, from school and now from his jealous wife.

Because she's just discovered his latest love affair and she's finally blown all the fuses. So this time he's clearing out and running for a lifetime of freedom.

But at forty years old, running away's not that easy. And freedom may not be that desirable after all . . .

'Genuine warmth and bursts of anarchic humour'
Sunday Times

'One of the geniuses of the modern-day comic novel'
Daily Express

'Comic and poignant'
Publishing News